Vaporbyte

Cat Connor

I0661497

9MM PRESS

Paperback ISBN : 978-047351950-6
Kindle ISBN: 978-047351952-0
Kindle ISBN: 978-047351953-7
ePub ISBN: 978-047351951-3
Draft2Digital ISBN: 978-1-0670072-8-7
Editor: Nicky Hurle

"Non-stop action in the 12th BYTE thriller starring Ellie Iverson super FBI agent and her team as they battle to stop a genetically enhanced pathogen being released just as the world is recovering from the COVID-19 pandemic. Vaporbyte takes the reader from Washington D.C. to New Zealand with an explosive climax."
- Nick Spill, The Jaded Spy

"Cat Connor's latest Byte novel, "Vaporbyte", takes her exquisite storytelling craft to a whole new level and onto the international stage, with a riveting quest to protect the world from a formidable contagion. Timely and breathtaking!"
-Lisa Towles, Award-winning crime novelist and author of The Unseen and Choke

"Part thriller, part mystery, Vaporbyte asks 'What happens if pandemics like Covid-19 are just the beginning?' I was drawn into the story right away, and eagerly followed along as FBI Special Agent in Charge Ellie Iverson and her team race to stop a deadly worldwide threat. Cat Connor combines wit, suspense, human characters, and a frighteningly realistic scenario into a story that made me wonder if any of us is ready for what could happen ..." - Margot Kinberg, author of the Joel Williams mysteries and the Patricia Stanley mysteries.

"Set amidst a threat of a worldwide pandemic with nefarious baddies, FBI SAC Ellie Iverson and the Delta teams battle to save the world.

Vaporbyte is a heck of a ride, with Cat Connor at her best for this last byte. Hope you enjoy this one as much as I did." - Bruce Melrose, author of the John Kelly novels.

For Breezy because she wanted an alternate ending to Terrorbyte and I did not do it!

"All of us knows, not what is expedient, not what is going to make us popular, not what the policy is, or the company policy - but in truth each of us knows what is the right thing to do. And that's how I am guided." — Maya Angelo

Chapter One

Let's Dance

The barista looked up and smiled as I walked toward him. "Hey, Ellie. Usual?"

I looked right at him, deadpan, and said, "Make it a black decaf, Jake."

He didn't miss a beat. "On your tab?"

"Please."

Jake had made my coffee almost every day for six years. He'd never made me a decaf anything.

The male on my right added, "I'll have a breve. Put it on her tab." His head tipped toward me.

Jake glanced at me for affirmation. I nodded. I kept my hands in sight. Not once did I venture toward the gun on my hip. Better to play it out than risk innocent bystanders. For now.

"Name for the cup?"

"John."

"With an h or without?" Jake held a black marker pen over the cup.

"With."

"Okay."

He busied himself then hurried out the back. He returned with milk. I waited. Jake's phone buzzed. The idiot with the gun in his pocket waited.

Jake carried on with the coffee orders in front of

him. No surreptitious glances in my direction. Jake's phone buzzed a few more times. He checked the messages.

John, the idiot with the gun, leaned on the counter, keeping his right hand in his pocket and watched Jake as he checked his phone. "What's with the phone?"

Jake showed him the screen without even looking up. "People text their orders, dude. It's the capital ... if you haven't noticed everyone's in a hurry."

I scanned the phone screen super quick. Three messages in a row.

Tony S: `Black.`
Kevin C: `Black.`
Dean W: `Double shot low-fat soy latte with cinnamon.`

Good work, Jake. He'd called the cavalry. I really appreciated the names Jake had chosen to use on his phone for Lee, Kurt, and Dane. Guess I wasn't the only one who saw Grange's lead guitarist Tony Sharron, Kevin Costner, and Dean Winchester when looking at my specialist crime investigation team, Delta A. For a split second, I wondered what he called me. I made a mental note to ask him one day.

"I'm about done here," I whispered to John with an 'h', hoping my voice did not betray the smile I felt growing. Typical Dane. Double shot low-fat soy latte with cinnamon, my ass!

John's eyes darted to me. "That's a shame."

"You've made a mistake. I can still help you correct it."

He snorted with derision. "There's no mistake here, Agent Iverson."

"I'll make sure that's carved on your tombstone."

"Pretty sure of yourself, given the situation." John wiggled the gun in his pocket. Jake clanged a milk jug, distracting the idiot's attention. "What's taking so long?"

"Coffee is a science. You want it good, or you want it fast?" Jake replied with a grin. I'd never seen him rattled by anything, and he'd seen me first thing in the morning and well under-caffeinated.

And we waited.

Other patrons came in, picked up phone orders, and left. Something pinged off to the side of my right eye. A flicker. My team.

"Where to next?" I turned to the man with me. He may have told Jake his name was John for his coffee, but I very much doubted that was true.

"Not your concern, Agent." He watched Jake intently.

"Glad you have a plan."

The flash in my peripheral vision increased.

"Hey, Jake?" Jake looked at me. "You got any of those cupcakes out the back?"

"I let you get coffee, cupcakes are pushing it," the gunman growled.

"You don't wanna be around me if I haven't eaten." I shrugged.

"I'll get you a couple, Ellie," Jake said with a smile, and disappeared. There would be no cupcakes.

Back-up was about to walk through the door.

The bell above the front door dinged. Lee crossed the floor with four easy strides, and stood as if he were waiting in line. He leaned around the gunman.

"Hey, Ellie. Didn't expect to see you here," he said, with a grin a mile wide. "We still on for racquetball later?"

"Looking forward to it," I replied. "That a new shirt?" Lee was more casual than Kurt, but still wore the 'regulation' black slacks and button-down long-sleeved shirt. He rarely wore a tie. Didn't matter what Lee did he always looked like a rock star. A tall muscular, ex-military, don't fuck with me, rock star.

"Yeah, like it?"

"Pale blue suits you."

Lee's eyebrow danced at the man between us. The door dinged again. I saw Kurt moving into line behind Lee. He wore a charcoal suit, white shirt, and diagonally striped tie in shades of gray. Definitely had a Kevin Costner look to him.

Beads of sweat appeared on John's forehead. He craned his neck to see out the back. "Hey, coffee guy, leave the cupcakes. We gotta go."

The door dinged once more. Dane strode in wearing jeans, cowboy boots, and a dark green tee shirt under his soft mid-brown leather jacket. Dane and I were more comfortable in jeans and boots. He tried wearing a suit once upon a time and it just wasn't him. Made him look awkward.

He came up behind me, leaned into my ear, and whispered just loud enough for John to hear, "Baby, I hope you ordered something special."

Biting back a chuckle, I let my voice rasp a bit as I whispered back Mae West style, "Double shot. Low fat. Soy latte."

John made a grab for me, but Dane flipped a handcuff on his wrist and gave his arm a twist. Lee reached over and took the gun from his pocket.

"Fucking amateur hour," he muttered, handing the weapon to Kurt.

"You okay?" Dane asked me, while pushing the cuffed man into Lee's waiting grip.

"Absolutely," I said, then leaned over the counter and called to Jake. "Hey, it's safe."

He emerged with a paper bag and handed it to me. I peered inside. Cupcakes. "Put these on my tab. And thanks for being cool."

"My treat. Not everyday someone tries to kidnap a federal agent in my coffee shop."

I reached over and shook Jake's hand. "Thank you."

"You're welcome."

Kurt and Lee escorted the prisoner. I heard Kurt reading the Miranda as he placed a hand on John's head while encouraging him into the back of his car.

Dane caught up with me on the pavement. He had a tray of coffees and a grin plastered on his face.

"Coffee first then interrogation?"

"I think so."

Kurt and Lee drove off. Dane and I climbed into his SUV and followed.

Chapter Two
The Width of a Circle

I sat at my desk drinking coffee and enjoying a chocolate cupcake. There were plenty of things wrong with the world, but chocolate and coffee were not on the list. Jake's cupcakes were as delicious as his coffee was strong and full of caffeine. Dane, Kurt, and Lee were observing our guest via the interrogation viewing room. I wanted him to sit for an hour. Just sit. No contact. As per the norm, the room was empty except for three chairs. Nowhere to hide.

I had a few minutes to gather my thoughts and finish my snack before a meeting with the Deputy Director to discuss current cases.

A Schrödinger meeting. My favorite, said no Special Agent in Charge ever.

Sandra swung the outer door open. I waited for her to enter my space before speaking.

"Can I help?"

"Deputy Director Vance has postponed until eleven-fifty."

"Still a Schrödinger or do we have a clue?"

Sandra laughed. "Good description. He sounded okay, if that helps?"

It did.

If it was a reaming he intended to dish out then he

would not sound okay. He would sound like the grumpiest fucker known to man. His crankiness put our new Assistant Director and the former SAC of Delta, Caine Grafton, to shame.

"Maybe I'll survive without an ass-kicking then."

"O Leader of the Ragtag, you are without a doubt, the best SAC Delta has ever had. I was never worried."

"Good to know." We laughed. "Re-jig my late morning meetings to accommodate Vance and I'll go down and see how John the idiot is doing in interrogation."

I wiped my hands and lips on a napkin, tossed the cupcake wrapper in the trash, downed the last of my coffee, and followed Sandra from my office.

Game face time. Made sense to stop by the bathroom so I did.

A few minutes later, I let myself into the viewing room.

"Hey, how is he?"

Kurt pushed off the back wall and joined me by the door. "No outbursts. He's sitting there like a little lamb."

"Interesting."

"Very."

"He moved at all?"

"Not a hair."

I could see him sitting upright in a chair. Feet planted firmly on the floor. Hands in his lap. Staring straight ahead. Under control. What happened to the interactive pain in the ass who attempted to abduct me earlier?

"Did he say anything?"

"No."

"He accepted his arrest, and sat ... like that ... without saying a word?"

"Yes."

"Houston, we have a different kind of weirdo," I muttered, watching him through the one-way mirror. "Finding out what makes him tick is going to be fun." I could feel it in my bones. My brain examined that thought for a second. Was it a hit from impending fun I felt or something more terror adjacent? Easy to confuse the two in my line of work. "Did we get a name?"

My phone chimed. "There's your name," Dane said.

I checked the alert.

Trace McAlester. McAlester worked for an accounting firm here in the city. I scrolled down the document looking for known criminal associates or anything that would point to him going from mild-mannered accountant to kidnapper. He'd been with the same company five years. Exemplary work record according to the company's Human Resources people. He was quiet but friendly.

Yeah, they're all quiet, and serial killers make magnificent neighbors.

Not much help. I read on. No prior arrests. No known dodgy friends. The regular type of social media.

Sandra had scratched the surface of his Facebook account and found bland family friendly posts. Nothing political. Nothing with inflammatory language. I watched the man for a moment.

"Why did McAlester do what he did this morning?" Lee voiced my question before I could.

"How about one of you go in there and find out?"

He grinned at me. "Thought you'd want this ..."

"Let's see what happens when you go in, Lee." Lee was the biggest of my team and the most imposing. He still carried himself like he was military and gave off a definite danger vibe, despite looking like the lead guitarist of a rock band.

"Stay tuned," Lee said, swinging the door open. He disappeared. The door closed. A moment later the door to the interview room opened and Lee walked in.

McAlester sat up a little straighter. Didn't know he could straighten his spine further, so that was impressive.

I turned the speaker up so we could hear Lee and McAlester.

"I'm Special Agent Davenport." Lee sat in front of the man. "And you are Trace McAlester." He attempted to make eye contact. McAlester stared straight ahead. Nothing registered on his face. Blank canvas sprang to mind. I imagined a fist connecting with his jaw, blood sprayed across the table.

"Do you like sports, Mr. McAlester?"

Nothing.

"Do you enjoy your job?" Lee glanced at his phone screen. "You're an accountant with a company here in the District."

Lee waited. Several seconds dragged by. It was going to be a long day if this lack of anything kept up.

"Worked there long?"

McAlester moved his head the smallest increment toward Lee. Kurt stepped forward. We watched barely breathing.

"You know how long I've worked there," McAlester said quietly.

"Maybe I wanted you to tell me," Lee replied, with a smile. "I like conversation."

McAlester reverted to a dead-pan, mid-distance stare.

"Was accounting your first choice as a profession?"

Nothing.

"Did little Trace McAlester want to be an accountant as a kindergartner?"

He didn't even blink.

Shit. Let's get into it before my patience vanishes completely.

I texted Lee.

SAC Iverson: Ask him, why me?

Lee shot me a look that said this is my interview, back off, but he still obliged.

"Why did you attempt to kidnap my boss?"

Lee stretched a leg out, giving the impression he was making himself comfortable. An easy smile lay on his lips.

"What was it you hoped to accomplish, Trace McAlester, fearless bean counter?"

McAlester rolled one eye to Lee, then back to the mid-distance stare.

I waited for him to say he wanted a lawyer, at least that would be something.

He sat like a bland statue with a broomstick up his ass. His spine really could not get any straighter.

Lee sat for five minutes just watching. Looking at ease. McAlester remained blank.

I leaned on the back wall. What was the point of his sloppy abduction or whatever that was? What would be the point of trying to take me?

Response time?

If someone needed to know how fast Delta A deployed, then attempting to kidnap the SAC would give them that information.

What else?

Pull our attention from another case? Kidnapping the SAC will cause a change of focus.

"What?" Kurt asked.

"What, what?"

"You, you thought of something, what?"

"What is the point of this?" I waved a hand toward McAlester. "What does he gain from this?"

Kurt shook his head slowly from side to side. "He

12

gains nothing. He loses a lot of hours to an interrogation room, and he'll end up paying a lawyer a lot of money. Lose-lose for McAlester."

Is it though?

What if he wanted to be locked up?

Dane stepped away from the window and turned toward me. "Which is it El? Response time, pulling our focus, or he wanted off the street for some reason ..."

Kurt smiled. "You two and your weird assed, same wave-length, mind reading routine are pretty creepy, ya know?"

"Jealous, much?"

"If you think I want a front row seat inside your mind, Iverson, you're more mentally hilarious than I thought," Kurt said. "I'll be revising my medical opinion to reflect that."

"Wiseass," I muttered under my breath.

"I heard that."

I shot Kurt a grin and shifted my attention to McAlester. "He wanted to be here, now. But why?" I said while I messaged Lee.

SAC Iverson: Ask him why he wanted to be in our building?

"Here? As in this building?" Kurt asked.

I nodded. "If he wanted to be arrested then police would be the way to go, but he chose one of us. He chose me."

This was a deliberate act, but why?

I focused on the interrogation room again. Lee glanced at my text. He shifted in his seat slightly, giving the impression he was getting more comfortable and then asked my question without looking like he'd read it from the phone screen.

McAlester remained blank.

"Let's explore that ...," Lee said. "You wanting to be in this building. If you wanted to be arrested, then any crime that got police involved would do. But if you wanted to be held and not turfed-out within a few hours, then perhaps the attempted abduction of a federal agent would be smart."

Nothing.

Lee waited for a beat before continuing, "What is it that is going happen outside these walls that makes you think this is a safe place? What did you stumble across while doing accounts?"

McAlester's expression flickered briefly to panic. A crack in the surface. Lee saw it too.

"It's time to talk, McAlester. If there is a situation developing, then now's the time to be a hero."

I took a breath. "Dane, get Sandra searching through McAlester's clients. Dig deep. We need to know if this is about a company client or someone he sees privately. Get a warrant for his personal computer and place of residence. Include his office. Something somewhere will tell us what's going on here."

"I'll deliver the message in person, and help." Dane

left the room.

I spun back to the window when I heard McAlester.

"It won't make a difference."

"What won't?"

"Talking."

And back to blank he went.

"Fuck," I muttered.

"You shouldn't go in there," Kurt said, straightening his tie. "Let Lee work."

I rubbed my temples. "I know. I know." It was me he tried to abduct or whatever that was he did at the coffee shop. "I don't think he's going to talk unless it's to me."

"Risky, Iverson."

"Life's a risk, Henderson."

He sighed. "You're going in, aren't you?"

"Yeah."

It's not because Lee can't do it. I need to be in there.

I swung the door open and let it slowly close behind me as I walked four yards to the interrogation room door. I rapped once and opened the door. McAlester did not look over. Lee stood and moved to the door. I slid into his warm chair and ignored the disturbance that was caused in my brain.

"I am Special Agent in Charge Ellie Iverson and have entered the interview at ..." I checked my watch. "Eleven-fourteen AM. Senior Special Agent Lee Davenport is still present."

With the formalities over, I gave McAlester my full

attention.

"We are in the process of obtaining search warrants for your residence, electronics, and office at the company you work for."

Nothing.

"Whatever it is that you aren't telling us, we will find it. If this is time sensitive then sharing what you know now, will work in your favor later."

He clamped his lips together.

Information about McAlester scrolled past on my internal screen. "Your parents live in Maryland, and you have one sister, who's two years older than you. Scarlett lives in Southern California with her husband. Guess she doesn't mind earthquakes."

Nothing.

"No significant other in your life. Or if there is, you've kept the relationship off social media."

His gaze pulled back from mid-distance; his eyes met mine.

"Agent Iverson, how many people did you lose to Qu?"

I steadied my voice before speaking. "Enough to know I don't want a repeat performance." Qu was a failure of a bio-terror attack. Hindsight is a helpful tool. We could now compare the Qu Pathogen release to the world changing emergence of COVID-19; it'd be true to say the former was measured and came up short.

He nodded. "Nor do I, but I don't think any of us ..."

Frown lines burrowed into his forehead. "I don't think *anyone* ... can stop it."

Fuckadoodledo.

"What do you know about Qu?"

His head shook slightly. "Someone I work for paid a lot of money to laboratories in New Zealand and Australia."

"For?"

"Research."

"Do you know what they paid the laboratories for, exactly?"

He nodded. "Research into the enhancement of the Qu Pathogen."

"I doubt that was written on an invoice. How did you find this information?"

"I was sent a document by mistake along with the invoice. The accounts I received clearly stated the payments made were for the research and development of a vaccine for Qu, but the accompanying documentation said the research was intended to enhance the pathogen and increase its deadliness."

"This is probably not what you want to hear, but we do dabble in bioweapons." I gave him a tight-lipped smile. "And companies don't undertake research for free."

"It's a private company."

"Uh huh, do you know for sure it isn't working under a government contract?"

He nodded. "This is not government funded, this is

private."

Guess an accountant should know that.

"Who is the client?"

He shifted in the chair. His lips set in a hard line and he slid back to the mid-distant stare.

"We will find out whether you tell us or not."

He blinked and looked at me. "I want protection and scratch the kidnapping charges."

"That decision will be made if it's deemed your information and testimony are required for the conviction of a felon."

"I'm as good as dead when I walk out the door."

Dramatic. But that's why the felony. If police picked him up for something, they might not have held him, and whoever is behind the research into Qu would still hear about it and take action in case of a security breach. Chatty loose ends don't have a long life expectancy.

"Say I believe you ... are you prepared for the consequences?"

"They're better than death."

I turned my head toward Lee, "Get me a US Marshal in case this is something we need to act on."

The door opened then closed. I texted Kurt.

SAC Iverson: secure the interrogation observation room. No one except Delta A is to enter. Check the electronic file is marked Delta A only.

I leaned forward and spoke quietly to McAlester. "Tell me exactly what you know and who is involved. Once the Marshal arrives, I will turn you over and they will bring you into the WITSEC program. You will not go home. You will not make contact with anyone from your life, which includes family. You will be a ghost." I paused. "You will be required to testify when told."

"Yes ma'am."

"Now, let's talk."

"Seven weeks ago, I first saw monies paid to laboratories in Australia and New Zealand by my client. I didn't think anything of it. They regularly paid money to labs for various research projects, mostly within the USA, but also in Europe and Canada. And they have Americans working in labs overseas, so they pay their wages."

"Okay, so they're Americans working for an American company based off-shore?"

"Yes and no. They're technically working for an American company because the company pays their wages, but they're on loan, I guess, to other companies."

"Okay."

"Seven weeks ago, was the first time I saw money go to Australia and New Zealand."

"Yep, you said that. Move on, pal."

He faltered, so I gave him a prompt. "If they pay wages to Americans overseas, why is this so

19

concerning? Couldn't this be more of the same, simply different locations?"

"Yes, but the accompanying documentation said they are paying them to create bioweapons on foreign soil."

Shit. Fuck. Shit. Wanna cause a panic in your immediate vicinity, all you have to do these days is cough. The merest suggestion of another disease roaming free killing people would dump us back into the midst of the COVID-19 craziness.

"Who is the client?"

"Exical."

"And you work for?" For clarification and our records.

"Cameron Chrysalis Business Services."

"Is Exical a private client of yours, or do they hire the company you work for?"

"The company."

That changed things.

"Who supplied the documents?"

"I don't know, there was no signature."

"Who has access to your work and your computer?"

He shook his head. "Only me."

"How about the company servers? Do they monitor communications?"

Some companies spy on their employees' email and internet use.

"I don't know."

"So, someone might know about the information you

found?"

"It did not arrive by email. It was a courier packet. The document was attached to a series of invoices. I think it was an accident. It's not information we would ask for, or that we need."

Was it an accident, or is this an anonymous whistleblower situation? If it was an accident, if the documents were gathered up with the invoices and whatever else was sent in the packet, then a name would be on something.

"Who sent you the packets?"

He clamped his mouth shut. I waited.

"Pam Straun."

"And where do I find her?" I wrote her name in my notebook.

"She works for their in-house accounting department."

"Do you have names of employees of Exical, who are recipients of the wages?"

"No. Their employees have numbers, like an SSN, but related to the company employee records."

"You're not paying their wages?"

He shook his head. "That's in-house accounting business. I get a spread sheet of employee numbers and wages paid."

"Okay." I need names and identifying information. A job for later. "The documents you have arrived as a hard copy?"

"Yes."

"Does anyone know you have it?"

"No. Except I guess Pam, unless it really was an accident."

"Where is it?"

"I destroyed it."

Holy crap on a cracker. "Tell me you stored it digitally first ..."

"I did."

"Okay, we need to retrieve it, where is it?"

"Can I use your pen and notebook, please?"

I passed both across the table to him. He wrote and handed it back. His handwriting was surprisingly beautiful cursive. "We will go pick this up, now."

"Do I stay here?"

"Yes. Do you need anything?"

"Water."

"Interview ceased," I said, then checked my watch, and added the time before I stood, switched the recording off at the panel by the door, and left the room with Lee. Something tweaked inside me and warned me not to speak the address.

I showed him the note. He nodded.

"Can we get our guest, water and a sandwich?"

"Sure. I'll get something from the bullpen for him. They just stocked the vending machine this morning."

"Thanks. I want you, Dane, and Kurt with me."

"Yes, Boss."

I walked to the stairwell. Once through the heavy smoke-stop doors, I ran up two flights, swung the next heavy door open, and hurried down the carpeted corridor, my footfalls deadened by the thick floor covering. At the fourth door on my right, I paused. Took a breath. Smoothed my shirt and knocked twice before opening the door into the atrium of an office, very similar to mine. It was slightly bigger with more commendations hanging from the walls. And this office had a gatekeeper.

"Reed, is he in?"

He nodded, picked up his phone and said, "SAC Iverson to see you, Sir." Reed replaced the receiver and smiled at me. "Go on in SAC."

"Thanks."

I knocked once on the interior door and opened it.

Grumpiness echoed across the expanse between the desk and door. "Ellie. A kidnapping?"

"That was fast," I said, grabbing a chair and placing it directly in front of Caine's desk. I sat. "I'm fine by the way."

"I know. I can see," he growled. "You asked for a Marshal?"

"I did. Our prisoner needs protection."

"You want someone who attempted to abduct you to have protection?" His growl became a long grave grumble.

"Long story. Not a real abduction more a mistake. He has information and is worth protecting." Maybe. "We are about to go and retrieve the proof."

Caine nodded. "He stays with us until you get back

here with whatever it is, he has. Then, we'll get the US Marshals involved."

"I've locked him down."

"Good call."

"I'll leave uniforms making sure no one enters the interrogation room or viewing room."

"Not Claude and Delta B?"

"Uniforms won't ask questions. Sandra will be emergency contact, just in case."

"Check in when you get back, Ellie."

"Yes, Sir."

I put the chair back where I'd found it, and left.

Chapter Three
Life on Mars

Back in my office, I looked up Exical and found their main reception phone number. Worth a shot. I dialed the number on my cell phone not wanting to leave an FBI calling card on their phone system.

The phone rang. I counted. Six rings. A voice followed. "Exical."

"I'm trying to reach Pam Straun."

"And you are?"

"Her cousin, Jenny."

"The extension you want is five-five-four, so type that in next time, Jenny. I'll put you through now."

"Thank you."

The phone rang again. After two rings I heard an out-of-office voice message. Damn. There was no time frame given, just a quick, "I'm out of the office. Please leave your name and number and I'll call you back."

So I did. "Hi, Pam, it's your cousin Jenny. Give me a call back on this number." I recited my cell number and then ended the call.

For all we knew, she might even have a cousin, Jenny. If she didn't, she could call back out of curiosity. In case plan A failed, there was a plan B. I summoned Kurt to my office.

"Can I borrow your cell phone please?"

He handed it to me without question. I entered the same phone number I'd called before, but before pressing the call button I handed it back to Kurt. "Press call and ask for their HR department. Then ask HR if Pamela Straun has a home phone number."

"And who do I say I am?"

"Her doctor."

He smiled. "Cunning."

"That's me."

Kurt pressed call. I listened to Kurt work magic on the receptionist and then speak to someone in Human Resources. He took a pen from his inside suit jacket pocket, then reached over and wrote a number on the blotter on my desk. After thanking the person on the other end, he raised an eyebrow in my direction.

Kurt pocketed his pen and his phone.

"They broke the rules," I said, smiling.

"They did. I can be quite persuasive."

"So I noticed." I used my desk phone and rang the number. It rang and rang. A river of cool tingles ran down my spine. Not a good sign. I gave up at fourteen rings. "Out, maybe."

I hoped nothing was wrong. Getting an address from HR would more than likely push them too far. Doctors usually have addresses, writing a number down wrong, now that's believable. Finding an address was a job for later.

Instead of all of Delta A leaving the building, I decided Kurt and I would go to the address McAlester gave me.

"Where are we going?" Kurt asked, pushing the key into the ignition.

"Reston."

"You've got more than that, I hope." Kurt drove out of the underground parking. "Reston it is."

I settled back and watched the city crawl past the window. It'd take us a while to get over the river and out to Reston. My phone rang. I checked the display hoping it was Pam Straun. Nope it was a confidential informant of mine: Jeremy Cotton.

"Hello, Ellie speaking."

"I have something that will interest you."

"When and where?

"There is an alleyway in the city."

"There are many alleyways in the city."

"Ask your colleague about the senator's wife and the alley way."

A memory shuffled forward. That was Sam's case. An Irish contractor was involved. Grace O'Malley. How the hell would Cotton know about that? Newspapers. Of course. It was splashed all over the papers at the time.

"I know the alley. Tomorrow?"

"Nine-thirty in the morning."

"I'll be there."

The call ended. Kurt glanced at me.

"All right?"

"One of my CI's has something for me."

"Related?"

"Timing suggests so." And the fact that Jeremy Cotton is a research scientist in the medical sector.

I let my thoughts go, and they drifted on a cloud barely visible on the horizon. All would be revealed in the fullness of time. There was little point scratching around trying to think up answers without the information. Twenty minutes passed along with a lot of scenery.

"Reston. Where?"

I gave Kurt the address. We drove past the house twice. Didn't seem to be anyone home. Kurt parked in the driveway. Usually we parked down the street from houses if we didn't want to advertise our presence, but this time, something told me it didn't matter. My arm bumped my holster as I exited the vehicle. Habit. A reminder that I was armed, and everything would be okay.

We looked at each other over the roof of the car.

"You good?" I asked with a smile.

"Yes." He smiled. "Is this McAlester's home?"

"Not according to property tax records, it's owned by a corporation." So is my house, so that doesn't mean much. It's a clever way to keep your name off property tax records though. "Doesn't mean he doesn't live here. But he has another home that shows up as his, and the other home is where we executed a search warrant."

We walked up the path that led to the front door. Small weeds grew in cracks in the pavement. A messy cobweb hung across the front door.

I knocked.

No one answered. Kurt peered in a window on the left of the door. "No sign of movement."

"What can you see?"

"An empty room."

"Void of life or actually empty?"

"Empty. There is nothing in this room."

Good chance no one lived here at all then. I knocked again and called out. "Hello, anyone home?" Maybe it was inhabited by ghosts and they might not like us coming in unannounced.

No answer. No signs of life or incorporeal beings.

"Where did McAlester say the documentation was?" Kurt asked. He turned to watch the street while I took a slip card from my wallet.

"Bathroom." I slid the card into the doorjamb by the lock and jiggled it into place. The door popped open. I pushed it all the way back then pocketed my handy slip card. We stepped into the hallway and closed the door.

"Hello! FBI!" Nothing. "Let's find the bathroom and get this over with." I opened the nearest door. An empty bedroom. "So far it doesn't look like McAlester lives here."

"Doesn't look like anyone lives here or has in some time," Kurt said, swinging another door open to reveal more emptiness.

The third door I opened was the bathroom. No toiletries. No towels. An empty laundry hamper. Not even a drip of water to indicate the shower or basin were used recently.

"Where?"

"In here," I said, and opened the cupboard under the vanity unit. Again, nothing to see. I crouched down and felt along the back wall behind the sink pipes. My fingers found a small bump. I felt for an edge and worked a fingernail under it. Grasping the lifted edge, I peeled the tape from the wall and withdrew my hand with the tape securely in my fingers. I dropped the thick white tape into Kurt's outstretched palm.

"A flash drive," Kurt said, peeling the tape away from the small object. It was barely longer than the USB slot in a computer. Just big enough to be removed without hassle, if you had fingernails. He handed it to me. I slipped it into my wallet and tucked the wallet back into my inside jacket pocket.

We did a fast walk through the house looking for any sign that someone had or did live there. The refrigerator in the kitchen was on. Inside the fridge I found a small block of cheddar cheese, a tomato, and a full bottle of milk. It was all fresh. No dishes in the sink or mess anywhere. Off the kitchen we found another room. That room was a furnished bedroom complete with a slept in, and unmade bed. A fast check of the drawers in the tallboy and the nightstands gave us little by way of information, but I was pretty sure the occupant was male. An old wind-up alarm clock revealed the person set an alarm for five-thirty. The alarm was off. I had a feeling McAlester had been hiding out here.

We found nothing to identify the occupant and left, locking the front door behind us.

Kurt opened the car.

"I'm going to check for mail," I said, and walked past the car to the mailbox. At first glance I saw junk mail and store mailers. I grabbed the handful of pamphlets and whatnot from the mailbox and flicked through it. In the middle of the pile I found a letter. A bill envelope addressed to Vaporcount Corporation. I shoved the junk mail back in the box and took the letter.

"Anything?" Kurt asked, as I settled into my seat.

I waved a bill at him. "Vaporcount Corporation."

"And they are?" The engine fired to life and rumbled.

"Wouldn't be surprised if they owned the house. We'll talk to McAlester about this when we get back."

Lulled by the noise of the road, my mind slipped through a rip in the fabric of life. Iridescent ether flowed over glittering sand. A single apparition formed on a delicate breeze. Luminous blue eyes watched and waited. Small familiar voices tumbled down a stony path to be swallowed by ethereal vapor before reaching the incorporeal eyes. A whirling frenzy swirled life into a fine mist until rampant darkness swallowed the light. And the blue eyes were gone.

A shudder ran through me. Whatever that was, it

wasn't good. I stared out the window at the traffic.

"You okay there, Iverson?" Kurt asked, glancing at me, then back at the road.

"Think so."

"Did you see or hear something? Is there anything you need to tell me about this case?" He tapped the turn signal briefly and changed lanes.

"Don't think it was relevant." My fingers crossed without my bidding.

Chapter Four
Two Out of Three Ain't Bad

Back at the office, I asked Cyber to scan the tiny flash drive before I plugged it into my laptop. No one wanted a disaster. While I waited for Cyber to bring the evidence back, I opened the letter addressed to Vaporcount. An electricity bill. The invoice was addressed to Vaporcount, attention Trace McAlester. I put it back into the envelope and dropped it into an evidence bag. That was all we had that connected Trace McAlester to the house, the corporation, and the flash drive.

I dug into Vaporcount and discovered they were a registered company owned by another company: Virginia Holdings. No mention of McAlester. Pretty stupid to have his name attached to an electric bill. I dug deeper. Virginia Holdings owned fifteen properties, and all were administered by Cameron Chrysalis Business Services.

McAlester waited. Before joining him, I made sure he'd been fed and had a bathroom break, and that a table was moved into the interview room.

Still no word from Pam Straun.

I looked up at a tentative knock on my door. The smallish frame of Clark Pendergast from Cyber. He was a civilian contracted to us.

"Hi, Clark," I said, waving him forward. He didn't move. "Come on in."

Clark blinked quickly and edged toward my desk, a small box held in his outstretched hand. He cleared his throat. "The flash drive."

"Thanks." I took the box as I made eye contact. His eyes shifted to a point over my shoulder. "Anything I need to know?"

"No."

"Good. Thanks again."

"No problem, SAC."

Clark scurried away. He gave the impression he was scared of his own shadow. I didn't know his story because he never hung around long enough to talk. One day.

My cell rang as I prepared to leave my office. Not Pam Straun. Damn. Caine.

"The Marshal is standing by, Ellie." His voice grumbled and vibrated into my ear. "They're waiting on you."

"I'm about to go down to the interview room and talk with McAlester."

"Let me know when you want the Marshal."

"Will do. Thanks Caine."

Caine ended the call leaving a growl suspended in the air over my desk. I watched as it collapsed into a heap of scratchy thorns on my blotter. A small yellow duckling squeezed from the nest of thorns, waddled to the edge of the desk, quacked once, and vanished. I shrugged, gathered my laptop, phone, the flash drive, and the evidence bag, and left the office.

* * *

The uniformed agent outside the interview room greeted me and swung the door open.

"Thank you, Agent."

"You're welcome, SAC. I'll be right outside." The door closed behind me.

I pressed a button on a panel on the wall near the door. "Special Agent in Charge Iverson resuming the interview with Trace McAlester." I juggled the things in my arms to check my watch and added the time.

McAlester looked up from whatever he was doing. As I neared, I saw it was *The Post* crossword.

"You like crosswords?" I asked, placing everything in my arms, on the table.

"Better than sitting here staring at myself in the mirror."

Imagine it would be.

"I have the flash drive," I said. "Depending on the contents, we have a Marshal standing by to take you into protective custody."

He folded the newspaper and moved it aside, placing the pencil on top of it.

"You haven't looked at it yet?"

"No. I just got it back from Cyber." I half-smiled and opened my laptop. "I don't plug anything into my laptop without vetting it first."

"Wise."

I broke the seal on the box and removed the tiny drive. "This is yours?"

He identified it with a nod.

"Can you audibly confirm please."

"Yes, that is my flash drive."

"Thanks." I pushed it into the USB port on my laptop. An icon popped up on my screen. I clicked it and opened the drive. Inside were a series of images. One by one I opened them on the desktop.

"Are these the only copies?"

"Yes."

"How did you take them?"

"With my phone. I moved them to my laptop at home, then to the flash drive. Once that was done, I wiped the images from my phone and from the laptop."

"You do know that deleted files aren't necessarily gone for good and are often recoverable?" We have people who specialize in that field.

"I do. I used a program we use at work to remove client files securely."

Let's hope that worked.

"Talk me through these," I said, and indicated he should bring his chair around so he could view the screen with me.

"I took a picture of every page of the document."

"I see that." There were eight images open on the screen.

"May I?" McAlester moved my laptop so he could reach the trackpad and ordered the photos. "This is the cover letter," he said, pointing with the cursor.

I studied the letter and the letterhead it was written on. By the time I reached the end of the page I knew two things. The name of the company paying for the research, and what they hoped to achieve. No wonder McAlester was nervous about his chances of survival.

Newgenic were a global entity and it appeared they were determined to weaponize the Qu Pathogen. By the end of page two I knew that Newgenic were using another company called Exical to move funds to laboratories to finance research offshore and to pay their scientists and chemical engineers. I also knew there was no way anyone outside of Newgenic should have this document.

"Who is the client you were working for?"

"Exical. I didn't know about their involvement with Newgenic until I saw that document."

"So somehow documentation was attached to the invoices sent to Cameron Chrysalis ... by Pam Straun."

"Yes."

"How long have you worked on the Exical accounts?"

"Since I started at Cameron Chrysalis."

"And you've never seen anything like this before?"

"No."

"I've tried to contact Ms. Straun, but she's out of the office."

Fear shot from his eyes.

"What if something happened to her. What if they know?"

Yeah, that thought crossed my mind too. If he's had the files for seven weeks trying to decide what to do with them, someone within the company may have found out.

"What exactly would they know?" That someone leaked documents saying they're weaponizing Qu and using American scientists to do it?

"That someone is creating a biological weapon."

I opened a search engine and then a bookmarked page. Pays to keep things handy, also pays to not sound like a wiki page but somethings can't be avoided.

"This is what the Biological Weapons Anti-Terrorism Act of 1989 says about, well, biological weapons." I took a breath and paraphrased the act. "The purpose of this Act is to implement the Biological Weapons Convention and to protect the United States from biological terrorism. This act amends the Federal criminal code to impose criminal penalties upon anyone who knowingly develops, produces, stockpiles, transfers, acquires, retains, or possesses any biological agent, toxin, or delivery system for use as a weapon, or assists a foreign state or any organization to do so."

"I knew it had to be illegal."

"And it is. This act provides for extraterritorial Federal jurisdiction over an offense committed by, or against, a U.S. national."

"Does that mean you can make arrests overseas?"

"Yes, it does. I just need the Attorney General on board to request the issuance of a warrant authorizing the seizure of any nasty bug and whatnot, and or the delivery system that exists to spread whatever is created. And we're going to need proof that this virus, or pathogen, is actually dangerous to humanity, or has been created in such a quantity that has no apparent justification for prophylactic, protective, or other peaceful purposes."

"That seems like a lot. What if you can't get proof?"

"That's my job, you don't have to worry about that."

"What happens to the virus once you've ascertained it is dangerous and it was created for criminal reasons?"

"We're authorized to seize and destroy all such toxins, or delivery systems upon probable cause, without a warrant, in exigent circumstances."

"You can just get rid of it all?"

"Yep." And save the world before anyone finds out what we are doing. Before the panic.

"I was right to come to you."

"Yes, you were. If it turns out that the agent, toxin, or delivery system is for a peaceful purpose and is of a quantity reasonable for that purpose, then we have the ability to allow it." I looked at McAlester. "I doubt that'll be the case though."

"It doesn't sound like it's for a peaceful purpose. Does it? I mean, what peaceful purpose could there possibly be for bioweapons?"

"Research springs to mind."

"They're making it off-shore and in secret. Do you think they have peaceful intentions?"

"I don't think anything yet. I simply told you what the Federal Government has to say about biological weapons and that as FBI, we can arrest Americans off-shore for doing bad things in other countries."

"What now?"

"I'm calling the Marshals in."

"Thank you, Agent."

I closed my laptop, leaving the flash drive where it was. I'd go over the rest of the document back in my office.

I tapped Caine's name on my recent calls list. The phone rang twice before he growled in my ear. "Marshals?"

"Yes."

McAlester looked at me. "What happens now?"

"You go with the US Marshals and you'll stay in their care. At some stage you'll hear from the DA, but that won't be until we have made our case."

"That's it for my life?"

"Just this part of it." I tried for a reassuring smile. "As soon as you leave with the Marshal, life as you know it today is over and Trace McAlester no longer exists."

"And I'll be safe?"

"Yes. As long as you do as you're told."

"What about Pam Straun?"

"We will try and locate her and offer her protection should she require it." I looked at the worried man. Gone was the semi-bravado of the early attempted kidnapping. Guess playing at secret agent isn't much fun when the stakes are this high. "Have you ever met Pam Straun?"

He shook his head.

"Any clue what she looks like?"

"No. None. I've never even talked to her on the telephone."

Such is life these days. Email and text have almost taken over in business communications; it was heading that way before COVID-19, but that event really ramped up our social-distancing.

"If you think of anything that might help us, tell the Marshal and they can get a message to me."

"Will I see you again?"

"No."

He sat, frown lines deepened on his brow. "This is how it has to be."

I stood, gathered everything into my arms, then remembered about the letter.

"I found mail in the mailbox of the Reston house that proves you had a link to the house."

"Does that help?"

"Yes, for us. It ties you to the place where we found the flash drive."

He nodded. "Cameron Chrysalis handles that

property."

"I know. It's one of many properties owned by Virginia Holdings and administered by the company you work for."

"How hard is it to get that information?"

"Not hard at all."

Panic resounded in his voice, "My name is on five of the houses as contact for various services."

"That doesn't really matter now does it?" I walked to the door. "Thank you for coming forward. Maybe don't attempt another abduction, it requires a skill set you clearly do not possess."

"I could've handled that better."

Chapter Five
In the Flesh

The day ran on, meetings blurred into more meetings. By early evening I knew McAlester was safe, and I'd heard from the DA. He was interested in the case; we were given the go-ahead to investigate Exical, and the parent company Newgenic, but carefully and without alerting the media to our investigation. Fine by me, nothing I disliked more than journalists poking around and destroying our ability to opt for a stealth approach. And nothing people needed less than the merest suggestion of another viral situation. We were just getting back to normal, going out and even traveling again.

The biggest thing for me, was to find Pam Straun, and get the names of the Americans working for Newgenic overseas. We needed solid intel. No knee-jerk reactions. Every action needed to be based on something tangible.

In the back of my mind all afternoon, was the phone call from Jeremy Cotton, and our meeting in the morning. Hearing from Cotton when I was looking into the weaponizing of Qu, did not sit well in my gut.

Lee ambled through my office door. "Shouldn't you be heading home?"

I glanced at the clocks on the wall above him. It was

getting late in the day. Still nothing from Pam Straun. One more call wouldn't hurt. She might be back at her desk or she might've finished up and gone home. Only one way to find out.

"Just need to make a phone call."

Lee plonked himself in one of the armchairs in the sitting area. "I'll wait."

Okay then. I rang the number in my notebook, then pressed the extension. The phone rang six times before cutting off. No out of office message. I rang back. It rang three times and the out of office message kicked in and I hit the end call icon. I didn't want to leave another message. Strange that the message didn't come on the first time I called. Didn't have to be anything though. Could just be a glitch. I called her home number. No answer after fifteen rings, and no voice mail.

"She's still not back."

"Who?"

"Pam Straun, the woman who *accidentally* attached the papers to the invoices sent to McAlester."

"Is she running, or is she on vacation, or has something happened?"

"He got those papers seven weeks ago. He's sat on them all this time and the minute he makes contact, the woman leaves her office ... and isn't answering her home phone."

"Change your route, okay?"

"I think McAlester was an anomaly," I said, with an

eye roll.

"Change it anyway. Humor me."

"Okay."

Whatever. Not happening.

"You know what. Screw it, I'm coming with you."

"Lee ... my car is chipped. I'm tracked all the time." I could tell by the tightness in his jaw that I wasn't winning. "It's me. I'll be fine."

Dane appeared at my door. "If you're leaving soon, El, I'll tag along."

Of course. I took a breath and released it slowly. They meant well.

Kurt's voice emerged from the gap between Dane and Lee, "We may as well all go out for dinner."

I rubbed the aching muscles in my neck.

"How about we have dinner at mine? Will that make you all happy?"

And get you off my back?

"You think Mitch would mind?" Lee said, and shot me a grin.

"Let's check shall we?"

I called Mitch and put him on speaker.

"Babe, you're on speaker. I have an office full of men who think I'm in danger of being abducted on my way home."

Mitch's laugh wrapped around my heart.

"Dinner at ours then?"

"Yeah."

"Okay, I'll pick the girls up and meet you all at

home."

A chorus of 'see you soon' rang out as I ended the call.

I packed up ready to leave. My team lurked in the outer office. Wasn't like them to be so obvious about their concern, especially as a unit. A twinge in my gut said something else was going on, something they'd kept to themselves. I sat back down at my desk, folded my arms, and waited. I hadn't picked anything up from Dane, which meant one of two things; there was nothing going on, or he'd blocked me. I went with the latter.

Thirty-seconds ticked by.

Lee walked through my door. "You ..." He stopped when he saw me.

"Me? I'm just waiting to see which of you is going to tell me exactly what's behind this sudden and OTT concern for my safety."

Kurt and Dane appeared behind him.

Dane muttered, "I told you she'd sense something."

Kurt grimaced.

"And I did. Now spill ..."

"It's probably nothing," Lee said with a dismissive shrug. "We're being over dramatic."

I narrowed my eyes and stared at him until I detected the merest flinch. Since when was Lee known for theatrics? I swear I could smell something brown and sticky.

"Nope, that won't cut it. Best you wipe the shit off

your boots and start talking."

Kurt cleared his throat. "Before you chew my head off ..."

He got my full attention. "Proceed."

"They filled me in a few minutes ago."

"So, you suggesting going out for dinner was a happy coincidence?" I don't think so, pal.

"Right before I suggested dinner," Kurt said. "The attempted abduction this morning might not be an isolated incident."

"He's not going to do it again. He's locked up and safe, remember?"

"Yeah, not him. Sandra found conversations on his laptop. He's been talking to people, or at least one person," Lee said.

"Were they clients? Because he's an accountant and I'm pretty sure that means he talks to people," I said with a sigh. "You can do better than that."

Lee dragged air over his teeth. "We have a name. The person he's been talking to is Hanzel Forberg. He's Scandinavian and here working for Newgenic."

"And how does that warrant so much concern for my safety?"

"He told Forberg he was planning to go to you with information. You, El, not anyone else."

"He said he'd told no one about the documents." I slumped in my chair, tapped my fingernails on the surface of the desk and thought for a moment. "Who else did he tell?"

"Exactly. Sandra is still going through conversation threads on his laptop."

Okay. He's an idiot. He wanted protection because he'd opened his stupid mouth. And that concerned my team. "There is no point worrying about it. Let's get out of here." A question popped up. "McAlester's client is Exical. He didn't know about Newgenic. Wonder how long he's been friends with a Newgenic employee? Did he mention Pam Straun?"

"Sandra will find out," Kurt said, and picked up my keys from the desk. "I'll drive." He glanced at Lee. "You happy to drop me home later?"

"Sure am."

Dane jangled his car keys. "I'll take my car."

I knew exactly what was going to happen next. Lee would be the lead car and Dane the rear car. They took McAlester's big mouth seriously, all right.

We'd switch places just before my driveway, as my car was chipped for the gates, theirs were not. They did, however, all have their own gate codes. It's just easier if my car approaches first, no need to zap down windows and lean out. It also meant less chance of disaster at the gate. As I walked down the hallway with my team, I wondered why I'd thought there could be a gate disaster. Wouldn't matter if we were first or middle in that instance, there would still be one of our cars in the rear.

The run down the stairs to the garage was fun, the noise of my boots on the concrete chased all thought of potential doom away. Kurt and I were halfway across the garage floor before Lee and Dane emerged. Guess they'd had to wait for the elevator upstairs. We waited in the car for Lee to pull out first. Kurt followed him, Dane close behind.

I settled into the passenger seat as our convoy entered the street. My phone buzzed in my lap. Emails. Nothing that looked urgent. My fingers rubbed my neck as I turned my head from side to side, hoping to ease the tightness in my neck muscles.

"All right there, Iverson?"

"Yep."

Kurt's mouth turned up into a slight smile. The look on his face was one of concentration. In the wing mirror I saw Dane's car. Then a dark sedan tried to pull out from a side street and sneak between us. Dane shortened the gap. Goodbye sedan. We managed to stay together through the first two sets of traffic lights. Ahead of us were the third set. Dane's voice pushed into my mind: Piss off.

I checked the wing mirror. A red car tried to slip in behind us. Kurt slowed, Dane closed the gap, and sat on our bumper.

"Someone trying to join our little convoy, again." I immediately regretted my choice of words, and squashed C.W. McCall's voice as music started in my mind. Listen here good buddy this is not the Rubber Duck. My mind answered: Ten-four. I'll catch you on the flip-flop. I took a breath as the imaginary convoy crashed the gate. "Impatient," I said, wishing I could flip people off, but that was frowned upon.

"That's Washington for you," Kurt muttered. "Everyone is in a hurry."

A dark sedan indicated and tried to get between us and Lee.

Kurt leaned on his horn. The driver changed their mind.

"Enough," he said, his hand grasped the radio and lifted it from the dash cradle. "Go for Davenport and Wesson. Full noise."

Lee's voice came back, "Done."

Dane replied, "Done."

Kurt replaced the radio and switched on the flashers and siren. His eyes flicked to the rearview mirror. We were surrounded by flashing lights and sirens. Maybe that would stop the impatience of the traffic.

The lights alone threatened to do my head in. I closed my eyes and let myself drift on the whine of the siren.

My internal world tipped; colored pencils drew a tornado of muted red, blue, and yellow riding up from a blank piece of cartridge paper. Black lines joined the foray. Bit by bit the scene changed. The colors came together to form an office, complete with a large glass topped desk, and chrome and black leather executive chair. My breathing slowed as I recognized the room and waited for the inevitable entrance of my longtime imaginary friend, Christopher Chance. Quite a while ago, it became apparent that I was not like other people. It's taken me years but I'm okay with that, and I'm okay with having a rich fantasy life that gives me insight into things I don't always see outright.

A door opened and Chance walked in, a smile on his face, and a coffee cup in one hand. "What's going on, El?"

"Not sure, but something, obviously," I replied, waving an arm around his office. "I'm not here to fuck frogs."

Chance laughed as he set his cup on the desk. "Grab a seat."

I turned and I saw a chair behind me. I sat. When I looked up, Chance was sitting behind his desk. Steam rose from his cup and curled through the air above us. He watched me. "Talk to me, El. I'm here to listen."

"There's a company trying to weaponize the Qu Pathogen."

"Wasn't it already weaponized?"

"Not really. Qu was modified, but not necessarily weaponized, by the terror cells that released it here and in the UK."

"Continue ..."

"An accountant brought it to our attention. It's supposedly happening in laboratories overseas and not within the US border or US territories, as far as we know."

"You have proof?"

"No, we have documents that outline what the

American company are doing, but we haven't confirmed their authenticity."

"What else?"

"The accountant is in protective custody, the person who sent him the papers from Exical is missing, perhaps. And it looks like he shared his concerns with at least one person from the parent company of the firm in question."

"That's not a smart play."

"Nope."

Depending on the person's loyalty or morality, any real evidence could've already disappeared.

"El, is there more to this?"

Maybe.

"I got a call from a source. He's given me information in the past but nothing huge. Usually more around animal rights activists and that type of behavior. He's a contact I made during the release of the Qu Pathogen."

"And?"

"He wants to meet me tomorrow, and it sounds important. Usually he's happy to use a burner phone and share information. Not this time."

"Could it be related to this new Qu thing?"

"That's a possibility."

Chance stood, pushing his chair back. He came around the side of his desk and perched on the edge near me. "El, you know this is related."

Maybe I didn't want to know that though.

I took a deep breath.

"I think I need to talk to Tahoma Whitehorse at the Centers for Disease Control and Prevention."

"Yes, you do."

"Thanks, Chance."

"What for?"

"Listening. As usual talking with you helps me see clearly."

"Happy to help, El." Chance grinned. "Hope you find the whistleblower. Now get outta here."

A tornado of color twisted across the room, sucked up the sketched furniture and then melted into the floor of the car. And real life resumed.

I looked out the windshield and took note of my surroundings. About twenty minutes from home.

"You're quiet," Kurt said.

"Thinking."

"Come up with anything?"

"I have a meeting tomorrow morning with an informant. Could be related to the McAlester situation. And I want to talk to Tahoma Whitehorse and his off-sider, Karen. Karen, um, what was her surname?"

"Schneider. Doctor Karen Schneider."

Yes. That was it.

I made a call to Doctor Tahoma Whitehorse and tapped the speaker icon. Five rings. Six rings. Seven rings.

Over a hum of voices and office noise, I heard a familiar voice, "You are speaking with Doctor

Whitehorse."

"Tahoma, it's Ellie Iverson."

"Ellie." I could almost hear the rampaging thoughts in his brain. "It is good to hear from you." He paused. "Is it good for me to hear from you?"

"Tahoma, I think I have bad news."

"I am listening." I heard a door close. All background noise ceased on his end. "Should I be concerned about the sirens I hear?"

"The sirens are unrelated to this phone call." I moved the phone on my lap. "Have you heard anything regarding research based on the Qu Pathogen?"

"Yes. There are several laboratories working on vaccines."

"Anything else, anyone doing anything less helpful?"

"No. What do you know?"

"There is a company called Newgenic. Do you know of them?"

"Yes. They are one of the companies that has live Qu Pathogen and are working on developing a vaccine."

"That's intriguing." In a 'here we go again with someone trying to end the world' way. "And if I told you I know something about that, and it's not pleasing, and we need to face-to-face?"

"Already I am becoming concerned."

"Can you come to us?"

"Yes. I will bring Doctor Schneider. We will get the first flight possible."

"Thank you. Travel well."

"We will."

The call ended.

I leaned back in my seat.

"How did he sound to you?" I said.

"He's hard to read," Kurt replied, glanced left fast then back at the road ahead of us. "Doesn't sound like he'd heard anything."

That's what I thought.

I turned my head as a loud crack exploded in the air and a thud hit somewhere forward of my door. Sudden braking propelled my body toward the dash. The seat belt grabbed. My head hit the headrest. I clanged a mental door shut to protect Mitch from anything that happened next.

"Okay?"

"Yep," I replied, and pressed my shoulders into the seat. Our car accelerated.

Another crack.

Small crazy paved chinks and cracks ran from a hole in Lee's rear window. Shit. I grabbed the radio.

"Break. Break. Agents under fire." I took a breath and depressed the button again. "Break. Break. SAC Iverson requiring immediate backup."

Chaos erupted. The lights and sirens that filled the car seemed to spiral with each gunshot. With a glance at Kurt, I saw his jaw clench. He gripped the wheel and followed Lee as closely as possible.

A voice filled the car from the radio. It was Claude. "SAC. What three words?"

Great time to try our new tool in the wild. I tapped the *What3Words* app icon on my phone and lifted the radio handset from my lap. "Waters. Buyers. Winter." The minute the words left my mouth, our convoy pulled off the road, edged along the shoulder, to stop with our car behind a set of donation clothing bins. About thirty yards away on the corner was a daycare center. This was not the ideal location. "Go for Claude." I didn't wait for a response. "There is a daycare." I released the button.

Claude spoke, "I see it on the map. Delta B four minutes away. Police notified." I leaned forward and hung the radio in the cradle.

Lee's door opened. I watched him ease out of the vehicle, pull a bulletproof vest on and fastened the side. I unbuckled my seat belt, slithered over the back of the seat, and then leaned into the very back of the SUV to retrieve our vests. I dragged them with me over the seat. I felt the weight go from my arm as Kurt grabbed the vests, enabling me to slide into the footwell and sit on the passenger seat. My phone rang in the center console, 'Eye of the Tiger' rocked under the sirens. I answered the call.

"You okay, Dane?"

"Yeah. I'm coming out. Don't shoot me."

I tapped the red end call button and swung my door open. Kurt grabbed my arm. "Stay in the car."

I shook his hand off, released my weapon from its holster, and kept moving. I ducked my head to stay below the clothing bins, and crept along the side of the car. Dane reached me as I heard Kurt open his door.

"We need to make sure anyone in there ..." He nodded his head toward the day care. " ... is safe."

A round hit the back of his car. We scrunched lower instinctively and watched back window glass blow all over the interior. The siren wound on and on. Ringing in my ears. I willed my brain to filter out the constant whine.

"Where is that coming from?"

"Window."

I smiled. Yeah nah. "The shooter. Where is the shooter?"

"A black pick-up, I think. The shooter is standing in back of the pick-up using the roof of the cab."

"Did you get a look at the weapon?"

"Long barrel. Rifle of some sort. The shooter has dark, short hair. That's about all I saw."

The truck meant he had a height advantage. The chances of us getting to the daycare building were slim, but a stray round from whatever rifle he was using, could make it that far.

"Unless they drive up, I don't think he can get a clear shot at any us as long as we're between the bins and the cars." I looked up at the side of the bins and let my mind work on trajectory calculations. Everything aligned. The shooter would have to drive up behind Dane's car, or get off the truck to put rounds through us. Thank you brain for not thinking about our gray matter splattered across donation bins.

We moved back toward the passenger door of the middle car. Kurt and Lee were crouched waiting. Shots smacked into Dane's car.

Pting.

Thud.

Crunch.

Kurt had a weapon in one hand and his phone in the other. He pressed a name on the screen with his thumb, then reached his thumb higher and touched the speaker.

A siren rang out over the phone line and then a voice slid under the noise, "Almost with you."

"Good."

Kurt hung up.

An engine roared, another round hit Dane's car. The engine roared again, and tires laid rubber on the road. A different siren pierced the air and followed the throaty engine away from our location. More sirens joined the chase.

A big black SUV parked beside ours. Claude, wearing an FBI vest, jumped from the driver's side, and ran over to us.

"Anyone need a medic?"

Heads shook as we stood up and took stock.

"Car damage," I said. "But I think we escaped harm."

"Police are chasing the truck. There's a roadblock further down Blake Lane. They'll stop him."

I hope so.

"Delta B does the interview, got it, Claude?"

"Yes, SAC."

"I want a report on my desk in the morning."

"Yes, SAC."

"Any link between those bozos and Exical, or Newgenic, is of utmost interest."

"Yes, SAC."

I did a quick inspection of the cars with Lee, then returned.

"After forensics are finished here, have Lee and Dane's cars trucked to the panel shop," I said to Claude, then spoke to Dane and Lee. "Grab your gear and put it in our car." They moved away. I called after them. "Leave anything with bullet holes or damage."

An hour later, we had given our statements to Claude, and left the scene.

I twisted in my seat so I could see all three of my team.

"Not a word about this to Mitch."

"Is that wise?" Dane asked.

"Nope, but, we're fine and I don't want him worrying about nothing."

Kurt adjusted the rearview mirror. "That wasn't nothing."

"It's over." My fingers crossed. "No one mentions the drive home."

He pulled into the beginning of the driveway, and the gate swung open. My breath caught in my throat. Kurt drove in, slowly, and waited while the gate closed behind us. I exhaled. It was over.

"And he won't wonder why we're all in the same car," Lee said.

"Just shush," I said, and planted a smile on my face as Kurt parked near the front door. As I climbed out of the car, Mitch opened the front door, light spilled across the steps and onto the path. "Sorry, car trouble," I said, stepping into his arms. His arms closed around me.

I heard the car doors open and close, one by one. Footsteps came up behind me. I ignored them for a moment and enjoyed a kiss. There was a definite reluctance on my part to leave Mitch's warm embrace.

"The girls are fed, bathed, and in their pajamas," Mitch whispered in my ear.

"Super dad strikes again," I replied, and kissed him again.

Mitch looked past me; I turned a little and saw Lee. "The leader of your fan club is still awake," Mitch said.

Lee laughed. "Then I better get in there and get me some snuggle time with ..." His tone changed from regular Lee to light and easy Uncle Lee as he called into the house, "Miss Isabella."

From the living room, I heard the delightful sing-song voice of Isabella, "Un-cool Leeee! Un-cool Leeee!"

He intercepted her as she ran toward the front door. Scooped into Lee's arms, Isabella giggled. She placed a hand on each side of his face, and pressed her forehead into his. "Un-cool Lee."

"That's me. Shall we go see Grace now?"

Isabella rubbed her forehead against his in a nod.

Lee strode down the hall and into the living room. We followed. Grace squealed with joy. They both loved Lee, but I think Isabella had Grace beat.

"Anyone want to say hello to mommy?" I said, and sat in my favorite squishy blue leather armchair. My weapon shifted against me, reminding me I was still armed.

Bad mommy.

Grace started to move toward me. I jumped to my feet. "Quick hug then mommy needs to go change."

I picked Grace up for a cuddle so I could position her away from the Glock I wore, kissed her head, and set her back on her feet. Smiling, she chose a toy to show Dane. Isabella looked over at me, smiled, and snuggled further into Lee. Guess she was all comfy then. For a second, I wondered if Delta were armed.

Dane heard the question in my mind. He looked up at me from the floor. "We left our work gear in the car safe."

I nodded. "Smart move. I'll be right back."

Chapter Six
Itchycoo Park

As requested, Claude left a report on my desk regarding the shooter and the Blake Lane incident. I set it aside for a few minutes and rang the home number for Pamela Straun.

The phone rang and rang. I let it go for twenty rings then stopped before it timed out. Still not home. It was too early for anyone in accounts to be at their office, but I tried anyway. It rang three times and went to voice mail. I ended the call before it wanted me to leave a message. Next, I checked on notes from Sandra. She was still working through information on McAlester's electronic devices and so far, Hanzel Forberg was the lone confidante of the secret document contents.

Didn't mean he didn't talk to someone face-to-face. Why would anyone risk a digital footprint if they had a secret like that? Stupid? Cocky? Unaware of consequences? We had feelers out looking for Forberg. I set it all aside and turned my attention to the report from Claude about last night's fun and games.

It made interesting reading. The shooter was a male, well-known to law enforcement: Craig Fallon. A gun for hire. Delightful. The driver was also known; Tyler Fergusson. He'd racked up one helluva lot of speeding tickets and fines for car related nonsense. Neither would speak. They lawyered up immediately. Claude added a note on the lawyers. I recognized the name of the firm. Why? Because I had arrested a partner of the firm a few years back, Charles Locke. Ol' Chuck was a renowned criminal lawyer for scum bags, and had some influential people holding public office, as friends. I rummaged in file notes searching for information I was sure I had regarding the firm and the last time we came across them.

Bingo.

Charles Locke was still serving time for multiple convictions including male assaults female times four, breach of a protection order, and evading arrest. The firm represented him, and among his friends he had several judges, so, hard time wasn't so much of an issue for the scumbag lawyer. He would be released by the end of this year after serving eighteen months plus time served. No doubt he'd resume his position within the firm as if nothing had happened. Asshole. I found a list of lawyers associated with Carter, Locke, and Cromwell, the firm in question. There were eight criminal lawyers listed and two of them were now representing the shooter and the driver.

Out of interest, I popped into Facebook to see what I could find in the public sphere about the two lawyers: Noah Bancroft and Lucas Ramirez. I found a few public photos of Ramirez partying. When I downloaded one photo and zoomed in on a few faces, I caught sight of someone I knew in the background. Caps. Holy shit balls, Batman. I zoomed in some more. He didn't seem to be part of the crowd. He was near the door. Working maybe.

I scrolled through my contacts until I found his cell phone number and gave him a call.

"Speak. This be Caps."

"Caps, it's Agent Ellie. Got a minute?" I braced myself waiting to see if he'd go with his usual speech style, or remember how hard I find translating ebonics on the fly.

"Good to hear from you."

I relaxed. "Quick question. Do you know a lawyer named Lucas Ramirez?"

"Don't know the name. What's he look like?"

"In coming." I copied the photo and sent it to Caps phone. When I heard his phone alert, I said, "He's the guy propping up the bar, front and center."

"That's The Sugar Shack. Don't know him, but I remember him and his crowd."

"Why do you remember him?"

"Mr. Money-bags. He comes in every few weeks with the same crowd." Doors opened and closed in the distance. Music played. "Maybe been doing that for most part of a year."

"And you work at The Sugar Shack?"

Caps laugh rumbled. "Yeah, since that Qu Flu. They were looking for someone who could handle themselves, and I got the job."

Curiosity rose. "You get Qu?"

"Yeah, that was some shit. Knocked me around for a week."

"It sure was." But it was still a terror fail. The regular flu took out more people than Qu, although Qu copped a lot of the blame, because that's how people roll. Only the immune compromised, otherwise weakened, or the incredibly unlucky with direct contact, died. Don't drink the water, echoed in my mind. I still didn't like drinking bottled water. Not a bad thing really. We don't need to add to the plastic waste in the world by buying water. Then came COVID-19 and more deaths. We really did not need another go-round with a virus.

"Agent Ellie, you still there?"

"Yep, sorry. How'd you fare through the last outbreak?"

"Didn't get that one. I wasn't part of the unlucky seven million."

Maybe it was luck. I glanced at the photo again. Not a mask in sight.

"What are you doing at The Sugar Shack?"

"Bouncer."

Good choice on their part. I just bet he was superb at it. "Ever had to throw any of Mr. Money-bags crowd out?"

"Not yet. Come close."

"When did you see him last?"

"Maybe the week before last." His voice dropped. "Something wrong, Agent Ellie?"

"You heard anything about a contract and my

name?"

Silence. A small hiss. "If I'd heard anything like that, you know, *you know,* I'd have ended it."

I did. I left his comment alone. "Give my love to your Aunt."

"For sure, Agent Ellie, for sure."

"Stay Frosty, my friend."

With care I pressed the end call icon and placed my phone on my desk. So, Ramirez liked to drink at The Sugar Shack. Caps would keep an eye on him and his drinking buddies.

I scanned Bancroft's Facebook profile. The only public information was that he worked for Carter, Locke, and Cromwell. No photos of him partying. A single profile picture that looked like a photo he'd use on a website. Perhaps he was smarter than his colleague. My hand delved into my desk drawer before I even realized it was happening. Next thing I was conscious of, was my fingers typing into a Facebook log on screen using an identity that Debbie Barnes created for me.

Welcome back to my world, Catherine Thomas. I checked the password for Catherine Thomas's Gmail address, then logged into her email account ready to verify the address for Facebook because it had been a while since I'd signed in or used Facebook as Catherine. Facebook did not ask for verification. Great. I got stuck in and wrote a post saying I was back from a trip. From the folder Debbie had provided I chose a few innocuous travel photos. Moments later I sent a friend request to Noah Bancroft.

Nice play, Shakespeare.

The clock above the door drew my attention. I checked my watch in case it was wrong. It's never wrong. Time to get to my meeting. A little voice in my deep dark subconscious said I should take Kurt, or at least tell someone where I was going. I shrugged it off. Best not to spook Jeremy Cotton.

Chapter Seven
Don't Think Twice, it's all Right.

"I said leave it." My voice bounced off the grubby red brick walls that created the alley way. The area was refreshingly free of urine stench and discarded fast food wrappers. The tall male with his back to me stopped in his tracks.

His hands rose to shoulder level as he took a step back. "Okay."

"Take another two steps backward and turn to face me."

He did.

"Now what?"

"Identify yourself." He shook his head slightly. There was no one else around. So much for meeting my informant at the end of the alley. Probably scared off by the presence of the spook.

That thought rolled around my brain. Felt right. My aim didn't falter. "Name?"

He said nothing.

"Hey Siri, What3words."

"Location: Giving. Noise. Expect."

"Siri call Dane." Siri made the call, and my phone never left my pocket. Somedays I love technology. Two rings and Dane answered.

"Dane, send Bomb Squad to me."

"Yes, Boss. What three words?"

"Giving. Noise. Expect."

"Got you."

The call ended.

"Extreme," the dark-haired man said, with a hint of New York, and a smirk. "Someone left a bag behind, that's all."

Yeah, nah.

Our terror alert is yellow and mine just hiked to orange.

"Keep walking backwards until I tell you to stop," I instructed. He looked over his shoulder as he moved. I walked with him, maintaining a suitable distance and keeping my weapon steady on him. I could see we were running out of room and heading for the road. When he'd moved about twenty feet, I stopped him. "Halt. Hands on your head, turn around."

He linked his fingers on top of his head and turned.

"Name?"

He shook his head slowly.

"You don't have a name, or you don't want to tell me?"

He shook his head again. Game over.

I moved closer, holstered my weapon, snatched my handcuffs from my belt, and clipped one bracelet onto his right wrist, twisting his arm down behind his back. I followed suit with the other wrist. His belt interested me; it was black leather, stylish, exactly what I'd expect with his black slacks, pale blue shirt, striped black and blue tie, and black leather jacket. The word spook sparkled in my mind. I slipped a finger underneath the belt and felt all the way around the inside. Three zippers.

Nice.

"Turn around."

He turned on a sigh. "What?"

"Your belt, it's very nice. Are you worried about muggings?"

"No."

"I'm undoing the belt for a closer look."

"Is this how you get all your boyfriends?" He smirked and tried to twist away. I reminded him he wasn't going anywhere. Sirens wound through the air. He looked over his shoulder then back at me. "I'm not in the mood, but I like attractive women who know what they want."

Awesome.

"Stand still," I growled, and undid his belt buckle. Carefully, I unthreaded the belt from his pant loops. Sure enough, the belt contained three hidden zippers. I choose a zip at the very back, the most likely spot for a handcuff key. He stood motionless and watched. "Nice belt."

"It's an expensive belt," he countered.

I showed him the key and a razor blade before slipping both back into their hiding place. "Everyone needs a handcuff key and a razor blade?"

"You never know," he replied, and rattled the cuffs

on his wrists behind his back.

Good point.

A siren burst through the alley on my left, and another ricocheted off the walls of the building behind me. I checked the other zippers in the belt. Folded money. Euros. Canadian dollars. American dollars.

"Planning a trip?"

"Always prepared."

"Bit old to be a Boy Scout." I zipped the folded money back where I found it. There were times in my life when I carried hidden emergency money in different currencies. There were times when I also carried razor blades, and a handcuff key. Okay, I still carried a hidden handcuff key.

Dane's voice came from behind the male, I peered around to see him.

"Boss, need a hand?"

"Yeah, search him, empty his pockets don't just pat him down. I want to see what he's carrying."

The timbre of another voice made me smile. I didn't take my eyes off the man Dane was searching, but I acknowledged Tony with a wave in his general direction. I could hear him giving instructions to his team, then the robot whir as it moved. Heavy booted footsteps came up behind me.

A voice I didn't recognize spoke, "We need you out of here, Agent Iverson."

"Okay." I glanced at Dane. He'd removed everything the man carried in his clothes and dropped it all into an evidence bag. He gave me the thumbs up. "Where do you want us?"

"Tony said for you to move out of the alleyway completely. There's a team out in the intersection, they've created a safe zone."

I nodded. I knew what that meant. Shields, sandbags, and ballistic blankets.

"Let's go," I said to the male, and Dane.

"I'm your escort," the bomb squad tech said, with a grin. "The name is Dakota, but everyone calls me Dak."

As we walked with Dak, I glanced at him a few times. There was something about him. Something I recognized as a memory. We walked out into an intersection. Lee greeted me from behind the barricade.

I turned to Dak. A memory flooded in from a long time ago. A little boy with coffee-colored eyes, straight black hair, on the pretty side of handsome. I dropped to one knee to talk to him after his mom was murdered in Richmond.

"Dakota Trevalli," I said.

He nodded and smiled. "You remember."

I remember everyone from every tragic scenario I've attended over my career. Everyone.

"I do."

Tony's voice echoed down the alley. Dak grinned at me and took off at a run to Tony.

Lee encouraged the cuffed man to sit on the ground near him. Dane and I sat a few feet away and went through the bag of things from his clothing. The contents of his wallet spoke volumes and smacked of a life lived in the shadows. Two credit cards, pre-paid with no name. No store cards. No ID. A credit card tool. And another credit card that was a flash drive. In the back of the wallet were an L-Rake and a small tension wrench.

"Nothing with a name," I muttered, dropping the wallet back into the bag. "Next?"

I fished out a set of keys on a keychain made of paracord. He really was prepared. I looked at each key in turn. Holding one in particular out to the cuffed man. "A bump key?" A set of three keys hung next to the bump key. "Jiggler keys. You really want to get in places, huh?"

No filing cabinet was safe with him around. I dropped the keys into the bag.

Dane handed me a piece of paper. Small, white, folded once. A phone number written in blue ink. I dragged out my phone and dialed the number on the paper.

The phone rang in my hand for six rings, then voice mail kicked in. I listened to the woman's voice. "Medial Data Services. Please leave a message and your phone number. We'll call back as soon as we can." Clever, but not clever enough. I did not leave a message. Medial Data Services. Yeah. Nah. I don't think so. Sounded awful like Central Intelligence Agency to me. Guess answering, "CIA, how may I direct your call?" would give the game away.

"What's your name?" I directed my question to the male in custody.

"Kevin."

"Last name?"

"Costner."

"Great." Because he didn't look anything like Kevin Costner. Before he could confirm or deny his bullshit name, I saw Kurt Henderson striding toward us in a dark gray suit. Now, he did look like Kevin Costner from back in *The Bodyguard* days. I stepped away from the man, leaving him in Dane's capable hands, and met Kurt. "Hey."

"What's going on?" Kurt asked, looking over my shoulder at the scene behind me. "Bomb Squad?"

"I dunno what's going on, but this guy here was about to pick up a potential bomb before I stopped him."

"Pick it up, or was he putting it down?"

"*Kevin Costner* here was picking it up. I had eyes on him the entire walk up the alley." And I did. I entered the alley eight steps behind him, and he didn't appear to notice. He certainly did not have a backpack with him when he entered. The backpack was sitting near the left-hand wall, about halfway along.

"Kevin Costner ..." Incredulousness sung in Kurt's voice.

"So, he says." Already intrigued, I had a feeling the situation was going to get entertaining real quick. I mean, Kevin Costner? "He's carrying what I'd describe as trade tools."

Kurt watched me. I knew the expression on his face from old. "I hope this isn't as alarming as the scary smile on your face indicates."

"It's been dull. Same ol' same ol' at work the last two weeks." I shrugged. If you call being nearly abducted same ol' same ol', and idiots opening fire on us, and the potential of bad guys developing a more lethal Qu. Run-of-the-mill stuff. My eyes rolled.

"Did your guy show?"

"Nope. There was no one in the alley but Costner there." I nodded toward the man. "Something feels hinky." My hink-dar was climbing by the second.

"I imagine it does. Not every day we find an IED in an alley in D.C."

We laughed. Not *every* day. I watched the man. He sat. A neutral expression on his face. At least the smirk was gone before I felt the urge to slap it away.

Mentally I ran through things we had found in alleys over the years. Trafficked underage girls. Lee's brother Mike. Dead bodies. Dumpsters. IEDs. Garbage. Money. Drugs. Tallying up the occurrences, dead bodies came out the clear winner. Such is life with Delta A. We know how to have fun.

"Is it an IED?" Kurt watched the goings on back in the alley.

"They'll tell us." My money was on yes. The answer is yes. "What's on the other side of that brick wall?"

A frown flitted across Kurt's forehead. "A clinic."

"What type of clinic?"

"Women's health."

"What are the odds of that bag being innocuous when it's next to a wall for a women's health clinic?"

Kurt nodded. My phone rang. I took the call.

"Sandra?"

"O Leader and Protector of us all, we have a situation unfolding."

"Us too, what's happening your end ..."

"Abandoned backpacks reported outside four clinics in the D.C. area. One exploded, blowing out a chunk of an exterior wall."

"Injuries?"

"None reported."

That was a relief. No one wants body parts strewn around, and puddles of guts on sidewalks.

"None of these explosives were placed near or in doorways, they were all on solid exterior walls."

"We have a potential IED at our location, same deal, it was left by a solid brick exterior wall."

"Instructions?"

"Get ahead of the media on this. Grab our liaison and left him know there will be a statement once we know what's going on. The media are to release zero information. We do not want our investigation compromised by idiots." I took a breath. "Until we have some idea who is behind this and what's happening. Anyone claiming responsibility?"

Bombing was an Army of God trademark.

Anti-abortionists were gaining traction country wide, with a dozen states rescinding or clamping down on their abortion laws in recent times. My mind whirred bringing up a prophecy from a dead man. I pushed it aside. Thinking about *The Handmaids Tale* and Sergeant Green would not help anyone. Move on, bury the dead with the past.

"Stay safe, O Fearless Seeker of the Truth."

I smiled. One day Sandra would run out of clever titles for me. Today was not that day. With Kurt next to me, I stepped closer to our handcuffed guest.

"Why did you try to pick the bag up?"

His eyes met mine. "I was going to move it."

"Where too?"

He tipped his head down the alley. "I saw a dumpster."

"So, you knew it was a bomb?"

Gee Golly, imagine that?

"No, but I guessed it wasn't just a backpack. People tend to remember putting them down."

"Who are you?"

"We're on the same side, Agent Iverson."

Are we though? I snapped a picture of him with my phone and sent it to Sandra asking for an ID. If it came back Kevin Costner, I'd buy rounds at Murphy's. More fun than eating an item of clothing.

"People on my side tend to provide a name when I ask."

"I bet they do," he mumbled, and moved his legs. "Do you take everyone's belt when you meet them? Leather fetish?"

Ignoring him wasn't difficult.

Sandra sent me a text with an ID.

"Why didn't you just say?" I said to him, as I knelt down and removed the handcuffs. I dropped my voice to a soft whisper. "Would it have killed you to tell me who you were and save any unpleasantness?"

His mouth lifted into a half smile and he whispered, "Maybe it's better for me if it looks like I'm a regular Joe." He coughed, and his normal speaking volume returned. "Thank you, Agent Iverson." He gave his wrists a rub, no doubt for the benefit of anyone watching. I stood and he followed suit.

"Enjoy the rest of your day," I said.

"You too, Agent."

I watched CIA Officer Peter Cooper walk away. He didn't look back.

Kurt joined me.

"What was that about?"

"He's CIA."

"And he just happened along the alleyway ..."

"Doubt it."

I doubt it very much.

Footsteps thundered in the alley. My eyes tracked Dak as he moved fast toward us.

"Cover!"

We ducked behind the barricade created by

sandbags and whatever else they used. Dak dove in dragging a ballistic blanket with him, snuffing out the light. A muffled bang resounded.

"Everyone all right?" Dak asked, from his position hunkered down next to Kurt.

"Yep," Kurt and I said.

"Couldn't defuse it then?" I muttered.

"We did. There was a secondary switch. Tamper-proof."

"Awesome."

Light poured in as the blanket moved away. Tony grinned down at us.

"We copacetic in here?"

"Yeah. You all good out there?" I said.

"Of course."

We clambered to our feet and dusted ourselves off. "You're going to be busy," Kurt said. "We have multiple reports of backpack IEDs and one other explosion."

"All the squads are out, attending. Emergency services are stretched." He watched his men working. "It's three explosions counting this one."

I glanced at Kurt and took a breath. We've been here before. A bomber in D.C. The difference being, this time it was aimed at clinics and not public buildings, tourist areas, or us, or the Navy. This time.

"You do your thing, Tony. We'll start picking up all the known homegrown terrorists."

"Stay safe," Tony said, motioning to Dak to follow him. Dak had definite puppy qualities.

Chapter Eight
Romeo and Juliet

The drive in gave me time to anticipate the irritation of the bazillion emails that lay in wait for me when I woke my laptop from its slumber. Pre-annoyance is real.

Already Wednesday felt shitty. I scrolled through my inbox taking note of anything pertaining to our newly developed alleyway IED situation. My gut said it was homegrown. Why? Because there was nothing to connect those acts of lunacy to offshore asshats. Yet.

Also, we had our own crazy bombers when it came to abortion clinics or reproductive rights. Such judgy assholes. Not helped by the current political climate. Reasoning with idiots is a fool's game. A smile dallied on my lips. I didn't plan on reasoning with anyone. Another thought grew legs and walked out from the shadows. What if there weren't any homegrown terrorists responsible, but the whole thing was orchestrated to cover something? Or cover someone's ass?

Extreme.

I dismissed the notion and any idea of investigating the bombings myself. Tapping an icon on my phone, I called the SSA of Delta C. Delta A had our hands full with the Newgenic/Exical situation.

"I want Delta C to investigate the bombings," I said,

as soon as Brody answered.

"Yes, SAC."

"Everything we have so far is in SENTINEL." I didn't say anything about the CIA or my informant. Best to let Brody and his team investigate without any sort of implied prejudice. There was nothing in SENTINEL about Jeremy Cotton, but Peter Cooper's name was listed as being on the scene. I forwarded Brody a bunch of emails I'd been sent about various groups known to use bombs, and correspondence from forensics.

"We'll get answers, SAC." I heard his email alert chime. "Thanks for the forwards."

"Might be something helpful there. Good luck."

I hung up. Before putting my phone down, I tried to get hold of Jeremy again.

Four times I'd attempted contact with no result. Good chance he saw who left the backpack, if he turned up, that is. Why wouldn't Jeremy Cotton make our meeting when it was his idea? He approached me. He wanted to talk about something he discovered in the scientific community.

Time to try Pamela Straun's work number again.

Same message as yesterday. Dammit. I typed her name into a Directory Search Engine and came up with nothing. Next I tried a social media search. Nothing. I added her name to our search engine. Nothing. Fan-fucking-tastic. Someone who has flown below the radar. Who has no social media? These days, no social media felt like a red flag.

A quiet ah-hem alerted me to a presence moments before my senses told me someone was in my office. Kurt. I'm definitely slipping. Used to know when someone was near me. At least I didn't jump this time.

"That's a creepy smile," he said, dragging a chair across the gray speckled utilitarian carpet.

"Just thinking."

"About squeezing the trigger?"

Couldn't argue with that, so I grinned and nodded. "It would be a nicer world if we could simply put the stupid down."

"That doesn't sound like you."

"I can't find this Pamela Straun woman. Is she the whistleblower? Or is it someone else who passed on the documents? And where is Cotton? And the Forberg man?"

"What does your gut say?"

"Nothing good."

"You'll find them."

"Will it matter if I do?" A sigh drifted from my mouth. It took zero effort. "If we manage to verify this information and stop the weaponization of Qu, will it stop there? Because I find it hard to believe there is only one company playing this dangerous game."

"Starting to sound a bit jaded there, Iverson."

"Maybe I'm tired of fixing other people's acts of stupidity only to find it's a full-on hydra and chopping off one head does nothing."

"One problem at a time. You know the drill. You

cannot fix everything at once."

Sensible advice, and yet it didn't feel like I was fixing anything.

"Maybe."

A familiar warm voice came from nowhere and startled me. "Maybe's ass."

"Hey, Iverson." Kurt leaned forward ready to stand. "You okay?"

My eyes searched the room for the origin. No one but Kurt. "I thought I heard Mac."

"No one here but us," Kurt said, visibly relaxing. "You haven't mentioned him in a while."

"I haven't heard him in a long time."

"How long's it been ... since ..."

"Since he was gunned down by a Russian while protecting Carla in a patrol car?" My voice remained light and even. That's how long it had been.

"Yeah, how long?"

"Eleven years." Eleven years, two months, one week, three days, and ten hours. But who's counting?

"Wow." A smile sauntered onto his face. "We've seen some shit since then." The smile vanished. Replaced with a flash of pain and guilt. Carla.

"It wasn't your fault, Henderson. She didn't want to stay. You did everything you could." A year after Mac died protecting Carla, I adopted her. Seven years, three months, two weeks, four days, and fifteen hours ago, she killed herself. "Sometimes I wonder about the shit we've been through. Does it have a purpose?"

"There were questions after Sam's death, that's for sure," Kurt said, his voice soft.

"We had zero chance of saving him by the time we found him."

"I know. Doesn't mean I don't go over losing Carla and Sam, looking for something I could've done differently."

"Me, too."

"We're still standing," he said, his smile almost found his eyes before retreating.

"Might be proof that miracles exist."

I pressed a number into the keypad on my desk phone, by heart. The waiting began. Two rings. Three. Four. Five.

"SAC Iverson, how can the CIA help you today?" Jonathon Tierney's voice scratched like claws on the bottom of a birdcage.

"Peter Cooper."

"What about him?"

"What do I need to know?"

"He's one of my best operatives."

I'd heard that before. Last time it ended badly.

"I need more than that, Tierney."

"Are you well? We heard someone tried to abduct you."

"It was nothing. Chalk it up to the full moon. Dealt with quickly and now over." My fingers crossed on my left hand. "About Peter Cooper ..."

"I hear he was in the right place at the right time.

Lucky as a new penny as always."

"I've got a missing CI."

"Careless of you, Agent."

"I didn't lose him, Jonathon. He was meeting me in the very alley, Peter Cooper turned up in. The very alley, where there was a bomb in a backpack." I paused. "You've known me long enough to understand my feeling on coincidental occurrences."

"Did your confidential informant plant the bomb?"

"Highly unlikely."

"Are you making the disappearance about Peter Cooper?"

"Look at you catching on. My CI is high enough up the scientific food chain to interest many people."

But he's an American on American soil, so off limits. Even so, I couldn't charge off looking for my CI with a bomb in the vicinity. And, that was on top of Peter Cooper being the CIA poster boy.

"Did you see Mr. Cooper with your confidential informant?"

"No."

"Do you have any evidence that Mr. Cooper knows, spoke with, or otherwise interacted, with your confidential informant?"

"No."

"Does this poor unfortunate have a name?"

"Not one you need to know."

"Been nice talking with you."

"If the CIA has something to do with the bomb, or

the missing CI, or ... knows anything about the development of a new bioweapon, I will find out."

"I don't recall a conversation about weapons."

"Just putting it out there, Tierney. You know, just in case."

"I do enjoy our little chats, Agent."

A split second of silence was followed by *beep, beep, beep*. Rude.

Did Cooper know about my meeting with my CI? If he did, Tierney didn't know his name. Surely that'd be something he would know? A light bulb flashed in my brain. I couldn't remember a time that I'd said his name out loud. Not here anyway. I couldn't remember if I'd mentioned the meeting while I was in the office or not. Something niggled. Overall, the hinkiness grew.

Shit.

I motioned to Kurt and we left the office. I wanted to find Lee.

"Something up?" Kurt asked, as he opened the bullpen door for me.

"Yeah, Tierney. I think my office is bugged."

"That statement added more disquiet than we need right now," Kurt said. "I have some calls to return. The DA wants to touch base. I'll handle that for the team. Let me know how you get on."

I nodded. He carried on to his office. I waved at Dane, and then tapped Lee on the shoulder. He looked up. "What's up, El?"

"Bring your RF detector toy and come with me."

"That sure answers my question." Lee delved into his desk drawer and dug out a small case.

And thus, began the process we all knew by heart. All devices were turned off and Lee fired up his handy toy.

"How often is your office swept?" He asked, as he stood in the hallway outside my office.

"Weekly."

"Here we go then."

Lee walked through the outer office and surveyed my office from the interior doorway. Sometimes I forget just how big a guy he is until he filled all available space with his six feet five bulky frame. He went left and passed the detector close to everything that could conceal a listening device. He paused by my desk and showed me the screen on his RF detector. It lit up like a Christmas tree.

Shit! Lee felt under the lip on the right side of my desk. He bent to see something, then removed a tiny object from the underside of the desk. He handed it to me. It was smaller than my little fingernail. Neither of us spoke until I found a shielded container in my bottom drawer and dropped the bug into it. And Lee swept the room again and then my outer office as well. Nothing.

"CIA?" Lee asked. He turned the machine off and placed it back in its case.

"Bit of a coincidence that we find a bug and my confidential informant goes missing. He must've had intelligence for me otherwise why set up a meet? How and why was the CIA's Mr. Peter Cooper in the alley, with a bomb." I leaned on my desk. "This has ookie spooky alphabet soupy printed all over it in large neon letters. Maybe I'll call Tierney back and let the denials begin." I looked at Lee. "Or, maybe, we'll put that little gadget back and feed it …"

"Like the all-the-way grown up folk we are."

"Laws have been broken. Last I looked, we," I waved my index finger between us. "We are American citizens. We are on American soil. The Central Interfering Agency is not only prohibited from collecting foreign intelligence concerning domestic activities of American citizens, but it is also not allowed to run around bugging Americans at home because this is America." A low growl filled my head. Since when did that stop anyone doing anything.

"Ballsy move on their part," Lee said.

"Yeah. I imagine someone was supposed to retrieve this before the next sweep." And that told me they knew when those sweeps happened. That's fan-fucking-tastic. Not like we haven't been here before.

"Do you think they have something on the Newgenic situation?"

"I just bet they do." They could even have my CI: Jeremy Cotton. Is that what happened to you, Jeremy? And what about the Straun woman and Forberg? And McAlester, did someone hear all that information?

"I can see how dropping that little device in your

office would be tempting, because we suspect that an American company is using off-shore laboratories for nefarious reasons."

I looked up at Lee. "Is nefarious your Word of the Day?"

He grinned. "Been waiting for one like this. You gotta admit it's a crackerjack of a word, El."

"No denying it." I nodded in agreement. "You got yourself a doozy there." He sure did lighten things up with his love of Word of the Day. Don't imagine he had to work too hard to use that one though.

My mind swung back to the idea that an American company has American scientists and chemical engineers inside the off-shore labs working. I stared at the little box with the bug in it. "I just bet they've come across something that's related to our case, in their swampy intelligence channels, but can't act on it."

"We can though?"

"Oh yeah we can. If they share."

Lee frowned. "How do you want to play this?"

"Close. Real close. Last thing we need is Adams getting a whiff of this."

Lee nodded. "He'd love nothing more than to make a song and dance about this. Then we'd have Counter Intelligence crawl all over us."

"Exactly. We don't need that."

He's certainly taken over from where Owen left off. Who knew the Evil Queen had a king? He sits there in his Counter Intelligence office like a marble statue.

Immovable and unwilling to acknowledge the many hues of gray that exist in the real world. Our world.

Adams would love to take Delta down, the last thing I needed was to give him ammunition by withholding information. Maybe it was me he was gunning for? I gave a mental shrug. I know a guy who can fix it.

"I need to talk to my mechanic. And I need you to sweep the outer office, meeting rooms, bullpen, and our cars. Run that toy of yours over everything and anything and do it without too many people noticing."

"You got it, El."

"I need a tech and a camera. Let's see if I can slide that through without alerting Adams to a problem on the floor." Fingers crossed.

"We'll put this little thing back after we've set up a camera, and one of our listening devices in that smoke detector, so we can see who comes to get it." I pointed to a smoke detector on the ceiling near the door. "Wait for a sec?"

"Okay." Lee sat in one of the armchairs in the corner of my office.

I scrolled through my contacts and chose: Mechanic.

SAC Iverson: Hey, Turner, I might have a leaky fuel injector.

Three dots popped up under my message as he typed.

Turner: I've got a minute. Call me.
SAC Iverson: Great

I grinned at Lee. "Here we go."

I called Turner's number.

"What's going on?"

"We have a situation, I need time to work on it and I don't want interference from up above."

"The situation?"

"My office was bugged. One of my team is about to do a quiet sweep of the floor."

"Anything else?"

"Yeah, I need a tech to put a camera in my office and I don't want Adams involved."

"Put the order through via me, I can action it and sit on the paperwork for a while."

"Thank you."

"What are you thinking?"

"Leaning toward CIA but I don't know, yet. I need time."

"I'll get you time. Remember if it's someone who knows their shit, there will be plans A through Z ..."

"I'm aware."

"I got your back. You do what you need to do and I'll keep an eye on this end. Tell the tech I'm writing the report."

"Thank you."

"I better get an invite to Murphy's."

I laughed. "Tequila's are on me."

Lee stood and walked to my desk. "I'll get a tech in here."

"Good thinking, Batman. Make sure the paperwork goes through Turner." I took a folder from my desk drawer, located an electronic surveillance form and filled out the relevant sections, signed the bottom, and handed it to Lee. I couldn't even bug my own office without paperwork. "I'll wait. Tell them it's urgent. We don't want the little device out of commission long. So, I'm putting it back now."

"All right."

Lee left with the form in his hand. I took the device from the shielded box and put it back where we'd found it.

Normal office noises resumed. I hoped whoever was monitoring would think I had just returned from somewhere.

I carried on trying to find Jeremy Cotton until my phone rang.

"SAC."

"We have a work order for your office, SAC."

"I have a minute now, if you're ready?"

"Yes, ma'am. I'll be right up."

I finished up, left my office, and closed the door behind me. Didn't have to wait long in the outer office for the tech to arrive. I met him in the corridor.

"As far as everyone is concerned you are replacing a smoke detector," I said. "The only thing you should say in my office is whatever it is you say when you've finished a job."

"Yes, SAC."

"In you go, I'll be in the outer office." I opened the doors for him so he could get through with his stepladder under one arm, and tool bag in the other.

Five minutes later, he called out, "All done, SAC."

"Thanks." I leaned in the doorway, and with a wink I asked, "Are you finished on this floor?"

He grinned. "Four more smoke alarms to replace up here."

He joined me in the outer office and closed the door behind him. He placed his bag and stepladder on the ground, took a card from his shirt pocket, and handed it to me. On one side was the app I needed to download to monitor the camera feed, and the other, the password.

"Let us know when it needs removing or replacing."

"What's the expected life?"

"Three months for that type."

"Thanks."

The tech hooked his bag into his hand and lifted the ladder until it was snug under his arm. I held the corridor door open for him.

Quietly, I walked back into my office and sat at my desk. I downloaded the app and used the password. Up popped the camera feed. I checked the settings and discovered I could set it to alert me when anyone came in.

Well, that'd stop anyone sneaking up on me in my

office.

I changed the settings so my phone would ping when anyone entered. If that became annoying, I could change it to screen banner only, but then I'd risk missing an alert. I checked the video feed. There I was at my desk. The screen looked like my phone camera screen complete with the ability to record video or take still shots. Clever. My brain wouldn't let me try to figure out how that worked.

My thumbs danced on the virtual keyboard of my phone as I messaged Tahoma Whitehorse.

SAC Iverson: Things are heating up. Let me know when you arrive.

Dane appeared in my office. I motioned for him to follow me out, then once in the outer office, I closed the door. Enjoy the nothing, you eaves-dropping motherfuckers.

"Boss?"

"Get Lee, get a warrant for personnel records, and go over to Exical. We need everything they have on Pamela Straun."

"What grounds?"

"She has information related to our case ..." That wouldn't work. The minute the FBI walk in, evidence will vanish. We need to hold off until we have everything then hit them fast. "Never mind. We're going stealth. Take Sandra to a quiet meeting room. I want you two to get the personnel files. We need to find Pamela Straun."

"When you say get?"

My eyes engaged his. "Don't care how that happens."

"Consider it done." He grinned like a little kid on Christmas morning and rubbed his hands together. "I love me some stealth."

For a second, I thought he was going to go deep into Dean Winchester mode and was about to say pie.

"Have fun, don't get snapped." Dane was already at Sandra's desk before my words reached his ears. He turned and grinned.

Time for me to talk to Frank at the front desk and see what his cameras have to show. No need to call ahead, he'd hear me coming. More accurately, he'd hear my cowboy boots on the concrete stairs long before I shoved the atrium door open.

I pushed through the heavy stairwell door into the hub of the ground floor.

No Frank.

The dull fog of confusion rolled over me. What day is it? Wednesday. Doh! Frank had Wednesday afternoons booked off for training. I leaned over the counter and picked up a notepad. With my pen, I scrawled a note for Frank letting him know I'd be down to see him first thing.

Late afternoon light drew streaks across the atrium floor. It was time I went home and turned from gun-toting crime fighter to super mom. I shook my head.

Sometimes I think some weird shit. But it was home time. Home was where I needed to be.

Chapter Nine
Everyone says Hi

The gate opened just after I turned into the beginning of our driveway. I edged the car through and watched the gate close in the rearview mirror. Satisfied all was well and no one had snuck in behind me, I drove up to the house and parked near the front door. Mitch's car wasn't out, guess he wasn't planning on going anywhere else tonight. At least one of us was certain they were home for the evening. I locked my weapon, holster, badge, and ID in the glove compartment.

The front door opened with the lightest touch. A joyful shriek met my ears. I pressed the door closed and waited. Skittering of paws, and more shrieking followed. Blonde curls, and black and tan fur, raced down the hallway to greet me.

Argo won.

"Hey boy," I said, as he skidded to a halt at my feet and dropped his backside to the floor. I reached down and gave him a hearty pat. "Good boy, Argo. Good boy." His tail swept the floor.

Curly headed little girls bobbed up and down next to Argo.

"Girls," I said, then addressed each child in turn. "Grace. Isabella." Smiles radiated from their small faces.

"Mommy, spin!" Grace squealed. "Spin!"

I bent down, tipped her upside down, and twirled her around before standing her on her feet. She giggled. "More Mommy!"

"One more time," I said, laughing and repeating the exercise. Once on her feet, Grace wobbled, then took off for the kitchen.

Isabella took my hand. I crouched down in front of her.

"How's my little Isabella?"

"Good. Mommy." She smiled, wrapped her arms around my neck, and squeezed. I stood, gathered her into my arms, and hugged her. "Mommy, home now."

"Yes, Isabella, Mommy is home." I knew she wouldn't relinquish her hold on me just yet. "Let's find Daddy."

Argo walked sedately beside me, glancing up at my face every two steps. Guess he liked me coming home too. I decided I'd take him to work in the morning. He'd had a couple of weeks off after a strained ligament, but he was much improved and ready to get back to it.

"Hey, Babe," Mitch said, crossing the kitchen floor to kiss me.

"I'm liking this welcome home thing ya'll have going." I leaned in for another kiss. Our lips met; warmth flooded me. I liked it a lot.

Isabella wriggled. I set her down. "Go and play with Grace. Until dinner."

"Mommy?" She paused, uncertainty shrouded her eyes.

"Mommy and Daddy will be right here."

Her smile dimpled her cheeks and she scampered over to join Grace near the window seat with their up-ended toy box. By the time Mitch had poured me a drink, the girls were playing with blocks and babbling at each other.

"This is nice," I said, sipping the tequila and lime concoction. "How was your day?"

"Good." Mitch peered through the glass in the oven door checking the cooking process. "Roast chicken tonight."

"I'm sure I can do that justice. Don't remember eating lunch." I leaned on the counter. "Tell me about your day ..."

"Everything went as planned."

My head shook slowly. "Unbelievable."

"I spent all day waiting for the other shoe to hit me in the head."

"I bet." I watched Isabella for a moment. "Has she been okay?"

Mitch watched the girls. "She has. She only gets clingy when you get home."

What is it with small people being perfectly happy until mommy arrives on the scene? "Nice that she's gaining some independence."

He nodded. "I can't believe we are about to be parents to two-year-olds."

"After dinner, baths, and once they're in bed, let's figure out what we want to do to celebrate that momentous occasion."

"Works for me." Mitch took my glass. "I'll freshen that for you."

"You've got awesome husband shenanigans down pat."

A Messenger alert banner popped up on my phone screen. Noah Bancroft sent me a message. I could read it without opening it. He asked if we'd met.

Now where would Catherine Thomas meet a thirty-something lawyer? Maybe I should've thought that through earlier. As long as I didn't open the message, he wouldn't know I'd seen it. I had time. That was a job for later. Now we would eat, as family, like we tried to do every night.

Mitch placed my drink in front of me. "About half an hour, then we'll eat."

My stomach growled, rumbling like a freight train coming into a station.

Argo's ears pricked. Mitch laughed. Neither of the girls seemed to notice the outburst from my stomach. I sipped my drink. Rogue thoughts regarding my missing informant and the bug in my office encroached upon my unwind time. That wouldn't do. I shoved it all aside.

Dinner was delicious. After dinner, we played with the girls for half an hour, then Mitch disappeared to draw their bath.

Noah Bancroft sent another message asking if we'd met.

Impatient.

I needed to talk to Debbie Barnes. The information I had on Catherine was at work. Catherine's bio was a hard copy hidden away in my desk drawer. But Debbie might have computer access to the file she created for me. I knew she'd been signing into the Facebook account of Catherine Thomas periodically, just so it didn't get deleted.

"Mommy!" Grace tugged my sleeve. "Look." She pointed to a precarious tower of blocks.

"Clever girl. That's high."

Grace beamed. "My tower."

Isabella reached around herself to grab for a block on the ground, missed and toppled over. Crash! Grace's tower hit the floor. Blocks flew across the tiles with an almighty clatter. Followed closely by an enormous angry wail from Grace.

Isabella burst into tears.

Mitch sauntered into the room trying to keep the smile off his face. I shook my head at him.

"There was a disaster," I said, hugging furious Grace and sobbing Isabella.

"I see that." He took Grace from the arm that held her. "Bath time."

"Yay, Daddy got your bath ready," I said to Isabella. "Go with Daddy and Grace. Mommy will tidy up."

Mitch hoisted her onto his right arm and off they all

went.

My phone alerted again. He really was impatient.

I gave Debbie a call. Someone answered on the fifth ring.

"Hey, it's Ellie. Who am I speaking with?" I learned a long time ago to never assume who answered the phone in their house. Michael and Debbie sounded identical.

"Hi there, El, it's Debbie. How can I help?"

"Not sure if you can yet, but I'm hoping I don't have to go back to the office tonight."

"All right. You better tell me what's going on."

"I'm using the Catherine Thomas profile on Facebook to interact with a target. And the target is messaging me wanting to know where we met ..."

"And he's a what? Is it a he?"

"It is and he's a lawyer with many scum bag clients. He works for Carter, Locke, and Cromwell."

"Charles Locke's firm?"

"Yep."

Silence for a couple of beats.

"I've got your file open. Catherine Thomas allegedly frequents some high-end bars and restaurants. Take your pick."

Sounded like she had quite a nice make-believe life.

"Probably a bar."

"Quill at The Jefferson," she said. "Be evasive. He probably won't want to admit if he hasn't been there."

I laughed. "Since when did a lawyer tell the truth,

right?"

"Are you planning on meeting him ever?"

"No, and Catherine won't be meeting him either. This is recon. I just want a look at his profile without having to get a warrant on a gut twinge."

"Okay. Have fun."

"Thanks Debbie."

I ended the call, opened Messenger, and wrote a reply to Noah Bancroft.

Catherine Thomas: `Quill at The Jefferson.`

I hauled a couple of names to the fore, people I remembered seeing at that bar because Mitch and I went there once or twice a couple of years back. Always smart to have a some names to drop. Nothing happened for a few minutes. I sat on the floor and began gathering the blocks. It required a bit of scooting about to corral them all. As I started putting the wooden blocks in the girls' toy box my phone buzzed. Him again.

Noah: `Do you go there often?`

Not super curious then, or maybe he hadn't been there and didn't know the in-crowd.

Catherine Thomas: `Been a few times.`

I dumped as many blocks as I could pick up at once, in the box. It was going to take quite a few handfuls to clear the floor.

Noah replied: `Perhaps I'll see you there next time.`

And just like that he accepted my friend request. Guess he saw dollar signs and a potential client. With a smile I finished putting the toys in the box. I picked up the box and carried it upstairs. The sound of splashing and giggles from the bathroom filled the hallway. My smile grew. I took the box into the girls' bedroom and put it in the bottom of the closet then closed the door. Out of sight, out of mind, was a real thing with small girls. With work now in the background, I joined Mitch in the bathroom in time to help with the exit from the bathtub. Neither child would get out until the plug was pulled, but the draining water caused panic. It was a race to get them out before the water left, just in case it took them with it.

"Mommy!" Isabella squealed, as the water rushed down the plughole.

I wrapped a towel around her and lifted her clear of the bath.

"All safe," I said, rubbing her dry.

Mitch did the same for Grace. We got them into their pajamas and into bed ready for their story in record time. Two stories later, and they were out to it.

We settled in the two-seater soft leather sofa in the living room with a notepad and pen each. Argo snored on his living room bed near the doorway.

"Bearing in mind that the girls will be two next weekend, have no friends yet, and won't remember this birthday anyway, how do you want to celebrate this milestone?" Mitch said, pen poised above his notepad.

"This is more for us, yeah?"

"That's a fat yes," Mitch replied.

"We're celebrating our tiny babies' survival to the ripe old age of two, we should acknowledge the support and help of our families."

"And friends," Mitch added.

"The usual suspects then?"

With a nod, he wrote something down. "Open house next Saturday? People can call in whenever with no pressure."

"Sure, and maybe those who feel like it can stay on for a barbecue that evening," I said, knowing that Delta A would stay on and celebrate with us. One big awesome family.

"Great idea," Mitch said.

I like anything that means less hassle for us and a barbecue is pretty simple to orchestrate. "Done then. That was remarkably easy."

A little bit reminiscent of their hurried arrival. Deep inside my head, in the midst of a protective fog, was the birth of the girls. Grace arrived three minutes before Isabella. So tiny, so perfect, so unexpectedly early.

"Penny for them?" Mitch said, touching my hand.

"Sometimes I still can't believe we created those two little people," I replied with a smile.

"I don't think that's everything, El. Why is so much of that day blanked out in your mind?"

"How much do you remember of the day the twins were born?" I answered his question with a question.

"Every second," he said with a smile. "Every second of the day that made me a father twice over."

Snap. I chewed the inside of my lip. Except I've spent two years trying to forget everything prior to their birth.

Mitch's voice slid under the fog. "Where were you that morning?"

"You don't recall?"

Mitch frowned a little. "You never told me. You just said you were wrapping up a case."

That day swung into focus. Full technicolor. And I couldn't stop it. It was not a case I ever wanted to revisit, and yet here I was back in the Barrington funeral home. Delta A and I had chased all over hells half-acre looking for missing boys from a D&D game. Three boys escaped captivity and raised the alarm, eventually. I'd felt off all day, but discovering what the Barrington's were really doing, pushed me over the edge. I swallowed hard and shoved the memory as hard as I could, but it stayed. It enveloped me and dragged me back.

There was only one way to deal with this intrusion. I opened my mind and let Mitch see:

"Guard." I touched Argo's head. He sat in front of Barrington Senior. He wasn't going to move, and no one would get past the dog. Not in one piece anyway. Senior got the message.

I said nothing to the man, and followed directions given to me by Dane.

At the bottom of the stairs the air was cool. Voices came from somewhere in front of me. I walked toward the sound.

Near an open doorway, I called out, "Iverson coming in!"

"Back here," Dane hollered.

When I walked in, the first thing I saw was a man in handcuffs face down on the concrete floor. Beyond the man, and the stainless steel table, was a cage built into the room. A jail cell. A jail cell with a terrified teenage boy locked in it.

Andrews unlocked the cell door.

"What the actual fuck," I muttered at Dane, as I stood next to him.

"What we can ascertain is that while they prep the room and so forth, check the orders on their ordering system, because yes, they have one." He flipped a thumb toward a laptop open on a counter. "They keep the victim in that cage over there." He gave the man on the ground a nudge with his booted foot. "I'm sure this gentleman will tell us if we're wrong."

The man on the ground groaned as Dane nudged him in the ribs. I peered at his face. He was the younger Barrington. The son. Jimmy Barrington.

I was on my phone before the third groan and talking to Detective Josh Konstram. "Argo has the owner in the foyer, arrest him on conspiracy to commit murder and kidnapping. And whatever other charges we have at our disposal regarding the sale and trafficking of human meat." Bile rose, I swallowed hard.

"Sorry, say that last part again?"

"I'd rather not."

Silence. Then a slow dawning.

"Holy shitballs. You said human meat."

I breathed in slowly through my nose to quell the nausea.

"Yeah, I did."

"I'll deal with the guy in the foyer, El."

I shoved my phone in my back pocket.

No way in hell did they build a fucking cage without the old man knowing about it. Family business.

A shudder ran through me. A dull ache in my back kicked up a gear. Maybe I should call my doctor.

Dane touched my arm. "You need to sit down, you don't look so good."

I ignored him and spoke to Andrews just as the heavy cell door swung back into the wall. "Come on. Let's get out of this place. It's giving me the creeps."

Andrews took the young man in the cage by the arm. I could hear his calm tone as he spoke inaudible words to the freed teenager.

My back was killing me, and I didn't want to puke in a crime scene. Time to go.

I made another call. "I want a forensic team to my location now."

When I hung up, I remembered that I thought someone was testing the kids. It seemed like a random thought at the time. Dane hauled our guy to his feet, and I got in his face.

"What lab are you using to determine their blood type for organ harvest?"

The guy leaned away, as if he was trying to distance himself from my question. Yeah, it's not that easy.

"Barrington, answer the fucking question," I growled.

He swung his head around to look at me, and with a small laugh, he said, "Yours."

Holy moly.

I walked into the hallway and called Stewart. "They've been using our fucking lab to type the blood. Find out who inside our lab is working for the Barrington family."

I ended the call before he could say anything.

Back in the room, I addressed the younger Barrington. "What was wrong with the three boys you didn't butcher?"

"They wasted our time. One was marinating himself

in Axe body spray, one was a smoker, and the other kid had a diet issue."

"What kind of diet issue?"

"He ate gross food. What thirteen-year-old eats asparagus and curry on a daily basis, and eats raw garlic as a snack?"

One who plays D&D and is scared of vampires? May you rot in hell you utter bastard. I looked at the unrepentant horror of a man in front of me. Evil hidden in a personable exterior. Evil walks among us and most people have no idea.

Nausea rose. My back ached. I had a bad feeling. Neither baby had moved or kicked in almost an hour.

"Dane, I gotta go."

"Yes you do, go call Mitch or I will." He threw me the keys. "You okay to drive?"

I nodded and hurried away.

My call to Mitch went to voice mail. I left a message. "Meet me at the hospital."

***

Mitch grabbed for my hand. "They were selling people meat?"

"Yeah, long pork. Harvested from teenagers and children. Cyber discovered they also traded in fetuses and placentas."

He turned a strange shade of green. "Why would anyone ..."

"No idea." My fingers wound around Mitch's. "I've managed not to think about that case at all since then, so thanks for trip down memory lane."

"Sorry. No wonder you went into early labor." He kissed the side of my head. "I remember you decided to take early maternity leave and you were looking forward to having a few months off before the babies." His hand squeezed mine. "And you didn't get any time."

"I kinda did. There was the four weeks while they were in the NICU." And I spent all day, every day, watching them try to breathe and fight to live. "Then another three weeks before we could bring them home."

"I think we should give moving to New Zealand, serious thought."

"And leave all this?"

"Yes. I can work remotely. I did it during the lockdown. I can do it permanently from another country. I'd quite like to step back and just design gadgets and drones again." He drew me into his arms. "Instead of all the daily grind of running the company and sourcing contracts, and the juggling acts we pull off every day to find enough time for the girls and us."

He had a point, or two. Could I though? Could I leave Delta A. Leave the FBI. Walk away and be a full-time mom?

"It's something to think about, for sure." I leaned my head on his shoulder. "I'm not dismissing this out of hand. I'm serious about giving it real thought."

"I know, babe."

My eyes closed, Mitch's arm wrapped tighter around my shoulders. Music filtered through the air on tiny waves of warmth that washed through me, a song I'd heard before but couldn't quite place. My thoughts flowed with the music, and I recognized Kenny Rogers voice. It was so clear, I kinda expected him to tap me on the shoulder. Wouldn't that just be amazing? I opened one eye. No Kenny. My eye closed. Mitch kissed my forehead.

A projector screen rolled down in my mind, an image wobbled, I blinked, and there on the screen was Kenny Rogers microphone in hand. White haired, white beard. I watched for a few seconds trying to work out what was happening.

Kenny was singing about old friends, another voice joined in before the owner came into view. Dolly Parton. This was something I needed to pay attention to. For reasons unknown, Kenny Rogers and Dolly Parton were singing 'You can't make old friends' to me. Waves created by the lyrics tumbled over me, leaving the faces of my team in the frothy wake. My whole team, not just the ones I had left.

I saw Sam and Lee, then Dane and Stewart, Mac, and finally Kurt. The song sung on, the images became clearer. It was Murphy's bar. We'd wrapped up a case. A half empty bottle of tequila sat on the table. Shot glasses in front of everyone. Laughter flowed like water rolling in and out on the tide. I started a story, Sam finished it. Lee poured another round, Kurt gave me a sideways look. It said, 'You're okay. We're all here. We survived another one.' Dane and Stewart ribbed each other over a miscommunication, both laughing. Sam chuckled and threw a napkin to Dane as his drink toppled. Mac passed the bottle to Lee.

The scene froze mid-everything. It didn't happen, it wasn't a memory, but a mashup of many memories.

The song ended.

Kenny and Dolly were right, you really can't make old friends. How the fuck could life go on without them?

Everyone slipped under a crashing wave when Mitch's voice broke through, "We probably do need a birthday cake. It's expected at a little person birthday."

And I was back.

"It's expected at *any* birthday, babe, don't forget it," I replied, the thought of trying to bake a cake, terrifying. Wonder if pancakes with a candle would be acceptable? I can do pancakes. All sorts of pancakes. I could do a big stack of assorted flavors. Banana. Blueberry. Raspberry. Chocolate chip. "You know what'd make a great faux cake?"

Mitch chuckled as he shook his head. "I'm vetoing the pancake cake idea. Seriously. no."

That's the problem with being on the same wavelength all the time, he can veto my amazing ideas way too quickly.

"You don't know how outstanding it would be, obviously. Just imagine it for a moment … all those delicious layers drizzled with maple syrup." Dammit, I wanted pancakes.

Argo woofed. I glanced at him. Fast asleep. His paws twitched. Must be a happy dream. Maybe he was dreaming about pancakes.

"El, let the pancakes go."

"I think we should go make pancakes."

"Right now?"

"Uh huh." I was on my feet heading for the door before Mitch put his notepad down. I moved around Argo careful to let him sleep.

"Hey, did you hear Kenny Rogers a few minutes ago?"

I paused in the doorway and arched an eyebrow at Mitch. "This is what happens when you wander around in my brain … aren't you lucky it wasn't 'Islands in the Stream'?"

His face crumpled. "No … that was cruel."

"You're welcome for the ear worm." I laughed and walked down the hallway. I got to the kitchen before I heard my phone chime.

"Your phone," Mitch said, catching me up and handing it to me. "Who is Noah Bancroft?"

I glanced at the screen and saw another message from Noah. He'd be at Quill on Friday night.

"He's a lawyer."

"A lawyer? Do you want to tell me something?"

A laugh bubbled forth. "Not really. It's a work thing."

"You're meeting him at Quill?"

"No. I'm not meeting him ever." Catherine Thomas might. No. Nope. Don't go there. No one is meeting anyone. "He's representing a low-life and it's a work thing. I can't talk about it." I clanged all the work doors closed in my mind before anything that alerted Mitch to the attack on our little convoy popped out and left the pancake thoughts in the open. "Pancakes, let's go."

Chapter Ten
One Cup of Coffee

Dane and Sandra were waiting in my outer office when I arrived at work. Argo greeted them with typical enthusiastic tail wagging.

"Morning. You got contact details for me?"

Sandra shook her head, her glasses slid, she repositioned them. "There is no personnel file for Pamela Straun. No Straun's at all."

"Bit odd, I spoke to reception who put me through to her phone the other day, so she was an employee."

Dane spoke, "I called reception this morning and asked for her extension, and they told me no one works there by that name. When pressed, they said to their knowledge no one ever had."

"That can't be good." We had nothing but a name. Couldn't put out an All-Points Bulletin with just a name. I needed more, a description or something. "Thanks for trying. Let's hope she surfaces at some stage."

"Sorry El," Sandra said. She gave Argo a rub on the head. He pushed her hand, so she'd do it again.

"Not your fault. I find it hard to believe they've scrubbed her from existence especially as someone knows her *cousin* was looking for her yesterday and her *doctor* called their Human Resources department."

I walked into my office, dropped my bag next to my chair, and put my laptop on my desk.

Argo settled on his bed while I checked email and messages.

Nothing earth shattering or requiring immediate attention lurked. Made a nice change. Then I thought about the case in front of us. That had earth shattering potential and ended the feeling that maybe today wouldn't be so bad. What happened to Straun, and where was Forberg, and who else knew about this situation?

Sandra was back behind her desk and Dane gone, when Argo and I emerged twenty minutes later. I held Argo's leash folded into my hand. It wasn't clipped to his harness, there was zero need for that inside our building.

Time to visit Frank.

Frank's voice rang across the atrium, "Morning, SAC. Morning, Agent Argo. How'd I know it was you two?"

"Always said your investigative skills were wasted behind a desk, Frank."

"Passing through?"

I smiled. "No. Came to see you Frank. I left you a note ..."

"You sure did. Hoped maybe you were on a coffee run ..."

Subtle.

"Later. I'll bring you your usual."

"What do you need from me, Ellie?" He bent down and gave Argo an affectionate pat on the shoulder.

"Looking for someone the front cameras might've picked up."

"Gimme a minute, I'll get Chadd in here to watch the desk, and we'll go through to the surveillance room."

"Awesome."

Less than thirty-seconds later, a uniformed agent came through the front doors and took Frank's place behind the desk. Frank let me and Argo into the surveillance room. A small, dimly lit room with no windows, and above a narrow desk that ran the length of one wall, was a bank of screens. They were arranged around a central larger screen. Was a new set up, and so far we all liked it.

Two office chairs sat side-by-side. Frank sat in one and motioned to me to sit.

He dragged a keyboard and trackpad closer to him.

"How far back do we need to go?"

Before I arranged to meet my CI. "Three days."

"And you know who you're looking for?"

Kinda. "A spook."

Frank gave me a side-eyed look. "We talking ghosts?" His head shook. "We're not are we?"

"Nope."

"And this person accessed our building?"

"Wanna check?"

Frank bought up a screen, clicked a box, and started typing. A list popped up. "Name?"

"Peter Cooper."

"No one by that name signed in."

So, he probably didn't do it himself then.

"Good to know. But I still need to know if he was in the vicinity."

Frank went back to the video screens. "Do you have a photo by any chance? It'd speed things up."

Do I? I did. I scrolled through my photos. Dammit. I must've deleted it after I got the ID.

"I don't, but I'll bet Tony does." Someone from the day of the bomb would've taken a scene photograph and he was bound to be on it. I sent a text to Tony asking for any photos from the alleyway.

Frank and I watched the main screen. Saw people I knew, and people I recognized from the area, but no Peter Cooper. My phone buzzed a photo from Tony.

"Can I use Bluetooth to get this into your system?" I showed Frank the image.

"Yes. It'll show under *other devices* as SENTINEL dot Frank."

I checked my Bluetooth settings and there it was. "Done."

The main screen changed, the image from that day filled the screen, and sure enough there was Peter Cooper with me. I sent a quick thank you text to Tony.

Good work.

"The guy with me, that's who I'm looking for."

Frank worked some magic and I crossed my fingers. "Now we wait, if he's been anywhere near this building, we'll find him."

Seconds ticked by as the computer searched for a face. After thirty-seconds, I stood and stretched. "Coffee?"

Frank chuckled. "Ants in your pants, SAC?"

I tipped my head toward Argo and headed for the door. "Americano?"

"Thanks."

"Argo, wait," I said at the main exit to the building. He stopped. I clipped his leash to his harness, and we carried on.

Ten minutes later I pushed through the café door and heard Jake's voice call out, "Hey Ellie."

"Hey, ya self."

He eyes shot past me and settled on Argo, then he grinned. "The usual?"

"Yes, and an Americano, and a couple of your fantastic chocolate muffins."

"Does he need a drink?"

"Wouldn't hurt." Jake passed a bowl of water over the counter to me. I put it on the floor out of the way and told Argo it was for him.

Five minutes later we left with two coffees and a couple of Jake's chocolate muffins. Everything balanced precariously from my left hand while my right held Argo's leash. I attempted a meander rather than my usual long stride, hoping to suck up some more time. A little voice way down deep in my skull muttered that the computer might be finished already.

A large shop window on my right caught my eye. Or rather, the reflection of someone across the road caught my eye. I paused to look at the merchandise displayed, when the man across the road turned, I saw his face in the window. Peter Cooper.

What were the odds?

Question time.

I checked the traffic and crossed between cars to step onto the pavement in front of Peter.

He faltered for a fraction of moment, then smiled. "Two coffees, guess one isn't for me ..." His eyes lit on the dog. "Your dog drinks coffee?"

"Usually he manages to get by with water. What brings you to this part of town?"

You know, right around the corner from the Hoover Building.

"Shopping."

I looked past him into the shop window. "Souvenirs? A map?" He didn't reply to my question. "Perhaps it's a tee-shirt you were after. Bet they have some with POTUS on them."

"Don't think that's the right kind of gift."

"You wouldn't know anything about a listening device planted in my office?"

Peter's eyes narrowed, he chewed the inside of his cheek for a moment. "We're not allowed to spy on the FBI."

"Since when has that stopped the CIA?"

"Don't know who you've dealt with in the past,

Iverson. But that's not how I operate."

I lowered my voice. "You work for Jonathon Tierney, so that is *exactly* how you operate."

He turned away. "We're done here."

Argo barked once.

"I don't think we are, Mr. Cooper. We'll be having another chat before long."

I crossed the road and walked back to work.

Who the hell was he kidding? Not how he operates, my ass.

My phone pinged. I tucked the leash in my back pocket and wriggled the phone from my front jeans pocket. Having twins made me a lot better at one-handed-almost-everything. The alert was the camera app. I opened the app and watched for a few seconds. Kurt. He walked in, saw I wasn't there, and walked out. Spying on my people felt weird.

Chapter Eleven
You Can Do Magic

I gave Frank his coffee and got him to take a muffin from the bag, on my way to the stairwell. He was still running through video footage.

Just as I swung the door open, his voice rang out behind me, "SAC, I got something."

I spun around, let the door close, and hurried to Frank's desk. "Wow us, Frank."

He smiled, patted Argo on the head, and pointed to an image on his screen. "I went back a few weeks out of curiosity. That there is ..."

"Peter Cooper." Hot damn. "Who is he talking with?"

"That's the interesting thing, SAC. Our facial recognition database returned a name. That there is Grant Hardcastle. He's British."

"And we have him on file, why?"

"He's a scientist, working here on a research program funded by the Federal Government." Frank gestured to the information on the screen.

"A virologist," I said. Well, fuckadoodledo. Another scientist. "That's very interesting. Can you send me a copy of all that, please?"

"It'll be waiting when you get upstairs, SAC."

"Thanks Frank."

My phone buzzed.

Tahoma Whitehorse: `Landed at Dulles. We are planning on being with you within the hour.`

"One other thing, Frank. A couple of CDC colleagues are coming to see me. Doctor Tahoma Whitehorse and Doctor Karen Schneider. Can you send them up once they're signed in?"

"Of course, SAC. They've been in before I remember the names."

"Nothing wrong with your memory," I said with a smile. "See you soon." I waved over my shoulder, dropped my now empty takeout cup in the trash by the stairwell door, and adjusted my grip on the muffin bag. Argo and I took off at a run up the concrete stairs.

Sandra looked up as I neared her desk. Argo panted, his tongue lolling from the side of his mouth.

"I know that look," she said, waving her hand at my face. "What's happening?"

I shrugged. "Dunno yet, but something is."

Sandra pushed her glasses into place and gave me a contemplative look. "Okay."

"Drs Whitehorse and Schneider are coming in. Show them to a meeting room when they arrive, please."

"Sure."

That should prevent whoever bugged my office from knowing about them, at least. A second after I walked into my office, the camera app pinged to let me know someone was in my office. Shame I couldn't tell it not to alert when it's me. I unclipped the dog's leash and he flopped on his bed.

True to his word, copies of the images and the file we had on Grant Hardcastle were waiting in my inbox.

I started digging around in my missing CI's information looking for a link to Hardcastle. After half an hour of searching through data, and cross-checking references, I found something.

They worked for the same company, ten years ago. Jeremy Cotton and Grant Hardcastle were both employed by Schröder Forschung, a German company situated in Berlin. Jeremy worked for Schröder for a period of five years and Grant was there six years. There was little else by way of information, nothing mentioned what they were employed as, or to do. They were working for the same company at the same facility. Good chance they'd met. That made Hardcastle's appearance intriguing. What I needed was a way to talk about Hardcastle and Cotton without anyone knowing who I was talking about. A way to keep Hardcastle out of the mix for now.

I stared at their names written in my notebook. Letters jumped off the page and floated above my desk. Jeremy Cotton's name glowed with an almost neon quality. The letters joggled, jiggled, twisted, and shuffled into new positions. It took a few attempts before the letters glowed bright, and brighter, then flashed. I wrote down the result. Damn that was super.

Joyce Tremont. The name dissolved into the ether. The letters of Grant Hardcastle's name grew in size, until they were nearly three inches high. They twisted and danced while they moved into various new places. The name Rachel emerged, glowed with a sun-like brilliance, and then faded into the background. The rest of the letters maneuvered into several positions and then pulsated as they moved again. The letters finally settled. The word Rachel emerged from the background and joined the rest of the now beaming name: Dr. Rachel Stantang.

I picked up my pen and added the new name to my notebook. Now that was fun. Yet another example of the enthralling machinations of my brain.

I called Kurt into my office. Before he arrived, I sent him a message.

SAC Iverson: There is an active bug in my office. Play along. Also, I have a camera in here.

He walked in the door with a smile on his face and his phone in his hand.

"What do you have?" Kurt moved a chair closer before sitting.

"An interesting potential link," I said, typing a few sentences into the case files before I looked up.

I picked up my cell phone and messaged Kurt.

SAC Iverson: Dr Rachel Stantang is Grant Hardcastle.

That way the CIA, or whoever it was, got no more information than they already had, and considering how much work happened in my office, they probably had plenty. "Doctor Rachel Stantang." Kurt read his phone message and nodded. "A new player in this game. Where do we jump from here?"

SAC Iverson: Joyce Tremont is Jeremy Cotton.

Kurt's phone chimed. He glanced at the phone in his hand and grinned at me.

"We need to have a conversation with Doctor Stantang and see what she knows about Joyce Tremont," I said.

"Have we come across the Tremont woman before?"

"Yes and no, it's been a while since I've seen her. An old acquaintance. But the appearance of the good doctor with a connection to Tremont is thought-provoking."

I typed a few words in the Delta team chat box to let them all know Delta A was out of the office. Then I typed in the private Delta A chat to summon Lee and Dane for a field trip.

My eyes met Kurt's. "I have a couple of meetings." I shook my head. "We'll locate Tremont and Stantang this afternoon and bring them in for a chat."

"Let me know when you're ready. I'll keep trying to track down witnesses who could have seen your CI in the alleyway."

"I'll be with the Chief if you need me."

Kurt left my office. I saw his shadow lurking in the outer office. I closed my laptop, gathered up everything I needed, including my iPad and Argo, and joined him. We didn't speak until the outer door was closed and we were nearly at the stairwell.

Kurt touched my arm. "Where did Tremont and Stantang come from?"

I shot him a grin a mile wide. "Think about it ..."

A frown burrowed into his brow. Thoughts raced across his eyes. I waited.

"How do you do that so fast?" Kurt muttered shaking his head. "Are they anagrams for Jeremy Cotton and Grant Hardcastle?"

"Yep. But it wasn't fast. I figured it out before you arrived." Probably best if I don't mention dancing letters and glowing words in the air. "As long as the CIA, or whoever owns the bug, think we are looking for two women and one of them is a doctor, we might buy ourselves enough time to find Hardcastle and Cotton."

"Your mind, Iverson, is ... it just is." He opened the smoke stop door. Yeah, he didn't need to know about the neon letters vying for position. That'd just worry Kurt and there wasn't anything to worry about. "Hold up, you said *whoever* owns the bug. Is there doubt in that steel trap of a mind of yours? Are you considering it might not be the CIA?"

"Open minds solve crimes."

I nudged him when I saw Lee and Dane walking toward us. We waited.

"Got an address?" Lee asked, motioning toward the elevator doors. "We'll take the elevator."

"Nope, but we'll get one," I replied, with a lot more positivity than I felt. The door closed quietly behind us, blocking out all noise from the Delta floor. There wasn't much time to come up with a direction. As long as it took me to run down to the parking garage. Argo panted at the bottom of the stairs, his tongue flopped out of his mouth. He won.

Kurt opened the back-passenger door for the dog and clipped him into his seat belt.

My phone rang as I climbed into the passenger seat. Sandra.

"O Leader of the Invincible Deltas, I have something for you."

"An address?"

"Indeed. Hardcastle lives in an apartment complex in Fairfax. Texting it through now."

"Thanks Sandra."

My phone buzzed in my hand. The address. I copied it to Lee, then told Kurt where we were going. Sandra texted me moments later with car information. Grant Hardcastle drove a blue Nissan Sentra. It was part of the Newgenic fleet. We had a file on him that said he was doing government funded research, but it did not mention Newgenic; the company he was supposedly working for was Dawn. So, was he working for both? Or was Dawn also part of Newgenic? If that was so, did that mean the government was funding Newgenic's research projects? Or maybe just one or two of their projects?

* * *

Forty-seven minutes later, I dropped a bulletproof vest over my head and fastened the Velcro on the left side. I added an FBI windbreaker to complete the look, then tied my long hair into a ponytail using the hair tie I carry on my wrist. Kurt joined me by the back of the car. He wore his vest and jacket. He handed me my cap. I shoved it on my head, threading my ponytail through the gap in the back, then wrapped Argo's leash around my left hand and gripped it tightly.

Lee and Dane appeared behind our car, similarly attired. Minus the dog leash.

"How we doing this?" Lee asked, while he checked his weapon.

I scanned the curbside parking out front and couldn't see a blue Nissan Sentra. He could be out. My gut said otherwise.

"Kurt and I will take the front, you two the back. His apartment is on the ground floor, one in from the corner. According to the map, there is access via an alleyway at the rear. Didn't look like there was parking out there, so maybe the only parking is out front, I don't see his car."

"Let's go shake the tree and see if a Brit falls out," Dane said. One glance told me he had his weapon in hand. Dane and Lee crossed the road.

Kurt and I released our weapons from their holsters on our walk down the street to the apartment complex.

I adjusted my grip on my weapon at the curb in front of Hardcastle's apartment. Lee and Dane vanished from site. One Mississippi. Two Mississippi. I tipped my head toward the door. Kurt nodded. Side-by-side we approached the front door. I banged on the door with my left hand, then stepped toward the hinge on the right side of the door. Kurt moved to the left.

A chair scraped on the balcony above us. A sliding door closed.

I leaned over and knocked again.

"Could be at work," Kurt said, peering into a window next to the door. "Think I saw movement."

I knocked again. "See anything?"

He nodded. The lace curtain over the window moved. A cat meowed. Argo jumped up to see where the noise came from. "Down," I said, softly. He dropped to his feet and watched.

"He's got a cat," Kurt said.

That's usually what meows, Sherlock.

"Suppose he drinks tea as well. Seems kinda clichéd British." The thought of a tea drinking cat lover made me smile. No idea why. If he wore a bowler hat and carried an umbrella, I'd be in real trouble.

"Crap," Kurt mumbled. "The cat's face is covered in something red."

I thought cats were fastidious self-cleaners.

"Maybe it just ate ... and we disturbed it before it could wash?"

"This cat eats well. Fresh meat judging by the coloration of the fur on its face."

I walked across the small stoop and looked in the window. A white and gray fluffy cat stretched a paw up the lace curtain leaving a smear of red. It pressed its face through the gap created by the movement. Red smooshed across the windowpane.

Argo grumbled beside me.

"The cat might be hurt." Definitely looked like blood smears. "We're going in," I said. Kurt called Lee. I holstered my weapon, handed the leash to Kurt, then used a slip card from my wallet to open the front door. As soon as the door popped open, I called out, "Mr. Hardcastle! Are you home?"

The cat meowed and rubbed around my legs, then took off down the hallway before I could grab it. Kurt handed me the leash and followed the cat. Argo whined. "Cat's are friends, not food," I whispered to the dog, and settled him by placing my hand on his head for a heartbeat. He knew. "Working here, pal."

I heard a door. Lee called out. "FBI entering."

"We're inside," I called back. I looked around the living room on my left. Tidy. There was a cup on a side table. On closer inspection it was the dregs of a cup of tea. Perfect. I wandered back to the hall. On the right was a bedroom. Nothing untoward. A dent where the cat probably slept on one of the pillows.

Kurt's voice rang out. Dane answered. A tap turned on in what I guessed was the kitchen. I found the kitchen, but no Kurt. Lee had filled the cat's bowl with water.

"Is it hurt?"

"Doesn't appear to be," Lee replied, stroking the cat as it drank the fresh water. "Thirsty little thing."

Kurt called out again, "Iverson, bathroom!"

"Coming," I hollered back.

"I'll take him," Lee said.

"Stay," I said to Argo, and handed Lee his leash. "With Lee."

Dane stood in the hallway outside the bathroom door.

"Henderson, you yelled?" I said, from the hallway next to Dane.

Dane's head swiveled. "Think we found Hardcastle."

"Come in here, Iverson. I don't think the cat is hurt," Kurt said.

My heart dropped so fast I thought I was going with it. I grabbed the doorframe for a second. Once I was sure I wasn't going to hit the floor, I took a breath and stepped through the door.

It was a regular sized bathroom, toilet on one side, bathtub on the back wall, then a decent vanity and basin. No immediately apparent body. Just Kurt near the shower in the corner next to the vanity.

"He's in there, isn't he?"

"Yes."

"Dead long?" I couldn't smell decomp, so he wasn't a big melty blob, yet.

"Few hours, maybe, since last night."

"Natural causes?" I knew it wasn't, but I hoped.

"Nope. Unless that's what we call slitting someone's throat these days."

Crapadoodledo. He moved over so I could see. A deceased male in the shower. He'd slumped to the bottom in a pool of congealed blood. Blood streaked the walls. He was naked, shriveled. My eyes were drawn to the bottom of the shower and the bathroom floor. Cat prints. I looked at Dane. "Did you get an ID?"

"Yes. Fingerprints match Grant Hardcastle."

I nodded. Of course they did. Our idiot talked to him and now he's dead.

"Kurt, was he chewed on?" From what I could see, it did not look like the cat had nibbled anywhere. But it's a cat, so it would not surprise me if it had.

"Maybe a little." Kurt pointed with a gloved hand to the lowest part of the deceased's neck.

Yeah, there we go, I won't be getting another cat anytime soon. Don't think Argo is overly fond of them anyway. The dog is smart.

I took gloves from my pocket and snapped them on. Time to have a chat with the deceased. "Room for me?"

I asked.

Kurt stood and moved back. "I'll be right here with Dane."

I didn't reply. Instead I crouched as close as I could to the body and spoke softly. "Mr. Hardcastle, I'm sorry your life ended this way." I took a breath. "Can you show me what happened?"

Cold seeped from the shower floor, up my feet, into my bones and my core. Deep breath. Someone shoved me smack into the wall. Another breath. Hot water poured over my face. Cold hands pushed water away, seeking the taps. Fingers slipped. Feet slipped. Another set of hands grabbed my shoulders pulling me back. Choked. Arms flailed. A blade in my periphery. I willed Hardcastle to turn his head. To look at his attacker. Instead he slumped through me onto the cold wet shower tray.

His dead eyes stared at the pool of coagulated blood. I touched his shoulder. "I need you to look at your attacker. Show me his face."

Hardcastle's head turned. Dead eyes animated beyond the cloudy surface. His hand reached for mine. He tugged my hand with surprising strength and unbalanced me. I fell into him. The warmth of my body vanished inside his coldness. Time rolled back. The arm that choked came from nowhere, and applied pressure to my throat.

I clawed at it with my right hand. Forcing my head to turn, I saw the attacker's profile. I took a breath. To get a better view, I dropped. The weight of my body forced the attacker to change positions, and his grip. The blade tweaked in the corner of my eye. From the ground I looked up and saw his face. Asian. I committed the snapshot to memory. Hardcastle shoved me hard and I landed outside the shower.

I blinked. Took a breath. And looked at Kurt.

"Okay?"

"Yep. Check under his fingernails. Right hand."

"Did you see the killer?" I could tell by his tone that he couldn't believe the words that came out of his own mouth.

Dane spoke, "She did. So did I." He dragged his notebook from his pocket and began sketching. Seconds later, he showed me the image of an Asian male with short cropped hair. "Could be Chinese."

"That's him, and that was my first thought too, Chinese."

"Good work," Kurt said, taking the notebook for a closer look. "Now we just have to find him."

"And check the body for DNA," I said. "I think he scratched the killer trying to get free."

Mixed memories of another case and multiple shower deaths, grew in intensity. Bodies collided with one another as the dead vied for attention. I felt Dane's eyes on me.

"You all right?"

The room closed in.

"I need ... air," I said, and tugged the neck of my

shirt away from my skin to create a breeze.

"Iverson, go outside," Kurt said. "Dane, take her out of here."

Dane's hand guided me. Bodies piled upon bodies. Stacked in a pristine shower. Dead eyes. Death masks. The dark earthy, slightly sweet scent of patchouli rose from the bodies. Voices mingled with images of their deaths. The faces of the dead with me forever. It took all my mental energy to force the memories into a vault and clang the door shut.

My vision cleared. I was sitting on the back step of Hardcastle's unit. Dane sat beside me.

"Better?" Dane asked.

"Yep."

"What was that case?"

"An artist liked to paint in blood. And a couple of thugs, a cop, and someone from our HR department, were involved in providing and draining the victims."

"Psychos everywhere," Dane muttered.

"Yeah, I definitely found it a bit Hitchcockian in the beginning."

"It wasn't long before Stewart and I came along was it?"

"Nope. It was a couple of months before you two joined us." And I nearly donated blood to the art project, unwillingly. I shoved that memory aside. "Let's get back in there and see if Hardcastle had any information on the Qu situation."

I stood. Nothing bad happened.

We rejoined Kurt, who must've gone out the front to grab his backpack from the car. The deceased wore paper bags over his hands to protect any evidence.

"I've called forensics and the ME."

"Good. Dane, get scene guards please. Use O'Hare Security. And send that image to Sandra." I turned and walked out of the room. Lee was in the kitchen. He'd fed the cat. "Did you search?"

"Whole house. Argo found a laptop under a bed. Way under, up against a wall it was pushed in so far." He tapped a large evidence bag. "He's a very good boy."

Yes, he is. Argo leaned on my leg.

"Anything else?"

"No. Not even a cell phone."

"Not often we come across someone without a cell phone. Killer might've taken that." Either didn't know there was a laptop or didn't have time to hang around looking.

"Figured the killer would take it if there was one."

On the wall next to the back door was a row of small hooks. I took a closer look. One set of keys. They weren't for a car. Did he drive home, get a cab, or ride share? Did he Uber?

"Did you find any car keys?"

Lee shook his head. "They might be with the cell phone."

"Wallet?"

"No. Good chance his wallet, keys, and cell phone were together, and are together."

I called Sandra at the office. "Hey, I need you to find out if Grant Hardcastle had a cell phone. If he does, we need access to all information stored on it, and his call records."

"Want to me write up the warrant."

"Yes. This is a murder investigation of a British national working here."

"I'm on it."

"Also, run the image Dane is going to send you through all of our databases."

"The image came through a minute or two ago. I'll run it now."

"Can you confirm that he still had use of the blue Nissan Sentra. We have no car on scene and no car keys."

"I'll contact HR at Newgenic. How much information do I give?"

"As little as possible."

"Okay."

"Thanks."

I shoved my phone in my pocket and leant on the edge of the kitchen table. The cat purred around my legs. Nope.

"What do you want to do with the cat?" Lee asked, bending down to pet the animal.

"Give the SPCA a call and tell them the cat's owner is deceased. Did you find a cat cage anywhere?"

"Actually yes, I did. In the closet of the master bedroom."

"You wanna put the furry demon creature in the carrier and drop it off?"

"Sure."

Chapter Twelve
Promises

It was almost dark when the medical examiner and forensics arrived. The scene guards turned up a few minutes later. Once we'd handed over to forensics we left. My phone pinged. I touched the notification and the camera app opened. I saw Sandra placing something on my desk. I watched her leave. It felt a lot like spying and I did not like it at all.

Dane accompanied Lee to drop the cat at the nearest SPCA animal shelter.

Kurt and I went straight back to the office. All hope of being home for dinner evaporated.

Sandra waved me over to her desk. "The information you asked for is waiting for you."

I know, I saw. I kept that creepiness to myself.

"Any problems?"

"No. His telco coughed it all up without a fuss." She continued typing.

"Good." Makes a nice change.

Sandra looked up from her screen. "You have a meeting with EAD Grafton in forty-minutes."

"Do I?"

"He scheduled it while you were out."

"Did Caine say what the meeting was for?"

"He did not."

It was pointless asking how he sounded. His usual was akin to a black bear woken from hibernation by someone throwing stones. "Reminder set?"

She adjusted her glasses. "Sure is."

"Whitehorse?"

"He and Karen have gone to check into a hotel. They'll be back first thing tomorrow."

"Great. Meeting room when they arrive."

"I haven't forgotten," Sandra said, with another glasses adjustment, and a perky smile.

"I'm taking this guy down to the break room for a snack," I said. Argo looked up at me with knowing eyes. I may not get home in time for dinner, but he would not go hungry.

There weren't many people around. I took Argo's bowl from the cabinet and poured a large cup of kibble from the container we kept on the counter. He sat and waited. I filled his water bowl and put both bowls down at the same time. He waited. I unclipped his leash.

"Argo, eat."

I gave him a pat as he chomped into the bowl of crunchy dog food then poured myself a glass of water. By the time he was finished eating and drinking, I'd finished my water. I washed his bowls and put them away, then we walked side-by-side back to my office. No leash required.

Argo settled on his bed in my office.

My phone pinged as I sat behind my desk. One glance at the screen showed it was the camera app. I touched the alert and there I was sitting at my desk. A smile lay on my lips as I closed the app and turned my attention to work. I could imagine the alerts getting old real quick. With a flip of my wrist the folder in front of me opened, and I began to read. Whoever had Hardcastle's phone could have the ability to see most of this information. Unless the phone was locked. I flicked the edge of the page as I read. A smile eased over me.

He had an iPhone X. Didn't matter who had his phone, they weren't getting anything except emergency information. Pleased, I ran my finger down the list of numbers called, and that called him, looking at call durations as I went. There were a lot of apparent missed calls and ones that ended within a few seconds from several numbers. I jotted the numbers into my notebook.

The text messages required scrutiny. He'd sent messages to the same three numbers on a regular basis. I added those numbers to my notebook. The next page had more messages, but only those sent to one number. Ah, they were sent as text not as iMessage. So, the other phone wasn't an iPhone.

The conversation was one-sided. I could only see Hardcastle's responses. From what I read, it appeared he was dating the person, or they were romantically involved in some capacity. Didn't think it was a friend's with benefits thing.

Dane pushed a word into my mind, "Fuck-buddy."

What a lovely term. I'm sure fathers really wanted their children referred to as fuck-buddies. I let it go and vowed to never say it out-loud.

I circled the number in my notebook. Worth giving it a call. I scanned the list of calls again. That number didn't feature until the day the messages started, and it got hot and heavy fast.

Timing. It's all about the timing.

McAlester and Hardcastle. Hardcastle and whoever was involved in the conversation. Hardcastle's death.

I sent the number to Sandra and asked her to trace all activity, then I called the number from my cell phone. Not particularly wanting to advertise I was FBI. As the phone rang Elvis rocked into my world with 'Suspicious Minds'. For a split second, I thought it was the ringing phone, but then realized the music was over the ringing. No doubt about my mind being suspicious, but was Hardcastle's? The phone rang on. Elvis gyrated in front of the microphone. What if the song was telling me about an old friend? But in what context? Was the sender of the message an old friend who caused suspicion? Was McAlester the old friend, and the text person was suspicious?

I was about to throw a crumb to the CIA. Let whoever is listening try and figure out what I'm up to.

"Hello."

Jolted from the Elvis performance, I answered, "Hello. Could I speak to Grant Hardcastle?"

"You have the wrong number," the female voice said.

"Sorry. Is this ..." I read her number out.

"Yes, that is *my* number, not whoever you are trying to reach."

"We must have glitch in our system."

"Who is this?" Suspicion hung in her words.

"Catherine Thomas from Doctor Stantang's office."

"I hope you manage to contact the person." And she was gone.

I did learn that whoever the woman was, she didn't want to admit to knowing Hardcastle. A message landed on my phone.

Sandra: The trace is running. She's already called Hardcastle's number.

SAC Iverson: Keep an eye on the activity. Can you get me a name for that phone number?

I wanted to know if she contacted any other numbers that might match the information from Hardcastle's telco. My phone buzzed.

Sandra: The phone number belongs to Pamela Straun of Virginia Beach.

Magnificent news. She's not dead then.

I stood with my cell phone in my hand; Argo looked at me. I shook my head and he went back to sleep. Instant sleep, it's not a bad life for a dog. I joined

Sandra at her desk. "That's her, Sandra. She's potentially the whistleblower."

"The mystery woman who doesn't exist, exists after all." Sandra pushed her long sleeves halfway up her forearms and wriggled her fingers over the keyboard. She opened an app, dragged Straun's phone number into it, then dragged mine into another screen. "Call her back, boss, I'm ready."

I tapped the phone number on my recent call list. One Mississippi. Two Mississippi.

A frustrated female voice answered and launched into a full sentence, "I told you I don't know the person you want. Don't call me again."

"You're in danger. I am Special Agent in Charge Ellie Iverson. And you no longer exist according to Exical."

Silence.

"Don't hang up. We can protect you."

Her voice faltered. "I don't know what you are talking about ..." A giant chasm opened and swallowed the rest of her words.

"Let me help you." I watched the screen on Sandra's computer, the map narrowed in on an address. It wasn't Virginia Beach. It was a swanky hotel in Washington.

"I don't need help." Another crack opened and filled with fissures of fear. "Please. Leave me alone."

"Has anyone else rung this number?"

"No. Please. Just leave me alone."

"At least use the security lock on your door and flush

the Sim in the phone you're using down the toilet. Someone has Hardcastle's phone."

"I ... I ... don't know that person."

"Flush the Sim card."

I spun on my heels and whistled. Argo charged from my office and skidded to a stop at my feet. "Working, Argo."

My whistle didn't just call the dog. Dane and Lee ran from the bullpen.

"What's up?" Dane asked.

"We found Straun. We're going now." I looked past Dane. "Where's Kurt?"

Argo turned his head, I caught the movement. Kurt was walking up behind me.

"O Protector of the Whistlers," Sandra said, to get my attention.

"Yep," I said, watching Kurt change Argo's vest from stab proof to bullet proof. "I added Straun's name to SENTINEL and we have nothing." All that meant was she hadn't come to our attention before. "I ran a quick all engine search looking for social media. She kept one social media account and it is a private account. There was absolutely nothing public except her name, and that she was from Virginia Beach. Her profile image was a flower."

"You found more than me then," I said, taking a vest offered to me from Lee and pulling it on. "Pamela Straun was a smart woman or maybe just naturally adept at being a ghost. But she screwed up when she registered that Sim card. Either way her fun with Hardcastle ended abruptly with his death."

Caine's office called. I growled at the phone in my hand as I walked toward the stairs, with Argo's leash wrapped around my right hand. Kurt on my left, Dane and Lee right behind me.

"Can we bring the meeting forward?" It was Caine, not his secretary.

"No. Out of office." I shoved my phone in my pocket and waved to Sandra on my way off the floor. "Go home!"

Chapter Thirteen
Rikki Don't Lose that Number

I climbed out of the car and opened the back door of our big black Suburban. Argo whined softly. Keen to get on with the job. He sat in the middle of the backseat. His dedicated seatbelt was positioned to protect him from side impacts. I leaned across and unclipped his belt. By the time I'd straightened up, he was already next to me on the ground. I clipped his short leash to his harness. Kurt reached behind the seat and hefted his backpack from the footwell. He hooked it over one shoulder.

The area was well lit, no one moving around. I love hotels with underground car parking. Lee and Dane parked next to us. Doors opened. Doors closed. We stood as a group in a circle.

"Do we have a room number?" Lee asked.

"No," I replied. "I'd like to get to reception without causing too much interest." My eyes ran over my team. Three tall men and a dog, everyone wearing an FBI emblazoned bulletproof vest. Totally invisible. Nothing to see here.

"Good luck with that," Dane mumbled.

"I know, right," I said, with a grin. "Let's get in there and find this woman before anyone else does."

"All for one," Lee said, sticking his hand out toward

me.

I slapped my palm against Lee's, our fingers curled around each other as we pulled our hands back. "Alert and safe."

"Always."

Dane and Kurt followed suit.

"Let's find this woman," I said, switching Argo to my left to free up my gun hand. Everything about the case felt hinky as fuck and if we found her location, who's to say that Chinese hadn't managed to figure it out. A deep silence fell over us. Even our footsteps on the concrete floor vanished. Lee and Dane took the elevator. Kurt, Argo, and I ran up the stairs.

It was a quick run up two flights of stairs to the reception. Kurt opened the heavy door and held it for us. Dane and Lee stepped out of the elevator as we crossed the floor to the desk. A young woman stood behind the front desk, taking selfies. She barely acknowledged our approach. I lifted my badge from the lanyard around my neck and held it toward her. She took one last pouty picture before sighing and putting her phone down.

"Special Agent Ellie Iverson. I need the room number of a guest, please. Pamela Straun."

She stared at me. I did not know someone could blink that fast and that often. No other movement. "Hello?" I scanned her blouse and spotted a name tag. It had toppled forward from the weight of the tag on the flimsy fabric and was unreadable.

Kurt snapped his fingers. She blinked once more and focused on him. "Room number for Pamela Straun," he said.

"I ... I ... I'm not allowed." Her phone made a familiar noise. Snapchat. She picked up the phone and smiled at it.

Christ on a cracker.

"Move over," I said, and dropped Argo's leash and stepped around the edge of the counter into her space. She backed away almost tripping over her own feet. "Maybe put the phone down for a hot minute." I looked from her to the booking system on the computer screen; it was open. Made it easier for me. The whole thing was simple to follow. All I did was type in Straun and up popped her details and room number. "Room one-seven-zero."

Lee locked the front door by pressing a red button on the wall. Dane locked down the elevator.

"You can't ..."

She was all of twenty-three. Did not look like she should be sole charge of a hotel front desk at night.

"What's your name?" I asked, as I removed all trace of Pamela Straun from their system. Then I found the spare keycard for room one-seven-zero. I shoved it in my pocket. The young woman stood, mouth flapping like a goldfish gasping for water. Step up from the kissy faces and the photo taking.

"Name?"

"Jessica." Jessica moved sideways.

"Right, Jessica, take a break. Go Snapchat your friends for twenty-minutes. Agents Wesson and Davenport will remain with you."

I glanced at Lee, who'd stationed himself in front of the stairwell door. He stood at parade rest. Dane stood in front of the elevators. He was mostly out of sight from the large glass front door.

Back at the front of the reception desk, I stooped and picked up Argo's leash. We walked two paces before Jessica squealed "O.M.G. you have a floof."

Argo looked up at me. "No idea, pal, just keep walking," I whispered.

"Can I pet him? He's adorable." Jessica appeared in front of us and dropped to her knees by Argo. One hand was about to grab his face. Her phone was in the other hand and she looked poised to take a selfie with my dog.

Nope. Big fat drooling nope.

I lowered my voice to something just above a growl, "He's working. Don't touch." It says right there on his harness. Do. Not. Touch.

"But he's ador-a-ble!" Her phone waved in Argo's face.

"Young lady, step away from the dog," I growled.

She bounced to her feet and narrowed her eyes at me. "Did you just assume my gender?"

Argo ignored her and moved closer to me.

Breathe.

"I did not mean any offense, Jessica." Her eyes

wandered toward Argo again. I snapped my fingers. She focused on me. "Now that I have your attention, leave my dog alone. Go Snapchat, or Insta, or TikTok, or whatever it is you do, and let me work."

We continued to the stair door. Lee swung it open. I could see a smile edging away from his eyes. I didn't have to look at Dane to know he was all in with a grin.

I stopped walking on the fourth stair and called Sandra.

"Questions. Banned apps, do you have a list? Is TikTok on that list?"

"One sec, O Genie of the app store." I imagined Sandras fingers flying across the keyboard in front of her. "Yes, boss, I do, and it is."

"Chinese developer?"

"I believe so."

"Can you check every Delta mobile against the list and in particular look for *TikTok*." Just don't ask me why. It just feels like a thing I should check.

"Yes, I can do that."

"Without anyone getting antsy? This is fact a finding exercise not a witch hunt."

"I could send through a routine update to all Delta cell phones that will check for us. I'd need an hour to modify a blank to the job."

"Do it. Also ..." We couldn't legally do that to their personal phones. "... personal phones, have anyone carrying a personal phone on the floor hand it over. They can collect them at the end of shift."

"Storage?"

"Faraday cage."

"Is there a problem I should know about, O Tireless Champion of Justice?"

"I'm hoping it's my overactive imagination. Let's do this quietly and carefully."

"And if anyone asks about private phones being locked up?"

"Tell them it's increased security due to a developing Delta A case and a direct order from me."

"Done."

"No one outside of Delta is to hear of this."

"Got it."

I hung up and ignored the brewing questions I felt from Kurt. We continued our upward journey to the required floor. Nice of the hotel to have numbers on the walls next to the stair exits. The arrows were a nice touch as well. Now we knew which direction to walk down the hall. The thick gray carpet deadened our footsteps and felt spongy under foot. Kurt motioned to the door, indicating it was the one we wanted.

I knocked.

Nothing.

I knocked again, then stepped back and held my badge up so it would be clearly seen via the peephole. Metal grated as the security lock disengaged. Then the door handle moved, and the door opened about eight inches.

"Agent Iverson?"

"Yes, and Agent Henderson."

"Come in." She stepped away from the door, allowing Argo and I entry. Kurt followed, closing the door and flipping the lock.

"Pamela Straun?" I said, showing the average height, tidy woman with a short blonde bob, my ID.

She passed my wallet back and nodded, then tucked wayward strands of hair behind her ears. "Nice hotel, was it your idea?"

"Yes, when I couldn't get hold of ..." She looked at me, resignation evident as her shoulders slumped. "When I couldn't get hold of Grant."

"Grant?"

"Hardcastle."

"Did you know that Exical have erased you from their employment records?"

She shook her head, but there was zero surprise on her face. "Can I sit?"

"Yes," I said. "Are you okay with dogs?"

"Absolutely," she replied. She lowered herself to the edge of the bed. A partial smile tweaked at one corner of her mouth.

"Argo, do your thing," I unclipped his leash. He looked up at me once, then ambled over to Straun and lay his head in her lap. "He's a very special dog."

I let Argo work his magic. Straun rubbed his ears and petted him, while Argo relaxed her without her noticing.

Animal hoodoo at its purest.

Once she appeared suitably less stressed, I crouched on the floor in front of her.

"Grant Hardcastle is dead." There is no polite or kind way to say someone was murdered. God knows I've tried over the years.

Her eyes met mine. "I thought something bad had happened."

"It did. His cat is with the SPCA. I'm not sure who to contact about the cat, with him being British an' all."

"One of his neighbors used to look after the cat sometimes, maybe he could take it." She rubbed Argo's ears. "I'd like to, but ..."

Yeah, you really can't. Not now.

"We'll talk about the cat situation later. For now, you need to be aware that you are in danger."

She stroked the dog and kept her attention focused on him. "This is about the bioweapons," she said, evenly, almost matter-of-fact in her tone. "I expected this to happen weeks ago. I don't know what took McAlester so long."

"We don't either." It was true. Why sit on something this important for seven weeks? Unless you wanted to leverage the knowledge. If he'd tried that, this would've been cleaned up weeks ago. We'd be finding bodies, and zero to connect back to overseas Americans developing bioweapons. "We need the names of the people employed by Newgenic overseas."

"If they've erased my record of employment, you can guarantee they no longer exist as far as Newgenic is concerned."

"Names, please."

"There's a document folder taped to the underside of the middle drawer of the bureau." She pointed across the room. "Do you mind?" Kurt asked, crossing to the dresser.

"No."

Kurt opened the middle drawer. I could see his arm moving as his hand felt along the underside. He stood up with a manilla folder in his hand and pushed the drawer closed.

He flipped the folder open, looked at a page, closed it, and handed the folder to me. My turn.

Inside the folder were two pieces of printer paper. The first had an image. An employee identity badge. Nicolaus Ng. A chemical engineer. I quickly read the paragraph below the image. He was in charge of a laboratory in Upper Hutt, New Zealand. Ng was a Chinese American who had worked for Newgenic for fifteen years; for two of those years he worked in China on a secondment. Not married. No children. His mother was alive and lived in Hong Kong.

The second page had the same type of image. Ken Chang. A chemical engineer in charge of a laboratory in New South Wales, Australia. There was a note saying that Chang moved the operation to Perth, Western Australia due to the bush fires of twenty-nineteen. They lost a lot of ground in the fire and were behind. Chang was also Chinese American. Unmarried, no children, no parents. Chang had worked for Newgenic for ten years, ten months of which were spent in China seconded to another company.

Most helpfully, we now had photos of the chemical engineers. It's much easier to make an arrest when you know who you're arresting, and what they look like.

"This is helpful, thank you."

"How useful is it if none of us exist in the Exical or Newgenic system? Can't they and won't they now deny all knowledge?"

I fully expect them to do exactly that.

"That's our problem. Your part is done."

"What does that mean?"

"That means that we will take you into protective custody and make sure you are safe." I handed the documents back to Kurt but remained watching Pamela. "Is there anything else?"

She shook her head. "I don't understand why McAlester took so long to use the documents I sent."

"One day, maybe, we can ask him."

Pamela slid a card from her pocket and handed it to me. "This is my lawyer, should I call him?"

"You're not under arrest. You've not broken any laws." I looked at the card. Noah Bancroft. Unbelievable. "How long has Mr. Bancroft been your lawyer?"

"He's not really. We're old friends, we went to high school together."

"Good to know." I smiled, keep it charming, keep it

together. "You can call him if you'd like, but it's not necessary."

Kurt sat down on the bed next to Straun. "The fewer people who know what's going on, the safer you will be."

"Speaking of which," I said. "Did you break the Sim from your phone?"

"Yes. Then I wrapped it in toilet paper and flushed it."

"Are you packed? Is there anything you need to grab before we go?"

She shook her head. "Can I use the bathroom?"

"Yes, then we can get out of here before anyone realizes something happened."

She stood and left the room. Argo watched her go.

"Handy having the names," I said to Kurt.

"Yes. She's right though, there'll be no record of those engineers on anything to do with Newgenic now."

"How far do you think they'll go?"

"They've crossed lines. I doubt there is anything they wouldn't do. Not now."

"So, erasing the electronic and paper trail is just the beginning ... hence Hardcastle is dead."

Didn't give me a lot of hope when it came to finding Jeremy Cotton alive and well.

Pamela stepped out of the bathroom. Something had changed. She gave off a different vibe. All my senses kicked into high gear as they tried to place the change.

159

She went to the bathroom and came out different. Drugs?

I threw a look at Kurt then signed: something is wrong.

Pamela spoke, "Why did you say something is wrong?"

"You speak American sign language?"

She signed as she spoke, "I'm rusty. It's been a long time."

Kurt used her distraction to slip into the bathroom. He stood in the doorway. Pamela had her back to him. He produced a bottle of pills and shook it. No noise. Empty?

Argo pushed his nose into Pamela's hand. She petted his head.

He knew something was wrong. She was calm. She didn't care anymore.

"Pamela?" Kurt said.

She turned and looked at him, and the bottle he held in his hand. "When did you fill this Ambien prescription?" His phone was in his other hand.

"Last week." There was no real emotional reaction. "Thursday."

"How many did you take tonight?"

"The last twenty," she said, without flinching.

"How long ago?"

"Half an hour, maybe longer."

Crap.

Kurt was already dialing on his phone. His voice was

low, but I heard him give our location and a quick summary to paramedics, stating he was a medical doctor and on scene. The next call was to Lee to let him know to open the door for the paramedics.

"Where's your backpack?" I said to Kurt. I was sure he had it with him. He always had it.

"Right here." He pointed to a backpack by one of the armchairs in the room. "It's not going to help this time. I carry Narcan ..." He didn't finish the sentence. He didn't have to. He carried Narcan because I sometimes needed Demerol for migraines.

I crouched down next to Pamela who still sat with Argo. "You know we're not going to let you kill yourself, right?"

Her eyes met mine. "You really should. You have all the information now, and if whoever murdered Grant finds me, I'm dead anyway."

So that was her plan? Commit suicide, but leave us the documentation? That spoke of utter desperation.

"Do you have any idea who that could be, who could find you?" I kept my voice even. We had time before the medicine in her system really kicked in, but even I knew it was too late to make her vomit it all up. I'd seen the bottle. We could reverse it, with luck. Major luck. "Who killed Grant?"

"I don't know. But last week I thought someone was watching us when we had lunch together."

"Did you have lunch together often?"

"Yes. Almost every day."

"Dating?"

"Friends." She almost smiled. "Very good friends."

That much I gathered from the partial texts I'd read.

She petted Argo. Kurt attracted my attention then mouthed the words, 'keep her talking'. I gave him a less than subtle thumbs up.

"Who else knows about this?"

"I didn't tell anyone except Grant. I told him what I'd found and that I'd attached the documents to the packet that went to our accountants. He said I should have given it to him." She sighed. "When it took so long for anything to happen, I started to think he was right."

"Do you know Jeremy Cotton?"

Her eyes flashed up to mine. then back to the dog. Yes. That was a yes.

"We went to high school together."

"Did you talk to Cotton about this?"

She shook her head. "No. I haven't spoken to him in years."

"You work for the same company."

"I know. It's a big company."

"You don't get on?"

She sighed. "He was an idiot in high school. Not a very nice person." The fingers on her left-hand stroked Argo's ear. "I didn't like him then, and there hasn't been anything to change my mind."

Fair enough.

There was a loud knock. Kurt swung the door open and two paramedics entered. They spoke to Kurt, who showed them his ID, and gave them the empty prescription bottle.

"Flumazenil will counteract the Ambien," Kurt said, as one paramedic knelt next to me in front of Pamela.

I touched Pamela on her arm. "Hey there, Pamela. I'm going to take Argo away. These people, and Kurt, are going to help you. We will keep you safe."

We'd try to keep her safe.

She looked up. Her eyes didn't quite make it to mine and her eyelids appeared heavy. Definitely time.

Argo followed me to the other side of the room. I clipped his leash and we waited. I hated everything about the situation. It was too familiar. I rubbed Argo's head and decided it was best to leave the room and join Lee and Dane. Protect myself from watching another person potentially die from a self-inflicted drug overdose. Not fun. Never fun.

The word Narcan curled around my windpipe and tried to choke me. The reason Kurt carried Narcan was because my teenage daughter and her best friend overdosed on medication, she took from my bathroom cabinet. Sometimes even administering the right medicine doesn't work. Sometimes God fucks up.

With my hand wrapped around Argo's leash, and the file tucked inside my jacket, I made my way past everyone and out into the hallway. A slow breath in through my nose and out through my mouth. A little floral scent stuck in my throat. I couldn't see flowers. I breathed in deeply again. Carpet freshener. That was the smell.

A faint noise came from the end of the floor. Argo's ears almost did a full circle before pricking toward the elevator. From where I stood, I couldn't quite see the doors. Argo bristled next to me. Someone was there and it wasn't Lee or Dane.

I flipped my badge, so it was right side out and obvious on the lanyard around my neck, then drew my weapon.

The dog stepped in front of me and watched.

One breath and a male came into view. Not tall. Wearing dark clothes. He walked straight toward us. The closer he got the easier he was to see. Asian male. My brain spun up the images I'd seen when we found Hardcastle. Was it him? Shit. Fuck. Maybe. My finger moved along the side of the barrel of my Glock. Edging closer to the trigger.

"Stop," I said clearly. My arm steady, my weapon aimed at the man. "FBI."

"I'm going to my room."

"Wait."

"It's just a few doors along." He took one step closer.

Argo growled, his hackles rose. He took a step toward the man.

"I said wait."

The man stopped moving.

"Show me your keycard."

He patted his pockets through the outside of his clothes. "It's here somewhere."

Enough. "Hands on the back of your head."

He continued patting his pockets.

"Stop. Hands on the back of your head," I repeated, slowly.

He froze for a split second, then his hand flew into his outer pocket. That wasn't a keycard. I let the dog go. Argo leaped at him with a snarl and grabbed his arm. A knife flew from the man's grip. Argo tugged him to the ground.

"Good boy." Argo held him. I took a nitrile glove from my pocket and picked up the knife by wrapping the glove around the handle. I stepped back. "Argo. Let go. Good boy."

The sound of Argo's attack drew Kurt from the room.

"You okay out here?"

"This guy isn't," I said, pointing to the man cradling his right forearm while sitting on the ground.

"And you are?" Kurt said, addressing the male.

"Brendon Wu."

"And you're here why?" I said, giving Argo a rub on the head.

"Going to my room, I'm staying here."

"Yet when I asked you to produce your key card you produced this ..." I held the knife up, still wrapped in the glove. "Funny looking keycard."

"It was an accident," Wu said, little traces of fear lurked in his words, but did not ring true as he looked at the blood on his sleeve. "I'm bleeding."

"That is a result of this," I replied, shaking the knife at him. "You're lucky I didn't shoot you."

Kurt made a call for another ambulance.

"You didn't come in from the reception area," I said. Fact. He did not. Lee or Dane did not call up saying someone wanted entry other than paramedics. "Where did you come from?"

I knew from the stair layout that no one could get from the main floors to the garages without going through reception. Sensible. Guess it prevented people skipping out on their bill back before everything was electronic.

"I was visiting a friend. Also staying here."

"We will need to verify that, and your room number."

Neither of us approached him. He sat on the floor, cradling his bitten arm. One of us was going to have to search him before the medics arrived. Kurt's eyes met mine, he tilted his head a touch to the right. Yeah sure. I'll do it.

He smoothly drew his weapon and trained it on the man on the floor. "Stay still while Agent Iverson searches you."

Argo growled from beside me, and walked two paces with me, then stopped. He edged a little closer, lip curled, teeth bared. Kurt positioned himself for a clear shot of the male's head.

"One move and it will be a competition to see if you're bitten or shot first," I said, quietly. "My money is

166

on the dog."

Wu changed. His face hardened. All faux fear gone. I grabbed his injured arm and encouraged him upward. "Stand."

He stood.

"Put your hands on your head, lace your fingers together."

He obliged.

With quick precision, I patted him down and removed a sidearm from the back of his waistband. I pushed the weapon in my waistband and continued. I found his wallet in his back trouser pocket. It contained credit cards and cash. I pried one of the credit cards out of the black leather wallet. The name on the card was Brendon Wu. The bank was First Century. There were two other cards and they were for a Chinese bank. I couldn't read the writing; it may or may not have said Brendon Wu. The cash was all American. No identification.

I threw the wallet toward Kurt. He'd get it once we were done. There was nothing in his trousers.

Shoes.

"Step out of your shoes," I instructed, stepping away to Argo's side. Wu extracted one foot from one shoe, then used that foot to remove the other. "Move back, five paces."

His hesitation caused a deep growl from Argo. He faltered, then stepped back five paces. I attracted Argo's attention and gave one fast hand signal. He picked up one shoe and gave it to me, then went back for the other. I inspected the inside of the first shoe. His right foot. Inside the leather loafer I found an identity card in Chinese. I flipped the card over and found an official looking seal. Dammit. The other shoe had nothing. I used my phone to snap a photo of the seal and then ran a search. Peoples Republic of China, Washington Embassy.

Argo returned the shoes to Wu. I kept the card.

"Why was your ID card inside your shoe?" I asked. "And why would you be staying in this hotel if you work at the embassy? Surely the embassy provides closer accommodation." I found no keycard. There was also that little gem. "No keycard. A knife, and a handgun."

A paramedic came out of Pamela's room. "We have to go," he said, looking from Kurt to me, and then the Chinese man standing shoeless in the hall. "Now."

"Okay," I said. I crossed the distance to Wu, slapped cuffs on him, and dragged him over to the wall. "Forehead on the wall. Do not move."

"You can't arrest me," he said. There was zero hint of an accent. He sounded American. If he was an American citizen then he was fair game, embassy or not. "I have diplomatic immunity."

"Until I know that for sure, I can and I am. Do not move."

Straun needed hospitalization, and Wu needed to shut the fuck up and be still.

Once Straun and the paramedics were gone, I called a friend at the State Department and told her what I'd done, and who I'd arrested. She agreed to take custody and continue the matter diplomatically. Her initial check showed Wu as a dual citizen of the United States and The Peoples Republic of China. Potentially a spy and an assassin. He could be stripped of his American citizenship and kicked out, if things went that far. Either way he'd be quiet for a while. Not quite enough for my liking, but at least he was out of our hair.

* * *

Caine's door stood open. Reed was not in attendance. Figured he'd gone home hours ago. Caine waved me through.

He launched into his pissed grizzly bear routine, "Was starting a diplomatic incident, the best use of your time this evening?"

"He had no real identification. He was armed and on the same floor as someone we needed to protect," I said. "In answer to your question, yes, it was the best use of my time."

"Full report."

"It's already underway. I turned him over to our State Department. They can deal with it, or Homeland can deal with it. He's a dual citizen." Just as long as he is out of the way and not our problem.

"And you think?"

"He's an assassin, maybe a spy." I sat in the chair in front of his desk.

Caine nodded. "The woman?"

"Coma. There is a police guard outside her hospital room door."

"Will she live?"

"No clue."

"Are you all right?" He sat with his hands clasped together near his chin, elbows on the walnut desk surface.

"Of course," I said. "Why?"

"I heard about this morning." His blood shot eyes pierced mine.

"Wasn't great for Hardcastle."

"The murder of a British national is newsworthy. We have a news block on this case at the moment. It's only matter of time before some reporter finds a way around it."

"I'm aware how tricky and slimy they are."

"Hanzel Forberg," Caine growled. "Talk to me about him."

"We know virtually nothing about him, except that McAlester talked to him and told him he was going to talk to me."

"He's Scandinavian, and is here working for Newgenic," Caine said, with a full bear growl punctuating his words.

"Are you worried he'll end up like Hardcastle?"

Caine nodded and grumbled, "We don't need

another foreign scientist murdered here."

"Especially another Newgenic employee."

"Yes."

"We'll find him. Whether he cooperates or not is another matter." That depended on his relationship with McAlester and Newgenic. "I have Tahoma Whitehorse and Karen Schneider here to consult on this case."

"CDC," Caine grumbled with approval.

"We might be dealing with an American company trying to weaponize the Qu Pathogen using foreign laboratories." Saying it out loud made the whole thing feel more real. It settled inside me like a piece of cold pointy quartz. One wrong move and it'd spear something vital.

"Evidence?"

"McAlester handed us documents that seem to back that up. I want Tahoma to look them over."

"Good call. Keep me in the loop."

"Will do." I stood and left.

Chapter Fourteen
Here You Come Again

After a few restless hours sleep, and a noisy breakfast with the twins, I strode along the corridor to Sandra's desk. Determined to have a better Thursday than I did Wednesday.

Sandra told me Tahoma and Karen waited in meeting room one. I swung through the door with a smile planted on my face.

"Karen, Tahoma, wonderful to see you both." I extended a hand to Karen and then Tahoma. "Have you had breakfast?"

"It is good to see you, Ellie. And yes, we ate breakfast at the hotel," Tahoma said. "I have something for you." He extracted a long black feather from inside his jacket and passed it to me. "For you."

"Thank you, a raven feather?" It was beautiful, blue black and shiny. I saw right away that there was rollerball nib at one end. A pen. "Did you make this?"

"Yes. I did. A raven was kind enough to leave me a feather. I believe it was for you."

"For me?"

"Raven told me you have met before. He teaches us how to hear messages from the other world. Raven is about transformation. He is your guide."

"Thank you, Tahoma." I stroked the feather and

breathed. A chill raced down my spine.

"Raven dropped his feather moments after you called to say we should meet in person. There is much to learn from raven."

With care I placed the feather on the table, stroked it once more, and then gave Tahoma and Karen my full attention. "I am very glad you are both here."

"I am not sure this is a good situation."

"It's not. Take a seat. I'll walk you through what we know, and it's not much. I'm hoping you two can fill in some blanks."

Sandra had chosen the room with a round table. Glasses were placed on the table in front of three chairs. In the middle of the table was a large pitcher of water.

"We will try," Tahoma said. Karen nodded.

"A man named Trace McAlester attempted to abduct me from a coffee shop. Once we got him in an interview room, he started to tell us about the events leading to that moment in his life." I reached for the glasses and filled all three from the pitcher. I took my glass and drank a mouthful. "He works as an accountant, and a client attached documents to an invoice by *accident* or so he initially thought. The documents seem to imply they are funding research into weaponizing Qu Pathogen."

"Can we see the documents?"

I nodded, and texted Sandra to bring my laptop. "They'll be here in a moment. Just after the McAlester incident, I received a call from a CI saying he needed to meet. My CI is a scientist."

"Auspicious timing," Karen said.

"That's what I thought. But wait there's more ..." I sipped more water. "We arranged for US Marshals to secure McAlester. I rang you from the car on my way home. About twenty minutes from home, someone opened fire on our cars."

"The shooting is linked?" Tahoma drank from his glass.

"I don't believe in coincidence. But the shooter and driver lawyered up immediately and have refused to answer questions."

"Could your CI confirm McAlester's fears?" Karen asked.

"No, because he disappeared and didn't make our morning meeting. There was a bomb in the alley where we were supposed to meet. There were a spate of similar bomb scares, none of them really powerful enough to do a lot of damage."

"Connected?" Tahoma asked.

"Waiting on Delta C to finish the investigation. There is no word from my CI. I cannot get hold of him. Since then, a Brit National, Grant Hardcastle, was murdered, and the woman who blew the whistle attempted suicide." But wait there's more. "We arrested a Chinese American a few doors from her hotel room, armed with a knife and a gun." I couldn't exactly say I thought Hardcastle was killed by a

Chinese agent because I had no proof, just what a dead man showed me. "Documents with the names of two Chemical Engineers working on the weaponization of Qu were given to us by the woman before she took an overdose of Ambien."

"There's a lot going on, Ellie," Karen said, as she finished making notes in her notebook.

"So much," I replied. "The State Department have Wu, who was the Chinese American we arrested in the vicinity of the woman's room." I took a breath. "She was a close friend of Grant Hardcastle's."

"That is sad news," Tahoma said. "Mr. Hardcastle is a virologist of great skill."

"You know him?"

Tahoma nodded. "We have attended many conferences together."

"I'm sorry for your loss."

"It is the world that has lost, Ellie. The world. He worked on the COVID-19 vaccine."

And the world that could be lost if these madmen get their way.

"Have you ever come across Hanzel Forberg?"

Karen stiffened. That was not the best possible response.

"Why?" She asked.

"It's a name that came up via McAlester."

She nodded and inhaled sharply. "He is a scientist. I have been at conferences that he has attended."

My spidey senses told me that wasn't the whole

truth, but maybe the only truth I'd get with Tahoma in the room. I stuck a pin in Hanzel Forberg for the moment.

Sandra swung the door open. Saved by the laptop.

"Thanks Sandra," I said, and took the offered laptop. She smiled and left, pulling the door shut.

I found the image files and loaded them for Tahoma and Karen to read. Tahoma looked over at me after he'd been reading for a few minutes.

"We must stop this."

"Just like that?"

Tahoma smiled, calm, almost serene. "Yes."

"Okay then."

"We will work alongside you, Ellie."

"I appreciate that."

"It is now our time to make a start and compare notes. We will get a plan in place."

Air flooded my lungs for what felt like the first time in days.

We got this.

My fingers stroked the feather on the table. Transformation? To what exactly? It wasn't the right time to contemplate the meaning of the raven feather. One day I will have the opportunity to explore the mysteries of the raven.

With Tahoma and Karen working with us, I could shift my attention to other matters inside the same overall case. More than anything I wanted to find Jeremy Cotton. I felt like I could take off and see if I could track him down and let the CDC work in peace.

I stood, stretched lightly, and tapped Karen on the shoulder. "Do you mind if I leave you both here. There's something I need to do."

"Of course. We will study this information and see what else we can uncover with our contacts," Karen said.

"Thank you."

I picked up the feather pen and left the room.

Chapter Fifteen
Don't Leave Me This Way

Dane reached around me and opened the heavy stairwell door.

"Going somewhere, Ellie?"

"Yeah."

"Want company?"

Something told me it wasn't a question as such. And the only acceptable answer was yes.

"Sure."

The nice thing about going anywhere with Dane was I didn't have to talk. If he really wanted to, he could figure out what I was thinking, unless I stopped him.

He pressed a button on the fob in his hand. My car chirped.

"You have my keys?"

"Imagine that," he said with a grin, swinging the driver door open and climbing in.

"You picked my pocket ..." I remembered him bumping me lightly as we descended the stairs. "On the stairs." I opened the passenger door.

"You made it easy," he said.

"Next time it won't be." Next time there might be a rat trap in my pocket.

"That's not nice, El." He still had a smile on his face. "Where do you want to start? The alleyway?"

"Yeah."

I settled into the seat. And remembered what I knew about the alleyway. It once housed an underground restaurant. Not literally *underground*, more illegal than underground. I had no idea how that nugget of information was useful in finding my missing informant, but maybe it was.

Dane parked a block away from the alley. "Which direction do you think he took to get there?"

"You thinking cameras?"

"I ain't thinking fairies."

Probably no fairies involved.

"So, we start here and walk to the alley checking for cameras. Then walk the other way and check there," I said. "Can't hurt."

But it felt like he was never there.

Dane stopped and turned to face me. His mouth didn't move, but I could clearly hear his words. "If he was never there, then where was he?"

Mentally I pushed an answer into his mind. "I don't know."

I carried on walking and scanning the exterior walls of shops and buildings for cameras. I looked up at a fire escape. An image emerged of a man scrambling up the fire escape ladder and into a window. A second-story window. I looked back at the street. He was followed. My eyes flicked from the street to the window. A shadow fell across the sidewalk just as the man's foot disappeared into the window. I waited.

Watched. Hardly dared to breathe. The shadow took form. Peter freaking Cooper. He kept walking and never looked up.

Was he following my guy? Did he just happen along?

Dane touched my arm. "Going up?"

I nodded, reached up and grabbed a cold steel rung, and started climbing. I could feel Dane behind me. His weight shifted the ladder. Don't break. Don't break. Careful to grab the rungs securely, I climbed until I reached the window. I saw the man go through. I stood on the small landing and peered into the grimy window. Couldn't see anything. Dane climbed up beside me. He gave the old wooden-sashed window a heave upward. It jerked but rose. I pushed a ratty curtain aside and revealed an old office. Abandoned by the look of it. Best way in looked to be from a seated position on the window sill, legs inside, then drop. I swung one leg over the sill then eased the other over. One quick drop and I was stumbling around a semi-dark room. Dane followed.

I found another window and threw back the old drapes. Light struggled through grime and grit to play in the sparkly airborne dust that swirled in the stale, musty air. Kinda looked like fairies lived here. A large partially rolled carpet lay on the wooden floor. An old dark wood desk with a wooden office chair. Apart from the meager furniture there was one door.

Dane tried the door. The doorknob gave a partial turn. "Locked."

I had a look. "I might need my tools."

"Do you have them?" Dane shook his head as I opened my wallet. "Silly question."

It took a wee bit of jiggling to get the old keyed lock to give. If felt like it had seized through lack of use. WD-40 would've been handy. I doubted Jeremy Cotton came this way.

"Give it a push," I said, and put my picks back in my wallet. Dane swung the door.

It opened into a larger room. Just as dusty and forgotten. A sneeze erupted before I could control it. Hardly breathing we waited for a second. There was no noise beyond the room. The whole floor was probably deserted.

No sign that anyone had been in there. Especially not in the last few days.

"I saw him." I gave that thought and re-worded my observation. "I saw someone climb in the window we came through." I turned in the doorway and looked back at the room. "Where did he go?"

Did he hide under the desk and then go back out the window? Is he under the carpet or in the carpet? I walked back into the first room. If he was in the rug, he'd be smelly in a few days or less.

"El?"

"I think he's still here," I said, walking to the rolled carpet. I shoved my hands in my jacket pockets looking for gloves. Pleased, I had some. I put the pink nitrile gloves on, the band snapped against my wrist. I heard the rubber *snap* as Dane did the same with his black gloves. "Give me a hand."

We stood one at each end of the long side of the carpet roll. Using our feet, we shoved it away from us. Took a few goes to get it to move. It was heavier than I expected. On the third big push it rolled once. Three more attempts. And we finally got the thing moving. It unrolled a few more turns and a man's black dress shoe fell out.

"Got a feeling that didn't get in there by itself," I said.

"I imagine there's another shoe."

"Think there's more than just another shoe."

Instead of pushing, we walked around to the other side, neither of us wanted to try to step over the now smaller roll. Dane nodded at me. We placed our hands on the carpet and rolled it toward us. All of a sudden, the remaining carpet moved faster than expected. Legs clad in dark blue jeans flopped onto the floor.

"Awesome," Dane muttered. "You were right."

"Wish I wasn't. One more roll should release the rest."

We tugged at the carpet. The body rolled with the last section.

Pffft. A foul gas expelled.

I held my breath.

It appeared to be a male body. He was face down in the last piece of the rug. Arms up over his head. One hand gripping the edge of the carpet. Oh, crap. It looked like he'd rolled himself into the carpet.

I made a call to the office.

"I need the medical examiner."

"Where are you?" Sandra tapped on her keyboard. "Oh, I can see you on the map. Notifying the ME now. Do you want forensics?"

"No. I don't think so. Let's wait until the ME is done."

"Okay. Tahoma and Karen are still working in the meeting room."

"Great. Make sure they have coffee and whatever they need." I looked at the phone screen as the call vanished, then pushed the phone back in my pocket.

I walked over to the dirty window and leaned out to get a breath of fresh air, and some relief from the dust that irritated my nose and eyes.

"Get an ID?" I asked Dane, without turning my head.

"Jeremy Alexander Cotton," Dane said. "Got his wallet. His phone is here too. It's on silent. Your number appears a few times."

I took a deep cleansing breath. It would. I'd been calling him.

"Now the big question ... accidental death or murder?"

I didn't see any marks on him at first glance. No blood. No wounds. No bruises.

Dane joined me at the window. "You think he hid in the carpet and suffocated ..."

"Yep. If Peter Cooper followed him up here there'd

be something, evidence, murder leaves traces."

"ME might find something."

"Or not. So, what was Peter Cooper doing out there?" I waved a hand to the street. "And then in the alleyway." Then I knew. "He was in the alleyway for the meeting. I think he wanted to intercept Cotton. But Cotton was spooked by the spook, so unbeknownst to Cooper our friendly neighborhood CIA officer, he scaled the fire escape and came up here."

"You're saying he didn't know Cotton shimmied on up here and he was telling the truth about not seeing him?"

"Shit. Am I?" I shook my head slowly. "Doesn't seem right." But it would be right if he didn't know who he was looking for in the alley. If he didn't know Cotton from a bar of soap.

Oh, this was bad. Worse than if the Central Interfering Agency had silenced Cotton. If the ME said this was accidental, I was going to have to apologize to Tierney and Cooper. Un-fucking-believable. I walked over to the body and crouched down. I laid a gloved hand on Jeremy Cotton's shoulder. If there was anything left of him, I might be able to see what happened. His head lifted a few inches off the carpet and turned enough for me to see an imprint of the fibers and his cloudy eyes.

"I'm here," I whispered. "I found you. but I was too late. I'm sorry."

His lips moved with no sound. The speaker was

disconnected. Fingers clawed at the edge of the carpet. A cold shiver ran through my veins. Again, the fingers clawed and got nowhere. The cloud in one eye drifted upward and left a dark blue stain. As I watched the stain became a screen and a series of images played as if I was seeing through his eyes. Walking. The sidewalk. Looked over his shoulder. A pause. Faster movement. He ran, looked up, and saw the ladder. No hesitation before the climb.

At the window. He pushed it up, fell in. Tumbled on the floor. Jumped up and closed the window. He peered out through the grime and saw the man continue on his way past the building. Everything blurred. He looked again. The man was walking back. Panic. He looked around the room. Tried the door. Locked. Didn't fit under the desk. Saw the half-rolled carpet and unfurled it. He lay down, grasped the top edge and rolled his body over and over, until fully encased. He held his breath. There was a noise. The landing outside the window creaked. The cloud in Jeremy's eye rolled back down. His head dropped.

"Dane ..." I pushed myself to my feet.

"I saw. Who was the man?"

"Peter Cooper."

Time to call Sean O'Hare. I ripped the gloves off my hands and tossed them on the floor near the body.

"Hey, it's me. I need a couple of scene guards."

"Again, El. You've been busy." The humor in his voice filled his words. "Send the address, I'll do the paperwork this end."

"Thanks."

I found the building address by asking Siri where I was, then told Siri to send the address to Sean. Back in the larger room, I used my handy tools and opened the lock on what I hoped was an outer door. Then swung the door wide and revealed a dark and somewhat dank hallway. Success.

I joined Dane and the body.

Twenty long minutes passed before I heard noises in the hallway outside the second room. Dane went to see and returned with the ME.

"Susan, hi," I said, meeting her in the middle of the room with my hand extended.

We shook. "Good to see you El. What do we have here?"

"Jeremy Cotton. I need a time and manner of death, as soon as you can, please."

"Absolutely." She tipped her head to the exterior door. "One of your cars arrived out front as I entered the building."

Didn't call for backup, so that's odd.

"I'll go down and see who it is shortly." My phone rang. "I'll get this then I'll be right with you." I plucked my phone from my pocket. Tahoma.

"Hey, I'll be in the office soon."

"We're here."

"Oh, right." Car mystery solved. "Come on up."

I pocketed the phone. Susan was already inspecting

the body. "Dane, I'm going to meet Tahoma and Karen. You okay here?"

"Yep."

The dark hallway gave me the creeps. I chose to go left. There was nothing to base my choice on. Perhaps I should've asked Susan. An internal sigh filled my mind. I walked with care. The heel of my boots clunked on the wooden flooring. Each *clunk* followed by the scrape of my foot. Sound bounced off the walls. The care was pointless. What was I afraid of, waking the dead? Announcing my arrival to the ghouls of the Christmas past? A small chuckle fell from my lips as I rounded a corner and came face to face with Tahoma and Karen.

"Something amusing?" Karen asked, as I turned and fell into step with them.

"Yeah me trying to walk quietly on wooden floors."

She nodded. "I see what you mean."

"All right, why is the CDC at a possible crime scene?"

"Because we found something and it has to do with a missing scientist," Karen said.

And I found a missing scientist dead.

"Did Sandra tell you anything?"

"No. She said you asked for the medical examiner which to me says you have a body," Karen replied.

We reached the first door.

"And you are here because?"

"If this is the scientist that Newgenic aren't saying is missing, then we may have a problem."

"You've spoken to someone in HR at Newgenic?"

187

"No. I spoke to someone who works with us, but is currently working on a Newgenic contract."

"And?"

"Our colleague said Jeremy Cotton disappeared on Wednesday. He didn't go to work. He is not answering his phone. He is not at his apartment." Karen took a deep breath. "I checked with our colleague and Mr. Cotton did not come in this morning either."

"The body is in there," I said, and pointed through the room to the other door. "It is Jeremy Cotton, but I have to say it looks like an accidental death."

"Did you touch the body?" Tahoma stepped in front of me. His intense brown eyes probed mine.

"Yes, with gloves on."

He nodded slowly. "Then you are probably all right."

Hold it. What now? Probably? All right? What the fuck?

Chapter Sixteen
(Don't Fear) The Reaper

Dane appeared in the doorway. "What the hell is going on?"

Tahoma moved toward him. "Did you touch the body?"

"Yes. With gloves."

"Then you are probably all right."

"What the actual fuck is happening?" Dane said. His eyes zoomed past Tahoma and hit mine. "Probably all right?"

My head shook in tiny increments. Tahoma and Karen put on masks and gloves, then went to see the body and the medical examiner, leaving Dane and I to stare at each other. A thought pressed into my mind from him: Not again.

"Where's the tequila?" I replied audibly. "Because if this is happening again, I want a lot of tequila. And I'm not staying in this dingy hole of a decrepit building."

"Damn straight. It's a nice hotel or they can get fucked," Dane growled. "What are the chances of it being us again?"

"Not high, I would've thought."

"Now what?"

"Let's wait until Tahoma comes back to talk to us."

Wait? We paced. Back and forth across the room.

My boots clunking, scraping, clunking. In comparison Dane made little noise with his boots.

Tahoma walked out the door and held his hand up to stop our movement.

"When you released the body from the carpet was there an expulsion of air?"

"Yes." It was highly unpleasant.

"This is a quarantine situation until we have more information about the death of this man."

Shit. Shit. Shitty McShitterson.

"Okay." Not okay. Not at all okay. But it is what it is. I needed to limit exposure to whatever the fuck this could be. "One sec." I gave Sean a call. "Hey, pull back those scene guards, we have CDC on site."

I could hear him typing. "Done. You need anything?"

"A containment facility that's not shit." I knew where we needed to go and obviously it was not home to those we loved. The Facility. "We're going to the bunker."

"I'll get Gerrard to re-stock it for you - he has the combination?"

"Yes. He does. Thanks, Sean."

"Give him an hour to do inventory and get everything you need."

"Make damn sure he gets us tequila."

"Us?"

"Me and Dane."

"Bad luck it being you two who need quarantine again."

Tell me about it. "Yeah."

That was that. Dane almost smiled but his mouth didn't cooperate. "We're going underground ... what about Susan?"

Karen appeared in the doorway. "Susan as well. You need a doctor with you, it'll be me. Any objections?"

"Not at all," I said. "Thank you."

"We will transport the body. From memory the facility you have has an autopsy room. A negative pressure autopsy room?"

"Yes."

Susan came out of the room.

"You can arrange transport," she said to Karen. Then looked at me. "So, we're bunk mates for a couple of days?"

"We are. Do you like tequila?"

Susan smiled. "Yes."

Then we'll get along just fine.

"We're waiting on the all-clear from a colleague who is re-stocking the Facility. Is there anything particular you require?"

"No."

I could hear Tahoma on the phone. He was calling in a CDC Hazmat unit. I knew that was to deal with the body and transport, and us.

Yay. Just what I wanted, to be showered with disinfectant and have my clothes destroyed, said no one ever.

Dammit. This was a shitty situation.

I turned to Susan. "Did they say what this could be?"

Her shoulder-length platinum-streaked blonde hair bounced as she shook her head. "No, they exchanged some long looks though."

Hmmm. Then they know, or they think they know.

"We're about to lose our clothes and end up in scrubs. I can get Gerrard to have clothes waiting."

"That would be great."

"You're a bit shorter than me, but the same size clothes wise, do you think?"

"I'd say so."

Neither of us had much to come and go on. A small laugh welled. Thanks Dad, for your excellent genes and weird sayings.

I called Gerrard.

"You all right, Ellie?"

"Just freaking peachy. We need clothes."

"You okay with trainers, because I doubt I can get cowboy boots to your liking?"

Well, he could if he went home and got my stuff. No reason why he couldn't.

"I'll call Mitch and he'll have my gear waiting. Can you pick it up?"

"Sure, who else needs clothes?"

"Susan, our medical examiner, and Dane."

"Okay, if they have someone who can pack gear for them, I can pick it all up."

"Thanks Noel. I'll text the addresses."

"Hang tight, Ellie."

We don't have a choice. Susan was already on the phone to her roommate or partner. I didn't know her well enough to make that judgment. Guess we'd all know more about each other after this. I motioned to Dane. He joined me.

"Wanna get Lee to swing by and pack for you?"

"Yeah."

He made a call to Lee. I walked to the doorway and phoned Mitch. The phone rang seven times before he picked up.

"Hey, Babe, was thinking we could go out for dinner tonight."

"Rain check, please. I need you to pack a go-bag for me. Put my iPad in there, and the charger, and boots. Imagine I'm naked and need everything."

"I like the naked part, not so much the rest, what's up."

"Dane and I were exposed to something. We're going to be quarantined."

"Jeez. You're okay?"

"Absolutely. It's a cautionary thing. We're fine." My fingers crossed. "We're fine. Gerrard will collect my bag."

"Noel Gerrard ... where are you going?"

"The Facility."

"El ... you said you were *fine.*"

Well, that was a bit of a slip on my part. I'm never fine. I'm okay. Not fine.

"I'm okay. I'll try and FaceTime you and the girls

tonight, just like if I was away for work. Okay?"

"Be okay, El. We need you."

"Love you, see you soon." My fingers cramped. It took effort and massage to release them. That'll teach me for crossing them to start with.

I stood and stared at the blank screen for a few seconds. Fuck balls. This was not how I expected the day to go.

With a deep breath I settled the queasiness in my gut and turned to Dane and Susan.

"Can I send Gerrard to collect bags?"

"Yeah, Lee is going to my place now," Dane said.

"My partner will have a bag ready in a few minutes," Susan said. "I'll send you my address."

Good. Then I could just forward that to Gerrard. Easy peasy.

I texted Gerrard with Dane's address, then said Mitch was packing, so do mine last. My phone buzzed in my hand, Susan's message. I forwarded it to Noel.

She didn't live far from me. Two-blocks away. Wow. I never knew we were almost neighbors.

Tahoma walked in, his brow furrowed, and concern shone from his brown eyes.

"Hazmat are setting up downstairs. A crew will come and secure the body."

I nodded. That's what I expected would happen. No sense letting it get to me. Could be worse. It. Could. Always. Be. Worse. Always. Way to go, Pollyanna.

I knew there would be a medical interview just in

case any of us had medical conditions that would make treatment of whatever the hell this was, difficult, or exacerbate any pre-existing illness.

"Can we get this over with?" Dane said, pushing off the wall he'd leant on. "There's tequila in our future."

Tahoma nodded. "I will walk you down, Dane."

Dane smiled at me as they left. He might be smiling, but I could hear the turmoil in his mind. A biohazard suit-clad team came in with a gurney. I noted they were wearing Elastomeric Full Face-piece Respirators. Basically, that just filtered the air. It did not provide them with their own air source. It. Could. Always. Be. Worse.

I watched them roll the gurney to the other room. When did the plastic appear over the doorway?

I nudged Susan. "When did the plastic doorway arrive?"

"About ten minutes ago."

"Why?"

"Because they're going to move the body and we don't know what it will expel."

Of course.

It would take some manhandling to get Cotton into a body bag. Glad I wasn't involved in that. See, proof it could always be worse.

Back in your box, Pollyanna.

We waited for Tahoma to return. Or Karen. I hadn't noticed her leave, but she had. I had a feeling she'd be back for us, and Tahoma would stay with Dane and do his interview.

Susan's phone rang. She answered the call, then politely told the person on the other end to call the next ME on the list as she was off-roster for the next few days.

Off-roster. That sounded better than quarantined.

Karen came in and beckoned to me.

Great. Let's get this over with. I shot a smile at Susan. "See you soon."

"Kurt is downstairs."

"Okay." Of course he was. Lee probably was as well. "Did he see Dane?"

"Yes." She ushered me from the room and into the hallway. There was no one around. I didn't think there would be, but it still felt empty and I didn't like it. We walked and talked. "Kurt wants to see you. He has a go-bag for you."

"How much does he know?" I figured if they knew what this was all about, they might tell him, because he's a doctor.

"He knows what we know."

"And would you care to share that with me? I'm not much enjoying being treated like a mushroom."

Karen smiled, but it didn't last. "Jeremy Cotton didn't just want to tell you something, Ellie. He wanted to *share* something with you."

Crap. That didn't sound super friendly.

"What?"

"A version of the Qu Pathogen."

"How was he intending to do that?" My core chilled to below freezing. "Karen, how?"

"A cough, a sneeze, breathing on you, if he had to, I imagine he'd spit."

"He infected himself?" He was a CI. A scientist. Why would he choose to infect himself just to get me? "It doesn't make sense."

"No, it doesn't, but it will once we start digging into his life. It usually does."

Usually? This is a thing that happens in the scientific community? My mind conjured a mad scientist in a white lab coat, crazy multi-colored hair sticking out at all angles, he turned and grinned. With a mental drop kick I sent the clown in a lab coat into a dark hole. Nope. "How do you know he was infected?"

"We don't yet, but our colleague has expressed concern about Cotton and his behavior. We know he was part of a team working on a vaccine for Qu17p."

We stopped walking at a plastic covered doorway.

"Qu17p? Was that the original pathogen?"

"No."

Well, ain't that just peachy?

"So why develop a vaccine for something that wasn't released into the world?"

"Because someone might."

"But it was modified by us? This is government funded research?"

She shook her head. "Not entirely. This version was created by the Chinese. We are funding the vaccine research."

A lump rose so fast in my throat I thought I was going to hurl. The plastic in front of me swayed.

"Ellie, you okay?"

Karen wrapped her hand around my upper arm. The swaying plastic stilled. I inhaled slowly. Okay. I got this.

"I'm fine."

"We're going through the doorway and into a plastic tunnel. Beyond that is a decontamination shower. All your clothes go into a biohazard bin for destruction. Your weapon, holster, belt, wallet, ID, and so forth go into a small plastic tray for decontamination."

"My boots?"

"We can decontaminate them."

"Good." I'm very attached to my steel-capped cowboy boots. They're handmade for me, and expensive.

"Here we go."

Chapter Seventeen
Hard Day's Night

My long hair dripped down my back as I dried off with a large white towel. Pointless with so much water running from my hair. I gathered the sopping lengths together and raked my cold fingers through it, dragging knots to the ends of my hair. Then rung it out and watched streams of water pour onto the ground. I side-stepped the puddle. Shivering, I reached for the hospital scrubs on a stand. The shower tent was opaque. I could see movement outside but not much more.

Once dressed I used the towel to attempt removing more water from my hair. My back was already soaked. I dumped the towel in a bin. Finding a patch of dry floor, I hopped on one foot, then the other, to tug on the provided socks. They weren't much help, warmth wise.

I opened the opaque plastic curtain into another short tunnel with another curtain at the end. It. Could. Be. Worse. Pollyanna did her best, but I wasn't buying her line this time. I took a deep breath, opened the curtain, and stepped through.

A voice said, "Mind the steps."

I climbed the three steps into the back of what looked like an ambulance. Dane waited. The person wearing a hazmat suit and another Elastomeric Full Face-piece respirator, wrapped a folded blanket around my shoulders. Shivering, I looked up when the person patted my shoulder. Kurt. He smiled.

"Doing okay there, Iverson?"

"Freezing," I said through chattering teeth, and sat next to Dane.

Dane shuffled closer. I could feel the warmth of his thigh through the flimsy fabric covering our legs. Kurt shook out another blanket and dropped it across our knees.

"That should help."

"Thanks," I said. "Hope you've got more of these." I tugged the blanket around my shoulders, closer. "Susan will be along soon."

"We have plenty. When you get to the Facility you can get into warm clothes. Gerrard picked up bags for you all and fully stocked the larder and fridge."

"And liquor cabinet?" Because I'm going nowhere if there isn't tequila waiting. Stubbornness reared. My heels dug in without any effort.

Kurt nodded. "Tequila, whiskey, and vodka."

Nice.

"Are you coming?"

"No. Someone has to help Lee get to the bottom of this mess."

A shudder ran through me. Dane pressed his blanket-covered shoulder into mine. Guess he felt that.

"Is Lee here?"

"Yes. He's outside. Not much room in here and he doesn't have a respirator like this." He pointed to his face. "They have to be fitted."

That made sense.

Best keep Lee out of harm's way; one of us needed to survive this. Jeez, where did that come from? Dane's shoulder nudged me. Oops.

"Sorry," I whispered.

"I know," he replied. "We're going to be okay, Ellie. We're made tough. It didn't get us last time."

"Good point." I drew my internal blackout curtains across the rest of my thoughts. No need to upset Dane. He didn't know it was different this time. That meant he was too preoccupied going through the decontamination and interview to tap into me when Karen and I were talking. Hey, I never had an interview.

"Henderson, wasn't I supposed to have an interview?"

"No need. I have all your medical records, remember?"

How could I forget?

"Do you have Dane's?"

"I hold all the Delta A medical records. We travel with them."

Guess they're not the bulky physical files they once were.

Dane spoke, "Makes it easier for shit like this."

"Yeah," I said. "What about Susan?"

"Karen will do her interview once she's through the shower and before she joins us."

Okay. Good. Really, I just wanted to get going. Get out of the ambulance and into warm clothes, I didn't even care that we'd be stuck at the Facility and confined to one underground floor. It wasn't that bad. We'd have a gym to use, a decent kitchen, games room with pool table, large living quarters, and comfortable beds. Could. Be. Worse.

"Badge?" I said. "How long before we get our personal belongings back?"

"I'll bring them tomorrow."

Tomorrow.

"Is Susan doing the autopsy?"

"Yes. She'll use the negative pressure procedure room at the Facility. Karen will assist."

The plastic moved near the doorway. Must be Susan.

Sure enough a few moments later it moved again, and Susan stepped inside the plastic. A voice said, "Mind the steps."

I looked around and couldn't see anyone else. Ah, probably automated.

Kurt was ready with a blanket. He wrapped it around Susan's shoulders. "Grab a seat. We should be ready to move in a few minutes."

"Are you coming?"

He shook his head. "Nope, I'm going through there." He pointed to the curtain. "To take this lot off and scrub my respirator."

"You make it sound like we're plague ridden," Dane said, his usual happy tone gone. "I'm not typhoid Mary."

Kurt smiled. "Let's hope you're not Qu Pathogen Dane."

"Enough with your cheerful banter," I said. "Get out of here so we can go get warm."

"I'll see you soon," Kurt said, and disappeared behind the plastic.

Chapter Eighteen
Baby Hold On

Warm clothes made all the difference. I went from feeling like a potential patient to feeling like me. Healthy.

We had our own bedrooms with private bathrooms. Our bags were waiting in our rooms, our names on the doors. Four rooms, four names. Gerrard was thorough. No doubt he had help from Kurt and Lee. They would've been able to move around freely before we were granted access. Now there was a big quarantine sign on the main doors, and no one could enter without suitable attire. Even Karen had to wear a mask. She wasn't wearing the big full-face thing Kurt wore earlier. She wore something that looked a lot like a really fitted surgical mask. It wasn't. It was called an N95 respirator or a filtering face-piece respirator. It was disposable. She also wore regular clothes, not a protective suit. Guess she wasn't that worried that we'd puke on her or whatever.

In the main living area there were two desks, four coffee tables, six armchairs and a large corner sofa. It was a big, but comfortable room. The weirdest thing was no view.

Being underground took some getting used to. It's not that I'm claustrophobic. And this isn't an elevator that could plummet to the ground at any point. I just like to know there's a world beyond my immediate vicinity. Maybe that's where hope comes from?

My mental ramblings were interrupted by the *smack* of a pool ball into another. *Clack.* I followed the sound from the living area to the games room. *Smack.*

Dane. He looked up as he lined up another shot. "Wanna game?" He grinned and sunk another ball into a hole. "Beats sitting around waiting to get sick."

He was right.

"Rack 'em up." It'd been a few years since my pool room days, but I was fairly confident I could still sink a few balls. "We playing Eight-ball?"

Dane nodded. I chose a cue and chalked it.

"Ladies first," Dane said, motioning to me to break.

Luck was on my side. I sank two solids on the break then another one, before I missed a shot. Dane sunk a couple of stripes, then the cue ball.

"Bad luck," I muttered, lining up another solid. I tapped it on the right side and sent it sailing into the middle left pocket.

Susan came in.

"This is where the fun is at,' she said, grinning. "Mind if I take over for you, Ellie. There's a call in the kitchen for you."

I handed her the cue. "Don't lose," I said with a grin, and went to find out who wanted to talk to me. Without our cell phones we were disconnected from the world and kinda living in a bubble. *The Boy in the*

Plastic Bubble. Don't go there, brain.

The phone sat on the large kitchen counter. It was tethered to the wall but on a long cord. Old school. Rotary phone. Half the population wouldn't even know how to use one.

I picked up the heavy receiver from the countertop. "Hello."

"You okay, kid?" Caine's voice graveled more than usual.

"So far so good."

"And Dane?"

"He's okay."

"You'll have your cell phones back tomorrow. Don't know if they'll be much use down there." His pause filled the airway with office noises. "Do you have your laptop?"

"Yes."

"You can plug into the internet cable and keep an eye on the investigation."

"I'll finish beating Dane at Eight-ball, then I'll check on the teams and see who's doing what." Confident I could run the Deltas despite the limitations being so far underground posed. "CDC?"

"Tahoma is running things topside. He is working with a CDC investigation team, and with Delta A."

Good. Maybe we'd get some answers and get out of here quicker.

"Karen said this virus or whatever it is, was designed, if that's the right word, by the Chinese. You should know that I think a Chinese male killed Hardcastle."

"What else should I know?"

"That someone bugged my office and I now can't monitor the camera I had installed to see who retrieves the device."

"How can I help?"

"Get my cell phone, download the app to your phone. Use my passcode. Monitor the camera for me."

A growl emanated from the phone. "Is there a Counter Intelligence report I need to know about?"

I took a breath. "Not yet."

"Be careful, Ellie. That's a dangerous game."

"I know."

"I'll access your phone and download the app. Passcode?"

"Your birthday."

A gruff growl spiked into a near laugh. "Take care, Ellie. We need you back up here. And get some sleep."

I'd forgotten how satisfying it was to hang up the receiver of a rotary phone. Did not miss the weight of the receiver though. And our cell phones were pretty heavy in their everything-proof cases.

I could hear Susan and Dane laughing when I left the kitchen. Sleep didn't seem like a thing any of us were keen on. My hand touched my wrist and there was nothing. No watch. No phone. No windows. Our ways of telling time were severely limited.

I didn't want to interrupt their jovial vibes with

work, so I went into the living area and set my laptop up on one of the desks. The desks had internet cables plugged into the wall next to them, and the free end plugged happily into my computer. And just like that, I wasn't so isolated any more. I saw the time on my screen. Almost eleven. I made myself a deal. I'd check for updates then tell the others the time, and attempt sleep.

With my secure log-in, I dove into SENTINEL and opened the case files attached to Trace McAlester. I saw the case number had a new prefix: Three-two-two dash HQ dash five-five-five-zero. When McAlester talked and went into witness protection, the file number was amended. It's changed from kidnapping to a bioterrorism risk assessment.

There was zero joy in knowing we were now part of that risk assessment.

Wouldn't help to dwell. I scrolled through the documents attached, to look for updates and something, anything, that said we were close to finding out what this was about, and that we would put an end to it.

I found plenty, but nothing like the positive news I wanted to see.

We failed to get an identity for the Asian, possibly Chinese male, I saw kill Hardcastle. Sandra attached a note saying she was still working on the identity and would forward photos of potential suspects to us via email. I added a comment: Thank you. She'd see it in the morning.

Lee added a note to a page about his investigation into the whereabouts of Hanzel Forberg. He'd visited his place of work, his home (same apartment complex as Hardcastle), and the places he was known to frequent. According to the document, he hadn't been seen since Thursday evening, but no one he spoke to thought that was unusual. Lee said he'd keep on it in the morning.

There was an addendum to the case notes added by Tahoma Whitehorse. He confirmed that Jeremy Cotton was part of the team working on creating a vaccine, but also said they were months away from a vaccine being a reality.

Fan-fucking-tastic.

He went on to say they found a large document on Cotton's laptop and were working through it.

Document or manifesto?

If he's released it anywhere, we'll know which it is.

I got up and shut the lid on the laptop. Out of sight, out of mind. In the kitchen, I opened a cabinet containing glasses and tequila, whiskey, and vodka. With a half-smile on my face I took three glasses and the tequila into the games room.

Susan was gone.

I placed the glasses on the pool table and waved the tequila at Dane.

He nodded.

"Where is everyone?"

"Karen came and got Susan, she wanted to get on with the autopsy."

"Just us then," I replied, and poured two generous tequilas. At least three fingers. "Wanna try and find a movie?"

"Sure."

Dane picked up his glass and the bottle. We moved away from the pool table to a cozy sitting area at the other end of the room. A comfortable looking sofa faced the wall. On the wall was a large flat screen television. On the coffee table in front of the sofa was a remote. We settled into the sofa with the bottle close by. I chucked the remote at Dane.

"You choose."

The screen sprang to life. There was a certain amount of happiness at the discovery of Netflix. "How about some Stand-up?"

"Hell yes," I replied, downing a generous swig of tequila.

"Preferences?"

"No one too sweary." After a few seconds thought I came up with someone. "I know, Katherine Ryan."

"Don't know if I've seen her."

"Then you're in for a treat, my friend."

I pointed to the screen and told him to choose the oldest one first. We settled into sipping tequila and laughter. There were worse ways to spend a night.

The banter rolled on, taking me with it. Before long nothing else mattered.

I reached for my glass and found it handed to me. The background wasn't a room, it was shaded pencil. The glass was drawn.

"Thanks," I said, looking from the realistic hand to the arm, and finally the face. Not Dane.

Chance. Everything changed. The room became a line drawing with sketched shading and all monotoned.

"Time for a chat?" he asked, looking from me to the screen. "Katherine Ryan. She's funny, right?"

"Sure is. And yeah, we can talk." I stood and followed Chance to the pool table. When I looked back the room was gone, no sofa, no television, no Dane. The pool table became a glass topped desk.

Back in Chance's office.

Felt like home.

"Have a seat."

I did.

"Is this the tequila, or is this an actual visit from my favorite imaginary friend?"

"A visit. We got interrupted last time and I had an inkling something was up."

"Lethal viral inkling was it?"

Chance grinned. His eyes sparked. "It's going to take more than a virus to take you out."

Holy shit. "What'd you say?"

"It's going to take more than a virus to take you out. Why?"

"Because someone hired a couple of thugs to try."

"The car attack?"

"Yeah. I spoke to Caps about a possible contract, but he hadn't heard anything. And we don't know why Cotton did what he did. Actually, we're not certain he did anything."

"What would make you a likely target of a scientist ..." He looked at me. I nodded. Yes, a scientist. "What have you done to him?"

I shrugged. "He was an informant. I met him during the aftermath of Qu. He's been giving me little bits of information ever since."

"You vetted him?"

"Of course."

"Back to what have you personally done to this man ..."

My head shook. "I honestly don't know how I could've done anything to him."

"How did you meet?"

"During the investigation into the release of the Qu Pathogen. I met a lot of scientists, virologists, and microbiologists. If it ends in ist and has anything to do with medical science, I probably had some form of contact with them."

"CDC?"

"We worked together to locate the bioterrorists responsible."

"And you met Jeremy Cotton."

"Yeah. Didn't have a lot to do with him. He volunteered some information about a laboratory that we were interested in. He worked there briefly."

"Did he lose anyone to the disease?"

Oh, maybe that was it. But how would that make me a target? It wouldn't. More likely to make Whitehorse or Schneider targets. I was just an FBI agent investigating a case. And really, I was investigating the death of our Director, it did not start out as a terrorism investigation. I swallowed more tequila.

"This needs refreshing," I said, holding the glass out to Chance.

He produced a bottle from a drawer in his desk and another glass. "I'll join you. Don't want you drinking alone." He poured the drinks. "Now, did Cotton lose anyone to the disease?"

People were less likely to lose someone to Qu than to the subsequent COVID-19 pandemic. But Qu was a terror act and that made a difference to reactions.

"I don't remember him ever saying."

"Perhaps he thought you knew. People assume all manner of things and often wrongly."

"But why arrange a meeting and not show? Instead of him at our meeting place, I came across a CIA officer and a bomb." I stuck a pin in Cotton's reasonings for a minute.

"Are those three things related?"

"They say not."

Chance gave a half-smile. "And they're known for being unscrupulously honest."

"Exactly."

"Someone bugged my office prior to the supposed

meeting."

"CIA?"

"Possibly."

"El, what do you think about the bomb? Was it an isolated incident?"

"No. There were a series that morning. Five or six bombs all near clinics." I passed the bombings on to Delta C while I concentrated on the new Qu information and Jeremy Cotton's disappearance. Why did I do that? Then it became clear. "I have a feeling the spate of clinic bombings are a smoke screen."

"Elaborate ...," Chance said, swirling the contents of his glass.

"But just the sort of thing ..."

"... Tierney would do to cover his tracks."

Our eyes met. "He's not an entirely trustworthy son of a bitch," I said. "But he is consistent."

Chance laughed. "Okay, so why didn't Cotton show?"

That I kinda knew. "He thought he was being followed. Well, he was being followed. He climbed a fire escape and hid inside a carpet."

"Why not climb back down once the danger passed and meet you?"

"He died in the carpet roll. I think he got stuck."

Chance suppressed a smile. "Karma?"

"Maybe. Except if he was infected with the intention of infecting me, he achieved his goal. I found him. Dane and I uncovered his hiding place." And I may have killed Dane and myself doing so.

"Do you think the CIA know something about Jeremy Cotton?"

I nodded. "They're denying knowing anything, or having anything to do with, what was then Jeremy's disappearance."

"But Tierney," Chance said, as he swirled his glass in the other direction.

Yeah. But Tierney. I didn't want to think he'd knowingly endanger lives.

"If this is personal. Cotton wanted revenge or some such. Then the means and the method are important. Most people don't immediately go for a lethal virus to exact revenge." Another big swallow of tequila. I enjoyed the heat as it traveled down my esophagus. "What if it's a two-fold scenario?"

Chance nodded.

"Infect you and then, before you know it, you've infected X number of people, and they've infected X number of people ... he gets to kill you, and release something into the world at the same time. He's infected already, he's dying. Had nothing to lose once he went down that path."

"Guess it'd really piss him off to know we were quarantined so fast, if he wanted a lot of people to fall ill or die." Something niggled in my gut. I let it fester and take shape. I needed more than a niggle. "It's a Chinese version of the Qu Pathogen."

"That Cotton had?"

"Yes."

"And we have it in this country?"

"Yes, for research purposes."

"Makes you wonder how they got it, doesn't it?"

"I figured it was stolen from a laboratory somewhere. They're hardly likely to hand it over to Americans."

"This whole thing could've been started by espionage and theft ... by Americans."

"Absolutely."

"Ever think we humans deserve all we get?"

All the time. All. The. Time.

Wasn't helpful, but Karma might just be coming back for a hard whack.

I set my glass on the desk. "Know what I hate?" Chance shook his head. "You're about to find out." I kept my voice quiet and controlled. "Limbo. Not knowing. Being trapped in a silent bubble. Not being able to see the sky. Not knowing what fucking time it is. Not putting Isabella and Grace to bed. Waiting. God, I hate waiting."

"This isn't how you die, El."

I lifted my eyes and looked deep into his. "You can't know that."

Cool blue stared through me into my soul. "But I can. And I do. And El, this isn't it."

"Okay. So, this isn't how I die. Feels very much like it might be."

"Trust me, El." His hand wrapped around mine. "Do you trust me?"

"I do."

His hand squeezed. Flesh on flesh. Warmth. Strength. Not bad for a drawing.

"Good. You're going to be okay. It does not end here."

"This is just a vacation then?"

A vacation underground in a fucking bunker away from the world and all those we care about. Not much of a vacation. My mind wandered along a dusty path at the end of which was an expanse of neatly clipped grass. Mikki. She's the only person who might enjoy a vacation like this. Although I had a feeling this was the shittiest writers retreat ever.

Mikki. Cait's sister. Cait O'Hare, our deceased Director. That's where this started. Cait. Her Mauryville property. Thor. The stable hand. Was that what he was? The person who told the bikers where she lived. The biker's sister. Whatnot girl. The biker and Whatnot girl. What was his name? Why couldn't I remember their names? Why is it important?

"Ellie?"

"I think this has something to do with Lexington, and that whole mess with the bikers, and Cait's death."

"Why?"

"I don't know ..."

I picked up my glass and took another big sip.

What were their names? My mind drifted back to Lexington and the place we met the girl. Stonewall Jackson Hospital parking lot. Dane and I were looking for a car and soon discovered she was too. I slipped into the memory; she was right there in front of me with her multi-colored over-sized sweater, braided hair, pink leggings, black Doc Martens, and the sweet earthy smell of dope rising from her clothes.

Her head nodded like one of those bobble-headed toys someone had flicked too hard. "It's absolutely the car and whatnot." Her face crumpled as she saw the broken window. "Someone is going to be mad and whatnot."

Shoot me now.

"Think you've got the wrong car. What's your name?" Dane said, steering her to me.

"Really, that's it," she squealed, trying to duck under his arm. "That's the blue car and whatnot."

A light bulb moment exploded. "Oh hey, do you know Jerry too?" I said, friendly, and opting for a name that sounded almost like Gregory.

The girl grinned her head bounced forward, then flew back. How does she not get whiplash nodding like a bobble-head?

"He's not feeling well. I thought I'd get him his phone and whatnot."

"I have it," I said. "I'll take it to him." I am so helpful.

Her face froze. I could see a dim light in her eyes grow brighter then fade. "Jerry asked me to get it. I should get it and whatnot."

I sipped my drink again and willed the memory to

move along to the bit where we found out her name. It sped up. Mental fast-forward.

"Jerry said we can both take it to him," I said. "What's your name? I'm Ellie."

"My name is Yvonne. Are you a special friend of Jerry's and whatnot?"

Fuck-a-duck. Her name is Yvonne.

Yvonne was a stoner and a wannabe scriptwriter. Her nasty older brother was Emmett the biker, and when he got mad, he had people hurt her. She had cigarette burns all up her arms and probably other places as well. I searched through more memories. Yvonne was sent to get something from a doctor's car; the doctor was infected with Qu by Juan Garcia; the pathogen was in a water bottle. Emmett stopped Yvonne drinking from a similar bottle. It was his phone that they wanted.

Did that help me now? No.

Their names helped. Emmett Garrison: head loser in The Inferno Jester Motorcycle Club. Emmett and Yvonne Garrison.

Why is this important? Because of Cotton and the new strain of Qu. But why?

"Chance … this has been enlightening as always, but I need to go do some digging."

"Go. I'm here whenever you need me."

I stood and walked to the pencil outlined door, at the door I looked back, and saw a white rectangular eraser moving back and forth across the room, taking everything in its path. My heart pounded. One step, and I was through the door and safe from the eraser, and solid flesh again.

Back in the living area and at the desk with my laptop, I started a search for Emmett Garrison.

A cough from the sofa alerted me to a presence. "Have you always been able to do that?"

"Walk across a room? Since I was ten months old, so Dad tells me."

"Always with the wise cracks."

"By the time I was two I could walk across a room without spilling a drink."

"You going to carry on like this all night?"

I smiled at him. "Perhaps ..."

"El, have you always been able to ..."

"See Chance?"

"Yeah." Dane stood, stretched, and yawned. "And we should both get some sleep."

"In answer to your question, no, I haven't always been able to see him or create the whole scene like that." I scanned Dane's tired face. "Have you always been able to tap into thoughts?"

Dane grinned, then yawned behind his hand. "With my brother, yes."

"How come you and I can do it?" Every now and then I wondered what made us so different. Kurt used to think my ability to glean information from people, and the way Mitch and I could connect, was head injury thing. Crossed wires or something. Mitch had never had a head injury, so that theory failed. I figured it was because we were so close. That didn't explain how Dane and I could hop in and out of each other's thought processes, or how he could see what I saw. Maybe somethings are best left as mysteries.

"Same wavelength. I dunno, El. Our minds just work differently to other peoples."

That was an understatement.

"And yeah, I think it's bedtime."

I left the search running. If there was anything to find, I'd find it.

Chapter Nineteen
Tell Her About It

Noises woke me.

People. Voices. Sounds of life. The darkness remained. No slivers of light edged through curtains or under the door. Dead dark. The same level of dark I imagined when the lid closes on a coffin. Don't suppose I'll hear the underlying buzz from voices when they close the lid on me. Or maybe I will? I lay, listening. The hum from voices continued. There was no way for me to know what time it was, but I knew I wasn't dead. I swung my legs over the side of the bed and found the floor under my feet. My hand fumbled for the bedside lamp on the nightstand.

Warm light bathed the immediate area but didn't reach the corners of the room. I stood and stretched.

Upright and mobile. Good start. I flicked the main light switch and filled the room with a cooler, brighter light. Here we go. Day one underground.

With little enthusiasm, I showered and dressed. Then I remembered I'd left a search running on my laptop. That could hold a clue or an answer to the Cotton question. I still had no idea why I thought Emmett Garrison would help me work out the Cotton issue. With a minuscule increase in vigor, I opened my door and strode into the hallway. Coffee wafted, carried on the lightest breeze. For a split second I thought there was a window open. I almost laughed. A voice in my mind said, "Get it together, Chicky" and it sounded very like Sam Jackson. Hot damn, I miss you, Sam. Guess that's a forever thing. Like Mac and Carla. Pushing thoughts of the dead aside, I went over to the computer and woke the screen. It was six in the morning. Good to know.

Screeds of information waited.

Satisfied I had something to do and I could somehow move the case forward, I wandered off to locate the coffee I smelt in the air.

Susan greeted me in the kitchen with a smile and a coffee. "Black?"

"Yes," I replied, taking the offered steaming mug. "Did you and Karen get any sleep?"

Susan nodded. "A few hours."

Karen still wore the respirator and was making breakfast. The mask would make eating and absorbing the required amount of caffeine tricky.

"Morning, Ellie. I'm taking a tray down to my room. I'll be back," Karen said. "Enjoy your breakfast. I'll take blood samples in an hour." She paused in the doorway. "Dane awake?"

"I don't know," I said. No doubt he'd wander out when he was.

She repositioned the laden tray and left.

Susan pushed the lever on a toaster, leaned a hip on the counter, and picked up her coffee. "Not quite how I thought I'd be spending the weekend."

"Wasn't part of my plan either." I'd planned on spending the weekend with the family and getting ready for the big birthday bash next Saturday. "It's a bit quieter here than at home."

"Toddlers, right?"

"Yep. Twin almost-two-year-old girls."

Be nice to be at their birthday and celebrate that milestone. Not dead.

"My kids are a bit older. Youngest will be fifteen in a month."

"Sorry I ruined your weekend, Susan." Depending on how the results of the bloods from Cotton, and our blood tests go, I might be apologizing for ruining her life next.

"I didn't feel much like watching teen sport." The toast popped. "But breakfast without having teens bickering and everyone in a rush to get out the door, now that sounds peaceful to me." She plucked a hot slice of toast from the machine. "Can I make you some?"

"I'll get breakfast later. You enjoy the peace. I'll take my coffee to the laptop. There's something I need to look at."

* * *

I woke the laptop again. And scrolled through information regarding Emmett Garrison while drinking my coffee. He was in prison. Although that was handy to know, it didn't mean much. He was situated in United States Penitentiary, Lee. And that was down in Lee County, Virginia. I dragged a map up from the bottom of my screen. It was near Pennington Gap. Some two-hundred and seventy something miles southish from Lexington. Damn near in Kentucky. A high security prison. Again, that didn't mean much. He obviously hadn't broken out, or that'd be plastered all over the file I read. I scanned, looking for his legal representation. Noah Bancroft. Well, would you look at that. Dammit. Now I really wanted a look at Noah's friends list, but couldn't access my alter ego's account. I'd signed out as Catherine Thomas and the information I needed to sign back in was on my phone or in my desk.

I left Emmett for a bit and looked for the sister. Yvonne. Nothing.

What did I remember about her? She was a victim. Dammit. I bet we put her into witness protection. What else did I know? She wanted to be a screenwriter. Good chance she still wanted that.

Dane might know more. I had a feeling he did read her script.

Absently I reached for my pocket. My jaw clenched as I patted my other pockets. A sigh struggled through my gritted teeth. Phone. Dammit, I need my phone. Another thought occurred. I didn't need my phone if I could use our internal messaging system. My finger traced on the trackpad, moving the cursor until I found the message icon. I scrolled for Debbie Barnes, found her and sent a message.

SAC Iverson: Debbie, Please video call me when you get in.

If we put Yvonne into our protection program, Debbie would know the details. She created the new identities for the FBI. She would know, but not necessarily divulge, that information. She would, however, be able to set me up in Catherine Thomas's Facebook account so I could check out Noah Bancroft's account with ease. I had a few hours before Debbie would get into the office, time to see if I could find out who visited Emmett Garrison in prison.

I emailed the prison with an official request for information and blank copied Sandra into the email. He was a convicted felon, so I didn't expect any push back from the prison, but you never know.

Time to read more of the information our system contained. There were links to other cases, not just ours. Not like I didn't have time to start at the beginning of Garrison's illustrious career in criminal gangs and get a full background on him and his buddies. As I read my fingers sought out a pen near my keyboard.

The first record of his name appeared ten years ago, and it was an assault charge, male on female, during a conversation with FBI about the murder of a rival gang member. He assaulted his female lawyer in front of the interviewing agents. Backhanded her across the face. He was arrested on the spot. Cleared of any wrongdoing regarding the murder and cautioned by a judge regarding the assault. Maybe if he'd been locked up, a lot of crap wouldn't have happened. No sense thinking about that. What if's are not helpful. I tapped the pen on the desk. Think.

He was my age, so what did he do before that first federal law enforcement encounter? Couldn't imagine it was anything legal and it wasn't back far enough to be a sealed juvenile record. There wasn't a link to any earlier crimes handled by Police. Perhaps he was smart enough to not get caught back then. Twirling the pen around my fingers, I gave that notion brain time. Yeah, I wasn't so sure that he was smarter back then. People don't usually get stupider as they grow older, well, without a defined reason anyway. And there wasn't anything to suggest he was mentally incapacitated. I'd met Garrison, and he was full of himself and seemed to think he was clever.

But would a smart guy assault a lawyer in front of FBI agents? Would a smart guy threaten a federal agent in front of police, and tell another agent to keep away from his sister? Would a smart man say, "The Doctor better hope he dies" in a threatening manner in front of federal agents and police?

I think not. Satisfied that I'd determined his intellect

wasn't of the highest caliber, I stared at the screen. There was an answer somewhere, I knew it. There was a hint of probability that dumb luck kept him off the law enforcement radar in his twenties.

"Come on Garrison, give me something ..." My whisper hit the screen, trickled down, and pooled along the top of my laptop. A fluffy little duckling popped out of the pool and shook. Water droplets covered the screen and keyboard. Its head dunked into the pool. Its little body tugged and tugged. All of a sudden, the duckling fell backward. In its orange beak, I saw a torn piece of paper. It waddled over and dropped the soggy, ripped paper on my keys. Quacked twice, turned around, and dove into the pool. Water splashed all over me. Tiny yellow feathers stuck to my hand. I picked the wet feathers off and lay them on the desk.

The ripped paper began to dry, on it, I saw writing. It was a large corner of a ledger page. From the corner of my eye, I saw the wet feathers dissolve.

Writing became clearer as the page dried. Two names. Bancroft and Zhang.

Another Chinese connection.

Shitballs and whatnot.

The names were underneath each other, and next to each name was a month, a year, and a number.

Bancroft: July, twenty-twenty, one hundred and fifty thousand.

Zhang: August, twenty-twenty, five hundred thousand.

I typed what I saw into a blank document.

Dane's voice rang out, "Morning!"

Dragging my eyes away from the ripped paper, I saw Dane wave from the doorway.

"Hey, come here a minute."

Dane ambled over. "I smell coffee ... can I get you a fresh cup?"

"Yep." I peered into my cup. Half-full. I touched the outside. Cold.

Dane picked the cold cup up. "Not like you to leave coffee to go cold. What gives?"

"This," I replied, pointing to the screen. Don't mention the duck. "I saw a torn piece of paper with these names and the month etcetera on it."

"In what context?"

"That's the thing. I don't really know the context. But, Dane, this is the third Chinese link."

"What do you think that means?"

"Nothing that will make us smile."

He nodded his agreement. "I'll be back with hot coffee and something to eat. Can I get you anything to go with the coffee?"

"No, thanks." Probably should be hungry by now, but I wasn't.

Time to stretch my legs. Standing, I rolled my shoulders a few times to loosen the muscles, then stretched. The other side of the room beckoned. Or rather the television on the wall beckoned. The lack of windows made me feel isolated even more than having no cell phone. Using the remote I turned the TV on and flipped channels until I found news I could stand to watch.

Local news. That would do nicely, thanks. I plopped into the squishy sofa cushions and watched the news presenters deliver the morning news. Curiosity drove my news interest. Journalists tended to like it when we withheld information; it gave them something to get all uppity over, and that in turn led them to start digging around looking for a leak. How long before Hardcastle's death would be a news item was anyone's guess, and now there was a second body discovered from the same company.

All it needed was one determined reporter with a connection to Newgenic and the buzz would start.

The phone rang. Even the ring tone sounded heavy.

Susan came in. "Phone, Ellie."

"Thanks," I said, pushing myself to my feet.

When I got to the kitchen door, I could hear Dane talking. He handed me the phone as soon as I walked through the doorway. "Kurt."

I smiled and took the receiver, wishing I could tap a speaker button, but no, we were old school down here.

"Hey, Henderson."

"Iverson, you doing okay?"

Nope. Not even close to okay. No point saying that. "Yep. What's up?"

"Newgenic and Exical closed ranks. They're saying our investigation is putting their employees at risk."

"And how would that happen?"

"I wondered the same," he said. "Their lawyers have formally asked us to back off, stating government contracts and their impeccable safety record."

"Really? And ours say?"

"Use a bigger shovel," Kurt said with a chuckle. "They're hiding something."

"We know that they're trying to hide their off-shore labs and the research into Qu."

"All we have to make that statement is the document from McAlester. Newgenic is saying that doesn't exist and was fabricated by a disgruntled accountant."

I had a feeling they'd released information.

"What did they do?"

Before Kurt could answer, Susan swung round the doorframe. "You will not believe what they're saying on the news ..."

Shitballs.

"What?"

"That there is a conspiracy to stop their vaccine research fronted by Trace McAlester of Vaporcount Corporation, and it involved forged documents implying that Newgenic is somehow responsible for the development of a new version of Qu."

"Holy flying brown stuff," I replied. "This situation is on a fast track to riveting."

Susan laughed. "I'm going to keep watching."

"Good thinking."

Kurt's voice grew louder in my ear. "Did she just say

that Newgenic are playing victim?"

"Yes," I replied. "According to the news."

"That's what I was about to tell you. They've gone public, crying about how Trace McAlester of Vaporcount Corporation is trying to discredit them and ruin their reputation. Newgenic says Vaporcount Corp are a competing biomedical research company."

"Well, now, that's new."

"How much do we know about Vaporcount?"

"They're owned by Virginia Holdings." I hauled in the information like a fisherman winding in the line. "They own property. The house we found the flash drive in was one of theirs. McAlester had his name on five properties as contact." So, he told us.

"I'll deep dive into Virginia Holdings and Vaporcount, see what I can turn up. Meanwhile, it looks very much like a smoke screen and they only go up when people are getting nervous."

"Keep the pressure on and let's see what boils over or goes up in flames."

"How's it going your end?"

"It's going." The walls are closing in. "My gut says Emmett Garrison has something to do with Jeremy Cotton and his desire to infect me ..."

There was silence for a beat. "Now that's a name from the not-to-distant past. And not one I wanted to hear again."

Kurt didn't deny my gut feeling or try to dissuade me. That meant something.

"Henderson, quick question ... if you were in a max-security prison and you still needed to conduct business, who would you trust?" I'd trust my lawyer.

"My lawyer."

"And if you needed records kept ..."

"My lawyer."

"Exactly. I think we're going to find some answers with Noah Bancroft, Garrison's lawyer."

"Lawyer client privilege ..."

"Life is full of quirky little workarounds, don't you find?"

"I do."

"Take care Henderson."

"Don't die, Iverson."

Chapter Twenty
And She Was

As much as I tried denying it, I was beginning to feel flu symptoms. Headachy, raw throat, tired, muscle aches. Of course, it could just be imagination.

That seemed more likely. I swallowed coffee without any problem. Probably nothing then.

Ignoring it, I settled to read more about Emmett Garrison. Two more pages of illegal activity later, I was over Emmett and his bullshit. Time to look into Jeremy Cotton. Maybe he'd be easier. He wasn't a biker so might've been more open on social media. At least that was a place to start.

What did I know about him? Not much apart from working at Schröder Forschung in Berlin at the same time as Grant Hardcastle, and that they both worked for Newgenic recently. And he was dead like Hardcastle.

I found two social media sites for Jeremy Cotton. Facebook and LinkedIn. The latter made sense, he was a professional. I clicked on people in the search tab and typed his name into the search field. Ten plus results. I scrolled down and smiled when I recognized his photograph. With a click I was looking at his profile and ready to discover how much I could actually see without signing in. I didn't want anyone knowing I was looking at his profile, was smarter to stay away from logging into any of my own accounts. The *About* heading contained a short biography. He worked in biomedical sciences and had an interest in astronomy. Under experience, he listed time spent with various organizations, and the roles he filled. Nothing I didn't already know. The *Present* day tab said he worked at Newgenic in biomedical research. Moving on, I found education. He did his Masters degree at the University of Buffalo, he also had a Bachelor's degree from the same university. His high school was listed at Princess Anne High School, Virginia Beach.

I added the high school information to the document I had open. I was starting to miss my notebook and pen as much as I missed my phone. I wondered about his high school years and checked out the high school website.

Absently the fingers of my left hand rubbed my temple where a dull ache resided. Fuzzy gray patches grew, making the screen hard to see. I ducked my head trying to look around them. Less than successful. I closed my left eye, leaned my elbow on the desk, and pressed the heel of my hand into my eye socket, hoping to stop the pain spikes before they took hold.

I opened a page on the website that contained yearbook photographs from nineteen-ninety-six onward. Nothing before that. Spikes jabbed into my brain from my eye. I pressed my left hand over my eye.

One-handed, I used keystrokes to bring up a search

box and then typed Jeremy Cotton into the box. Several entries popped up. His first high school photograph and a class photo caught my eye. With a click, I zoomed in on the class photo. It filled the screen. One by one I looked at the faces. Finding Cotton was easy. Another boy seemed familiar. Using the mouse pointer, I hovered over his face. Noah Bancroft.

Fuckadoodledo.

Running my right eye over all the male faces, I found another face with a hint a familiarity. I hovered until a name popped up. Emmett Garrison.

What were the odds?

Fucking astronomical, I would've thought.

A sudden violent pain jabbed my brain. The part that still functioned tried to piece together the contents of the bag Mitch packed for me, trying to determine if he'd put the migraine synergy, or my meds, in the bag. Or both. I hadn't needed any for nearly ten months. Then I remembered the small zippered bag in with my toiletries. He did.

A soothing voice flowed through me. Mitch: Of course, I did.

Another voice spoke and was closer. Dane.

"Where are your meds?"

"I'll get them," I said, standing. Bad move. I clamped my hand over my eye.

"How about you sit, and I get them?" Dane's warm hand held my elbow.

"I ..." A massive jolt from behind my left eyeball spiked deep into my brain, nausea swirled around my uvula. "I need to get out of here."

It was going to be bad. Another jab from a red-hot knife jammed into my brain. I needed dark. Demerol. Anti-nausea meds. Tylenol. Too late for synergy.

Dark. A small smile tried to escape. I'm underground. Dark is everywhere.

Dane's hand stayed on my elbow. My one operational eye said the doorway was getting closer. I was moving.

"Wait here," Dane said, leaning me against a wall. I saw him go into my room, then return. "I turned the main light out. Just the lamp now. Once I get you the meds, I'll switch that out."

Okay. Whatever. More movement. It wasn't good. The bed sank as I sat down. Dane pressed a cold glass of water into my hand. Gratefully I took a sip.

"Where in your bag?" Dane whispered.

"Inside my toilet bag."

Zippers opened and closed. The air moved as he got closer to me. He removed the glass from my hand. The clunk reverberated as he put it on the nightstand, shock waves flowed through my brain.

"Sorry," he whispered. "Hold out your hand, there are two tablets and one red capsule."

Ibuprofen times two. Meperidine combined with promethazine times one. Capsule first. I swallowed that easier than the two round tablets. Gingerly, I laid back on the bed and waited for the magic to happen. I knew I had about twenty minutes of hell to get through before the anti-nausea and sedation properties of the promethazine kicked in, along with the pain killing Meperidine. If Kurt was here, he would've injected Demerol and it'd be faster. He wasn't. My eyes closed. Lightning bolts of pain surged. I knew Dane was nearby, but the torturous light was gone.

I grabbed the end of the pillow and folded it over my head.

The storm raged on and on until I heard a voice, soft at first, then louder and more insistent. I held the pillow tighter over my head, but the voice continued to grow in intensity. Words began to make sense. A bolt of pain speared a sentence to a black wall. Shimmering words hung suspended by a lightning bolt. "What did Seamus say?"

My shoulder moved. Jiggled. A hand pressed into my shoulder and shook it.

"El, this is important. Wake up." My eyes refused to open. Under the warm blanket of fluff caused by the drugs, the voice tried again. "El. It's important. What did Seamus say?"

"Chance?"

My mind dropped. Free fall. Spinning into the great beyond. Chance's voice followed me, "What did Seamus say?"

Behind closed eyes the spinning slowed, then stopped. My right eye opened. Confusion reigned. This wasn't the bedroom in the Facility. A restaurant. Why? Dim lighting and the thrum of voices soaked the room. I knew this place. Seamus Kennedy waved from a corner booth. A roadhouse. When was this? Time and place cemented in my semi-functional brain. After Director O'Hare was killed, but before we knew about Qu.

Another voice, familiar, quiet. I glanced to my left. Chance. "Listen El."

Okay.

"To what?"

"To what Seamus tells you."

"Okay."

Chance nudged me forward. "He's waiting for you."

Everything froze. I looked around. No one moved. Noises stopped. The world around me zoomed backward. Then jolted to a stop. Gathering my bearings, I slid into the booth opposite my long-time friend Seamus Kennedy. Life continued, but not life as I knew it. Life as it was.

"What do you know?"

"There's chatter suggesting a biological attack," Kennedy said.

Shit. "Do any of our agencies know?"

"They should, if they're listening." His expression changed from neutral to grim. "I have no idea. Initially, this came from my own intel network and I confirmed with sources within my reach, on the quiet." Seamus took a sip of water.

"How did Five-Eyes not pick this up?"

"We don't know they haven't." Seamus finished his glass of water.

Sarcasm crept into my voice without me noticing, "Really? Because I'd expect this to make their weekly newsletter."

A small smile flickered across his face. "You've heard nothing?"

"Correct. I haven't heard even a whisper." Dammit. I should know this. We should all know this. My mouth opened and recent events spilled. "Cait O'Hare is dead. Iain Campbell was killed in a hit-and-run." Information sources are endangered.

"What? I heard on the way down here that O'Hare was treated and discharged from hospital, after an unfortunate riding accident."

"Yes, but we did not say she was alive."

Seamus inclined his head slightly to let me know someone was coming.

"Two medium rare steaks," a girl said, sliding the plates in front of us.

I smiled and thanked her.

"I'll be right back with some more water." She picked up the empty water jug from the table and disappeared from my view. Seamus watched her for a few seconds.

Steak, fries, and salad awaited my fork. My stomach growled.

"Hungry, Iverson," Seamus commented, slicing a

piece of steak and ramming it into his mouth.

I nodded and did the same. I'm always hungry.

Water arrived. I filled our glasses.

We'd eaten half our meals before either of us spoke again. I rested my fork on the edge of the plate. "Tell me about this chatter," I said, and leaned on my elbows.

"Finish eating first."

"I'm taking a break," I said with a smile.

"We've pieced together chatter from multiple sources and it looks like a series of biological attacks is on the agenda," he said.

I smiled, it had to look like old friends catching up. "The threat is what? Anthrax?"

"No. Or at least that's unlikely. It never works quite as well as those bozos expect."

"So, what then?" Visions of a zombie apocalypse loomed.

"Viral something."

"Okay. How and where will this potential killer flu be released?"

"It's gone quiet."

Shit. "Soon then."

He nodded. "As for where, from what I gleaned … multiple locations within the US, the UK, Canada, and Australia."

"And those countries all have what in common?" I knew full well what it was. Five-Eyes. They were countries which provided intelligence. Everything I knew about Five-Eyes came to the fore. A country was missing. That's gotta be something, or maybe it was designed to have us chasing our tails. "Why'd they miss New Zealand?"

"My guess would be isolation and small population."

Chance pushed my arm, I slid over and let him sit down. That's not weird at all.

He extended his hand to Seamus. "Christopher Chance, you must be Seamus Kennedy."

Kennedy's mouth twitched into half a smile. He shook Chance's hand. "This is what it's like to talk to El's invisible friend?"

"Welcome aboard the crazy train," Chance said, with a grin. "But we're here for a reason, and it has to do with New Zealand."

The fog in my head parted just enough for the whole scene I was embroiled in to make a bit of sense.

I remembered our conversation, and how I'd thought it was time to re-locate south, and that Mitch had suggested we move back to New Zealand well before we knew about Qu. The fog closed. I was back at the table with Seamus and Chance.

I said exactly what I said the first time I heard about the new threat. "How the hell are we going to deal with this? We'll need anti-viral medicine, quarantine stations, shut the borders, vaccines." Disaster. This could be a total disaster. "CDC? Are they at least in the loop?"

The beginning of a notion wiggled, catching

lightning bolts and pushing them away from my brain.

Chance spoke, "It could have been a total disaster ..."

"But it fucking wasn't, was it, Chance?"

He shook his head, a small smile on his lips. "No, it wasn't." He looked at Seamus who'd paused, fork halfway to his mouth, and stared back at Chance.

"The question becomes, why ... why wasn't it a total disaster?" I said.

Seamus nodded. "It was a trial release." His deliberate words fell into his plate, gravy splashed over the edge onto the table.

"Now you're thinking," Chance said.

I remembered how we talked about open-sourced intelligence regarding the bio-threat situation. We thought our agencies might have overlooked open-source intelligence, and that was why no one seemed to pick up what was happening or going to happen.

"Chance, if it was a trial release and there was nothing to pick up, what does that tell us?" I pushed the plate in front of me away and leaned on my elbows.

"You know what it says ..."

"It says the planning and execution was above and beyond anything we've ever seen from a terror cell or known terror organization."

Seamus spoke, "It's not one virus."

"That is the other important information," Chance said.

"We lost important people within our intelligence community, very quickly," I said, and one was replaced with my nemesis, Owen. Assistant Deputy Director Owen. She sat on the IC in our Director's place. And she never filed a report about the meeting that should have included the potential viral threat. Owen disappeared soon after.

Shit-fuck-shit.

Memories swam around in the gravy on Seamus's plate. People in prominent places or agencies were dying or suddenly unavailable.

"Houston, we have a problem," I whispered.

"Iverson, we have the beginning of a catastrophe," Seamus said.

"I concur," Chance added. "Who specifically are we talking about when it comes to the IC?"

"Deputy Director of NSA is dead. Director of FBI is dead. The newly appointed Deputy Assistant Director of our Intelligence Branch has mysteriously gone on leave. Iain Campbell, Assistant Secretary of the Bureau of Intelligence and Research, is dead." I hauled in information that tied them together.

The intelligence community: that's what ties all of them together.

Seamus leaned across the table. "I have one to add, but he's not yours."

I rubbed my temples trying to stop the pain shards returning and instantly regretted the word that left my mouth. "Who?" I knew who. I didn't want to be here again.

"Misha Praskovya."

Shock from Kennedy's words still vibrated through my body. Not Misha. My eyes flicked up to Kennedy's. "Not Misha."

I did not want to relive his loss again. But I couldn't stop the memory.

Misha stepped straight off a Mills and Boon romance cover and into our team ten years ago. He was our FSB counterpart. We'd worked cases together over the years. Misha was a friend. He taught me Russian and how to drink Vodka. I brushed tears from my eyes before they fell. He was Isabella's godfather. Just fuck.

"I'm sorry, Iverson. I know you were close."

"How?" My voice cracked, and a single word was all I could cope with.

"He was working a case in Minsk. There was an explosion. Misha died at the scene."

Now I know why Seamus made the journey to see me. "Is it connected?" I swallowed tears, and a giant lump in my throat. Now was not the time for emotional outbursts or grief. People depended on me doing my job. With one final swallow, the lump in my throat dislodged and sank.

"My intel didn't mention Russia or Europe beyond the United Kingdom," Seamus said

"Sure, okay, but what do you know about the case he was working?"

"He was tracking a known terrorist. Last I spoke to him, he said he was close, and it had something to do with a laboratory explosion in St Petersburg."

"A laboratory?" I felt my internal threat-level monitor zoom up the scale. "How is this not connected?"

"Because nothing I've heard mentioned anyone or anything in Russia connected to this fecking viral disaster."

Hashtag apocalypse. "Open minds."

Chance interceded, "Seamus, go back, think, it was a laboratory. He died at one in Minsk? And part of his investigation involved a lab in St. Petersburg? Who owned the labs?"

I watched Kennedy's face. A struggle ensued that involved his features, a moment or two later his facial muscles relaxed. "Schröder Forschung. Both of them."

Oh, man.

"They're German," I said. "We have two dead scientists now, and at one time both worked for Schröder Forschung."

But what did that mean?

"Someone killed a Russian FSB officer at a laboratory owned by a German company, but situated in Russia?" Chance asked. "But two laboratories owned by the same company exploded?"

Seamus nodded.

Chance continued, "And now an American and a British scientist are dead, and they have a connection to the same German company."

"Let's not forget one of those men wanted to infect me with a modified version of Qu created by the

Chinese," I said. "And he might've. This whole migraine crazed time-slip, whatever the fuck this is," I waved an arm over the table. "Could be a Qu fueled hallucination ..."

"Maintain an open mind, Iverson." Seamus said. His Irish brogue softened, "You don't die like this."

I smiled. "So people keep telling me. When I say people, I refer to imaginary friends ... so ..."

"Don't know about Seamus, but I'm hardly ever wrong," Chance said, with a laugh. "Now, you know there is a definite link to a German company."

I nodded. True. But it didn't feel like they were behind any of it. Why? I circled back.

"Talk to me about the trial, Chance ... I'm trying to get a feel for what's happening here. You're telling me that when this began, some important people died, and a Deputy Director of Intelligence disappeared?" Seamus said. "And that happened, that's not disputed."

Chance nodded. "Go back to the multiple threats."

Seamus took a deep breath. "My intel, not Government intelligence, said more than one virus would be released in each country."

"Origin of the viruses?" I asked.

"I could not determine where they came from."

"In the beginning we considered Russia as the source. They'd been involved in the unfortunate Novichok situation," I said. "But it's easy to blame the Russian's and it's never sat right."

"Would be easy to also point to the Germans,"

Seamus said. "You have a connection."

"Why would they destroy their own labs? We're talking multi-million-dollar equipment and research gone ... doesn't make sense." I said. "Who would want us to point fingers all over the map? Who benefits from raised suspicions? How was this kept from our combined intelligence communities until it was too late? Why not New Zealand?" I slumped into the seat; lightning flashed in across my vision. "This is no one we know. Someone with a vast network, and ability to conceal their true motive and silence their arms, and it feels like they're multi-armed like an octopus." Someone released the Kraken. "It was the bio-terror threat that never really was." Mist shrouded my thoughts covering the first time we tangled with Qu Pathogen in a fine blanket. Vaporware. "Qu Pathogen was like vaporware. Except we did it, we were the ones who hyped the release, after the fact, and ran the media campaign for the terrorists."

"People died," Seamus said, his voice hardened.

"Not enough to make it an effective release, but enough to make us think we foiled the plot." When we were in the middle of the mess, it felt like the world was sinking, but in reality, it did not. It was not. "We were played."

"Or it was an experiment to see how far Qu would spread once released ..." Chance said.

"And what? New Zealand was the control group?" I queried.

Chance shrugged. "Maybe. You need to get well. You have a job to do."

"As I said, Houston, we have a problem."

"How so?" Seamus pushed his plate away. "We're closer now than before."

"Hello! Neither of you exist and I'm basically talking to myself while fueled by a version of Demerol."

"What do you mean I don't exist?" Seamus grumbled into his water glass. "I fecking exist, Iverson."

A tear slid down my face as the thought of never seeing Seamus or Misha again crept over me. I clung to the images of the last time I saw Misha, in church when we christened the twins. He took his role as Isabella's godfather seriously. The font wavered and shimmered, holy water splashed over the edge dripping into a puddle that spread across the floor. I followed it with my eyes. Gun fire erupted around me. Seamus called out, "We're good here, Iverson. Do your thing."

A hard, painful lump grew in my throat. I swallowed. The gun fire went on forever. I saw him. Seamus. On the floor, covered in blood, with paramedics working, their bags wide open. They grabbed for what they needed without looking. A helicopter's rotors thumped the air. Sirens screamed. What would I do without them?

Warmth touched my hand. Seamus watched me.

"It's never easy, Iverson, letting go, moving on." The warmth in his lilting voice surprised me. "Are you going back to wherever you came from?"

"Yes. I wish you could come with." I felt work pushing sadness aside and I encouraged the shift. "I need to find out who is behind the Qu bullshit."

I no longer believed they were created within each border, like we originally thought.

"If I could, Iverson, I'd be there with you."

"I know ... but you leaked a bit of blood and took the easy way out."

Seamus's laughter rang like a series of big bells. I imagined that was how humongous leprechauns laughed. "That's more like it, Iverson," he said. "Me and my special skills won't ever truly leave you."

Before my eyes, he morphed into Liam Neeson, and not for the first time. Seamus had a unique set of skills and we would miss them. I missed him.

I sank under the misty vapor. Most people talk about Qu like it was a bad flu season, people died, and most have put it aside as the past. Its origin was never made public because we didn't know exactly where it came from, just that it was a mutant version of Qu Fever and spread through water and body fluid. And now, if the last release was a trial run, the next release will be fucking deadly. And we'd already had one very recent deadly pandemic.

My mind circled a gurgling drain. What could we say? Nothing without proof. I've been here before. I was still there. The same thoughts.

Saying anything would cause more panic and that would lead to more death, especially if they were spread in different ways. Airborne and touch. Hard to avoid multiple viruses. I used to think I'd spread Black Death, and follow it up with smallpox, and maybe chuck in some swine or bird flu for added oomph. But, now, I think I'd release something that doesn't spread by itself very far, then wait eighteen months or so, then release something that looks the same but, surprise, it isn't, and now you're dead.

It wasn't the first time I realized I'd be a fairly effective bad guy. One day that might be important.

What was the world in the grip of right now that is preventable? English measles. Why? Because too many people aren't vaccinated. Leave it to us and we'll kill ourselves with preventable illness. Thoughts snuggled up together in a dark corner of my mind. Is that part of the plan? Using unvaccinated pockets of the world population to spread a preventable disease far and wide? Not difficult.

An example sprang to mind, because I heard about it via a police officer friend in New Zealand, and I couldn't figure out how so many people got sick. Someone got on a a plane or maybe multiple someones and the disease ran rampant in Samoa and other places in the world. People died. A lot of children died or became very ill. How could that happen? Because adults are spreading the disease, those who didn't have all their vaccinations as a child, or missed that one for whatever reason. And there were a lot of unvaccinated children or children who were too young to have complete the vaccination program.

What if the worldwide measles outbreak is also a trial? Measles is one of the most contagious diseases ever. Imagine if the contagion power of measles was harnessed and used? Everything came to a screeching halt. COVID-19 was the opposite. The people worst effected were over fifty, but we only just had a vaccine for that, and as far as I knew, it was a novel virus that jumped from animals to humans.

"We need to know where the killer viruses are coming from, or going to come from?" I said, as space and time wound around me like a corkscrew.

"A research facility in another country," Chance replied. "What's the connection you made with Emmet Garrison?" His words spiraled on threads of time. Separating as they went.

"The Chinese connection?"

"Yes, the high school connection is something else entirely."

"China ... Chance, are you saying China is behind this?"

"I'm saying they haven't been third world for a very long time, and no one seems to grasp just what a superpower they've become."

"People know ..."

"Not really, El. Governments still treat them like they're the western world's poor cousin. And they have us beat in so many ways."

Be nice if we could weaponize vaccines or cures and

blast the world with that. My mind drifted on a sea of used needles. There were already concerns about China and their growing investment in bio-science and looser ethics around gene-editing. Other cutting-edge technology and integration between government and academia raised the specter of such pathogens being weaponized. Canada reputedly sent a nasty emerging germ to China for research purposes. Who's to say another germ wasn't sent over? Who's to say they didn't create whatever was sent over to start with and are just playing innocent? But if they were innocent, and then were sent a pathogen, then that could mean an offensive agent, or a modified germ let loose by proxies, for which only China has the treatment or vaccine. My mind ran that scenario and nothing good came out of it. The world held to ransom by a superpower. Was it better or worse than a world nuclear threat?

"We've been up against it before, Iverson," Seamus's voice curled upward from the middle of the warped time spiral.

"Not like this," I called down, and watched my words break apart and travel independently.

"You should go." His voice struggled to find me. "Leave the country, take your family," he said, from the depths.

A small laugh escaped as I recalled how that conversation went last time. "That's never been my thing. It's fucking tempting, but this is me, and this is what I do."

Words spilled from the center of the now black hole. "Is there a safe place?"

If the world is at risk from a new weaponized virus or whatever, then nowhere is safe. Except the Facility. I'm in it. This is it. And I may already be infected. Where the fuck are you now, Pollyanna?

Chapter Twenty-one
Here Comes the Sun

My eyes opened slowly, and with caution. Blackness. Did I fall in the hole? Probably not. Although, who knows? I turned my head to the left. Far away in the dark, I saw a soft glow. My eyes adjusted to the night. The glow illuminated Dane's face. Dane was in the hole too. Nice.

My first attempt at speech caught somewhere behind my teeth. I swallowed, and tried again, "Hey."

The glow moved. It grew in height and came closer, before fading to nothing.

"Hi, how are you feeling?"

"Not sure." There was a temptation to ask where I was. I fought it. I should know where I am. My head felt foggy and tired, and left inner elbow felt bruised. Nothing else seemed out of place.

"You've been out about four hours."

"Did you stay with me the whole time?" I tried to shove myself upward. Too soon. I lowered my head onto the pillow.

"Yes. Karen came in a few times to check on you. She took bloods as well."

Ah, that accounts for the elbow thing.

"Did I behave?"

"I think you were asleep."

Good. That means I didn't punch her. I've been known to get combative during a migraine. Depending on the situation, I guess. Sometimes after a migraine, when I can't remember what's happened, I get a bit punchy. This time, I at least knew who I was and what happened.

"Anything else happen?"

"Yeah. I saw, El, I saw it all."

"Saw what?" God, what'd I do? I scrambled around in the recesses of my still foggy brain, trying to find a glimmer of a spark that'd tell me what I did.

"It's okay. You didn't do anything." He was close now. The bed shifted as he sat. "I saw you and Seamus and Chance."

"Oh, okay, and what were we doing?" Little flickers of potential images started deep down in my mind. "Did I hold some kinda weird-ass seance?"

"I guess you did." Dane chuckled. "I think that's exactly what you did."

"Good to know."

"There are a few things we need to really delve into. One is the potential Chinese connection, and the other is whether or not the release of the Qu Pathogen was akin to vaporware. It was supposed to happen, but it never really did situation."

"Damn. Seems I was busy in my drug-induced stupor ..."

"You were."

"Anything else?"

"The vaporware idea - it's a good one. The thought that New Zealand was the control group is creepy as fuck, but plausible. Probably not in everyone's world, but in ours, it definitely holds water."

Feels more as if it leaked like Eliza's bucket.

"Have you told Karen anything?"

"No. I wanted to wait to see what you thought and how you were." Dane shifted his weight. "Also, how the hell do I say what I saw, and not end up in front of our friendly team psychologist?"

"Good point." Ashley would just love that. We'd find ourselves a part of some fucked-up research program operated by the CIA. CIA? I gave a mental shrug. Felt about right.

"We need to build our case."

"If what you are telling me, is what I was doing ... then, the case will build itself. The information we need exists we just don't know where yet."

"You mean we have it?"

"Yes. We have some of it. Karen and Tahoma have some of it. Emmett Garrison has some of it."

"You're kidding me?"

"Nope. He, Jeremy Cotton, and the lawyer, Noah Bancroft, they all went to High School together in Virginia Beach."

"So, it's not a drug thing with him?"

"It might be, but there's more to it." I memory rolled in my mind from a discussion about biker gangs with one of our task force agents. "Money, Dane. They're about making money and they don't much care how or where it comes from. Drugs, prostitution, breaking people's legs, brokering dodgy deals, selling viruses to the highest bidder ... being part of a distribution chain ..." Guns for hire for whoever can pay. Wet work specialists, as long as you don't want it to look like an accident.

Whoa, what? My brain spun back over my thoughts. Selling viruses? Where did the selling virus thing come from? How would Emmett get hold of a virus? From Cotton? Or was Zhang a delivery boy of extra special viral contagions? So maybe the virus was incoming, not outgoing?

Oh, dear lord.

Chance's voice curled in my mind, "People always act in their own best interests."

How is letting a lethal virus loose inside our boarder, in anyone's best interest? It isn't, unless you're happily vaccinated. My mind circled around a plot from *Designated Survivor*. What if the virus was altered to attack people with certain traits or genes?

I slammed that thought into a blackhole. No. Don't go there.

A quiet knock on the door startled me. Karen's voice followed and the door opened. She stepped in before closing the door and shutting out the bright light beyond. The dimmed bedroom lighting was about all I could cope with. I looked up and saw the mask was gone. That could be a forward positive thing. I blinked as my eyes focused again. Still a mask, dumbass.

"Good to see you're awake," she said, sitting in the chair near the wall opposite the bed. "How are you feeling?"

"Better than I was." No sense doing my usual 'I'm okay' routine. We all knew it was crap. "Anything exciting happen in my absence?"

"As a matter of fact, it did." Karen crossed her legs. "Jeremy Cotton's blood work showed a new strain of the Qu Pathogen."

Bile rose rapidly. I swallowed hard. Shit. He was infected.

Dane jumped to his feet. Then sat back down. His eyes found mine as he pushed words into my mind: That's not what we wanted to hear.

No kidding, Einstein.

"And us?" I asked, without taking my eyes off Dane.

"Still waiting on results."

"What are our chances?" Dane asked.

"That depends on how contagious it is, and how it's spread."

"Worst case scenario ..."

"Airborne, and you show symptoms within twenty-four hours."

"What does *within* mean?"

"Anything from four hours to twenty-four." She watched us for a moment. "But we don't know yet how this virus was designed, what the intent behind it is, or how virile a strain this is."

"I doubt it's cold strength with a side of man flu," I said.

Karen nodded. "There is a slim probability that because you both contracted the Qu Pathogen and survived, that your bodies might recognize this Qu and destroy it."

"Slim ..." Dane muttered. "Could be worse."

I dropped my gaze.

"Yes, it could be. It could've been Kurt or Lee who found Cotton, they'd have no chance of fighting this off," Karen said.

"What about Susan?" I sat up and swung my legs over the side of the bed. Nothing bad happened. Apart from the familiar dull ache behind my eye, and a bit of fog in my brain, I was okay. "Was she exposed in the last go-round?"

Karen shook her head. "Susan is already showing symptoms."

Crapadoodledo.

And we aren't, apart from my raw feeling throat early this morning which seemed to have sorted itself. Perhaps our slim chance kicked in? Or perhaps it was designed to target a trait she had, and we did not? That thought tumbled in my brain, picking up speed before shooting off a ledge into the blackness. Best place for it.

"How sick is she?" I made an attempt at standing and changed my mind. "Can we see her?"

"Yes, you can. She's showing flu symptoms, it came on suddenly, and is progressing fairly quickly."

"Is there anything you can do?"

"Support her, monitor her symptoms, and treat those as they arise."

That's not enough.

"There must be something. Weren't labs working on vaccines or cures or something?"

"Yes, but not for this strain."

"But we haven't been exposed to this strain before ..."

"I have asked Tahoma to look into our research, and your potential immunity, or at least slow uptake of the new version. If there is something we can do, he will find it. The only other person who could possibly do that is ..." Her jaw tightened. "Hanzel Forberg."

Ah, the elusive Mr. Forberg.

I looked from Karen to Dane. "We need to find Forberg."

"If you two aren't showing symptoms in the next twenty-four hours, I will release you from quarantine. And then you can get back to work."

"And Susan?"

"Cross your fingers that Tahoma can find something to help, or that Forberg turns up. I've always thought that the original release of the Qu Pathogen was to see how it behaved in the wild so to speak."

Well, snap!

"And now?"

"I still believe that. I can't prove it, but I believe it." She crossed her right leg over the left. "Do you remember the measles outbreak in twenty-nineteen?"

"Yes, I do, it was worrisome for us with partially vaccinated toddlers."

"We were most interested in the way the virus spread in New Zealand from an infected person traveling from Indonesia."

"Why?"

"Because they never got Qu down there."

"Because it didn't spread like it maybe should have?"

"Precisely. But measles did, especially in Auckland where there is a higher percentage of unvaccinated immigrants. From there it spread to Western Australia with a tourist, and within two weeks there were twenty-four confirmed cases from that one tourist. Then it spread to a mining camp in Western Australia by a fly-in-fly-out worker and infected another twenty-three people."

"Contagious ..."

"Very. New Zealand began to plateau at about the eighteen-hundred mark, but it all happened at a rapid rate."

"Okay, and?"

"Imagine if you wanted to test the contagion level of a virus on live subjects. What better way than to use a highly contagious disease that we vaccinate against. You're going to kill people, make others ill enough to require hospital treatment, but the majority are immune. In fact, in New Zealand, a lot of people over fifty had measles as children so they have natural immunity. They consider people over fifty, immune."

"That gives them a target population group," Dane said.

"Yes, it does. Anti-vaxxers, young children who haven't yet been vaccinated, and those who haven't received their booster because it was forgotten, and they could be any age from four to fifty." She took a breath. "Anyone born after nineteen-sixty-nine was offered the vaccine as part of the regular vaccine schedule for children."

"Targeting age groups."

She nodded. "And watching how the disease spreads."

"What about COVID?"

Karen shrugged, "That appeared to target the missed age groups, those over fifty. Again, you could use that to study virus spread and the reaction of the world to it."

Somewhere beyond my room, a phone rang. "I'll get that, you take it easy for a bit longer," Karen said, touching my shoulder as she left the room.

Chapter Twenty-two
Home

The door opened. Karen stepped in.

"You have a phone call, Ellie."

"Okay." I swung my legs over the side of the bed and sat for a moment. Everything seemed okay so I stood.

"Okay?" Dane asked.

"Yes."

"I'll come with," he said.

Karen left the room and waited outside for us. "I'll be in with Susan if you need me."

"Thanks," Dane said.

I smiled. "I'm feeling better. But thank you."

The phone on the kitchen counter was off the hook. I lifted the receiver to my ear. "Hello, Ellie Iverson speaking."

"Ellie, it's Debbie Barnes. Can we meet?"

I paused for a split second to gather my thoughts. Fog encroached making clear concise thinking difficult, but not impossible. "I should be back at work in forty-eight hours." I glanced at Dane for confirmation. He nodded.

"All right. Let me know when you're back. I think I've come across something that might pertain to your current situation."

"Which one?" We have a few on the boil.

"The missing scientist. He was instrumental in releasing something we are describing as brochureware."

Intriguing.

"What is brochureware?"

"Brochureware (noun): A published specification about a product, either a current or future product, that the reader has usually not physically seen yet. Generally, this is thought of as a brochure, but can be any sort of marketing material, for example advertisement, web page, etcetera. The information in the brochure is usually around features or capabilities of the product, which the reader can only assume is true, knowing that reality may prove different."

"Okay, and the missing scientist created a brochure with wild claims and the product is not living up to them?"

"Yes, something like that. Some marketing material arrived a few weeks ago and I've just seen it. There is a product on the market that claims to fool biometric scanners into thinking your face matches the one on the stolen passport."

"How does it work?"

Debbie laughed lightly. "It doesn't."

"Okay, and?"

"I've got the product in my office, and Hanzel Forberg is supposedly the creator and scientist behind this."

"I'm interested."

"So am I. Come see me when you're out."

"Looking forward to it."

I dropped the receiver into the cradle.

A gurgling noise and the smell of fresh coffee snapped me from thoughts of Forberg. Dane passed a mug to me.

"Pretty sure this will help," he said, sliding a sugar bowl across the countertop.

Probably.

I added a spoonful of sugar to my black coffee and stirred.

The phone rang. I jumped. Dane laughed. I lifted the receiver. "Dungeon of Doom. You've reached SAC Iverson."

"Doom, huh?" A male voice said.

"Mike?"

"At least you can still recognize my voice."

"I'm not incapacitated Mike, just quarantined." I took a sip of coffee. God it was magic. "How are you?"

"Fine. I think."

Hmmm. Not the answer I expected. "What's up, Mike?"

"Can we get together?"

"Not right now. What with the quarantine and whatnot. Problem?"

"Someone gave me something today."

"And?"

"And it's weird."

"I'm the Queen of weird." And curiosity. The Queen

of curious weird shit. "Are you concerned?"

"Nah, it's probably nothing. You know what we should do? Cotopaxi in the Fall."

"Fall's better than winter."

"That's the spirit, El."

The heavy receiver dropped harder than I expected. Oops.

Dane leaned on the counter, cradling his coffee in his hands. "Mike Davenport?"

"Yep."

"Everything okay?"

"Not sure."

"Did he say Cotopaxi in the Fall?"

I sipped more coffee and looked at him. "Yep."

"What does that mean?"

"It's a mountain we've always wanted to climb."

Dane's right eyebrow rose. "Wiseass."

"We have a way of keeping in touch. If one of us says Cotopaxi the other knows to go check for a message."

"I bet there's more to it."

"Winter is bad, Fall is concerning, Summer is all okay, Spring is somewhere between okay and concerning."

"Ah, I should've guessed it was something like that."

"Yep. You should have."

I joined Dane in leaning on the counter. So, Debbie needed to see me, and someone gave Mike something that caused him to contact me, not Lee. Life didn't need to get any more interesting.

It really did not. What we needed was to get out of here. What I needed was my phone back.

What did the person give Mike? I finished my coffee and went into the main living room and settled at the computer. Looking at a screen wasn't going to please my brain any, but I needed to find out what Mike sent me.

After a few moments staring at the message service home screen, I remembered my login details. A small sigh of relief escaped as I added the information, and the screen changed to my inbox. And there I saw a message from Mike with an attachment.

One click opened the message and revealed an image under the text. A photograph of a piece of paper.

Mike was correct it was weird. My eyes skimmed the jumble of letters and numbers contained in the image. They weren't words. I'd seen similar things left on blog posts and TripAdvisor. They usually disappeared fairly fast. I was looking at a code.

Zb7r qapb 9rv8 cdr cog356 eqj f2pu9 cdsf 8w2j 35 l1jrqa 4u8l j1lpb w39 fdw7al8j6.

Or maybe a password. All that was missing was the special characters and the blood of your first born.

I replied to Mike: Got it. Thanks. Let me know if contact is made again.

Dane appeared next to me with a pen and notebook. He passed them to me. "Thought you might need these."

"Thanks," I said, taking them and turning the screen

a fraction toward him so he could better see what I was looking at. "What do you think?"

"A cipher. But which one? Could that be Base 64?"

I shook my head. Pain shot into my eyeball leading to instant regret. "No. That tends to have jumbled upper and lower case, and often includes equals signs at the end."

"Caesar?"

"Don't think so. I think it's something with a little more gumption than that."

"Gumption? Who are you now, my grandma?"

"Feel like it at the moment. What about a Homophonic Substitution cipher?"

Dane nodded slowly. "They're the ones that layer the most common letters, right?"

"Yep."

"This could take a while depending on the depth."

It sure could.

We needed a starting point, one letter that we could work with. Skimming the collections of letters again, I let my mind form whatever it wanted, and hoped it'd find something I could latch onto. And there it was. J.

"Dane, if J is R, how many three letter words can you think of that end in R?"

"Air, bar, car, ear, jar, for, war, tar, our, fur, far, fir, sir, par, per, how's that?"

"Great. Write them down for me."

Dane picked up the pen and notebook and wrote his three-letter words ending in R on the first blank page, then handed it to me.

"Logically, a message for me from an UnSub isn't likely to talk of fur, or fir trees, so let's get rid of them. Also, jar, ear, and tar."

"Are you sure about that? I mean we've come across some sick individuals and they might be telling you about ears in jars of tar."

"Not helping, Dane," I said with a grin. "But maybe!"

A cipher doesn't usually contain waste words. With that in mind I crossed per, par, and sir off the list. Then removed bar for shits and giggles. We were left with car, air, war, far, our, for.

I drew a line through our and far. For fun I did the same to car. My eyes closed for a long blink. When they opened again. I saw it. The word. For.

"Okay, the word is for. O will be deeply layered because it's a vowel and common, but we have at least one R with potential layering there as well and we have an F. It's doubtful F would be layered."

"Even so, this is going to take time." Dane dragged a chair over, sat next to me, and rubbed his hands together. "Been awhile since we had something to challenge our gray matter."

Yes, it had.

Half an hour later, I stood and stretched. We were sure we had two words and were on the way to uncovering more. We had letters; O=8, T=U, V=W, P=L. The beginnings of words grew and groaned under the weight of our combined consciousness.

"I'm going to see Susan," I said over my shoulder as I neared the door.

"I'll keep on this."

I knocked on Susan's door. Karen called out, "Come in."

With a smile splashed across my face, I held onto the door handle. Here we go. She's not dead yet. That might not even be the outcome here. Come on Pollyanna, get the Glad Game happening. I'm glad Karen is here to increase Susan's chance of survival.

The door opened effortlessly, causing me to catch it before it hit the doorstop. Susan lay on her bed. Pale, faded, ill. She looked over. Machines beeped at a steady rate from next to her.

"Hey," I said, acknowledging Karen with a smile, and turning my attention to Susan. "How you doin'?"

Susan smiled back, it was weak, but there. "You doing okay?" She asked, trying to push herself up. One machine beeped faster.

"I'm fine. Nothing some modern medicine and rest didn't fix. How about you?"

"Not feeling great but getting some expert care." She lowered her upper body to the mattress. Her eyes closed. "Sorry. Tired."

"You should rest. I just wanted to stop in and say hello."

"Are you making progress?"

"Think I'll make more once we're out of here, but we're trying to track someone down who can help." My fingers crossed behind my back. We hope he can help. Maybe he can help.

An unusual feeling wormed into my conscious mind. It began as a shimmer and grew into a dark patch. Migraine? Was it back? I looked up at the wall. No holes in my vision. Then a word jumped out of the dark patch and flamed. Dane.

Shit.

"I'll be back," I said, and left the room. I hurried into the living area. Dane was at the desk, his head in his hands. No. No. No. I touched his shoulder. "What's going on?"

"Really bad headache."

"Let's get you on the sofa."

I helped him stand. "I can walk," he grumbled, and shook my hand away.

"Then walk," I said, backing off.

He stumbled toward the sofa and lowered himself into the cushions. Dane's eyes closed. "Didn't that mechanic in Mauryville start with a bad headache?"

"Yeah." I sat next to him. "But I had a migraine and scratchy throat and I'm fine, so maybe it's just a headache." I crossed my fingers. Just a headache. We're under stress. A headache is reasonable.

"Maybe."

Dane didn't get headaches. I knew that.

"I'll go get Karen. Don't move."

Dane gave a weak laugh. "I'll try not to."

My mind spun thoughts behind an impenetrable

vault door. Don't die, Dane. Not now. Not like this. Just don't. I can't. We can't. We've lost too many people we care about.

Chapter Twenty-three
Old Habits Die Hard

Karen crouched next to the sofa and spoke to Dane. She had a penlight in her hand and her bag open in the floor. I watched, unaware that I'd backed away, until a wall stopped me. It felt better to have something solid behind me. My hand plunged into my pocket, half expecting to hit my phone. Disappointment flowed from the emptiness.

Come on. You can't fall apart. You have to crack that cipher. Find Forberg. And get the fuck outta here. Buck up, Ellie. You got this. A rich, deep voice came from a crack in the corner of my mind. "Chicky Babe. Get it together."

"Dammit, Sam. I need Dane." My eyes closed as I slid down the wall. And there was Sam. Kneeling in front of me. Looking like he always looked. Big, solid muscle, shaved head, dark brown eyes, and perfectly straight white teeth against a dark coffee colored background. Sam landed a massive hand on my knee. Warmth seeped into my bones, radiating from his incorporeal hand.

"No. You don't. You got this."

I shook my head. "They're both sick Sam. I can't fix this."

"You aren't. Concentrate. You're no quitter." Sam's

voice softened to a velvety chocolate custard. "We went through hell as a team and you never let us down. Never, Ellie."

I blinked. It'd been years since I'd heard him call me by name. Before Mac died. Before Carla. Just before.

"There's a first time for everything Sam."

His smile vanished. Eyes hardened. "Cowboy the fuck up," he growled. "There isn't a choice, Chicky Babe. Get your shit together and do it now."

"What if ... ?"

"What if my incorporeal ass slaps you upside the head, because that's the only what fucking if, right now."

A small chuckle rose fast and splashed over Sam. He grinned. His eyes lightened to a softer brown.

"You're going to slap me upside the head?" I whispered. "Go ahead and try."

"Now, see ... that's my Chicky Babe." Sam grabbed my hand and helped me to my feet, dragged me into a bear hug, then disappeared.

Before I knew it, I was in front of the computer blocking out everything happening on the other side of the room.

Next time I looked over it was to say something to Dane.

"You better be alive."

"I am."

"I got it, I think."

"What does it say?" He said, rolling over to face me.

The grimace on his face told me a lot about how he felt, so I didn't ask.

"It says 'Eyes Only. ASIO has HUMINT for Delta. Hand over in person. Stop. Reply via Davenport.'"

"Human what?"

"Brain a little foggy there, Dane?"

"Doesn't want to work."

"Human Intelligence."

"And A. S. what was it?"

Guess I should've expanded on that as well. That one made me think when I first saw it, because it wasn't what I expected to see.

"ASIO is the Australian Security Intelligence Organization."

"And just like that our shit got weirder," Dane said. "The Aussies went through an actor ..."

"Yep." Sneaky of them. "This must be big, and they must be worried, if they didn't just reach out through the usual tried and true channels."

"I reckon." Dane smiled at me. His face half squashed into a cushion. "You can reply in the same cipher?"

"I'll change it, make it mine. Just in case someone else figured this out or intercepts it and whatnot."

"Good thinking."

"Rest. I'll get on with this." I opened the site I used to communicate with Mike and then opened a new message screen. I wrote quickly instructing Mike to copy the cipher to a piece of paper and keep it on his person until he sees whoever gave him the note for me again.

"What are you telling them?" Dane asked.

"That we're coming A-sap. We'll make it happen from our end. This is the last communication via Davenport. I will be in New Zealand as soon as I can arrange it."

"I've always wanted to go to New Zealand," Dane said from the sofa.

"Then let's make that happen," I said with a smile, and finished rearranging the cipher to create my own version. "Hey, didn't Karen do blood tests?"

"She did."

"As soon as I'm done here, I'll go find out about those blood tests."

"El, how will ASIO know you're in New Zealand?"

I twisted in my chair to look at him. "Oh, they'll know. Everyone in the intelligence community will know."

The Bioterrorism Act gave us the power to go to New Zealand and bring back the scientists or chemical engineers and any other American's involved, but we didn't have enough concrete evidence to do that. We had a smear campaign started by Newgenic, screaming about how they were victimized, and a legitimate research company. There was no way I could enact the act to get us to New Zealand without more evidence. Hard to get dead bodies and a comatose person to corroborate our findings.

A frown danced along the top of his brow. "What does that mean?"

"I'm accepting a position I was offered by the Director."

"What? Why?" Dane staggered to his feet. "You're leaving?"

"Yes, but not without Delta A. Sit your ass down."

"When, what, how?"

"Remember when Director O'Hare said I had my pick of assignments ... I just figured that died a natural death after her murder. It didn't. The new Director offered me several overseas embassy postings. All limited to eighteen months or two years." Quite possibly to get me out of his hair, or out of Washington for an extended period.

"Why do I get the feeling there is more to this?"

"Because I said not without my team and after some intense negotiation, he agreed." I also pushed the boundaries when it came to my final decision. My call when we left.

"Kurt, Lee, and me?"

"Yep."

"But ..." The wheels were turning.

While they turned, I emailed Caine and told him I was ready. He replied quickly with a less than enthusiastic tone. This too would pass. It's not forever. It's for now.

"Kurt has a family," Dane finally said.

"I am aware." So do I.

"What about his family?"

"Dane. We are not leaving families behind. No one is expecting us to leave our families. This is a relocation deal. We're overseas for at least eighteen months."

"Does anyone know?"

"Not yet." I grinned at him. I really hoped no one would push back on this, and that my team, my full team would follow me to the end of the earth. "Get better. We've got travel plans to make."

Dane lay back down. "I'll close my eyes for a moment."

"Good thinking, Batman. You look like shit." I watched him for a split second and willed him to get well before leaving the room. "I'll be in the kitchen. Have a call to make."

No one was around. Not a surprise. Karen was either working on lab stuff or in with Susan trying to keep her alive.

With a sigh, I picked up the heavy white receiver. People must've had well developed telephone hands back in the day. I dialed a number I knew by heart. Numbers are our friends. It pays to retain some phone numbers and not rely a hundred percent on smart phones.

There was a click at the other end and a voice scratched at my ear drum. "Jonathon Tierney speaking." I was glad I'd memorized his private secure line all those years ago.

"It's Ellie Iverson." Part of me expected him to hang

up. He didn't.

"Is there something I can do for you, SAC?"

"Get me a face-to-face with Peter Cooper."

"I thought we established that Mr. Cooper had no involvement with your missing CI."

"You did. I did not. Just get me a meeting with your golden boy, Tierney."

"I'm afraid that won't be possible, SAC."

A sigh escaped unchecked. "It's important."

"I don't doubt the importance of your request. It's simply not possible to see Mr. Cooper at present."

Ka-ching. A dime dropped and rolled away.

"Where is he Tierney?"

"Working."

"Somewhere southern?"

"I couldn't say."

I banged my head against the wall - not hard - but hard enough.

"Australia."

"Why would you say that, Ellie?"

"You sent him to Australia." Another coin hit the ground and rolled away. "Why? Why did you do that?"

"I didn't send Mr. Cooper to Australia."

"So, what, he went by himself?"

Imagining Tierney's beady black eyes darting across the three screens in front of him, trying to work out how I knew, pleased me. I only thought Australia because of the note from Mike Davenport, but now it felt like I was onto something.

"Do you know Hanzel Forberg?" He said on a long wisp of air.

"No, I do not." That's one hundred percent true. We have never met.

"You should make his acquaintance - sooner the better."

The line clicked.

"Tierney?"

Beep. Beep. Beep.

Dammit. I slammed the receiver home and stomped from the room. Annoyed at myself as much as Tierney.

"Ellie?" Dane pushed himself up on the couch.

"Sorry. Didn't mean to wake you." Or maybe I did.

"I've slept enough. What's going on?"

"I want to see Cooper, but Tierney won't say where he is or set up a meeting." I paused, reconsidered my crankiness, and ambled over to Dane with what I hoped was a pleasant smile on my face. "How are you feeling?"

"Better."

"Then get up I need you." I tapped his leg to make him move over, then sat down. "Are you really better?" Nothing in his mind refuted his improvement.

"Headache is going. No other symptoms, so, yeah." He smiled. "When do we get out of this place?"

Everything spiraled as a song took over. The Animals. We definitely gotta get out of this place.

Thanks Dad, for my truly awesome taste in music.

"As fast as possible." Dane's legs moved against my

lower back as he tried to prop himself up. "Tierney thinks we should be finding Forberg."

"We should," Dane replied, dragging himself further into a sitting position. "What about Susan?"

She won't be finding anyone.

My head shook. "Bad."

"Karen?"

"I think she's okay. Tahoma was supposed to be trying to locate Forberg, but I haven't heard anything." Debbie popped into my consciousness. I needed to see her as well. Fuck me. Perhaps it was time to look into cloning?

The kitchen phone rang.

Dane nudged me. "Probably for you."

"Yeah."

Chapter Twenty-four
Angel of the Morning

"How fucked are we?"

His voice echoed down the line. "Fully. Is that what you want to hear?"

"Ding, wrong answer. Try again."

"We can't find Forberg."

"I don't want to hear that either, Henderson." I sighed. "You're pretty shit at this game."

"How's it going underground?"

"Lemme see ... I had a migraine. Dane has a really bad headache and looks like shit, but says he's improving. Susan is probably not going to make it." I leaned on the counter. "Forberg could stop that."

"He's a ghost."

Let's hope he's not a literal ghost.

"Rattle Tierney's cage. He knows something." My foot kicked back and hit something solid with a bang.

"What was that?"

"My foot and the side of the kitchen island." I turned around and leaned on my elbow. The receiver was annoying in my hand, so I tucked it between my shoulder and chin. A memory of mom doing the same while she painted her nails and talked to her friends surfaced. I blinked it away. Not helpful. "Henderson, I need out of here. Get Whitehorse, get my fucking blood results, and get me out of here."

"How'd you know Karen sent the bloods out of the facility?"

"I guessed. But I was right, wasn't I?" She's got her hands full with Susan's rapidly declining health. Dane and I haven't helped much either.

"Tahoma took them to our forensic lab."

"We need results."

"Science, Iverson. It takes time."

"We're running out of time."

"I'll chase them up."

"Then get us out of here, we've got shit to do." My decision to leave with my team jumped onto my tongue and fell from my mouth. "I'm taking the offer from the Director. Delta A is moving to New Zealand. Obviously, it's your choice if you come or not. Families are included in the package. Might be smarter to settle first then go back and bring Rachel and Olivia over. The term is set for two years."

Silence.

"Henderson. Just so we're clear. I want you with me."

"Does Lee know?"

"Not yet. Bring him when you break us out ..." I should call him before that happens. "Where is he?"

"In the office somewhere."

"Find him for me and I'll tell him now."

I could hear movement. Kurt was walking around looking for Lee. I heard him pass the phone over. "Hey,

Ellie, you two doing okay in there?"

"Kinda. Hey, Lee, I'm accepting a posting in New Zealand. I want you, Kurt, and Dane with me." A sudden wild thought encroached. What if Director Thomas rescinded on the deal? I shoved that aside. Not helpful. Mom's voice screeched from the depths, "Don't be naïve, Gabrielle. I didn't raise a gullible girl." Supportive as always.

Lee's voice chased mom away. "Ellie, you serious?"

"Yeah."

"Seems sudden, is it something to do with this situation."

"Big part of it. It gives me a legit reason to be in New Zealand. There's intel waiting for me in Australia. Those labs creating Qu bullshit are in New Zealand and Australia."

"I'm in."

"Thank you."

He didn't even ask how long we'd be gone. "It's two years, Lee."

"Not a problem, Ellie. It's a beautiful country. I'd like a chance to see more of it."

"Okay. As soon as we're out of here, I'll get the arrangements made."

The next call was to Caine. "We're going to New Zealand. Can you let the Director know? Full team plus families. Can we have Sandra too?"

"Give me a minute on the Sandra thing. As for the rest, we'll get arrangements for travel made and accommodation organized for you and Delta and the families who want to go." His gruff voice rasped in my ear.

"Hanzel Forberg?"

"Nothing this end. So far."

"That's not ideal. The longer it takes to find him, the worse this is going to get."

"I'm aware. There are agents turning his life upside down and inside out." He paused for a beat. "I'll see the Director and call you back."

"Thank you."

I leaned on the countertop while I thought about the encroaching negative feelings regarding the New Zealand posting. It made no sense for Director Thomas to renege on the deal. We're not exactly pals, good chance he still wants me gone.

A shadow fell over me. I turned my head toward the doorway. Karen. The grim line of her mouth and sad eyes, gave much away.

"Something wrong?"

"Susan ..."

"Gone?"

"Not yet, but she's not going make it. The pathogen has too big a hold on her. Even if we get help, we can't reverse the damage to her body."

I moved around the counter to the coffee pot and poured a cup for Karen. She peeled off her gloves, rolling them inside each other and removed her mask. Her skin looked flushed. Beads of sweat trickled down her brow. She accepted the cup with a grateful nod.

"Are you feeling all right?"

"Yeah, it's hot wearing the respirator and so forth."

"Are you at risk?" Sounded like a stupid question, but it wasn't. She might've been exposed when we were back during the first go round with Qu.

"Probably not. Not like the general population anyway."

"Vaccine?"

"Yeah, I don't know how effective that will be against this new version, but like you and Dane, I might escape with a headache if I'm exposed again now."

Here's hoping.

"How long does she have?"

"Hours."

"Is she conscious?"

"On and off." Karen sipped the coffee. Her eyes flicked around the room, then settled on me. "We need to eat."

I opened the refrigerator and took stock of the contents. "How about a fruit yogurt?"

"Sounds tasty."

Don't know if tasty is the best description. I placed two small yogurt pots on the counter and produced spoons from a drawer. Karen chose raspberry, leaving the blueberry one for me. Dane's voice flowed from the doorway. "Are there more?"

"Yes," I replied, and grabbed another yogurt from the fridge.

He smiled and took it from me. The pain in his eyes told me he knew about Susan. Saved me explaining, so I left it alone.

I'd eaten half my pottle when the phone rang. We all looked at each other for a beat. I answered the call.

"SAC Iverson?"

"Speaking." I waited. Not quite sure who was on the line.

"Director Thomas here, SAC. How long before you and Agent Wesson will be released from quarantine?"

"Unclear as yet, Director. Hoping within the next thirty-six hours."

"This isn't something I want to do over the phone, but you need to know. You and Delta A are better utilized here." He paused then took a breath. "I am formally denying the posting to New Zealand."

Shit. My mind spun off its axis.

"Why?"

"You are needed here."

"Sir, I was granted the ability to choose my own posting for my service to the FBI by Director O'Hare."

"I am well aware why you were given the choice of posts. You are needed here. And that is where you will stay."

I counted to ten and forced my tone to remain reasonable. "I believe the only way to get to the bottom of what's going on, Sir, is to have boots on the ground in New Zealand. Delta A boots. On. The. Ground. Sir."

"Having my most experienced Delta team leave the

country is not in the FBI's best interest."

No amount of counting to ten helped. "With all due respect Sir, this is utter bull ..."

"Don't finish that sentence SAC."

"And when this explodes and sprays weaponized Qu all over The United States of America, I hope you're happy with your decision. I hope you'll understand that it's on you, as you watch those you love die." A voice in my head cautioned me to pull it back and settle. I growled a deep internal, fuck off. "People will die."

"My decision is final."

"Then the deaths are on you, Sir."

I slammed the receiver into the cradle. "Fuck!" With a shove the phone jerked away from me. "Fuck!"

Anger and disbelief roiled until I couldn't think straight.

Dane touched my hand. "Finish your yogurt."

I picked up the spoon and jabbed it at the creamy blob in the bottom of the pottle. My appetite gone. Wasn't exactly starving to start with.

Karen rinsed her pot then tossed it in the garbage. She washed and carefully dried her hands then put on fresh gloves from a box on the counter. Before she put the mask back on, she said, "Eat. We'll be out of here soon and then we can worry about the rest. I'll be with Susan." She smiled, put her mask on and left.

Leaving Dane and I staring at each other. Eventually he spoke, "Why are you so determined to get to New Zealand?"

"You know why. I need to face-to-face someone from the ASIO in Australia, and New Zealand is a jumping off point." And I want to see the labs. I want to be there when they're raided. Then it hit me. A work around. "Fran."

Dane's eyebrows shot up. "Your friend in the New Zealand Police?"

"Yeah. She's a senior detective. If she asks us for help ..."

"Then it'd be rude not to help."

"But Director Thomas ..." my voice trailed off as I thought, then strengthened again when I had a plan, "We've worked with her before. So, we have a relationship. Theoretically, she could ask for Delta help, and if he offers one of the other teams, she could suggest us, and use our past joint cases."

"Would she?"

"Only one way to find out." Fingers crossed she has something that she can spin to need our help.

"Are you going to call New Zealand?"

I shook my head. "Yeah, nah. We have a way of communicating that isn't monitored or paid for by the FBI."

Dane grinned. "As I'd expect. Is this like how you can talk with Mike Davenport?"

"Yes. Just like that, except I can't text her our code this time, so I'll email it via my private email."

"If she makes the request today, Thomas will deny it."

"Yep. I'll explain to Fran. Get her to wait a couple of days and send the request via me, I am the SAC after all, and copy in Caine. We might not need to go any further than him. It's day-to-day business in the crime division, not something Thomas would be normally informed about."

"Except he grounded you."

"Did he though?" I stepped back and finished the yogurt.

"What were his exact words?"

"I am formally denying the posting to New Zealand."

We smiled at each other. He said 'posting' he didn't say we can't visit. I headed for the computer. Over my shoulder I said, "Let Kurt and Lee know we've had the posting quashed. Don't say anything else."

"Got it."

Chapter Twenty-five

Queen of Hearts

I utilized the Onion and a VPN, opened one of my private email accounts, and emailed Fran a single word: Coropuna

No denying my love of mountains, especially South American stratovolcanoes, dormant or not.

I closed everything down and purged my laptop. If this idea didn't work, I'd take vacation time. Pretty sure we all had at least four weeks owing. The country might have shut down for a two-month period, but we did not. Turns out criminals don't stop for viruses or shelter-in-place orders. Who knew? Me, I knew. There were two significant benefits of working during the lockdown, way less traffic on the roads, and some things could be fast tracked through the system.

My mind loaded spreadsheets and scanned them. Yep. We all had oodles of vacation time. And I could get my Foundation to foot the bill. We've done that before. Years ago. Last time we went to New Zealand, semi-off the books, to find Hudson Hawk. The Butterfly Foundation funded that excursion and I supplied the petty cash on credit cards. If that was how it had to happen, then, I could pull the same thing off again. Mitch might not love the idea, but it would work. I was fairly confident Delta A would follow me to the end of the earth. They have before. Don't let me down this time, boys.

Without the benefit of a single glance at the multi time zone clocks in my office, I had to use math to work out the difference between us and New Zealand. It'd be a few hours before I heard back from Fran.

I ducked my head around the kitchen door. "Plans are in motion. We got this."

He was still talking on the phone. Dane grinned, and gave me a thumbs up.

"I'm going to see Susan." I waved and hurried down to Susan's room. With a soft knock I opened the door. Karen was sitting on a chair next to the bed. She motioned for me to take the chair as she stood.

"Hey, Susan, how you doin'?" I touched her hand. No reaction. Not even a flicker from her closed eyelids. "You need to hang in there, Sue. We're going to find the scientist who can help. Just don't give up, not now."

My head turned to see Karen. She'd moved another chair next to mine.

"While you're here, let's talk," Karen said, setting her notes aside. She rested the clipboard against a chair leg. I was getting used to seeing her masked and gowned. But it still made me feel like Typhoid Mary, or maybe that should be Qu Ellie? Enough, brain.

"Sure, talk to me about what the hell is going on, please, tell me something that doesn't end in death."

"I had an email from Tahoma. He's doing his best to

get us medical help in the form of a vaccine or treatment plan."

"That's comforting."

"Any research into viruses, bacteria, and fungal organisms has the potential for dual-use. It can be used for good or evil." She stopped talking to read a printout from a machine next to Susan. Karen ripped the paper off the machine and added it to her clipboard of notes. She continued, "Scientists have a moral obligation to alert their institutional review boards to any experiments of concern. And five years ago, someone alerted a review board, to research using the Q Fever bacterium, Coxiella burnetii."

"Okay, so someone knew someone was researching Q Fever and … ?"

"That research was undertaken by a German company actually in Germany."

A German company. Now I was paying attention. The Q Fever bacteria was being messed around with in Europe. Fantastic. Why doesn't everyone pile on?

I shook my head slightly. "Let me guess, you're going to tell me it's Schröder Forschung?"

"Yes. They are one of the world's largest biomedical enterprises. The board that were told about the research deemed it dual-use and nothing else was said."

That's just peachy.

"But someone was concerned, do we know who?"

"Hanzel Forberg. He went to the board."

I hauled information together from everything I'd discovered about Cotton and Hardcastle. "Cotton and Hardcastle were not working at Schröder Forschung five years ago."

"Are you certain?"

"No, not really." But why would anyone falsify company employment records? Doh! Because they were hiding something. "And all three of them ended up here. Now. And two of them are dead."

Yeah, something doesn't compute.

Karen shook her head slowly. "I wonder if Forberg followed them here, if he thought they were still working with C. burnetii?"

"C what now?"

"Q Fever."

Oh, right.

"The link via Forberg was through Trace McAlester the accountant. We'd found no tie between him, Hardcastle, and Cotton." And McAlester is snuggled away inside the WITSEC system until we need him to testify.

"Do you think there is one now?" She asked.

"The company is a link. Is there a personal link? I find it hard to believe there isn't." I pressed my lower back into the chair. "I think it's time you told me your story when it comes to Hanzel Forberg. What is it about him that makes you uncomfortable?"

A small smile met my gaze.

"We had a fling." She shrugged. "Met up at a few

conferences. Away from home, drinking, getting our nerd on with a hotel full of scientists and doctors in the medical profession ..."

Regret? Was that what I heard? Regret that it happened, or that it ended?

"Shit happens. I take it, it's over?"

"Yes. We were younger, sillier, it's over."

"How much younger, I mean are we talking, right out of college, or are we talking ten years ago?"

"More like six years."

"Okay, so before he got squeamish about Q Fever research."

"Yes."

"He didn't mention it to you?"

"No. We weren't on the best terms at that point."

"Are you still in touch?"

"We'd see each other across the room at conferences and avoid each other like we were plague ridden."

I stuck a pin in that, I was coming back to it.

"Right. Got it."

I watched Susan. She looked so still, so peaceful. Karen noticed as well. She motioned for me to move back a bit so she could lean closer. Karen put her stethoscope in her ears and placed the other end on Susan's chest. She listened for a few seconds. Then nodded at me.

"Still with us."

"Good. Now, why did you talk about seeing Forberg in past tense?"

Karen faltered. Her words somehow sticking as she tried to speak. "Not ... no."

I waited.

She gathered momentum. "No. That's not what I meant. He wasn't at the last conference, that's all. And then conferences were cancelled so it's been a couple of years since I've seen him."

Okay.

"Do you know where he is? Or how to contact him?"

She shook her head. "I reached out and got nothing but bounced email and a 'this number is no longer in service' message on his old phone number."

"Thank you for trying."

"Tahoma said the measles outbreak in the Congo, wasn't measles."

"The fuck what?"

"He's been working on analyzing the blood samples and it's another chimera. Measles and Qu17p."

"That's why it's so deadly?"

She nodded. "Nearly five thousand people died in DR Congo in twenty-nineteen. Disease spread to all provinces in the country. A quarter of a million people were infected."

"Isn't it usually Ebola over there?"

"Yes. And this epidemic killed twice the number of people that Ebola killed in fifteen months, and it only took a few months."

Jesus. "So, someone caused the deaths?"

"Yes. And the world looked on thinking it was

measles, because we were in the throes of a measles pandemic. Vaccination programs were set up as quickly as possible."

"How do you vaccinate against a disease that is two diseases and no one knew?"

"You can't. So, the deaths were attributed to the poor infrastructure, attacks on health centers, and lack of access to routine healthcare, which hindered efforts to halt the spread of the disease."

"What happened to people who were vaccinated?"

"Initially, the majority of deaths were unvaccinated infants, which is what you'd expect. What we didn't expect was the next wave of deaths being vaccinated children and adults, and adults who had survived measles as children."

"That was never released was it?"

"Nope. We're still running tests on the Congo blood samples, and we've extended our reach, looking at other severe outbreaks worldwide." She picked up her notes from the floor. "Anywhere a large number of cases were reported with a second wave of deaths."

"How fucked are we now?"

"All is not lost, Ellie, but it's heading to a bad, bad place." She squinted at me. I felt a subject change coming. "Did you ever see Married with Children?" Karen shot me a half smile. "You would've been a kid."

I wrestled with memories of my childhood. Mom was a blonde-haired, insane Peggy Bundy. High-heels an' all. I'd seen re-runs on Prime Video, and every time

I tried to watch it made me shudder. "I kinda remember it, why?"

"Forberg was a fancier Al Bundy."

"Sexist asshole?"

"All that, and much more."

"What did you see in him?"

"No idea. A moment of crazy that kept popping back up." She grinned. "He knew his way around, if you know what I mean ..."

"He wasn't all Al Bundy then?"

We laughed. The desperate apocalyptic feeling of doom lifted.

Dane poked his head around the door. "Nice to hear laughter," he said. "El, phone."

I nodded and rose from the chair.

"I'll sit with Susan," Dane said, as I moved past him in the doorway.

* * *

The receiver lay on the counter. I picked it up and spoke. "SAC Iverson."

"Iverson, you okay down there?"

"Great, Henderson, just fucking awesome."

"I got something." A door closed and all background noise vanished. "Cotton had contact with Emmett Garrison two days before his disappearance."

"Why didn't that float to the surface when I asked for a list of Garrison's visitors?"

"Guess."

"Someone on the inside is on his payroll."

"Yep."

"How'd you find out?"

"Sandra got me into the prison security footage. We could only access the external cameras and they have several in the parking lot. We have Cotton on film accepting something from an Asian male outside the prison two days before he went missing."

"Crap, I was right about the Asian link then."

"I took stills of the video images and had an agent go shake things up at the prison. Turns out Cotton visited Garrison three times in a six-week period."

"I know they went to High School together, but what would entice Cotton to visit a Federal Penitentiary three times? And what did the Asian give him?"

"Garrison is not talking. He refused to see FBI, which is his right. He's already locked up for a long, long time. He does not have to talk to us."

"But now we have a current solid link between Garrison the biker and Cotton the scientist. Could that Asian be the one who killed Hardcastle?"

"We're running his image through everything we can think of, we'll find out who he is."

"Try looking up Zhang Fo-hsing."

Silence for a beat.

"Okay, where'd that come from?"

"I caught a glimpse of a piece of paper from a ledger." Don't say it was a hallucination.

"Anything else you'd like to add?"

"Nope."

"Okay. I'll get on with things my end." He paused. I held my breath expecting a question about the ledger. "How's Susan?"

Whew.

"It's not going well for her at all. We could really use a miracle, and Forberg."

"Message received."

Five minutes later I was sitting on the sofa in the main living area with Dane.

"Our biggest problem, Dane, is security. I can't just jump into another identity and turn up in New Zealand, like I could before."

Dane nodded. "Tech, surveillance cameras, biometrics, smart passports, the way everything can be linked. It's fantastic for us as tools to catch criminals and terrorists, but not so much fun when we need to fly under the radar."

Pretty useless for flying under the radar.

"What we need, seriously need, is boots on the ground, and HUMINT. Nothing beats talking face-to-face."

"How much intel can we gather from here?" He circled his index finger in the air.

I shrugged. "Not a lot. I can get Debbie to monitor the fake Facebook page we have set up and carry on keeping tabs on the lawyer, Noah Bancroft. Caps is in a valuable position to gather intel on the other lawyer."

"You're using a gangbanger to bring in intelligence?"

"Dude, you've met Caps. He's a likable rogue and people tell him things."

Dane nodded. "Because they're too fucking scared not to."

"Whatever. It works."

"Okay that's the lawyers covered, what about finding Forberg?"

"That's the thing that's most puzzling. His passport hasn't pinged at a border. So, he's still in the United States, somewhere. We've plugged his photo into everything, and nothing has come back. He's not anywhere there are cameras that we can gather data from."

"Is he dead?"

"If he's not and he suddenly pops up I'm going to be a tad suspicious of anything he has to say."

"Fair enough."

"I think the Chinese got to him."

"You're pretty certain they're the bad guys here," Dane said, with a half a smile. "You know they're scarier than thinking the Russians are behind anything."

He wasn't wrong.

"You know what?"

"What?"

"This is scarier than the Cuban Missile Crisis, and it's scarier than that day in June Twenty-fifteen when the Office of Personnel Management announced there had been a data breach." A twinge in my gut caught my attention. I acknowledged it but wasn't sure where it was going.

"I remember that, twenty-one million records breached."

"By the Chinese, and we think some were sold to the Russians."

Dane nodded. "Pretty much everything was out there for the taking."

"Yep. Except records we held ourselves and didn't store off site."

We looked at each other for a beat. Dane's thoughts gathered like a storm in his eyes. Lightning shot from the dense clouds in the middle.

"Fuckadoodledo," I whispered.

Dane rallied. "The List. Someone would have to know about the list to turn someone else and get them to hand that information over."

"Who knew about it?"

I felt my eyes widen as a lump formed in my throat. When we were chasing all over Virginia trying to bring ex-agents and current agents to safety because The List was compromised, it looked like an organized crime case with a smattering of revenge thrown into the pot.

"Two and a half years ago ... we were wrong."

"What?"

A memory hauled to the surface. Kurt was shot. I'd shot the bad guy, Dave Smith. Tyler from THU came to the rescue and while we waited for ambulances, we started piecing the craziness together. My brother-in-law, Chris Iverson was involved, or rather caught up in the terror. Kidnapped along with his wife, and daughter. I slid into the memory and took Dane with me. Kinda propped him in the corner so he could see what I saw and what I remembered. Sometimes it's handy having special talents.

Tyler was on his phone as well; by the look on his face, I'd say he was Googling up a storm. "Two years ago, see who the guest speakers were at Oakton High career day."

Smith didn't look happy. Beads of perspiration gathered on his forehead. Clammy, pale, shocky. Not a good look.

"Got it," Tyler said. "Guest speakers at senior career day ... Chris Iverson, talking about Iverson Tech and his philanthropic work designing software to help charities. Second speaker, Debbie Barnes with the FBI. Her specialty subject was undercover work within the Bureau, and the third and final speaker for the day was Dave Smith, talking about graphic design."

Kurt leaned back. He was pale but holding it together. "That's the link we couldn't work out, Iverson. That's where it all came together. Something Chris talked about during the career day triggered a spark in Moretti."

"Let's hope Chris and Susan make it out of this alive."

Smith started to laugh, but pain took over fast. "If

he'd just done what Nazario wanted, it would've been so much easier."

I ignored him. Because Debbie Barnes was there that day too. "Who gave you your new life?"

"Michael Addison," Smith said, under a groan.

I had no idea he'd been doing that job for so long. "I'm going to have a stab in the dark here … two years ago, three people came together at Oakton high school. Jenoah Moretti was one of the teachers present. He listened to Chris Iverson talk about his passion for drone design, and knowing Chris, he probably had a demonstration model with him."

I heard sirens. Time to pick up the pace. "I bet Chris talked about his charity work and how he was designing software to help locate child traffickers and bring trafficked kids home."

Smith groaned. I figured I was on the right track. "Debbie talked about the FBI and how she creates new identities for people and about her work with undercover agents. Bet that sounded super exciting to a criminal like Moretti."

Another groan. "And then there was Dave Smith, someone who knew about new identities firsthand but couldn't say anything. Who used to have a cool job but couldn't say anything. He got to talk about graphic design. Bet that didn't sound real exciting to the kids after the other speakers."

Tyler chuckled; when I looked over, he was crouched down by Kurt taking his pulse.

"Poor Dave, boring old Dave. But he was friends with Jenoah Moretti because his wife worked with him, and when Jenoah had a few drinks one night and said how cool it would be to steal a drone and hack into the FBI database and find all those new identities ... bet that caused a bit of panic."

"Jenoah is a smart guy ..." Smith said, rallying. "He doesn't do things for fun."

Sirens screamed up the street. "Why did he hack the database?"

"I can't tell you that."

"Won't and can't are different."

"Jenoah wanted to find the guy who married his sister. He was supposed to be dead, but someone said they saw him at Dulles airport about five years ago. Then he heard Jeb Warner had a new identity."

"Heard from whom?"

"I don't know."

"That wasn't so hard, was it? And kidnapping Harley Iverson and Chris Iverson?"

Smith's groan became a moan. "Iverson designed software that helped put his brother in jail. If hadn't been for him, they never would've caught Angelo."

"You seem to know the family quite well," I arched an eyebrow at Kurt.

He attempted a smile in return, but it wasn't quite there, and his ghastly appearance told me he needed to be in hospital.

Green flight suits hurried past the window.

Paramedics. Tyler went to meet them. He pointed them to Kurt. The second crew would deal with Smith. Kurt was quiet, Smith wasn't.

"My wife is Christina Moretti. She's a cousin."

"How many times did you blow scopolamine in some innocent person's face and make them do something unspeakable?"

"Four times."

"Is the whole family involved?"

"Yes, the whole stinking lot of them."

"You're a dead man walking." I left him to his pain and walked outside beside the gurney Kurt was on. "You going to be okay, Henderson."

I distanced myself from the memory, from the entire scene. Shook it all off and settled myself.

"Dane ..."

"I saw it all. But who saw Jeb Warner at Dulles airport?"

Bits and pieces of that time in our lives collided in my brain. I recalled how I'd considered Debbie Barnes and Michael Addison, who are in fact the same person, or rather inhabit the same physical space, and were perfectly placed within the FBI to provide information on undercover identities. When we found out she was there that day at the school, another nail rammed into the lid of the coffin ... but we extracted that nail when it all came back to organized crime. The Moretti situation blanketed everything and suppressed my initial feeling that either Debbie or Michael had something to do with the compromising of the list.

I thought out loud. "The person who saw Jeb Warner ... he'd aged, he wasn't Jeb Warner anymore, and he really did not look like Jeb Warner. I don't think I would've recognized him. Maybe something about him would feel familiar but think about it, how many people feel a bit familiar?"

"A lot. So how was he recognized at an airport?"

"If someone was using facial recognition software and scanning the CCTV ..." I jammed my hand into my right jean pocket. My fingers wrapped around a small piece of paper. I extracted it and unfurled the crumpled note. Two words: Call Debbie.

"But why would Warner be someone anyone was looking for? He was supposed to be dead."

"Who knew he wasn't?"

"Debbie."

"But why would she be looking?"

"Exactly, it makes no sense. She already knew, she could've told them straight up where to find him or at least that he was alive." A roll of coins dropped. Coins spun all over the ground. "But accessing the full list would leave a digital footprint and that's traceable."

Would she have made a copy way back when the list first became a thing, way back when our former Director Cait O'Hare was working with Delta A and Delta A was mostly involved in undercover cases?

Why would someone do that? Insurance? Just plain old security? Making a backup in case of corruption of the original file? How would anyone outside the immediate circle know there was a list? And if they did, did they also know about The Wayward Son Protocol? Or was that a surprise to them too?

"Who would want to cause a shit ton of trouble and implicate our own people? Who wanted the list more than the Moretti family?"

"Russians, Chinese, North Koreans, anyone who has a spy presence in the US and that we're not working with?"

I nodded. "How many of the agents we helped relocate are alive now?"

"You think Debbie was turned ..."

"Maybe it was Michael ..."

That sent my mind whirring over the whole transgender/gender fluid Debbie and Michael thing. Easier for me to just think about Debbie, it was her I had a friend and work relationship with.

"Dane, who knew about The Wayward Son Protocol?"

"No one who wasn't involved. Everything was locked down, only the Director could access that information."

"Your names were changed ..."

And Debbie was the master of new identities.

"Awesome. That's just fucking awesome. We were handed new identity cards and passports and Social Security numbers - the whole nine. Our employment records were sealed and replaced with the new identities. Dane Wesson and Stewart Smith."

"And who provided those covers?"

Dane shook his head. "I don't know. We were handed them and everything else was gone. We had a new apartment, and our former digital footprints were wiped away."

"You became ghosts?"

"Pretty much. Me and Stu had no other family, so we were the perfect ghosts."

"Friends though?"

"Of course."

"And the explanation?"

"I believe we died in a car accident."

The old standby. Bet there was an explosion.

"Debbie Barnes or Michael Addison would've put it all together and taken everything else apart, that's what they do."

"What are you saying?"

"You know what I'm saying Dane." A heavy sigh punctuated my words. "They were turned."

"Not possibly turned, not maybe they were turned. But an absolute?"

"Yes."

"What do we do?"

"Business as usual until we have proof."

"And who do you think turned them?"

"The Chinese."

"Figured you were going there." He nodded. "It makes sense. They were behind the OPM breach, and this data wasn't part of it. If they wanted more, they'd have to turn someone with access."

Yeah, and someone with more access than a janitor.

"If the Chinese dangled the existence of the List over the Moretti's, then it's possible they have at least one organized crime family right where they want them."

"We need to get out of here. Now."

Chapter Twenty-six
Wasted Time

Kurt dropped me home. Mixed feelings rumbled and grumbled. The joy of seeing my family, and the sadness of losing Susan, fought a battle within. But it was all overshadowed by the knowledge that I needed to talk to Debbie, and I had no proof of any of the ramblings and craziness Dane and I concocted.

No proof except my gut. My gut screamed so loud I couldn't ignore it. But I also couldn't act openly on a gut feeling. She was my friend.

She visited our home and played with our babies. And Michael, well, he was Caine's pal. They golfed together. A large rusty can toppled over. Worms wriggled into knots trying to escape the daylight. From my pocket, a little fluffy yellow duckling emerged, shook and started snapping up the knot of worms. He yanked one worm, it stretched, and stretched, before snapping back into the contorted bundle. The little duck tried again. He grasped another worm in his little orange beak and tugged. The worm broke free, and the little duckling toppled over with the wriggler firmly in its beak. It lay there on its back gobbling the long worm until it was gone. Satiated, the duckling waddled past the large knot of worms and climbed back into my pocket.

I watched the worms tie themselves tightly together, before the image faded into nothing and I was left staring at wooden blocks on the floor. Wooden blocks. My energy shifted. I was home. Sitting on the floor in the family area of the kitchen. Argo nudged me. My fingers slid into his thick fur. Grounded again.

"You're a very good boy, Argo." I buried my face in his neck. "You are the best boy."

Little feet clattered on the tiles behind me. "Mommy!" I turned my head in time to see Grace run up behind me. Isabella followed her with a grin on her face.

With one arm still around Argo, I scooped the girls into my lap with my left arm.

"My girls," I said, kissing each child on the head. "Mommy missed you."

Mitch's voice called down the hallway from the front door. "Babe, you're back."

His smile lit his face as he walked toward me. I set the girls on the floor, patted Argo one last time, and stood. The girls spotted their abandoned blocks and busied themselves building. Nothing impacted their drive to play for long.

Mitch's arms circled me. His mouth found mine. Soft, sweet, warmth. I could stay here forever. Screw the world and its problems. Fuck 'em all.

Me and my family, safe in our house.

And the phone rang. Loud, unrelenting, the noise bouncing off the walls and onto the tiled floor. It circled us like a shark after blood.

Mitch gently eased away. "That'll be for you, babe."

"I know." Can't we just ignore the world?

Mitch smiled. "I heard that. You have to save the world, so, ignoring it isn't an option."

The ringing intensified. So did my power to ignore it.

"No pressure." A chuckle rose and spilled over Mitch's chest. "So dramatic. Saving the world."

"It is what it is."

Yeah. Whatever. And bam I had Doris Day singing in my head. 'Que Sera Sera.' Come on brain, that's unfair. The phone stopped and then beeped as our voice mail kicked in. I heard Mitch's voice say we were unable to get to the phone, blah blah blah.

Grace squealed. Isabella snatched a block from her and shuffled away on her bottom.

"I'll referee," Mitch said, moving toward the girls and the squealing. "You go check that message."

"How about we do this the other way around?"

Mitch laughed. "But you're the superhero, I'm just super dad!" He lifted Grace from the floor and flew her around the room in his arms until the irritated squeal was replaced by giggles.

I leaned on the kitchen counter and pressed the flashing message icon. Must have missed a few calls. There were sixteen new messages. Jeez. I looked at Mitch. "Sixteen?"

"You've been gone a few days, and we all know if the

house phone rings it's for you."

"Thanks." I pressed to hear the latest message and while it was loading said, "You could've cleared the messages though."

"Sorry," Mitch said, sitting on the floor with the girls.

The message I'd just missed was from Debbie Barnes. Hot damn. Were her ears burning?

I played it again when I realized I hadn't heard it the first time.

She wanted to meet for coffee in half-an-hour. Okay. Lets fucking do it then.

"Babe, I'm going to meet Debbie for coffee. Do you want me to pick anything up?"

"Milk and string cheese," Mitch replied.

"Okay." I stooped to kiss him, then made my escape while the girls were happy playing. Argo slunk up behind me at the door. "You coming with?"

I swear he nodded. As I opened the front door I called out, "I have the dog."

Argo jumped into the backseat of my car and sat. I rummaged in the trunk area for his spare harness and short leash. I tossed the leash onto the passenger seat, then fitted the harness on Argo and threaded his seatbelt through the D ring and clipped it securely. His soft tongue licked the side of my face before I moved back to close his door. Sneaky.

I drove and talked to Argo. He was a first-rate listener.

"Wonder what Debbie wants? Guess it's something to do with that brochureware thing she told me about. Forberg created something or other to do with fooling biometric databases."

Argo huffed.

My sentiments exactly.

Where the actual fuck is Forberg?

I edged the car into a parking space outside the coffee shop Debbie had chosen. I zapped the back windows down six inches and twisted in my seat to see Argo. "Stay. I'll be right inside. Any trouble, and you call me."

He whined once. I took that to mean he understood his directive.

"You're such a good boy. I'll be just there." I pointed to the coffee shop before exiting the vehicle and locking the doors with the fob. Argo watched me walk inside. I knew he'd stay watching until I returned and that gave me a warm feeling of security. I was pretty sure that if he thought he had to, he would find a way out of the car and to me.

I scanned the dim room and saw Debbie in a back-corner booth. Her blonde curly hair visible over the back of the seats. Tall people were definitely easier to spot from a distance. Debbie was six feet two. That qualified as tall. I ordered coffee and pointed to the booth I'd be in. The barista wrote down the table number.

One deep breath, a smile planted on my face, and I

joined Debbie.

"Hi," she said, smiling. "Glad you have survived your ordeal."

"You and me both."

"The girls would've been excited to see you."

I nodded. "They were."

Small talk continued until my coffee arrived. As much as I wanted to hurry things along, I also did not. I had no clue how I was going to drag the past back into the future and bring up the subject of being a Chinese spy, and her potential treacherous behavior.

I sipped the coffee. "This is delicious."

"That's why I like this place."

"So, tell me about Forberg and this ... what'd you call it? Brochureware?"

"That's right. Apparently Hanzel Forberg developed software that enables someone to trick biometric databases."

"To what end?"

"The company he apparently designed it for are marketing it to agencies and the private sector. They're claiming that agencies can use it to keep aliases functioning in today's highly computerized and surveillance orientated environment."

"And?"

"It's bullshit."

"So, the plan is to make a shit load of money with a product that doesn't work ... seems like a fast way to involve yourself in a lawsuit." I took another sip of coffee. "Not a smart move."

"Except if it's released all at once, sales are made, the product shipped, and by the time anyone figures it out, the company is long gone with the cash."

"Could that happen? Agencies don't pay right away, most companies don't pay immediately, there's an invoice system and accounting departments."

"Yes, there are. So probably not."

"How would it even work? Would it rely on people's ability to get the software into, let's say, TSA systems?"

"It says the software embeds code into images that change how the image appears when read by electronic means."

"It what now?"

"Exactly ..."

"Hanzel Forberg is a scientist but as far as I know he's not into software development. He's into creating vaccines for diseases we don't even have yet."

"Could there be two Hanzel Forberg's?"

I shrugged. Maybe. Doubtful that they'd both come to our attention at once. Bit too coincidental. And the whole software thing made no fucking sense at all. Just like thinking Debbie was turned by the Chinese. How could she?

"Explain the brochureware thing to me again ..."

"I have a fun example," Debbie said smiling. "I've wanted to use it for a while now."

"Okay, then let me have it."

"Remember the photoshopped photo of POTUS as a

half-naked boxer, six-pack, gloves an' all?"

"The one he released on his Twitter account? That had a Putin feel to it, that one?"

"Yes."

"Been trying to erase that from my memory for the last year or so, thanks for the reminder." I stifled a chuckle. "Just when I thought we couldn't fall any further in the eyes of the world."

"It's a fine example of brochureware."

"The picture on the box may differ to the actual contents?"

"Yes."

"And the claims are exaggerated?"

Debbie laughed. "Now you've got it."

"Would it also apply to someone who outwardly displays total loyalty and is a real team player, but underneath is selling secrets to the Chinese?"

Her face froze as her laugh switched to terror. Contorted and frightful. She bounced back. "That's a strange analogy."

"But is it correct?" I allowed a small smile to rest on my lips. "Would that be a form of brochureware or is it just plain old treason?"

"Is there something wrong?"

"You tell me, is everything all right in your part of the world, Debbie? Nothing you haven't told me, or want to tell me, but didn't know how?"

She pressed her lips together, flipped her hair over her shoulder, and shook her head.

I lifted the cup to my lips and took another sip. "This is really remarkable coffee. But I better get going. Have some family time to catch up on." I placed the cup on the table. "Before I forget, we're having a birthday bash for the girls next Saturday. We'd love you to come."

A hint of confusion flittered across her eyes, before disappearing, as a smile lit her face. "Of course. I would love to be there."

"Twoish on Saturday afternoon."

I left without looking back. There was no need. I'd given her something to think about and think she would. If she was guilty, then she'd be wondering how much I knew and when the guillotine would fall. If she was innocent, she'd think I was stressed due to the situation and let it go.

* * *

I drove through the city and to work. Argo and I ran up the stairs from the parking garage, neck and neck. I'm sure that if he could've laughed, he would have. We walked sedately down the corridor to Sandra's desk. She was on the phone, but waved and grinned. I signed that I'd be in my office.

She gave me a thumbs up.

Argo and I went into the office. My phone alerted. Oh yeah, my camera. I sat at my desk and checked the alerts. My phone recorded every alert and linked it to the exact time in the camera app. All I had to do was tap each alert.

Didn't realize how often people popped into my office until I started opening each alert. No wonder some days it felt like Union Station in here. Argo lay under my desk. He settled in, guess he knew how many people came in and out every day. I knew every face, every face. The one that surprised me was Michael Addison. What was he doing in my office? I watched. He walked in, walked to my desk, looked over his shoulder, paused, then removed the bug from the edge of the desk. Well, fuckadoodledo. Michael Addison planted the bug. So, it wasn't the CIA listening, it was the Chinese? Maybe that was a big leap. I rolled it back to not the CIA. That much I knew. Because Addison did not work for the CIA. Neither he nor Debbie Barnes names came up in any context in all my dealings with the CIA.

So did Addison plant the bug or simply retrieve it? Because Debbie had access to my office. I wished I'd thought to have a camera installed in my office earlier. Just for such situations. All the time it took for me to rebuild trust in the people outside of Delta that I dealt with on a daily basis, swam before my eyes. We'd been here before. Back in the day, we had a media liaison attached to the Delta teams. She sold out to the highest bidder and got a friend of mine killed.

Then there was Troy. He was an FNG attached to us, I was supposed to be mentoring him. He sold his soul to the devil. And now, we're fucking here again. In a place that makes me wish I had surveillance running in my own office. Fuckadoodledo, maybe I do need a change of career. I gave a massive internal eye roll and I shoved traitors of the past off a mental cliff. It wasn't necessarily a repeat of past performances.

We had cameras in the corridor near the elevator. Frank had access to the feeds, for security reasons.

"Argo, we're going downstairs."

Argo crawled out from under my desk and waited for me at the door.

"Hey, I was just coming to see you," Sandra said.

"Be right back. I need to check something," I said over my shoulder, as I strode to the stairwell door. Argo and I ran down the stairs and barged through the bottom door into the foyer.

Frank looked up from his desk, shook his head slowly, and grinned. "Every time SAC, every time."

I grinned back as I crossed the large open tiled floorspace to his desk. "Got a question for ya, Frank."

"Okay, shoot."

"When we were looking for Cooper outside the building and anyone who shouldn't be on our floor, did you see Debbie Barnes or Michael Addison?"

"I think we better go through to the back room and have a look at that search again." He picked up his radio and pressed the talk button. "Chitra, come on in. I need you at the desk, over."

"Roger that, Frank," came a disembodied female voice from the handset.

The main door opened, and a uniformed woman walked across the floor. She nodded at me and took Frank's place behind the desk.

"Won't be long," he said.

Argo, Frank, and I entered the back room. He retrieved the history for our last search and this time he used the database to locate Debbie Barnes or Michael Addison on our floor.

Argo leaned his hairy body against my leg, encouraging my hand to pet his head. Images scrolled past my eyes, but nothing really registered until Frank spoke, "SAC, look at this."

I looked at the main screen. There was Debbie, having just stepped out the elevator. She walked toward the camera, which meant she was walking toward my office, but we couldn't see if she went that far. We watched. She came back, less than a minute later, and took the stairs instead of the elevator.

"Okay, that's weird." I squinted at the date and time on the screen. "I didn't meet with her at all that week, but she may have been there to see someone else."

Who else would she visit on my floor? Debbie hardly left her office suite down in the sub-basement. Maybe she came to see me, and I wasn't there? But there was no mention of it or no message, and Sandra can't have been at her desk.

"Roll it back for me Frank, does Sandra leave the floor before Barnes arrives?"

Frank did as I asked. "Here you go, SAC. Agent

Sinclair taking the elevator, looks like she's going up."

"Up, okay." I made a mental note to ask Sandra why she left her desk that day.

"You need any more?"

"Yeah, but can you do this and let me know if you find Barnes or Addison on my floor at any other time between ..." I paused while I thought about the bug sweep days. Sunday. Sunday night the crew come through our floor. "Between ten o'clock Sunday night and today."

"Of course, SAC. I probably owe you for those muffins you bring me."

"Thanks, Frank. I'll be in my office."

Argo and I ran back up the stairs. Sandra was working, but not talking, so I interrupted.

"Hey, a few days ago, did you get called upstairs for something?"

She pushed her bright green glasses further up the bridge of her nose, her eyes sparked. "Yes. Talk about annoying."

"Okay, what happened?"

"Someone called me and said there was a problem with a pay slip and I needed to go to HR to get it sorted."

"And?"

"It was rubbish. Wasn't anything. They didn't know why I got the call, and said it was probably another Sinclair."

"And you didn't think anything else of it ..."

"Nope, just an annoying interruption was all." She pushed her glasses again and raised an eyebrow at me. "Why?"

"Because someone was on the floor at the same time you were gone, and it might be a bit suspicious."

"Are you serious?"

"Yes. Did you recognize the voice?"

"No. It was male though. Maybe."

"Thanks."

"Is something wrong?"

I shook my head. "Nope. I'll be in my office. My laptop?"

"Here," she said, reaching down and picking up a laptop from her bottom drawer. "Kurt dropped it off."

"Thank you." I took it and hurried into my office with Argo on my heels.

Back at my desk I opened the laptop and signed in.

The other thing I had to do was see if Fran had made contact regarding needing Delta's help with anything.

There was an email. I opened it and read the contents.

She was formerly asking for Delta help on a case. One person was dead and five others extremely unwell in a house in a suburb of Wellington. There was a second crime scene with two dead and four in critical condition. Her concern was it looked like a poison. They didn't know what caused the illness and she thought we might have come across something like this before. I forwarded the email to Caine making it top priority. That was an excellent email, and it would be hard to ignore. She stopped short of saying Novichok, but damned if the contents didn't suggest something like that.

I jumped into our private messaging system using a private browser and a VPN and messaged Fran.

Rubber Duck: Is that true?

Mother Goose: Yes and no.

Rubber Duck: Enlighten me.

Mother Goose: I have dead people and I have unwell people, looks like poison.

Rubber Duck: Could it be Qu, COVID-19, or something new?

Mother Goose: It could, but looks like poison and all the people were in contact with the same takeaway place.

Rubber Duck: Keep that part quiet.

Mother Goose: See you soon. I just got an email from your boss saying he was sending Delta A.

Rubber Duck: Fantastic.

I closed the browser and turned off the VPN.

On my screen was a request from Caine. More like a demand really. He wanted to see me A-sap.

"Come on Argo, the boss wants us."

Minutes later, I knocked on the outer door. Reed beckoned me in.

"Go through SAC, he's waiting, and take the beast with you."

"Thanks."

He gave me a cold stare. "Don't thank me."

Okay then. I can see why they get along so well. Grumpy and Grumpier. Anyway, who doesn't like dogs? Weirdos, that's who.

"Agent Iverson, Agent Argo," Caine said on a long growl. "Be seated."

I sat in the chair in front of his desk. Argo sat on the floor next to me. "You wanted to see me."

"You've connived your way to New Zealand."

"No conniving. Fran asked for help." I gave my very best wide-eyed innocent look.

"That might work on your father, or your husband, but I'm not buying," he grouched. "Get organized. You'll need to be on a flight within twenty-four hours, or The Director might get wind of it and pull the plug."

"Where is he?"

"Golf tournament for three days."

"Lucky that."

He narrowed his eyes and leaned forward. "Did you know?"

I shook my head. I actually did not. Sometimes the stars do align. "No knowledge of golfing at all." True story. Can't see the sense in it.

"I've instructed Sandra to make the necessary travel arrangements, and also to liaise with Mitch. I believe the twins have a birthday coming up and if he's in agreement then you should all travel together."

Whoa. "You're suggesting what exactly?"

"That when this is over, that you stay on in New Zealand for a vacation with your family. You have plenty of vacation time owing, and this is the perfect opportunity."

"You don't want me back until The Director has cooled off ..."

"There's that too. The rest of Delta A followed orders. You, however, gave them, so, be smart about this Ellie. Let him cool off."

I nodded.

"Argo?"

"He stays. Sandra will take him."

Argo stood and stretched. His head landed on my lap. "She'll love having you pal."

"Go, get organized, solve this crisis."

"Tahoma and Karen?"

"I forwarded the email to them."

His email alert sounded, and my phone chimed. We both checked. Tahoma Whitehorse saying they'd meet us in New Zealand.

Caine looked over his laptop screen at me. "Did you get the same email?"

"Tahoma?"

He nodded.

"Now get out of here and save the world."

"What if I can't ..."

"If you don't try then you won't." Caine dismissed us

with a wave. "Get out of my office."

Chapter Twenty-seven
Sorrow

Ding.

"Kia Ora, welcome to Auckland, New Zealand. The temperature outside is twenty-three degrees, sunny with a light northerly. Please remain seated until the seatbelt sign turns off. On behalf of the flight deck and cabin crew, I'd like to thank you for choosing to fly Air New Zealand." A pause then the Captain spoke again. "A reminder all passengers must collect their bags and pass through customs."

My head swiveled toward Mitch. I glanced down at Isabella in my lap when she wriggled, then looked up to see Mitch grin at me. Grace's curls jiggled. I sensed her impatience before it became obvious. They'd done well to cope with the five-hour trip from Dulles to San Francisco, then the twelve hours to Auckland.

"One more flight and we can relax."

Grace grabbed Isabella's hand. "Go."

"Not yet, Grace. We wait until the plane stops moving, and the flight attendant tells us it's time to go," Mitch said.

She wriggled in the seat belt, attached to his seat belt. "Daddy. Go."

"Grace, soon."

Lee peered around Mitch. "What's up little lady?"

"Uncle Lee, go!"

"Soon." Lee leaned back. Across the aisle I caught sight of Kurt, and beyond him, Dane.

"We clear customs and immigration, then Delta are met by an attaché?" Mitch asked.

That's where we part ways.

"Yes. And a representative from the New Zealand State Department."

"What's the game plan?"

"They escort us to Wellington." One more flight. "We check into our hotel. Maybe have time for a nap, then Delta A meets with police and health department representatives."

"Simon and I take the girls to Wellington on a later flight, then we pick up the rental car, and car seats." He glanced at his watch. "We're on an evening sailing to Picton."

"Works for me," Dad said, from across the aisle on my left. "Been a long time since I was in Wellington, or on a Ferry." His voice was light. "We might have time for a walk along the waterfront before we sail."

Isabella grizzled. Lee leaned forward. "My turn?"

"Looks that way." I unclipped her seat belt and passed her across Mitch and Grace to Lee's waiting arms. She snuggled in and sighed. Her happy place definitely involved Uncle Lee.

The trip held promise. Not a vacation for me, but if we had time once we'd finished doing what had to be done, then maybe I'd be able to join the family on their vacation. I knew Mitch hoped the vacation would become our lives and that I'd agree to stay. Would be nice if all of us could spend some down time in the Marlborough Sounds. Not like Mitch's place isn't big enough to accommodate the team.

"Is Whitehorse already in New Zealand?" Kurt asked, leaning forward to look around Lee.

"I don't know," I replied. "Hope so. I'd like to hit the ground running on this situation."

It's either hit the ground running, or don't hit it at all. The muscles in my forehead cramped into a frown. That's not an option. Was bringing the girls to New Zealand really a smart idea?

Bit late to walk that road.

Dane's voice floated through the ether and into my mind. "There was nothing to suggest the terrorists plan on releasing anything in New Zealand. Probably safer having them here."

I thanked him mentally.

He was right. Close is safe. Tucked away in the Marlborough Sounds is safe. Back home, not so much.

People around us moved. Opening overhead lockers, gathering belongings. We waited. Let them hurry. We'll catch them up anyway. I relished the last few family moments before work took over.

Grace squawked and grabbed at my sleeve.

"Problem?" I said, giving her a mom look.

"Argo," she replied, with a frown.

"He's at home with Sandra."

"Argo!" Her voice rose.

Isabella leaned forward. "Argo, mommy?"

"At home with Sandra, Isabella."

Unhappiness grew flailing arms and legs. When it's two sets of flailing arms and legs, it's a little like trying to tame a windmill. Lee wrapped his arms around Isabella, and Mitch wrapped his around Grace. People smiled down at them as they passed. I sensed their relief at exiting. Couldn't blame them. Couldn't blame the girls for wanting Argo either. They weren't the only ones missing the big hairy comforting German Shepherd.

Mitch and I said our goodbyes before customs. Delta was going out the same gate as the airplane crew. Our bags would be x-rayed, and the attaché would be waiting with police, to escort us from the area. Such is our life. Mitch, Dad, and the girls were going out in the next line, and with nothing to declare, probably straight through.

Chapter Twenty-eight
Here We Go Again

A tallish, muscular man, wearing a leather jacket and black boots, fell into step beside me at the bottom of the stairs into Te Papa. Five o'clock shadow evident on his weathered face. Questions stacked in my mind. I had no idea what Dave Crocker looked like, just that I was meeting a man. Could he be the spy? Or maybe he's just visiting the national museum for cultural reasons. Time would tell. He walked next to me up the large staircase. I noticed a tattoo on his outer wrist as his jacket moved. I couldn't make out what it was, before his sleeve dropped and covered the ink.

Halfway up the stairs, he started a conversation.

"Been here before?" He asked, with a crooked smile. "You look like a tourist."

"How astute," I replied, smiling. Don't exactly sound like a local either but nor did he. "I've been here before, but it was a long time ago."

"Anything in particular you'd like to see again?"

That was the cue for my prearranged reply.

"The Britten."

"Don't blame you, that's one helluva machine."

"John Britten was a talented man."

"Maybe I'll see you over there," he said, as we reached the top of the staircase.

I looked for a map and he disappeared from view. So that was Dave Crocker. Looked more biker than spy, but whatever.

Something needled in my mind. Why did he seem familiar? Where and why would I have come across an Australian biker?

With a mental shrug, I checked a display board.

The Britten was up more stairs. I wandered through a sea display, where above me hung a blue whale skeleton. It ran the full length of the enormous hall. An imposing mammal. Can't say I'd want to meet one face to face in the ocean. Be more like face to giant eyeball.

For almost half an hour I explored dioramas of the ocean depths. A coffee shop lured me to it and satisfied my need for nerve-soothing black deliciousness. I made my way to the Britten display with a takeout coffee cup in my hand. Dave Crocker bumped into me as I stood watching a video about John Britten. My coffee sloshed.

"Sorry," he said, and placed a friendly hand on my forearm. "You okay?"

"No harm done."

He nodded. "I'm Crockett." He moved to enable a handshake.

I took the offered hand and shook it. "Ellie," I said. "Crockett? As in Davy Crockett?"

"That's me, King of the wild frontier."

Definitely my meeting then. "The man who doesn't know fear," I replied, with a small smile. "Killed many bears as a toddler?"

Crockett chuckled. "No ma'am."

"Shall we walk or sit?"

"Allow me to be your guide and we'll walk," he said, his accent more American than Australian.

"All right then lead the way," I said, with a smile.

"It'll be a pleasure." He indicated our direction with his hand. "I think Phar Lap is a satisfactory place to start."

We walked, throngs of people milled around, looking at exhibits, or talking.

"Why do you look familiar?" I asked, when he came to a stop in front of a large glass case containing a horse skeleton.

"We'll get to that, but for now, I think I can help you piece together some of your current puzzle."

"How so?" I moved around the case, reading the information.

"A Chinese agent has defected to ASIO. He confirmed the People's Republic of China funded research to further weaponize the Qu Pathogen."

Movement caught my eye. Someone hurried in our direction. An Asian male. Crockett saw him. His hand grabbed my arm and steered me through a group of tourists listening to their guide talk about the horse, up a ramp, and then behind a pillar.

My brain jumped back to another museum and a trap that left me bleeding from a knife wound. Fun times. What the hell is it about me that attracts that shit? I fished a mirror from my bag and angled it to see what was happening.

"I don't think he saw where we went," I said. I adjusted the angle trying to see where he went. The people moved in groups of two or three, affording me a visual gap. The man was standing near the skeleton, turning on the spot. "He's lost us. I hope."

"Good. There are meeting rooms around somewhere, think we should head on up here and find one."

"Keep us out of harm's way." Or more importantly, keep the public out of harm's way. Crockett held my arm. Guess he didn't want to lose me. A small smile wiggled in my brain. I'm definitely mellowing with age. Once upon a time, I would've smacked a hand away regardless of the reason for it. But here I was being led through a museum in Wellington, New Zealand by a big ass biker-looking dude. A biker-looking dude? My heels planted. All movement stopped. "Why do you look familiar, and why is your accent more East Coast USA than Australian?"

"Not now. When we get to a safer space."

I spotted a door two paces from me. I dislodged his hand. In two strides I had a door handle in my grip. With a twist the door popped open. I poked my head around it. Empty of people. It was a small conference room complete with long table and chairs.

"This will do." I stepped inside. Crockett followed me. I closed the door and turned the lock. "Talk."

"We've never met, if that's what you're wondering."

I sat in a chair, he sat opposite me. An image swam into view. Crosshairs. Looking down a rifle scope. The scope moved across the driveway of Cait O'Hare's home, pausing on a male who looked up once before walking away. Him. The scope moved again, this time settling on another man. That man had an SRAW on his shoulder. I squeezed the trigger. The side of his head blew out in a fine red mist. My mind rolled back and refocused on the first man.

"Lexington. Actually, Mauryville, at Director O'Hare's property. Inferno Jesters." I sprang to my feet, fighting to control an urge to reach over the table and punch him. "You.Were.There."

I knew at the time that one of the Inferno Jesters, or Brotherhood, was an undercover agent, but not who it was. There was probably more than one.

His brown eyes met mine, without flinching. "I was."

"DEA or ASIO which is it?"

"ASIO."

"What the hell is ASIO doing infiltrating American gangs?"

"Not just American. Jesters are Australian too." He planted his hands flat on the table in front of him. "Before the guy running all over the museum looking for us breaks down that door, I need to pass information. We can discuss my role in the unfortunate incident in Mauryville later."

The door handle rattled. Crockett pressed a finger to

his lips. We waited for nearly a minute, but no other noise followed. We both scanned the room looking for another way in or out. There was none. Crockett stood, picked up a chair, and wedged the back under the door handle. Just in case. Good thing it was an inward opening door.

We moved to the other end of the room and kept our voices low.

"Okay, so, you're a Jester and ASIO. You can finish that story later. Tell me what I need to know about the Chinese."

"Instead of creating a vaccine for the Qu Pathogen, they've created a way to initially deliver the virus, followed by a booster shot eight weeks later. It's the booster shot which triggers the new version of Qu. Basically it makes it lethal to certain ethnicities and biological traits."

"Holy shit."

"No wonder no one wanted to go through channels. How long can you keep your guy safe?"

"Unknown, but ..." He waved a hand to the locked door. "It didn't take long for them to send someone after us. The thing is, he also said Federal Police are compromised, and so is ASIS. Foreign agents are embedded in the justice system and the political system."

"Fuck." I changed my position and leaned differently on the table edge. "I have secure CDC contacts."

"We know. If anyone moves openly on this, they'll

move up the program."

I dragged my phone from my pocket, held my finger up to signal to Crockett to wait for a moment, and called Tahoma. He answered on the fifth Mississippi.

"Ellie Iverson, what can I do for you?"

"Stay in the US."

"You do not want me with you?"

"I do not want this situation to become one I cannot control, and the movement of the CDC's top virologists will draw unwanted attention."

Cough once and the world gives you the filthiest look. Imagine what our CDC doctors traveling overseas would do?

Silence. Then the soft sound of a laptop in use.

"Do not worry, my friend, Karen and I have a workshop to attend. We are currently waiting a boarding call in San Francisco."

"Where are you going?"

"Auckland University Medical school, conferring with others in our field on the measles outbreak in Samoa last year," Tahoma said. "This is a World Health Organization sponsored think tank."

"Excellent."

"Stay well, Ellie."

I intend to. Crockett waited. "And?"

"They'll be in Auckland at a workshop/think tank to do with the measles outbreak."

"Good timing."

"The stars aligned." Maybe the universe isn't ready

to relinquish its hold on humanity yet. "Can we get samples of both vaccines?" I said, while trying to think my way through getting the samples to Tahoma Whitehorse at the University of Auckland.

He rummaged in a messenger bag he carried and passed me a small box. "They're marked with batch numbers, and also which dose they are."

"Do I have to keep them cold or anything special?"

He shook his head. "Just don't sit them in front of a heat source or anything silly."

"Where did you get these?" I said, putting the box in my bag.

"A laboratory here. These people are using labs in Aussie and New Zealand to manufacture this shit under the guise of vaccines."

"Anywhere else?"

"Not as far as we know. But I'd be surprised if there weren't European manufacturing plants."

"I've heard of a German company that has the Q Fever bacteria."

"Worth taking a closer look at."

A noise on the other side of the wall gave us pause for a minute.

I whispered, "Is that it for now?"

"Yeah," he replied, matching my hushed tone.

"So, tell me how an ASIO agent ended up inside The Inferno Jesters in Virginia."

"Garrison invited me over to set up a new distribution chain for some of his product."

"And ..."

"I stayed."

"How long?"

"Seven years."

Shit. "And now?"

"I hung around after Garrison went to prison. Tidied up some stuff, and then took his distribution ideas back to Australia."

"Is that what you're doing now?"

"Yes. I'm going back to the States soon."

"Why?"

"Garrison trusts me. He's still operating the club, but seventy percent of everything he's involved in runs through me."

"And you are trusting me?"

"Done my homework, Iverson."

"Okay, so you're close to Garrison. Ever heard the name Jeremy Cotton."

"Yes."

"What's the link that binds Cotton to Garrison?"

"There's back story that I don't know, because Garrison hasn't talked about it, but I do know he ordered Cotton's girlfriend abducted eight days ago."

"Okay. That's a big thing." I gave it a beat. "I figured they were once friends?"

"Maybe. But the order was given by Garrison to snatch the girl. He wanted leverage."

Cotton was a scientist. Why would he want leverage? Drugs?

"Are we looking at a *Breaking Bad* situation here?"

"The kidnapping did coincide with one of our best cooks meeting an unfortunate end."

"Did Garrison know Cotton was my CI?"

Interest flicked up a notch in Crockett's eyes. "Not as far as I know."

"Is Garrison working with the Chinese?"

"Yes."

Well, ain't that just the cat's pajamas?

"Doing what?"

"Distribution. Chinese drugs."

"Drugs?"

"It's our biggest revenue stream. Remember the UPS bust?"

"Sure do."

"They were bringing a huge quantity of product in for us, and when that stopped, we had a demand and supply discrepancy. In came the Chinese."

"Great, they're making bioweapons and meth."

"Iverson, they have their sticky little fingers in everything. It's all about the One China."

"Cotton tried to infect me with Qu17P. Did that come from Garrison?"

"If it did, it did not go through me."

"He was involved in the release of Qu last time."

"Ah, you see, that's not correct intelligence. We were security, not distribution."

"Really? And Cait O'Hare and my men?"

"O'Hare was the target. Your men were collateral

damage."

Thoughts rampaged. I stepped back and jammed my hands in my pockets. Don't hit him. Do. Not. Hit. Him.

Hold it.

"Back up the bus ... if the new Qu is delivered by vaccine, how did Cotton infect us by expelling air?"

"Multiple delivery systems. The trial suggested the first Qu did not spread as far or as fast as they expected. The new version becomes airborne once patients are infected."

"Even if you're not vaccinated twice ..."

"Precisely, if you get one vaccine and come in contact with someone who is infected, they can still trigger your dormant virus by coughing or breathing near you."

"Flaw - Dane and I were exposed to the original pathogen and survived."

"We know."

"Cotton failed to make us ill."

"We know that too, and you better believe the Chinese are aware."

"There are other people out there who were exposed and survived."

"Yes, but not as many as you'd think."

"It wasn't as devastating as it should've been ..."

"True, it was mostly direct infections, with very few people becoming ill from human transmission."

"Guess we were unlucky."

"Turns out you were very lucky."

Tahoma Whitehorse told us we had a natural immunity to the known forms of Qu, including the recent Qu17P, but it didn't hurt to hear it from someone who has had contact with a spy. "So, we can't die from this?"

"Highly unlikely. Steer clear of anyone offering vaccines though. Don't tempt fate."

"When people start to work out that the so-called vaccines are not - it'll undermine the government's efforts to help. Trust will go. The populations will turn on their governments." We had an effective taste of how people behave in crisis, with COVID-19. And people would be fairly receptive to a new vaccine because of that, and the vaccine that halted the spread, and restored life to the locked down world.

"Before that happens, WHO will declare the next potential pandemic to be Qu17P, and start delivering more vaccines, and the first people offered vaccines will be medical personnel, armed services, emergency responders ..."

"This is really how the apocalypse starts?"

"Yes."

"Is anyone working on legitimate vaccines?" I asked.

"Yes, but ..."

"How do we know?"

"Exactly," Crockett said, shifting his weight from foot-to-foot.

"Trust no one."

"If I can help more, I will."

I turned to face him. "Thank you." We shook hands. Then he slipped a bottle of hand sanitizer into my palm. "Thank you again."

"Don't thank me Iverson, find a way to stop this bullshit before they win," he said.

"I'll do my best."

"We know, that's why you're the one we needed to talk with."

"Can I get hold of you?"

"No, I'll reach out to you. Safer that way."

Our eyes met. "Ah, crap," I said, as I realized what the Chinese guy running around trying to find us, was capable of. "You can't go back."

Crockett's brow knitted. "I'm not finished with the Jesters yet, nor with Garrison."

"That guy," I thumbed toward the door. "He knew who he was looking for, but was it me, or was it you? And he potentially saw us together."

"I wasn't planning on waltzing back into the club house without putting some feelers out first, Iverson." He smiled. "I always check which way the wind is blowing. I've been doing this a long time."

"You must have a cast iron gut and titanium nerves."

"I'll be in touch."

Chapter Twenty-nine
Trust Yourself

I dropped my sunglasses over my eyes as I walked out of Te Papa. It was cold, but not freezing, and the clear blue sky over head promised no rain. Spring in Wellington seemed okay so far. I'd heard that the weather could be changeable all the way through to the start of summer in December. I zipped my jacket up, as a gust of frigid wind caught me by surprise, on my walk along the waterfront to the hotel. If the wind keeps up, I'll be changing my mind about Wellington in the spring. People meandered along in small groups. The occasional runner passed me. No one seemed in much of a hurry. Sun glistened off the water in the harbor. I threaded my way through a group of people, tourist-types, all gathered in a large group stretched across the walkway.

"Sorry, excuse me," I said, squeezing past a man, no taller than me.

He smiled, looked away, and pressed something into my hand. I didn't look and kept moving. Instead of walking along the waterfront, I turned and made my way to the street. Among the noise of traffic and bustle of people, it was easy to vanish. I paused and looked into a large store window. Busy inside. Perfect. I pushed the door open and began the task of browsing for clothing.

Clothes shopping is my least favorite form of shopping. Out of view of the street, I looked at the piece of paper curled in my palm. An address and two words: Fake sable.

I added it to my phone and a map appeared. It was a shop two streets away.

I called Kurt.

"I'm meeting someone ... I'll send the address."

"What's it about?"

"No idea. Was passed a slip of paper with an address."

"How'd it go with your last meeting?"

"Yeah, okay. Fill you in when I get back to the hotel."

"And Fran?"

I glanced at my watch. Shit. I was supposed to be at her place in an hour. "Might end up going straight to Fran's. Meet me there?"

"Sure, I'll bring Lee and Dane. They've taken a drive out to locate the first place of interest."

"Track me."

"Of course. Text the address and I'll watch. If you need back up, yell."

By yell, he meant text our prearranged safety word.

"Of course."

I checked the map and left the store.

The address was a fabric shop. Made sense if I wanted fake sable. Still weird though, but whatever. I walked through the open door.

A retail assistant looked up, her passive expression matched her tired words, "Can I help you with something today?"

"Not sure. I was given this address. Perhaps I have the wrong shop." I glanced at the fabric displays. I couldn't see any fur.

"What is it you are looking for?"

"Fake sable."

"I see. We keep the fur out the back, even the fake fur." She waved toward the rear of the store. "People are funny about fur these days."

True. I followed her across the store, through a doorway, and down a short corridor. She knocked once. A Russian male voice called out, "*Voyti*." Enter.

Fascinating.

She opened the door for me and indicated for me to enter.

My hand held my phone in my pocket ready to press the panic button. Panic text really.

An imposing looking man in a black suit, sat behind a large desk. He nodded at me.

"*Chto ya mogu sdelat' dlya Federal'nogo byuro rassledovaniy?*" What can I do for the Federal Bureau of Investigation?

He pointed to a chair next to his desk. Okay, I'll play. I sat.

Memories surfaced of long conversations with Misha Praskovya, and his patience with me as he helped me learn his mother tongue.

"A man passed me a note with this address on it. *Ty zval menya.*" You called me.

"*Vozmozhno ya sdelal.*" Maybe I did.

My eyebrows rose. "*U menya net vremeni na igry. Chego ty khochesh'?*" I don't have time for games. What do you want?

"*Pochemu odin iz luchshikh agentov FBR v Novoy Zelandii?*" Why is one of the best FBI agents in New Zealand?

Compliments. Unexpected and alien. I sized the man up for a moment. In my mind, I opened a manilla folder that contained everything I knew about Misha Praskovya's colleagues, and also photos he had shown me over the years. Mentally flipping through the photos, I placed the man behind the desk and replied with care, "That is quite a compliment. *YA v otpuske.*" I am on vacation.

"*Ty znayesh' kto ya?*" You know who I am?

"*Da. Josef Baranov.*" Yes. Josef Baranov.

"*Khorosho.*" Good.

"Why did you want to see me?"

He frowned. I dredged up more Russian and asked my question again, "*Pochemu ty khochesh' menya uvidet'?*"

"*Vy vstretili avstraliytsa v muzeye.*" You met an Australian at the museum.

Imagine my total lack of surprise at discovering I was being watched? Then multiply it by a hundred. Everyone is always watching everyone. Especially now.

"You have someone watching me."

"Kak obespokoyennyy drug." Like a worried friend.

Yeah right. Many thoughts converged, but the loudest of all was the one that told me Misha's death had something to do with what's happening now. And the Russians dropped the ball. Butter fingers. He died in a laboratory explosion right when the Qu Pathogen became a problem. Could I prove it was linked? No. But I couldn't prove it wasn't either.

I opened my mouth and the words fell, "Perhaps if you had shown more concern for Misha Praskovya's death, we wouldn't be on the verge of annihilation now."

His eyes narrowed. *"Chto eto oboznachayet?"* What does that mean?

I said it again, this time using his mother tongue, *"Vozmozhno, yesli by vy proyavili bol'she bespokoystva po povodu smerti Mishi Praskov'i, my by seychas ne byli na grani unichtozheniya."*

He stiffened. His shoulders squared. He slowly shook his head.

"It means you sat on your hands and did nothing, and we're all in danger." I made direct eye contact with Josef. "Misha Praskovya was my friend and colleague. I believe his death is related to the manufacture of Qu Pathogen."

His eyebrows rose. *"U vas yest' dokazatel'stva?"* Do you have any evidence?

"Net." No.

Surprise registered on his face. He didn't look so scary when surprised. *"I vse zhe vy govorite, chto yego smert' proizoshla iz-za etogo vozbuditelya?"* And yet you say his death was due to the pathogen?

I shrugged.

"You wanted me to come here, remember?"

"Vozmozhno, ya khotel luchshe ponyat', chto vy delayete?" Perhaps I wanted to better understand what you are doing? He sighed and spoke English. "I did not expect you to blame me."

"I told you why I was here." I pushed my rising anger down. "I did not expect Misha to die for nothing." A puff of air blew over my lips as I attempted calm. *"Vyyasnit', pochemu Misha byl ubit, pomozhet nam oboim."* Finding out why Misha was killed will help both of us.

His head shook. *"Nam ne nuzhna vasha pomoshch'."* We do not need your help.

"Okay." I stood, smoothed my jacket, and gave him a quick smile. *"Spasibo za to, chto vyslushal menya."* Thank you for listening to me.

What the actual fuck did he want? What was the point? I spun and headed for the door. Enough time wasted for one day. I had vials of Qu17P to deliver to Tahoma.

Before I could grasp the door handle, his voice called out, *"Podozhdite."* Wait.

I turned to face him. *"Za chto?"* For what?

"Skazhite, pochemu vy tak daleko ot doma i

pochemu cherez vosemnadtsat' mesyatsev vas interesuyet bezvremennaya smert' ofitsera Praskov'i?" Tell me, why are you so far from home and why, after eighteen months, are you interested in the untimely death of Officer Praskovya?

I held my hand up while I tried to translate his words. Maybe I was tired, it was getting harder and harder to keep up.

Why was I interested in Misha's death? Because this is starting to feel like genocide, and anyone who doesn't fit the 'One China' directive has their head on the chopping block. I jammed that thought deep into my gut. And rallied something easier to translate into Russian.

"YA ustal zhdat' otvetov." I'm tired of waiting for answers.

"Agent Ayverson, udovletvori moye lyubopytstvo." Agent Iverson, Satisfy my curiosity.

"Yest' li v Rossii laboratorii, rabotayushchiye nad vaktsinami dlya Qu17P?" Are there any laboratories in Russia working on vaccine for Qu17P?

He cocked his head slightly to the left. It'd be bird-like if he wasn't such a brawny man. Instead of a bird, he was more like a curious bear. Capable of swiping me off the face of the earth with one giant paw.

"Russia is a big country. Watching scientists is not my business."

I walked back to the desk and sat in the chair. "It's not my business either, Josef. But it is important. This is not about Russia, America, or New Zealand." This is about the continuation of life. I paused and let that sink in for a moment. Then continued, *"Dzhozef, mne nuzhen kollega, a ne tot, kto boitsya ispachkat' ruki."* Josef, I need a colleague, not someone who is afraid to get their hands dirty. His expression remained blank. *"Yesli ty ne khochesh' pomoch', ya seychas uydu."* If you don't want to help, I will leave now.

My mind scrambled over the translations and thoughts, making sure I was saying what I thought I was saying. I was fucking tired of speaking and thinking Russian.

"Ya etogo ne govoril." I did not say that.

Actually, you did say you didn't want my help, which implies you don't want to help me, but whatever and whatnot. I opened photos on my phone, clicked on the photo I'd snapped of the Asian at the museum. I had nothing to lose so I passed him my phone.

"Ty znayesh' etogo cheloveka?" Do you know this person?

He looked at the image for too long. I knew he recognized the man. His eyes lifted slowly from the phone to me.

"Kitayskiy shpion." Chinese spy.

Okay, enough Russian. My head was starting to ache in a way that warned me of impending doom and disaster. "Can we speak English please?"

He nodded, his accent wrapped snuggly around English words, "What do you need from me, Ellie

Iverson?"

"Help me find that man." I took the phone from Josef.

His face twisted into half a smile. "He will find you before you find him."

"Josef, we need to work together."

"Your president does not like that situation."

I swallowed hard. "I'm aware." He also doesn't understand how wind works, or what windmills do. And thinks disinfectant injections might kill viruses, so, there's that. Maybe someone should tie him to a windmill and give him a disinfectant injection before he starts tweeting about something else.

I reeled my conscious thoughts back. Don't go there. You've got a job to do.

"Doesn't change the fact that we need to work together to stop the spread of Qu17P. I can't do this alone, and there aren't that many people left that I trust."

He pointed to himself. "And you trust a man you met fifteen minutes ago?"

"I trusted Misha Praskovya with my life and the life of my children. You were his commanding officer for fifteen years, and he trusted you."

You get my trust by default.

"Mrs. Iverson, I know who you are very well." His mouth twisted sideways. "For many years I watch you work. I see the kind of people that ..." he circled his hand above his desk. "Surround, that is the word?"

I nodded. "I think so."

"The people that surround you are admirable. I see that you have no tolerance for corruption and ..." he paused again. *"Vran'ye."* Lies.

"You see a lot."

"You and the Delta team are of interest to the FSB for over twelve years."

Well, that can't be a good thing.

"I didn't know I was so captivating."

Josef opened his desk and withdrew a piece of paper. He lay it carefully on the polished wooden surface and pushed it to me. It was an image from a security camera. Peter Cooper.

"This man arrived Wellington late last night. You know him?"

"He is Peter Cooper. CIA."

Josef nodded. "He is worthy man."

"Is that a question or a statement?"

"We know Peter Cooper. It is statement."

I was beginning to think that way myself but couldn't quite make it fit. Why was Cooper here?

"Okay."

Josef produced another sheet of paper from his desk. He lay it face down, his hand on top of it. "This is something you must know. We did not do this. This is something we uncovered a few years ago and have monitored."

My stomach dropped. What now?

I steeled myself for what was to come. Josef turned

the paper over. Two photographs. Debbie Barnes and Michael Addison.

So, the Russians knew before we did. Nice. If the channels of cooperation hadn't been muddied by the latest administration, maybe they would've shared earlier. I pushed that away. We don't know that. Just leave it.

"And?" I said, hoping my single word answer didn't giveaway that I suspected Debbie of being a double agent.

"This persons." His brow wrinkled. "What is this?"

"Transgender."

He nodded. "This persons, they, have secrets."

"Most people do, Josef. What secret in particular?"

My gut twisted.

"A man called Lui Jin made contact with the lady person over five years ago."

"Perhaps they're friends."

He frowned at me. "Friends do not ask other friends to reveal FBI files."

"And you knew about this for all this time and said nothing ..." That's not very friendly.

"It didn't suit us to offer information."

That was brutally honest.

"Why now?"

"Things have changed. You should know the events that led to Agent Jackson's death were started by one of your own."

Freezing cold thickened my blood and stopped my

heart. With a bang it all came back. Even when I suspected Debbie of working with the Chinese, I didn't let myself think of the real consequences to us, to Delta. I didn't allow myself to connect those dots. Not those ones. I couldn't do that and be in the same room with her.

"Josef, I know about Debbie. We worked it out but had no proof. Do you have proof?"

He produced a flash drive and passed it to me. "Our surveillance."

Fuck. Shit. Fuck. Shit.

I closed my hand around the small drive. "What is it?"

"Audio and video. Spanning six years."

"Thank you." What else could I say. I needed to sit down somewhere safe and view the files, and then work out how to use them. I couldn't very well say I was handed them by a Russian spy. Or maybe I could.

"In the spirit of cooperation and preventing world-wide deaths, I will help you."

Wow.

"Thank you again. How much will this cost me?"

He shook his head. "For Misha."

Josef rose to his feet, slowly. He walked around the expansive desk and held out his hand. We shook. My hand disappeared into his large warm hand. Before letting me go, he held me closer, and kissed both my cheeks. "It is a pleasure to meet you, Mrs. Iverson."

"And you, Mister Baranov."

I shoved the flash drive deep into my pocket. From another pocket I took a card and handed it to Josef. "Easier if you can contact me directly."

He too produced a card from a pocket, but it was an inside pocket of his suit jacket. "Private numbers," he said, pressing the card into my hand.

"Thank you. I'll be in touch."

I walked away thinking how strange life was and how much kinder it felt now we could shake hands and greet each other in time honored fashion once again.

Chapter Thirty
In the City

I rang Kurt's cell phone. "Hey, I'm going to Fran's. There are developments. Bring my laptop please."

"Okay, be there soon. You okay?"

"Let's say yes for now."

"Iverson ..."

"See ya soon."

I jumped in the first taxi I saw and gave the driver the address. Was much easier using cabs in Wellington than this driving on the wrong side of the road palaver. Too many years driving like an American made being a driver in the Southern Hemisphere a little dodgy. I paid the driver and climbed out of the car. The view, from the hill Fran lived on, was magnificent. The house overlooked the harbor. I took a breath of cool clean air and let it wash through me for a moment, before walking down the path and knocking on the white-painted front door. Fran swung the door wide. Warmth hit me.

"Come on in, it's chilly out," she said. "I've got the wood-burner on."

"Wood-burner?"

"Fire, we don't have open fireplaces anymore. Not heat efficient."

"Okay, then. But it's not that cold, is it?"

She laughed. "It will be later, and better to keep the house warm than let it cool right off."

"Kitchen or living room?"

"Kitchen," I said. "I like kitchens."

She nodded and led the way. "Me, too."

Sun bathed the kitchen via large windows. The whole house was cozy, but the kitchen was warmly inviting. Pale wooden counter tops, with soft cream-colored walls and cabinetry, some of the higher cabinets had glass doors displaying fine china in a range of pastel blues, greens, and pinks. A large, functional, rectangular polished pine table sat in the middle of the expansive room.

I settled into a straight-backed wooden chair at Fran's kitchen table, and carefully removed the small box from my bag. "Do you have a nice cool cabinet this could rest in?"

"And it is?"

"Lethal ... both vaccines that the Chinese are developing for Qu17P."

"Shouldn't that be helpful, not lethal?"

You'd think. I lifted my chin. "Yes indeed, but it's not helpful, and it very much is lethal."

"Fridge?"

"Nope, just somewhere not too warm."

She took the small box and placed it in the pantry on a low shelf. "It'll be safe there."

"Thanks, now, who do we trust in the New Zealand police?"

"I want to say the entire police force, but I didn't come down in the last shower."

"Good answer."

"Let's limit this to my partner, Rawiri Rakete, and keep it out of the station as much as possible."

"All right." I took the flash drive from my pocket. "When Kurt arrives, I'll need to look at this, but until then, I have a new Russian contact who is willing to help us."

"Here in New Zealand?"

"Yes. Though I'd prefer him to be back in Russia. There is a lab situation I'd like him to look at."

"Okay. You said before you arrived that there was a lab here? Do you know where?"

Our sources pointed to a suburb of Upper Hutt. "Upper Hutt."

"Surveillance?"

"Lee and Dane are doing recon today. Serious full-time surveillance would be helpful." I chewed my lip and looked at the closed pantry door. "I'd like to hit all known labs at once - in all countries."

"Without anyone but the team having prior knowledge."

"You got it."

"Can we do that?"

"We're going to be spread pretty thin and will need police cooperation, but yeah, we can." I crossed my fingers. A covert operation spanning at least two, but possibly four, countries with only us knowing exactly what was happening, and why things were exploding. Sure, why not? That's right, Pollyanna. We got this. I also needed to confirm with Tahoma that exploding the lab would kill the pathogen. Not all nasty germs died in fires, some were fireproof little delights.

Fran rose from her seat at the sound of footsteps on the path outside the window.

"Expecting someone?"

"No," she replied, moving closer to the window and peering out the net curtains. "Dark haired male about to knock on the door."

Kurt wasn't dark-haired, so it wasn't him. I slid my Glock from my holster.

Fran smiled. "I forgot you were armed."

We looked at each other when there was a light knock on the front door. I whispered, "Answer the door."

She walked across the room and down the hallway. I followed. Another knock. This time a little firmer. Fran twisted the deadlock and the door handle simultaneously. She opened the door still holding onto it.

"Hello. How can I help?" she asked, her tone pleasant. "If it's religion your peddling you can toddle off."

A voice I recognized replied, "I'm looking for Ellie Iverson."

"And you are?"

"Cooper, Peter Cooper," I said, from behind Fran.

"He's CIA, and a long way from home."

She swung the door wide and I stepped forward. "Why are you here?" I asked, as I grabbed his arm and drew him over the doorstep. Fran closed the door and snipped the deadbolt.

"Hello, Ellie," Peter said, dusting himself off theatrically the second I let his arm go. "Is this how you treat all your guests?"

"Shut it, Cooper. You're not a guest, you're an interloper." I holstered my weapon.

Fran herded him into the kitchen. She stopped by the table and offered him her hand. "I'm Fran."

"Detective," Cooper replied, shaking her hand before sitting at the table. "I've heard about you." My eyes rolled all by themselves. Of course, he had. "Your skills are wasted in the police department."

"So, people like you tell me," Fran responded with a touch of abrasion. "Now what are you doing in my home?"

"You invited me in," he quipped.

"Always with the wise cracks, Cooper," I said with a growl.

"There's a situation," he replied.

"Yeah, we're a bit screwed mate," Fran said. "Next you'll be telling me you're here to save the world."

I buried a smirk inside a yawn. "Tiresome Cooper. Does Tierney know you're here?"

He blinked and lifted his brow. Of course, he did.

"Have you met anyone significant since arriving in

this beautiful country?" Cooper addressed me by turning his head a fraction.

I countered his question with a look of confusion. "What do you mean?"

"Anyone offering help?"

"No."

My fingers crossed behind my back. Technically it was on the edge of truth. Crocker was working deep cover and had his own shit to deal with, and Josef, well, he was an unknown, unproven, potential ally.

"How are you planning on handling the next phase?"

"We're still gathering intel. How about I let you know, later. Where are you staying?"

A smile broke his face in two. Neither half matched.

"That thing your face is doing, stop it, it's scary," Fran said, pointing at his face. "Looks a bit like constipation. You a bit out of whack from traveling?"

"Not a topic of conversation at many kitchen tables, I'd warrant."

"Welcome to New Zealand," Fran said with a smile. "Can I get you a coffee."

Coffee makes ya poop.

Relief registered on his features. "For a moment I thought you were going to offer me prune juice."

Fran laughed. "All out, just coffee, tea and perhaps ..." She opened a canister on the table. "Milo. Yes, Milo."

Cooper and I made eye contact. My eyebrows scrunched in the middle to match his.

"Milo ..." A memory lurched from the part of my childhood spent in New Zealand, bringing with it the deliciousness of malted chocolate. "Malty chocolate goodness in a mug. Yes, please, to the Milo."

"Make that two, I'm intrigued," Cooper said.

"I ordered Milo from Amazon once. It was a can of disappointment," I said.

"Probably Australian rather than ours," Fran said, and scooped heaped teaspoonfuls of Milo into mugs, then topped them off with hot milk. "Theirs isn't as delicious. Never could figure out what was wrong with it, but it doesn't taste right - not as malty perhaps."

Fran passed me a mug. The first sip transported me into my childhood. Back when my biggest worry was whether mom would keep her shit together long enough to make dinner for me and my little brother. None of this save the world bullshit, I just had to save Aidan from mom. Those were the days.

Carefree, hazy days of youth.

Nothing was said as we enjoyed the Milo. Everyone had their own thoughts, and mine were not ones I wanted to share. My fucked-up childhood was best kept under wraps.

My phone buzzed with a message from Kurt.

Henderson: Be there in five minutes.
SAC Iverson: Peter Cooper is here.
Henderson: Friend or Foe?
SAC Iverson: I'm leaning toward friend,

but with an open mind.

I placed my phone face down on the table.

"Delta A are incoming," I said.

"Good," Cooper replied. "I would very much like to meet our team."

"Presumptuous," I said. "My team."

Fran interjected, "Let me give you a piece of advice, Cooper. Always blow on the pie."

Cooper shot me a look of utter confusion. Me too, pal. Had a feeling we'd both understand what Fran was saying one day.

* * *

Cooper went on a coffee and burger run. I asked him to get enough burgers and fries for the six of us, as Delta would be here by the time he returned. I gave him our coffee order as well, stopping short of ordering Dane a low-fat triple shot soy latte with cinnamon and extra foam. It would've amused me, just to hear Cooper order it. Instead, Dane got his usual black coffee. I opted for beef burgers with *everything* for everyone. Easy peasy. Fran agreed that was easiest and assured us that the closest burger joint to her made the best burgers ever. That was where we sent Cooper the interloper.

I got comfortable with my laptop and checked messages and email. Time consuming at the best of times, but even more so with so much going on. Delta B and C were self-governing under Caine's semi-watchful eye, so I didn't have them to worry about, too much. My concern was more for the high-stakes crazy that surrounded the Qu17P adventure we were on.

Utilizing private email, not FBI email, meant I had to remember to check it regularly. Fran worked quietly on the other side of the table. She was working from home to help us. She spoke, "Hey, my partner, Rawiri, will join us later tonight. He's wrapping up paperwork on a serial burglary we were working."

"Excellent. What happened about those families who were suddenly taken ill?"

"Food poisoning from a local Thai takeaway."

"Glad we opted for burgers."

"Me, too."

I opened an email from Josef. Fast work. I didn't expect to hear from him so quickly.

"Fran ..." I stared in disbelief at an image on my screen sent via the email. Holy thermo-nuclear pie filling. Mac. Why the actual fuck would Josef send me a photo of Mac?

"Un huh?" She looked over from where she was working on her laptop. "What's up?"

"You knew my first husband, right?"

A frown creased her forehead. She fiddled with the gold sleeper earring in her left ear. "Are you talking about Mac Connelly?"

I nodded. "I am. I know he was working down here

before we met." I knew that, even though he never told me, and was happily lying about his life as a stockbroker. I knew, because after his death, when his twin brother caused all manner of shit, and came out of the dark, Tierney told me the truth at the behest of our Director. The memory of meeting Chad, and how much he resembled Mac, burned over the memory of my teenage daughter's death. Flames raged. Chance ran in with a fire extinguisher. He squeezed the trigger enveloping me in foam. Gave me a thumbs up and disappeared. I wiped white foam from my clothes and shook it off my hands. Big globs of it landed on the table. Some slid down my laptop screen. I swished it away.

Mac was still there.

"Where are we going with this?" Fran said. "Because this is old news and it will do no one any good to revisit it." She lifted her eyes up to see me. "You all right?"

"Yeah. Nah. Come and look at this."

She pushed her chair back and came over. Fran peered over my shoulder. "It's been a long time ... but that looks like Mac Connelly when I knew him."

"He didn't look any different when I knew him either really." I enlarged the photo to read writing on a signpost in the distance. "Cuba Street."

"Look at the area." Fran pointed to the shops behind Mac. "It's definitely here and definitely Cuba Street, but not now, this is an old image."

That was comforting. Don't think I could handle him

returning from the dead.

"How old?" I wanted to know if it was Mac or his brother Chad. The mess that was that family, tightened into a knot in my stomach.

Fran looked thoughtful for a moment as she sat in a chair next to me. She tugged the elastic tie from her short ponytail, smoothed wayward strands, and re-tied the ponytail. "I'm going to say about fifteen years ago."

"And I'm going to say it's Mac and not his twin Chad," I said, adding a dismissive-do-not-want-to-go-there tone to my words.

"But why would Josef send it to you now?"

I shut the file and opened the email it arrived in and looked at the size of the attached image. It didn't appear any bigger than I expected it to be. I read the email again. Okay, I got it now.

"He sent it because the image contains something I need to see, not immediately visible." Man, I wished Sandra was with me to work her magical powers and open whatever the image contained. A voice that sounded very like Christopher Chance, filled my mind, "Come on, El, you can do this, you've seen her do it enough times."

"Yeah I can."

"What?" Fran grinned at me. "Talking to yourself?"

Yeah, let's go with that. I smiled back and searched my computer for OpenPuff. No clue if that's what was used, but I knew how to use that software, without waking Sandra in the middle of the night and sending her the image to crack for me.

Two minutes later I made a guess at a possible password and the image revealed its secret contents.

"Holy shitballs, Batman," I said, as I tapped a link inside the image, and it sent me to a secure site. I used the same password as before, and the screen changed to a video. I pressed play.

"What is this?" Fran asked, as we watched Mac walk across the floor of what looked like a warehouse.

"Dunno. Old security cam feed from somewhere."

It was definitely Mac, that was his walk, I'd recognize it anywhere, no matter how much time passed. He walked to huge double doors, opened one, then the other. Another man walked in from a loading dock. Yeah, that's what it was. A truck backed up. The other male was of interest. I fiddled around with the video controls and discovered I could zoom in on parts of the screen. I zoomed in and took a screenshot of the man's face, opening it on the right of my screen. I paused the video. And stared at the familiar face of Sean O'Hare.

"Who is he?" Fran asked.

"You haven't met?"

She shook her head. "He's not bad looking, and I'd remember meeting him."

"He is Sean O'Hare. Owns O'Hare Security in the States. His company is almost a private army." I could feel an inkling begin as soon as I mentioned his company. I knew it was something usable. On the large hessian pin board in my mind, I stuck a big red pin in the words 'O'Hare Security'.

"Tell me more about the hunky looking Sean O'Hare," Fran said, licking her lips.

"Apart from the bad boy vibe he cultivates and drops all over the place?"

"Yeah, his company does what?"

"Quick low down. He started out monitoring and installing alarms, then he added Close Protection Details and scene guards. All his employees are ex-military or ex-SWAT. Last conversation we had, was about some of his people doing protection work over in Iran and Saudi Arabia. He has people protecting all types of US citizens all over the world. He's also the brother of our deceased Director, and a close friend." I swallowed. "He lived in Christchurch for a while, once upon a time. I'm guessing while this whatever-the-hell-it-is was going on." I waved a hand at the screen. "He's been a friend for a lot of years and never once did he mention being in New Zealand with Mac. Not fucking once." He'd keep. I was sure I'd get a chance to have a long in-depth conversation with Sean O'Hare. I scrabbled over the contents of my mind regarding Mac and Sean. Everything twisted into a vortex of bullshit. What did Sean tell me right before Carla died?

I fell into the moment and remembered hearing Sean tell me that Mac was agency well before he met me, and supposedly went through Quantico to become an FBI agent. The secrets we bury eventually come to light. The conversation spiraled around me, but at no point did Sean say he was working with Mac anywhere. He told me Mac was working on a long running CIA operation when he died, and I thought he was working with me. I thought my husband was FBI. The lies were deep.

I didn't know him at all.

I pressed play again. Sean and Mac walked into the back of the truck and began unloading boxes. They didn't look heavy. We watched them take twelve boxes into the warehouse and stack them. The edge of the driver's door was just visible so I figured it was open. A man emerged and climbed up on the loading dock. I zoomed in, took a screenshot, and managed to get his face. Asian-looking guy. I took a closer look. I'd seen him before. He killed Hardcastle. He was the man I saw when I talked to Hardcastle's dead body. Let's not say that out loud to someone who hasn't come across my weird shit before. That means Sean knows who this guy is.

"Who is he?" Fran asked, pointing to the Asian dude.

"A bad, bad man," I said. "But now I know someone who can give me a name and maybe a bit more about this guy. Pretty sure he's Chinese."

I pressed play again. The Chinese male shook Mac's hand. They spoke briefly. Sean then stepped closer and shook his hand. A short conversation ensued, then the driver got back in the truck and left. Sean definitely knows the guy. He shook his hand. He'll have a name, and possibly more than that.

The video finished as Sean and Mac closed the doors and locked them.

"That was strange," Fran said, shaking her head at the screen.

I took Josef's card from my pocket and called the number on the bottom.

"It's me, *spasibo*." Thank you.

"Expect a visitor."

He hung up.

I leaned back in my chair. Expect a visitor? Yeah, all right. Fran moved a chair next to mine and sat down. For a split second I wondered how he'd known where I was. A chuckle escaped.

"What's funny?" Fran asked, as she stared at the frozen image on my screen. Sean and Mac standing by the closed warehouse doors.

"Me being naïve. For a hot second I thought no one knows where I am unless I've told them."

"That is pretty funny."

"I know, right?"

"What was that we watched?" Fran pointed at the screen as she stood and went back to her computer.

"Undercover operation, I guess, maybe a joint one, or maybe one the Russian's were watching. Either way, I get the feeling they haven't been able to ID the Chinese male, and they know I can, and that they can now ask."

"Why is he so important?"

"Don't know why from the Russian perspective, but he killed a scientist in Virginia."

"Could he be here?"

"I'd say so, there was a Chinese man who appeared to be chasing me at Te Papa." But it wasn't him. I would've recognized him. "This image was taken, you think fifteen years ago, so this man has probably moved up the food chain since then. I think he's an assassin, but I'm sure the Chinese wouldn't cop to that."

"What do you think that operation was about?" She waved a hand at my laptop. "A warehouse and a delivery. What's in those boxes?"

I shrugged. "No clue, but I'm going to ask when I get the opportunity." Questions are piling up. And Sean is someone I really want to have a sit-down chat with.

Josef's comment popped back up. Expect a visitor. Could that be the other reason I needed to see the video? I doubt the ghost of my first husband will turn up. Sean then? Or the Chinese assassin. Or Josef himself. I hoped it was Sean. I could tell when Sean was holding something back, or outright lying. Known him long enough to know his tells. That was a perk. And I didn't feel like taking on a Chinese assassin today.

Someone knocked at the door. I jumped. Fran startled. Neither of us heard footsteps approach. My weapon was in my hand before Fran moved to answer the knock. I followed her to the door. Through the frosted glass I saw two tall shapes and a taller darkness behind one. Kurt, Dane, and Lee behind them, was my guess.

Fran looked from me to the door. "Look like they belong to you."

"Sure do," I replied, keeping the weapon in my hand. She opened the door.

Kurt and Dane smiled. I holstered my weapon.

"We made it," Lee said from the back, then spun around as footsteps approached.

"I come in peace, bearing offerings of food and coffee," Cooper said, as Lee stepped forward to challenge his presence.

"All right then," Lee said, low and quiet. "The things that are dragged up halfway around the world ..."

"Davenport, isn't it?" Cooper said, lifting a paper bag full of burgers in one hand, and a large tray of coffee in the other. "We're on the same side, and as I said, I come bearing sustenance."

"Guess the same side thing depends on what's in the bag," Lee said, his tone changed to moderately friendly.

"Come on in," Fran said with a warm smile. "It's nice to see you *all*, welcome to my humble abode."

Much shuffling and reorganizing took place in the kitchen. Lucky Fran had a decent sized table that seated six. Fran and I moved our laptops to the safety of the kitchen counter. Food was spread around. The atmosphere hung on the fringe of convivial. I could live with that. Better than it being cold and distrustful.

Chapter Thirty-one
Old Time Rock and Roll

By the time we'd finished our meal, everyone was getting along-ish. Best description really. Tahoma and Karen would be on their flight to Auckland. I still needed to get the evidence to Auckland for Tahoma's arrival. Time to have a word with Kurt, that kinda thing was in his wheelhouse and he'd know the best way to proceed. I motioned to Kurt. He followed me into the living room, making sure no one else followed along.

"I have the vaccines. Both of them. Or at least samples of them. The ones that they're using to 'vaccinate' people with, then give them a booster and watch them die."

"I'm sorry what?"

"Intel from ASIO, they had a spy defect, he had a tale to tell about the supposed vaccines for Qu17P."

"This is what he shared when you met at the museum?"

"Yes. That and more." We sat on the sofa, and I filled him in on everything Crockett told me.

"That makes everything more exciting," Kurt said, when I finished.

"Yeah, let's call it that."

Kurt dropped his voice, "I take it Cooper doesn't know about the vaccines you have?"

"Only you and Fran know about them."

"Seems the best way to play this for now." He leaned closer. "What else happened?"

"Misha's commanding officer, happened."

"That's a story I need to hear."

I filled him in, then told him about the flash drive and the video, and that he said to expect a visitor.

"Crafty bastard, couldn't just say who, then?"

"Apparently the cloak and dagger thing is more fun." It kinda was, to be honest. But I was all funned out.

"So who is the visitor? Was it Cooper he was talking about?"

"Don't think so, he told me Cooper was in Wellington when I met him. He said to expect a visitor after I thanked him for the video."

I handed Kurt my phone with the photo I'd snapped of the Chinese guy talking with Sean and Mac.

"Wow. That's proof positive that Mac was involved in something with a group of alphabet letters prior to you meeting him."

He was smack in the middle of the alphabet soup.

"Sure is." Also proof that Sean knows more than he's ever said.

"Sean can identify this male ..."

"Yeah."

"And it's not the guy you saw in the museum?"

I shook my head. "No, it's the guy who killed Hardcastle."

Kurt swallowed hard. "One hundred percent?"

"Yep."

He passed the phone to me, and I dropped it in my lap. Kurt and I leaned back on the sofa. "Guess we wait to see who shows up next?" he said, releasing his weapon from his holster doing a quick press check then setting the weapon on the side table within easy reach.

That's exactly how I felt. Jumpy as cat on a hot tin roof.

"We need to talk to Dane and Lee," I said. "I don't want anyone unaware with the Chinese chasing us around town. The guy at the museum was an assassin according to Josef."

Assassin. Had a finality to it. Grace's giggle hit me full force reminding me how much life I still had to live. That's a big no to any assassination attempt on my life, thanks.

"Can we trust Cooper?"

"Don't think we have a choice now." I closed my eyes and kept them shut while I spoke, quietly. "Debbie Barnes and Michael Addison were turned by the Chinese five years ago. Josef gave me a flash drive with surveillance photos and videos and audio tracks. I haven't looked at it yet. I need to, but that's best done at the hotel, after Lee's swept the room." My eye lids lifted, but the sense of disappointment did not.

"You okay?"

"Sure, why wouldn't I be?"

"Because you have a relationship. You're friends."

"And she did what others before her have done.

Trust no one, Kurt, you know how it goes."

"All for one ..."

"And one for all."

"Us, El, always us."

Yeah. Always. Us. I handed Kurt the flash drive. "Hold on to it." He put it in his inside suit jacket pocket without a word.

My phone buzzed and flashed like a demented Christmas decoration. I checked it before answering and showed Kurt the caller's name.

A video call from Sean O'Hare. Surprise, surprise.

I answered, holding the phone up so he could see me, but not Kurt. "Sean, what can I do for you?"

He didn't look happy.

"Tell me where you are."

"Helping someone with an unexpected death and illness case."

"El." His arm jerked, and another man came into view, I got the merest glimpse. "Tell me where you are."

I could see Sean on my phone, but not the other man.

"No. Who is with you?"

"A friend of Karen Schneider's."

Had he found Forberg?

"A close friend?"

"Yes."

"I'll text you."

I closed FaceTime. Sean disappeared. Kurt nudged

me. I ignored him for a moment and texted Sean.

"What?" Kurt said. He stood, picked up his weapon from the table and holstered it. His hand reached for mine. Kurt helped me to my feet with a smile. "I know that look, Iverson. You saw something on the screen."

"Sean has someone with him, and I got the impression he's not in Kansas anymore."

"Who?"

"You heard him say it was a friend of Karen Schneider's."

"I don't really know Schneider well enough to know her friends."

That's right he didn't. He wasn't quarantined with her.

"It could be Forberg."

"And he got him out?"

"I don't know."

"Could he have had him this whole time?"

Quite possibly. We didn't publicly announce we were looking for a Scandinavian scientist named Forberg. I didn't talk to Sean about cases unless I needed his help with scene guards or Close Protection Details, and even then, I didn't give him details. He's not actually one of us.

"Guess we'll find out when he does whatever he's going to do with the address I sent him."

Expect a visitor.

Okay. But, is this the visitor Josef meant, or is that still to be discovered?

The feeling of restlessness flowed through the walls from the kitchen. I sensed Dane wanted to get on with the job, and that he also had information to share.

When we walked into the room, the table was clear of wrappers and coffee cups. Water droplets glistened on the clean surface. Dane rinsed a cloth under the faucet, and Fran wiped the table over with a dish towel. Lee and Cooper were looking out the window. Everyone appeared to be getting along. That would help move things forward.

Kurt and I made eye contact, I moved my head in tiny increments, no. Dane spun around. His eyes glittered in the fading spring sun.

"O'Hare," he said.

Damn. Didn't put the conversation behind a wall and Dane piggy-backed on my thoughts.

"We'll see," I replied, giving him a look that said, 'not now and not here'. He shot me a fast smile.

"Lee?" I said to get his attention.

He turned. "Boss?"

"Tell me what you saw today?"

His eyes flicked to Cooper, then back to me. I nodded.

"Fran have you got a map?"

She tugged a folded paper from an overstuffed drawer. "Yes."

I spread the map out on the table top. Weird using paper, but this way we could all see. We were low-tech until we had this situation controlled and could be back inside a law enforcement office with all the bells and whistles.

"We think the lab manufacturing one of the vaccines is here," Lee said, circling an area on the map. Wallaceville, Upper Hutt. "Ideally, we need a few days for surveillance, but we might have to make do with a couple of trips out that way."

"We have to make do with today and maybe a surveillance drone," I said. "We don't have time for much more than that."

Chapter Thirty-two
It's All Over Now, Baby Blue

I walked out the front door and over to the deep blue Holden sedan waiting at the curb. Sean leaned across the front passenger seat and opened the door for me.

Such a gentleman.

"El," he said, by way of a greeting. "Get in."

I glanced into the back. We were alone. Not what I'd hoped.

"Where is he?" I asked and slid into the passenger seat then pulled the door shut.

"Safe."

The engine roared to life. Sean drove, negotiating the weird driving on the left thing like it was normal. It was not. Ten semi-terrifying minutes later, he drove into a parking lot surrounded by trees.

"Where are we?"

"Botanic gardens. Thought fresh air would be nice."

Did you now?

I said nothing as I checked the area visually before opening my door and climbing out.

"Come on," Sean said. The car beeped as we walked away. "Should be quiet in here, being mid-week and cold."

Was it mid-week? I'd lost all track of time and days. Did that mean I'd missed my babies second birthday or was it this coming weekend? Not helpful.

We fell into step.

"I have questions," I said. "First, is it Forberg you have?"

"Yes."

"Right, I have something eating at me I need to clear up." The whole Debbie Barnes and the facial recognition software thing breached in my mind and seemed like utter and total bullcrap to me. "Do you know anything about some kind of software product he was supposed to have developed? It was a total scam."

"I know he did not develop it and that a group wanted him discredited."

"Gonna need more than that, Sean."

"My people did their own investigation ..." He steered me toward a pathway. "Forberg expressed concern about a line of research using the Qu Pathogen in a laboratory in Germany."

"I know about that."

"When he wouldn't be quiet, measures were taken by the company to discredit him in the eyes of his peers."

"But he's a chemical engineer or scientist. How does that fit with software development, surely his peers would see through that and work out something bad was happening?"

"Yes, but unluckily for him, it was no secret that he was working on a piece of software, and no one knew exactly what it entailed, because he didn't talk about it more than to say it would rock the world."

"What was it?"

"A game."

"You are kidding me?"

"No, a game that allowed players to create viruses and other nasty bugs, and then play God and kill the world."

"Oh, great." I'd seen various forms of those games and always thought they were in poor taste, and now, they definitely were. "Should've just killed him like they did Hardcastle."

"Yes, indeed. I do know that Forberg's death would have triggered an investigation back then, because he was vocal about the research and how dangerous it was." He paused for a moment. "It was a couple of years ago that he was supposedly involved in dodgy software. Whereas Hardcastle's involvement, or at least knowledge of what was happening, was recent."

"Okay. Who is the company?"

"Schroder Forschung."

"Who are they owned by?" I stopped near a park bench and sat down. "You do know?"

Sean sat next to me. "I dug around and the company is owned by The Peoples Republic of China. That was buried deep and took a lot of digging."

"Who created the brochureware to discredit Forberg?"

"The Chinese."

"Did you know Debbie Barnes told me about that

while we were looking for Forberg?"

"No." Sean watched something. I followed his line of sight to see two people walking down a path. "What's wrong?" Sean asked.

"You mean other than the Chinese trying to kill us?"

"Yeah. I'm sensing something closer to home."

"My new Russian friend gave me evidence that Barnes was turned over five years ago."

"I'm sorry El. You've had more than your fair share of that type of bullcrap." He turned his head to me. "New Russian?" Skepticism rang in his voice.

"Misha's former commanding officer."

Sean's steel-gray eyes sparked. "Josef Baranov. He's here?"

"Yes, he is. You know him?"

"By reputation only. Misha and Kennedy had utmost respect for Baranov."

Good to know. Maybe trusting him isn't a mistake.

"You need to keep Forberg under wraps until we finish our job."

"And then?"

"And then re-unite him with CDC Doctor's Karen Schneider and Tahoma Whitehorse. They're either in Auckland at the University for a workshop or arriving there soon."

It occurred to me that Karen wouldn't be that thrilled, but she knew he could help anyone already infected, and we didn't know how many that was.

"I can do that. He's safe. He's with my people and

he'll stay with them until this is over."

"Might pay to leave written instructions."

"Jeez, El, defeatist. Where's the Pollyanna I know and love?"

"She got tired. It's not defeatist, it's practical." I watched someone walk toward us then veer off down another track. "I get a gut twinge the size of Texas every time I think about what we need to do."

"I get it."

Curiosity grew and grew and mingled with what felt like the end of times. Would we win?

"How did you get Forberg out of the US?"

"Ah, I wondered when you'd ask," Sean said with a smile. "When McAlester opened his mouth to Forberg, he reached out, within hours. We had him in Canada weeks before McAlester made his decision and involved the FBI."

That explained why we couldn't find him. It also made the 'last sighting of him on Thursday' bogus. Guess the bad guys couldn't find him either, so in case we did, they wanted him discredited as a scam artist or whatever by one of our own, Barnes. Insidious fuckers are everywhere. Cold bit through my jeans and into my knees. Time to move.

"So, you're onboard?"

"El, what's your favorite saying?"

"I didn't come here to fuck frogs." I smiled. "Now take me back. You need to meet the team."

"You have more than Delta here?"

"Oh, you really need to meet the team." Had a feeling this team was one that needed to be seen, or he wouldn't believe it. We were sinking further into multinational Black Op territory every second. I just wasn't willing to say it out loud.

Sean stood and hauled me to my feet. His arms swallowed me for a second. "Cait would be proud."

I sucked back a tear and pushed him away. "Let's go. We have a job to do."

Chapter Thirty-three
Battle Hymn of The Republic

"When we are finished, you and I are going to have a conversation about how well you knew my former husband. But for now, who is this?" I handed Sean my phone with the old photo of the Asian male.

"Zhang."

"Thanks."

I looked at Kurt and Fran. "What do you do here when someone is wanted?"

"Media release and notify all police, I'm on it," Fran replied typing. "Send me the photo."

I airdropped it to her. "It might not be that easy," I said. "He might have, okay probably does have, the protection of the Chinese Embassy."

"We'll find out when they grab him and deal with it then."

Fair enough. My attention returned to Sean. "Now, Sean, we need people and you have resources."

"Exactly what do you need?"

"Potentially a drone strike without starting World War three."

He gave a small laugh. "If you believe the news, that was supposed to happen already with the death of Iranian General Qasem Soleimani."

"He was lucky to live as long as he did. No world war

just a bunch of sensationalized garbage overshadowed very quickly by a pandemic ..." I shook it off. "But let's not cause a war or fresh pandemic now."

"Deal." Sean smiled, but it stopped short of his steel gray eyes. "Where do you want me?"

"Berlin, Germany."

Josef spoke, "I am helping with St Petersburg, Russia."

"Anywhere else?"

"We really need someone on the ground in Australia. Anyone know a likely candidate?" I glanced around the table.

"Dave Crocker?" Kurt offered.

"I got the impression he was heading back, he's working a job." Shame though, he'd be helpful.

"You don't want much," Sean said, lowering himself into the nearest chair.

"We can't do anything about a lot of things. It's too late for the Congo and Samoa, they were infected with something way nastier than measles. But we can limit this shit. We can destroy the plants creating more evil. We can stop the Chinese threat that's right in front of us."

"I've seen that look in your eye before," Sean said.

"Really?"

Imagine?

"Lookie here, Cait point oh. I'm on board so long as ..."

"Really? Criteria?" A hard laugh hit the table.

He didn't flinch. "So long as ... you go home to those babies of yours when this is over."

That I could do.

"Done." We shook hands. "I mean actually done. I'm out once we stop this."

Let's save the world, one last time.

Sean grinned, this time his eyes lightened to a brighter steel, more stainless in variety. "Whoa, without an argument, and then you add to it? Are you growing up on my watch?"

Yeah. Nah.

I laughed. "We're going to talk later."

Josef passed me his phone with a time stamped photo on the screen. Zhang and the museum guy on Willis Street, fifteen minutes ago. I passed it to Fran. "Can we get these two picked up before they bumble into our operation?"

She typed quickly into what looked like a chat window. Guess they had the same kind of set up we had, direct contact with their teams and whatnot. "All police in the Wellington area are alerted to their presence, and they're marked dangerous."

"Thank you."

What did I need? What did we need? Imaging. We needed clear imaging of the areas we were about to hit. Real time imaging. Satellites. Josef moved in his chair and caught my attention.

"We need real time imaging. Can you help us Josef?"

"*Net*." No.

"Wrong answer."

"How about you, CIA?"

Cooper smiled. "Possibly."

Josef spoke, "Maybe not impossible."

Ah, was that a smidge of rivalry?

"We have multiple scenes to coordinate. The more satellites the better." Or drones. Do we need drones? The answer to that question, is always yes.

"Hey Sean, those drone swarms, swarm drones? Is that a real thing or just something Mitch was talking about?"

"You're talking to the wrong man. Russia was supposedly working on that. Something called Flock-93. Last I heard it was purely conceptual."

"That sounds familiar." Remnants of conversations with Mitch gathered. "That was a kamikaze like swarm, each drone armed with a five-point-five-pound warhead." Sounds delightful. "The question is, is it real, or is it vaporware?"

"Sean is correct," said Josef. "Russia is interested in swarm drones, but controlling more than a hundred drones at once, is not so easy."

"Who was actually working on that?" I said, remembering how interested in it, Mitch was.

"Zhukovsky Air Force Academy and private industry."

Bit more info than I expected considering he was FSB not Air Force. The private industry bit interested me. I made a mental note to talk to Mitch as soon as I could.

"And the tech doesn't exist?"

He shrugged. "We have the Kalashnikov ZALA-KYB. It is attack drone."

"Can we use it if we need it?"

"Perhaps."

"What about you CIA? Can you get us surveillance and the potential to neutralize the threat from the air?"

"You know you're now running a black op, right?" Cooper said. "They will disavow us the second it looks like we've lost control of the op."

Not my first rodeo. I knew the minute I got the coded message via Mike Davenport, that I would end up running a Black op, just didn't know I'd be including foreign nationals in my team.

"And you know you're here, because Tierney wants you here to fucking babysit," I countered.

"He's always had faith in you, but I'm not convinced."

"Fine. Whatever. If it's not something you can do, I'll ask Tierney myself." I suppressed a smile. "If you don't have the authority, you don't have the authority." Guess he wasn't as excellent at his job as Iain Campbell. Hot damn, another massive loss to our out-sourcing ability died with him. Not just a friend and colleague, but a trustworthy man who got shit done. He's going to have to try a bit harder to fill Campbell's shoes.

I rose from the table, rotated my tight shoulders,

and walked away rubbing my neck. Fresh cool air hit me. I'd wandered outside into what amounted to Fran's backyard. A small section of lawn with a rotary clothesline set off center on the left. A shiver ran through me as a gust of wind hit me in the face. The lawn overlooked the harbor. Choppy whitecaps danced in the distance. My thoughts spun around the unfolding apocalyptic disaster. What I wouldn't give to have Iain Campbell, Misha Praskovya, Seamus Kennedy, Sam Jackson, and Stewart Smith, back. Stupid death fucks everything over.

Everything felt sideways, like I couldn't get my footing. Life beyond the walls came into focus. People walking. Cars driving. Life living. I tipped my head from side-to-side in an attempt to loosen my tight muscles.

Life is just a blur of subversion hidden behind a screen of smoke and mirrors. What's the actual point? Why do people always do such horrible things to each other? All the bioterrorism bullshit served to prove, is that there is always funding for terrorism, and evil never sleeps. Qu wasn't as bad as it could've been, but this new version could destroy entire population groups. Genocide disguised as the flu. People suck. This was a fucking disaster and I wanted all my team back. All of them.

A deep velvety voice rumbled within, "Buckle up Buttercup."

Sam.

They're not gone, they just not physical anymore. You can't destroy energy. I've got people around me who want to help. I've got an incorporeal team that can still kick ass. We fucking got this.

Chapter Thirty-four
The Chain

On Kurt's advice, I handed the vials Crockett gave me to Lee and asked him to get them on an urgent courier to Tahoma. Best case scenario, he would have them in about six hours. That gave us six hours to accumulate more intelligence via surveillance and get everything we needed in place for the operation. Coordinating attacks on four locations worldwide, wasn't going to be easy. I needed to run; energy required burning.

"Anyone keen on a run?"

"Yeah," Kurt said. "Come on, you and me. We'll head back to the hotel and pound some southern hemisphere pavement."

Heaven.

I eyed Kurt in his pristine suit and wondered if he packed anything less FBI along with his sweats.

"Everyone else okay with their tasks?" I said, looking from person to person.

Josef's lips tightened across his teeth in what I thought might be a smile. "I will meet you where? There are things I must do."

"Here?" I glanced at Fran, she nodded. "Then here."

Josef nodded. "Here, five hours?"

"Da, does that give you enough time?" I walked with Josef to the front door.

"There is time."

"Five hours. Don't be late." I opened the door for Josef and watched him walk toward the road and his car. When his car door closed, I shut the front door and rejoined those who were left.

Cooper and Rawiri were talking in the kitchen. Dane had gone with Lee to get the vials to Tahoma. Sean was in the living room talking to Fran. Kurt was nowhere to be seen.

"I take it you two have some catching up to do," I said, and sat in an armchair, close to the wood-burner. Flames crackled behind the thick glass. I watched the fire as orange and yellow danced over a hunk of wood. I didn't look up when I felt Fran and Sean's eyes on me. "Kurt and I are heading out in a few minutes."

"Is that wise?" Fran asked. "We don't know if police have picked up Zhang and his mate."

"I need to get out of here. We'll all meet back in five hours. Hopefully by then we'll have everything we need in place." I stood when I heard a toilet flush. Guess that's where Kurt was. "You two carry on catching up. We'll talk about how you know each other. And how you both worked with Mac, later. It can wait."

Kurt called out from the doorway. "Ready, Iverson?"

"Absolutely," I replied, and joined him. I looked over my shoulder at Sean and Fran. "I don't care that you all worked together, but why lie about knowing each other?"

Kurt and I left without saying anything to anyone

else.

The drive to the hotel was uneventful. Kurt opened the hotel room door with his keycard. We were used to sharing space. It was normal for our team to book two rooms not four. I rummaged in my suitcase for my sweats, then changed in the bathroom. When I emerged, Kurt was similarly attired. Instead of academy sweats like we usually wore, we'd both opted for less FBI, more covert. Dark gray, no markings. I jammed a baseball cap on my head. Kurt reached over and flipped it off.

"Hey," I said, leaning down to grab it. Before I could, he stuck a different cap on my head. I looked in the mirror. "Oh." The cap was pink and had no distinguishing marks. He tossed my usual cap onto the dresser with his. They were navy blue with FBI across the back. Yeah. Nah. I took running shoes from my suitcase and put them on, double tying the long laces. Kurt handed me my phone which I put in my sweatpants pocket. Kurt did the same with his.

"Keycard?"

Kurt nodded. "Let's go."

We ran down the stairs and out into the foyer, then the street. Feet pounding pavement felt good. Running while dodging pedestrians was fun. It was just fun. Kurt tapped my arm and motioned to a sign that said: Plimmer Steps. We ran past a bronze statue of a man in a top hat with a small dog skipping beside him at the beginning of the alleyway that led to the steps. At the bottom of the steps we grinned as each other.

"Race ya," I said, taking off a step ahead of Kurt.

Plimmer Steps was a workout. At the top, doubled over, I waited for Kurt to climb the last few steps. Not at all competitive.

"Fun, yeah?" I said, as Kurt panted next to me.

"Jeez," he muttered. "Suppose you want to run down now?"

"Yep," I said, beaming a grin at him. I took off two steps ahead of him. By the time I was halfway down, he was almost with me. At the bottom a hand shot out, grabbed my arm, and twisted me sideways. I spun, still moving forward, taking the hand with me.

"Whoa!"

The voice registered as one I'd heard before. My heart pounded through my chest as I tried to understand what was happening and focus on the face.

A split second later, Kurt's voice rang out. "Let her go!"

I snapped out of the adrenaline rush from the steps, and the abrupt stop. Kurt had a weapon trained on the male. I shoved his hand off my arm and stepped backwards.

"Hey, it's me," he said. "Crockett."

Kurt slowly lowered his arm. "Crockett?"

I took a deep breath to quell the desire to punch him. "What the fuck is your malfunction, Crockett?" His lip twisted into a half a smile. "I thought you were gone."

Kurt's weapon vanished back into his concealed holster. He strode forward. "That was dangerous."

I breathed. Deep and slow.

"Why?" I said, on a slow exhale. "Why, are you here?"

"I want to help."

I looked at him. Black leather well-worn biker jacket, black tee shirt, black jeans, scuffed black boots that looked a lot like a pair of Steel Blues. If they were, then they were heavy boots. I kinda liked that he wore steel caps. Man after my own heart.

"We're running, can you keep up?"

He shrugged one shoulder. "Might attract a bit of attention."

"Might look like you're chasing us," I said with a smile. "So, we're walking then."

I heard a quiet sigh of relief from Kurt. "Henderson has had enough anyway."

He didn't refute my comment. I introduced them properly. There was a brief handshake.

The occasional person took a tiny amount of notice as we made our way along the streets back to the hotel. The thing I liked about Wellington the most, was that the suits were intent on their own thing and not interested in anyone else sharing the sidewalk, as long as no one got in their way.

The three of us walked with our heads on swivel, looking for any sign of trouble. If Crockett followed us, or happened upon us, then unfriendlies could too. I didn't much like the idea of an assassin making a move on a city street.

It was a relief to be back in our hotel room. I hit the shower first. That allowed Kurt some time with Crockett and meant I didn't have to listen to the Crockett story again. It's not that it's a bad story, I just didn't want to hear about the Inferno Jesters and have him explain about that day Seamus and Stewart died, *again*.

By the time I finished in the bathroom, Kurt and Crockett were well acquainted and laughing. Crockett was sitting in our lone armchair. Kurt sat on the end of his bed. For a change we had two singles instead of having to flip coins over who got the double and who got the single.

"Tag you're it," I said to Kurt.

Kurt grinned, and vanished into the bathroom.

I brushed my hair and said, "Thought you were going back to Virginia."

"So did I," Crockett replied. "Change of plans."

"Why?" I tugged the brush through a stubborn knot.

"Garrison."

The brush freed. "Okay, what about him?"

"His mate Bancroft told me not to return."

"They know who you are ..."

"That fucker in the museum must've got a photo of us before we saw him."

That'd be right.

"What happens now?"

"I'm here, that's what happens."

"Inferno Jesters?" I was trying to gauge his usefulness. If he was hiding or running, then whatever he was hiding or running from, was a threat to our operation.

"There's a hefty price on my head. Think I'll stay in New Zealand for a while."

"Will that stop them?"

"Oh, hell no. But it will slow them down. There is no affiliated gang here, and generally speaking, bikers can't travel freely across borders."

Awesome. I imagined they were plenty resourceful, and the difficulty of border crossings wouldn't slow them down for long.

"Okay, whatever you say. Meanwhile - talk to me about Bancroft and Garrison."

"Old high school friends."

"I know that."

"He's on retainer ... him and the firm he works for represent the Richmond chapter of Inferno Jesters."

"Does he know about the kidnapping of Cotton's girlfriend? Does he know what the deal was with Cotton?"

"I imagine so. No doubt it's all tied up in a lawyer client privilege bow."

"No doubt."

We could maybe use it though. I made a mental note to tell Caine then changed my mind. No time like the present.

I threw my hairbrush onto my bed, sat down, grabbed my laptop, and opened it up. One click, and I was in SENTINEL. I added case notes to our current case. The first notes were about Bancroft and Garrison and potential kidnapping, the second notes were about Cotton with a big ol' question mark regarding how much Bancroft knew. I knew Caine well enough to know he'd find a way of confirming and acting. The third note told him to open the attached files. I marked the note 'Caine Grafton's Eyes Only.'

The flash drive from Josef was still in Kurt's suit jacket pocket. His jacket was lying on his bed. I reached over and fished out the flash drive, then stuck it in the USB port on my laptop. It popped up on my screen. I clicked the drive and found it contained audio, video, and document files. The oldest file was dated twenty-fourteen. I chose a document file and opened it.

It was in Russian. Great. My eyes scanned the text looking for familiar words and a jumping off point, just as I would if it were written in a code. Didn't take me long to get the gist. Nausea curled around my uvula as I read notes from a surveillance operation undertaken by the FSB. The officer wrote about how Debbie Barnes met with Chinese agents, when, where, for how long, and the topics of conversation. The notes that went with the audio and video files were observational comments by various officers.

I closed the file I'd read and attached everything

from the flash drive to the Eyes Only note to Caine.

"Something wrong?" Crockett asked, as he poured himself a glass of water.

"Nope, just another day."

Another day that confirmed that *trust no one* is the best way forward. Another day that confirmed I wanted out of this life. I finished writing my notes, checked the files were all attached, and closed SENTINEL. Regardless of what happened with the laboratories, the FBI now had everything they needed to remove a traitor from our midst.

No matter how much that betrayal stung, I had to move forward. I knew I was on the verge of making a life changing decision. Transformative. My mind caressed the feather pen Tahoma gave me. Maybe this was my transformation. Moving from FBI Special Agent in Charge to full time mom. I knew deep down that it was time to devote my energy to being a mom. It was also time to be honest with myself and those around me.

Kurt came out of the bathroom wearing jeans and a button-down shirt. So, he did have something less FBI in his suitcase after all. "There's a weird vibe in here," he stated. "What's going on?"

I shrugged. "Your imagination?" I closed my laptop. The only way I could walk away from my life as I knew it, was to take Mitch up on his offer to stay in New Zealand. "I need to make a phone call," I said. "Could I have the room please?"

The men nodded, picked up their cell phones and left the room. As the door shut, I pressed Mitch's name on my recent calls list. The phone rang and rang. I stopped counting just before voice mail kicked in.

"Babe, it's me. Let's stay here. You're right, it's time. I love you. Kiss the girls for me." I paused then added, "I'll see you tomorrow night." With that I opened the door. "All clear."

Both men wandered in. A tingle raced down my spine picking up sparks as it went. Could've been a lot of things, but I knew it was the beginning of an adrenaline buzz. We had a job to do. A multifaceted complicated death-defying operation, and with that Pollyanna vanished and work began.

"Crockett if you're in, then we need you to liaise with ASIS or ASIO or whoever you trust, and can get eyes on the Perth laboratory, and the ability to strike."

"Consider it done. I'll get hold of some people. You want satellite imaging as well as strike capability via drone?"

"It'll make their jobs easier if they have the whole picture, so yes." I could feel the buzz vibrating through me. "You'll need a team who can handle the assault. There's an American in that lab, we want him." Very much. "I can get FBI flown out of Canberra to make the arrest."

"You sort that, leave the strike force to me."

Happy too. "That Perth lab. Is it in a built-up area? Suburban?"

"Satellite will confirm, but I think it's an industrial zone."

Good news. The less civilian casualties the better. A certain amount of collateral damage was inevitable with an operation this big. Satellites would help us make the assaults as clean as possible.

"Time difference?"

"Four hours."

Crockett started making calls, he opted to utilize the small counter as a work surface, a pen in one hand poised over a notebook, and his phone in the other. I left him to work and joined Kurt near the windows. He leaned on the wall next to the window and looked out over the city.

"Beautiful isn't it?" I said, standing next to him.

"You're not coming back with us, are you?" He didn't move to look at me.

"No."

"It's going to be a surprise to Lee and Dane."

"No, it's not."

"Figured one day you'd leave Delta, but it didn't occur to me that you'd leave the FBI."

I shrugged. "It's been inevitable since the twins' birth."

"It's not going to be the same without you."

"I'm not gone yet." I bumped his shoulder with mine. "We still have to save the world."

He bumped me back, turned quickly and kissed my cheek, then ducked before I reacted.

"Chicken," I said, as he slunk away laughing. You can't make old friends. It was not going to be easy leaving my team.

Crockett finished his calls and joined me by the window. "We've got a team. ASIO will make the arrest on your behalf. That means we don't have to wait for flights from Canberra."

"Great."

"Crockett?" Kurt's voice rose slightly and floated across the room.

"Yeah?"

"Can you keep an eye on Iverson when we're gone?"

Crockett grinned. "Pretty sure that'd go down like a lead balloon."

I laughed, because it was true.

"I'm retiring Henderson, to the Marlborough Sounds. The only danger there is a rogue fishhook."

"For normal people, Iverson. I recall you finding excitement last time you were there."

Jeez, find one dead body on a beach, and a crazy killer hiding in a potting shed, and no one will let you forget it. Do I know how to have a fun vacation, or what?

"That wasn't the last time, that was the first time."

Kurt laughed. Crockett smiled.

"If it makes you feel better Henderson, I'll check in on Iverson every now and then. Always wanted to go to the Marlborough Sounds and fish."

"Thanks."

I interrupted them. "Boys, we've got some sketchy shit to do out in Upper Hutt. Think we should get ready, and eat. And by eat, I mean call for room service because we've still got a couple of assholes out there looking for us."

"Good call," Kurt said, and threw me a menu.

Our meals arrived. The atmosphere felt lighter. Kurt and I were happy working together, Crockett was an okay guy. He joined in on the banter. We all had a beer. No telling when we'd get a chance to relax again.

"Henderson, I have a question," I said, waving the Corona bottle in my hand.

"Just one?"

"No, but I'll start with one." I took a swig then carried on. "What's your take on Qu17P?"

"Considering the scientific community are still working on more effective vaccines for COVID-19, and the timing of this potential new threat. This is extra." He downed some of his beer.

"What age groups are most affected by COVID-19?"

"Iverson, I think I know where you're going with this."

"What age groups?" I asked again.

Kurt put his beer on the coffee table and picked up his phone. He scrolled a bit then found the information he was looking for.

"The stats that came out of China regarding age brackets, were that most infections were in the thirty to sixty-nine age bracket," he said.

"Us then," Crockett said, placing his empty bottle on the table.

"And deaths?" I said.

Kurt scrolled again. "Most deaths via stats are in the eighty plus bracket. Also more men than woman, but these are stats from Chinese studies, and more men smoke, and if the patient has other medical conditions their chance of death is higher, and to be honest a lot of the eighty plus people have other medical conditions." Kurt looked up from his phone. "We're still learning. Relatively young people are dying after recovery from strokes and heart attacks. COVID attacks the body in many ways not just lungs. We're talking vascular and neurological as well. Studies are on going, all over the world." He moved his finger across his phone screen. "Don't over look the Chinese studies just keep in mind, everyone has their own agenda."

He had a point. How much of the information was hidden or skewed, to make it look like whatever agenda they were told to report to?

"And Qu17P is capable of doing what if we fail? If it's released now while the world is still trying to control COVID-19?"

He looked at me and closed his phone. "It'll pick off a lot of the people who are weakened by COVID, that had no comorbidity previously."

"How about kids? If they're mostly surviving COVID, if they're healthy to start with ..."

"Iverson, if everything we suspect so far is correct

and Qu17P is targeting genetic markers, we could be fucked regardless."

Fucked up beyond all recognition.

"Ever feel like we're living smack in the middle of a conspiracy theory and there is no escape?"

Crockett chuckled. "We have science, Ellie."

"That's what all the nuts say, when they drag out stats to prove their point."

Kurt looked at me. "We have real science. And the girls are safe in Marlborough away from people."

I swallowed another mouthful of beer and hit pause on my runaway thoughts. They were safe. That's what matters.

Crockett motioned to the empty Corona bottles on the table. "Ironic."

Chapter Thirty-five
Dancing in the Dark

Again, I found myself in Fran's backyard enjoying fresh air and solitude. I could breathe. Cold nipped at my fingers. I plunged my hands into my jacket pockets. My phone rang in my ear. Sometimes EarPods were the way to go, especially when it was chilly out, and my hands were finally warming up.

I answered the call. "Ellie Iverson."

"This is Tahoma."

"Didn't think I would hear from you yet."

"Information has come to light from the scientific community. It is not good."

I blew air out. "Tell me."

The call tone changed. Video call. Dammit. I tugged my phone from my pocket and pressed end and accept. And there was Tahoma, looking at me from the screen.

"I want to see your face," he said.

"Good to see you."

"Ellie, do not fail your task. It will take years to recover from the release of Qu17p. It will be another pandemic, and we are already tired from fighting two back-to-back and overlapping, pandemics."

"Surely it can't be that bad?"

"The worst-case scenario has come to fruition. Mankind destroying mankind."

Words and images swam in the quagmire within my mind. "I heard a rumor, before the first time we encountered the Qu Pathogen. I heard that China built a lab to study SARS and Ebola in Wuhan, and that our experts worried that a virus could escape the facility." I assembled pieces of a puzzle. "That's the same city where the Coronavirus outbreak began?"

"Yes. I also heard that rumor."

"Is this worse than COVID-19?"

"About the same. But it is a manmade bioweapon existing at what we hope is the tail end of the COVID-19 pandemic. If that was not bad enough, it is also flu season. We have swine flu, ebola, and there is also the measles situation." He shook his head. "And we know the measles virus in the Congo was a bioweapon."

"No pressure, right?"

Tahoma frowned. "China is where almost all the pandemic viruses have come from in the last fifty years."

"What are you saying?"

"Just an observation."

"You're not surprised they are behind Qu17p ..."

Tahoma raised his eyes to meet mine. Warm brown eyes switched to dark, almost black. "I am surprised by nothing man does. I am disappointed."

"Did they really manufacture the coronavirus and blame bats?"

An image of a bat in a soup bowl floated in my mind.

Yuck. Followed by a video of a young man biting into a live animal. Sometimes social media sucks. I couldn't unsee it and I only watched two-seconds of that clip.

He shook his head. "We do not know. Do not fail, Ellie. We are talking about yet another virus created to kill, and hundreds of millions of people will die if it is released." I nodded at Tahoma. Holding my phone a little higher in my cold hand. "There is more. We have reports of a highly pathogenic strain of H5N1 killing chickens."

"Where did that start?"

Tahoma frowned, glanced down, and then back up at me. "Mexico, Brazil, South Africa, Italy, France, Spain, Britain."

"But where did it start?"

"Simultaneous reports from the countries I listed, but nothing reported from our teams who study wild birds. We did not expect this. There were no signs in the wild population."

"What does that mean?"

"It means we have more than one fire to fight." He licked his lips. "It means culling a food source by the millions, and the potential for this bird flu to cross to humans."

Shit.

Okay. Not my problem. Our part was in front of us. "Any tips for our operation?"

"Yes. To kill the virus, you will need extreme heat."

"I am waiting for confirmation on drone's armed

with warheads."

"That will do it. Go well my friend."

"Talk soon."

I pocketed my phone and stared out over the sea. Failure is not an option. Time ticked by as clouds gathered.

A voice came from behind me, Peter Cooper. "Sorry to interrupt."

I turned around. "You're not." Sam's deep voice chuckled in my head. I pushed my thoughts at his incorporeal image: What was I supposed to say? I think we're all going to die, and I don't know how to fix this?

"I can get us eyes in the sky, and strike capability," Cooper said.

Of course, he could. That was why Tierney sent him. Well, the other reason. First task, babysitting, second, getting me whatever I need. For all his faults, and there were many, Tierney usually came through for us.

"Good. Because short of nukes the only other option to destroy this goddamn virus, and the so-called vaccines, is, extreme heat."

"All right, then that's what we do."

"Yep."

"Next?"

"Get everyone in the same room and make sure they have pens, paper, and envelopes."

Cooper nodded. "Final letters," he said, his voice held a modicum of resignation.

"There's no guarantees here, Cooper. No guarantees

at all." I turned back to the view across the harbor. Calm stretches of water, then small whitecaps, drew my eyes to a large white ship that moved across the harbor. Wind blew my hair into my face. I gathered it with both hands and secured it into a ponytail with a hair-tie from my wrist.

"You coming in?" Cooper asked.

"Yeah." I filled my lungs with clean cold air and exhaled slowly. "Lead the way."

Dane waited inside the backdoor. Cooper excused himself and disappeared into the house.

"Tahoma texted Kurt and confirmed that extreme heat is the only option for destruction." Dane's eyes narrowed as he tried to read me. "But you already knew that, how?"

"I just got off a call with Tahoma, he told me." He also said not to fail. Fuck. A massive weight crushed me. Pressing me into the floor. Just breathe. I stood for a moment staring at Dane and counting each breath.

"This isn't it El, this isn't the end of us."

I pushed a massive steel door closed in my mind. It effectively shut both Dane and Mitch out of my inner most thoughts, out of the place I kept the truth as I saw it. I switched a light on in my eyes and smiled, here comes Pollyanna.

"We got this Dane, I know that."

"What now?"

"We all have letters to write before we do this."

Dane shook his head. "Defeatist talk."

"No, Dane, sensible. At any point, this operation could go sideways. If, and only if, that happens, then those we leave behind deserve a goodbye." I could do a better job of explaining that, so I tried again. "Think about from my point of view Dane. I need all of us focused on the prize and the best way to do that, in this case, is with us all knowing we said what we needed to say."

He swallowed hard. "I don't like it."

"Me neither, but this is what we do before any big operation."

He frowned. "Maybe you do, but I've never ..."

"I haven't for a long time. Once upon a time, Dane, I was in Wellington bringing back a traitor or terrorist, whatever your point of view is ... it was a coordinated operation and someone leaked information, blah blah blah."

"Hold it, how were you involved?"

"Seconded to a CIA task force in Iraq. And ending up in New Zealand was my choice, Tierney agreed, and sent me over here. It's a long story that ended badly for quite a few people, me included."

"That was the last time you wrote a final letter?"

"Yes." Ominous. "We're doing this. Once it's done, we can concentrate on making sure they're never delivered." I hooked my arm in his and turned him toward the interior of the house. "Come on, we've got a job to do."

"Okay."

I extracted my arm at the living room door. Dane lowered his head slightly and whispered in my ear, "I know what you really think." Then he walked down the hall to the kitchen. I know you do.

Had a feeling I wasn't quick enough to shut that steel trap door in my mind. Nothing I could do about that, except hope we had this, and we all made it through. We were dealing with people, and people make the whole process unpredictable.

People are the problem. I shook that off. Not helpful. My job was people. Like it or not human nature provided me job security, just as human nature provided pay insecurity. Our pay was at the whim and behest of a tyrannical child who used it as a bargaining chip. That knowledge made the decision to stay in New Zealand and raise our girls easier, and maybe I could use my skills as part of the New Zealand police force. That's definitely a plan, and one Mitch and I had discussed. I'd held our family back thus far.

Me.

My inability to break away from Delta A and the FBI. From the life I knew. Now it was time for that fresh start and new life. A hand waved from across the room. Time to drag myself out of my thoughts and pay attention. The hand waved again. Kurt.

"Iverson, come over here," he said, then frowned. "Iverson?"

"Sure, coming." I dodged a sofa and coffee table to join Kurt on a two-seater under a window.

"You all right?" He asked.

"I'm okay."

"And again, and this time with feeling," Kurt said, half a smile crossed his lips and vanished.

"Cooper got the drone."

"He said."

Dane and Lee were sitting on a sofa adjacent to us. I could hear their conversation.

"Thinking about the lockdown rolled out to try and stop the spread of COVID-19. All the travel restrictions, how closed the world was, and in some cases, is still. And the western world's crazy toilet paper and dry pasta panic buying ..." Lee scratched his head. "And how we shut down. Our borders to Europe closed. Schools shut. Events were shit-canned. People couldn't gather to pray. The whole thing was surreal as fuck. We couldn't even go to a bar or out to eat. Or travel. Jobs were lost. It was fucked and it's still fucked. The world is still a goddamn disaster."

"Yeah, go on," Dane said.

"How do you think people will react to this new threat if someone figures out what's happening and what we're doing?"

"Badly, very badly."

"Did you see the rumor that the coronavirus was manmade and created to assassinate POTUS?"

I listened without comment. That rumor circulated on social media, and every now and then, some crackpot brought it back up again.

"No, but it doesn't surprise me, no doubt that one sprang from a handshake ...," Dane said.

"The world was behaving like it was the end times."

"And then some."

Lee and Dane turned their heads in my direction when I cleared my throat. "Best we don't fail. Keep our mission under wraps and throw no crumbs to the rumor mill."

"Are we going to win?" Lee said. That was the first time I could ever remember him having any doubt in our ability as a team.

"We have to win, Lee. It's on us," I said.

A little yellow duckling squeezed from the sofa cushions between Lee and Dane, and gave a violent shake. A tiny cloud of fluffy yellow down floated in the air. It quacked and climbed onto Lee's leg by using its little orange beak to grab a seam and pull itself up. As I watched it waddled along his thigh, quacking and snapping at colorful spiky balls suspended from what looked like a double helix, that spun slowly in mid-air. When all the colorful balls were gone the duckling quacked, shook, and vanished into a cloud of yellow fluff.

With no clue what the duckling meant, I let the images fade from my mind. Dane's eyes held questions. Guess he saw that too.

I shrugged at him. "I have no explanation."

Dane nodded.

Lee frowned. "What did I miss?"

"A duckling eating what I think were virus cells suspended on a double helix ..." No sense denying my colorful brain antics. "On your leg."

"Okay, for a second I thought it was something weird."

Dane laughed.

"Lee. We'll win, we don't have a choice," I said with a smile. We got this.

Kurt nudged me. "Iverson, you are without a doubt the most mentally peculiar person I've ever come across. Duckling hallucinations?"

Guess I'd not mentioned them before. My bad.

I checked the time on my watch. "Let's get on with this. The clock is ticking." I stood up and whistled. My team knew what that meant, and I couldn't imagine the others not picking up on it. "I want final letters written by everyone before we move."

"Good call," Kurt replied.

Everyone assembled in the living room. Fran came in last. I stood up and addressed the room.

"The next fifteen minutes are for the last briefing, then I want letters written. Everyone writes a letter to loved ones. End of story. Once they're done, the letters will be left here at Fran's place."

"I'll find a box for them," Fran said.

"Excellent." Eyes watched me. Some held questions, and some were simply attentive. "We will divide into two teams for the operation." I looked at Josef. "Josef, do you have clearance from Russia?"

"Ya. I have control from this ..." He held up his tablet. "FSB team standing by, a block away from laboratory."

"The drone?"

"Armed and waiting for orders."

"Good." I turned my attention to Crockett. "You?"

"ASIO are a block away from the Perth lab. We have the area secure. Drone armed and ready."

"Awesome. Your team does know we want the American chemical engineer, Ken Chang, alive, right?"

"Sure do. They'll do their level best to make that happen."

Good enough.

"Cooper?"

"We have a drone, it's armed. We have eyes on the entire Upper Hutt facility, live." He held up a tablet. "They're using a local security company to patrol the grounds. Twice a day and twice during the night."

"We haven't had eyes on long enough to know that ..."

Cooper smiled. "Might've hacked the security company and grabbed that data."

I smiled back. "Good work."

"Sean, Germany?"

"We have a ground team and a strike drone."

"Who?"

"A few of my men."

"Where were they?"

"Private security for a traveling VIP, in France.

They've been replaced by a couple of locals."

"And the drone?"

"I don't think you need that information."

Fair enough.

"So, we're okay. The whole operation kicks off in exactly ..." I checked my watch again. "Eighty-nine minutes."

We all checked our watches and tablets, making sure we had exactly the same time. Four completely different countries, four teams, four strike drones, on standby. This was the biggest operation I'd ever been involved with, and it terrified me. So many lives trusting me to get this right.

"Give us our team assignments, SAC," Cooper said.

"We're hitting the Upper Hutt laboratory as a cohesive unit. I'm taking Delta A in with Fran and Rawiri."

Cooper shook his head. "Not without me. Drone, remember?"

"I was getting to you Cooper. You are with me."

I felt Sean's energy change from fluid to fixed, solid, stubborn, and looked at him. "Problem Sean?"

"Yes. I don't want you going in. What if this turns to custard?"

"I'm not letting my team go anywhere I'm not prepared to go."

"El ..."

"Sean," I countered. "It's not a discussion. My op, my rules." I leveled a stare right through him. "You,

Josef, and Crockett have your own off-shore teams to worry about."

Crockett waved a finger in my direction. "We are more than capable of monitoring our teams while helping you. The place you are going is huge. We've all seen the images."

He was right. There were four interconnected main buildings, and five other buildings scattered around a central area.

Josef cleared his throat. Great, lets everyone wade in.

"Iverson, we are here to help. Allow it."

Okay, fine. What we have here is a communal death wish.

I let all their opinions and observations fall around me and reassemble into a plan that involved everyone in the room. I did not like it. What I needed was to make sure the people monitoring off-shore teams and drone, were protected.

"Okay, this is how it's going to work. Lee and Dane, you will have Crockett with you. You are now team one. Rawiri, Cooper, Sean, and Fran you are team two. Kurt, Josef and I, are team three. Three teams, three entry points." I took a deep breath and let it out slowly as everyone shuffled around until they were in their teams. "We have induction mics for everyone. That will be our means of communication. Kurt will pass them out in a second." I heard him open the box he had near him on the floor. He was ready. "Gear: side arms, go-bags, bullet proof vests. If you don't have your own, talk to Kurt, we have extras."

The faces in front of me changed. I recognized the shift in energy. Everyone had their own pre-game rituals.

"Collect your induction mics, then go write those letters. We leave here in twenty minutes. Find time to familiarize yourselves with the plans of the compound and buildings you have on your phones." No one moved. They maintained their focus on me. "The main laboratory is in the center of the main building. There are no windows to the outside world."

"That means we can't set up a sniper position," Lee said to me, with a wry smile. "And I know how much you love to be on the end of a rifle."

I'd lost count years ago of how many times I'd been able to do just that. I trained with SWAT for years, and they trusted me enough to put a rifle in my hands and let me work with them. I'm a damn fine shot with an M40A5.

"We'll have to make do."

"No fun for you this go-round," Kurt added.

All teams appeared to mill about, but they weren't. They were collecting hardware and settling into their teams. Banter filled the room, punctuated by the laughter. From the edges, I could get an overview. They would work well together. Josef loosened up and fitted in with everyone. Cooper, wasn't such a dick. Crockett, I quite liked. And Sean? Delta A had a long working relationship with Sean O'Hare. We were solid.

I tapped Cooper on the arm. "Can I have a quick word?"

He nodded. "Here or?"

"Here's fine. I just wanted to say, I'm sorry for not giving you the benefit of the doubt when we met. You're not a dick and you're not the enemy."

He smiled all the way up to his eyes. "Apology accepted."

My phone rang. Caine. I looked at Cooper, "We okay?"

"Yes."

I answered Caine's call and left the room.

"You all okay down there, kid?"

"Yep. We got this." My fingers of my right hand crossed without my bidding.

"I know you do. I trained you," Caine growled. "We got Wu."

"Thank you."

"Straun passed away a couple of hours ago."

"She lived longer than I thought she would," I said. "Tell me about Wu?"

"Remember the new virus that emerged in China?"

"Yes, Tahoma suspected it to be Qu17P, or another variation of Qu."

"According to the information Wu had on him, Tahoma is correct on both counts. They tested Qu17P on their own people, it was airborne. Then they introduced another version via a vaccine."

"What the actual fuck is wrong with these people?"

"The vaccine made the virus lethal to only people carrying specific genetic markers."

"Great."

"Do you know where this all came from." I uncrossed my fingers at a twinge of cramp. Silently I willed Caine not to say mainland China.

"Russia and Germany."

"Both?"

"The initial airborne virus was apparently created in Germany, and the vaccine containing the genetic marker, came from Russia."

"Confirm laboratory of origin and the coordinates, please."

Caine sent two map images to my phone. I looked at the images. Positive confirmation that the viruses came from the labs we'd identified in German and Russia. Schroder Forschung laboratories.

"Okay, thank you. See you when this is over."

"Wait. There's more. We have reason to believe that at least two laboratories have automated delivery systems."

That sounded bad.

"How did you get that information. I doubt Wu would know shit about the labs."

"We have the Chief Science Officer for Newgenic."

"And she's cooperating?"

"She tried to flee the country and was stopped at the border." Caine's voice grated like an old washer woman's hands on a washboard. "I had a chat with her and now she's talking."

I don't doubt she'd talk after Caine spoke with her.

My mind swung back to the automated delivery systems. "What exactly does automated delivery system mean to us?"

"There is a device built into two of the buildings, that we know of, and it can release the viruses as an aerosol of sorts."

"How?"

"It's triggered from within the lab, it's basically a giant bug bomb."

"I'm guessing, because we know these viruses burn in extreme heat, that the bug bomb is more pressurized air or something, but nothing explosive?"

"Yes."

My guts tied into a knot. Before Caine said anything, I knew one of the delivery systems was in Upper Hutt. "Where?"

"New Zealand and Russia."

"What about Germany and Australia?"

"We can confirm New Zealand and Russia, but not the others."

And the chances of only two having something like that seemed ridiculously low.

"Thanks, Caine."

"You can't un-ring this bell, Ellie," his voice growled into my ear and almost tickled.

"I'm aware."

"Stay safe kid."

"That *is* my intention."

Caine's call ended.

I walked back into the living room. Kurt was writing. Fran sat in an armchair and wrote. Everyone else was gone to wherever they felt comfortable to write their letters. I took a notebook from my back pocket and sat on the sofa. A voice in my head reminded me I had little time, and to keep it short. Don't think about it, just write.

Chapter Thirty-six
Fire and Ice

At dusk, we sat in the car across the road from a fish and chip shop, far enough from the nearest streetlamp that we remained in the growing shadows. The streetlights flicked on, and yellowish pools of light dropped at regular intervals, onto the cold pavement. Down the street was the place we were going. Shrouded by the creeping night, was a collection of buildings set in park like surroundings that used to be a government research facility. Guess it still was used for research, just not a government sanctioned anymore.

Darkness closed in as we sat and waited. The other cars were parked along Ward Street. We were all close enough to move fast. Cooper had a surveillance drone with night vision watching the area. No sign of any movement. It took everything I had to prevent me climbing out of my skin. The ten-minute wait felt like ten hours. Each breath tightened my diaphragm. The tension in the car ramped so high it was tangible. Electricity filled the air.

Breathe.

I closed my eyes and let go of everything that wasn't now. As almost all of the extraneous thoughts washed away on a river of light, my pre-game ritual began. I grasped the side of the barrel and pulled back the slide until I glimpsed a round in the pipe. Satisfied I released my grip and the slide slipped back into position.

I knew my magazine was full. Seventeen rounds in the magazine, one in the pipe. Two spare magazines on my belt. I slid the weapon back into my holster. We'd been through a lot, me and my Glock. Pretty much everyone had moved to Gen 4 and I stuck with my trusty old friend. We had a way to go yet. Let's not screw it up.

Breathe.

Checked my two spare magazines. Rotated my shoulders, clenched and unclenched my fists, and tried to clear my mind of the one remaining thought that encroached: Mitch.

Breathe.

The tightness returned.

Breathe.

Mitch was hard to dislodge. His blue eyes twinkled, as his smile filled me.

Breathe.

I exhaled slowly, and knew I needed to distract myself for a little while. Put my EarPods in, loaded a podcast on my phone, and pressed play.

Two minutes later Kurt tapped my arm. "What are you listening to?"

"A podcast." I hit pause.

"Now's the time you choose a podcast?"

"Brain break."

"Gimme." He held out his hand. I took my left EarPod out and handed it to him. He inserted it and I pressed play.

Five minutes later, Kurt tapped my shoulder. "Who is this guy?"

"Pete A Turner. We're listening to the *Break it Down Show*."

"Turner?"

"Uh huh."

Kurt turned his head to face me. "The guy you call your mechanic is Turner, is that a coincidence?"

"You have to ask? This is him utilizing his downtime."

"Guess everyone has life beyond the FBI. Who is he talking with?"

"Dana Commandatore - she was on Great American Baker."

"A podcast about a baker?"

"Yeah."

"I'm confused."

I could see how he would be. If I'd opted for one of the spy vs spy episodes, it would probably have made sense for Kurt. I shot him a smile. "Maybe I'll be a baker in my next life."

"Maybe pigs will fly," Kurt said half under his breath. "How many ways can you do pancakes?"

"Wiseass."

Exactly half a sentence later, the alarm on my phone buzzed, overriding the podcast. Thoughts of being a baker would have to wait. I shut it down. Kurt handed me back the EarPod he'd borrowed.

Time to go. All the car doors opened. We were not driving in.

I jammed my cap on my head, felt the weight of the Glock in my hand, pushed my phone deep into my pocket, and crossed the road with Kurt and Josef. Kurt held a pair of bolt cutters. Team One approached from the farthest gate and were to make their entrance into the main buildings, from the back. Team Two took the middle and were to enter the main building from the front. My team had the gate closest to our car, and would enter the building from the far right. Rooms would be cleared as everyone made their way to the central laboratory we'd seen on the floor plans. That was the most likely place to house the viruses.

Sean, Crockett, and Josef had their tablets and monitored their respective areas: Germany, Western Australia, and Russia. The order was given before we left Fran's, that as soon as the facilities were clear, the drones would strike. We had to take out the dispersal methods before anyone could activate them. It wasn't a choice, it was what we absolutely had to do, to protect the population of the cities housing the laboratories, and therefore the regions, and then the world.

Cooper's eyes in the sky watched the facility as we moved steadily toward. Everybody knew the people inside had the ability to release the viruses before we got to them, or once they realized we were there. No one wanted that scenario to play out. Way up in the dusky sky was a MQ-9 Reaper. It saw and recorded everything while it waited for the strike command from Cooper.

The gates opened without much effort. Darkness deepened. The area lighting was minimal. That worked in our favor.

We moved up our various paths connected by comms, but not by sight. I hoped everyone was in position by the time Cooper gave us the go-ahead to open doors. As far as we knew, there were ten people working the evening shift. One of them was Nicolaus Ng, and we wanted to repatriate him on behalf of our government. There were charges and potential jail terms waiting.

Cooper's voice flowed into my ear. "All Tango, this is Tango Two. Okay for door breaches, out."

"All Tango, this is Echo, go, go, go, over," I said, quietly. They could hear me if I whispered so there was no need to speak any louder. For a second, I wondered if my heartbeat was louder than my voice.

Kurt lay the bolt cutters on the ground next to the door we were entering. He tried the door handle. The door moved. One-second later, we were in a dimly lit hallway, moving toward the main laboratory area in the center of the building. Tango Two was moving to meet us, sweeping the area as they went. Pre-ordained entrance.

Tango One was on the other side of the buildings,

sweeping and making their way to the laboratory from that direction. The constant stream of voices in my head told me where everyone was, and what was happening. The whispers from my team in my ear was the only noise, there was external silence all around us. I heard encounters with personnel as rooms were cleared. Kurt and I swept four rooms and two hallways, before we found the main laboratory. We waited by the main lab door with Josef and remained out of sight. until Team Two joined us.

No one had come across Ng so far. Kurt pointed to a window into the room beyond. I nodded. He slipped over and used a small mirror to see inside without giving himself away. He ducked quickly pulling his arm down. I froze. Footsteps approached from the other side of the wall. Kurt's voice rasped in my head, "Fuck. Armed guard."

"Shit, wait one," I replied.

The footsteps moved away. I breathed out, and whispered, "Charlie One this is Echo, armed guards. Out."

None of the surveillance warned about armed guards. New Zealand was not an armed country.

Cooper's voice tickled my ear as he spoke, "Echo, this is Charlie One. Not armed outside, must have an armory within the building. Over."

What else didn't we know?

I heard Rawiri. "Tango Three, this is Tango Two. We're here. You okay? Out."

Kurt replied, "Tango Two, this is Kilo. Affirmative. Move. Out."

He nudged me. Hand signals came into play. He told me to let him and Sean go first. I acquiesced, because there was no time. I shoved the feeling of doom aside.

We were not going to fail.

Not on my watch.

Sean took the first door out with two shot gun blasts to the hinges. Kurt and I stormed into the room. A figure moved past a window in the next room. I followed the movement. Kurt looked over. I waved two fingers to my right. He nodded. We moved right. Another shadowy figure appeared. Kurt grabbed my arm and yanked me down. He whispered in my ear, "That's the main laboratory."

Two quick shots fired, and darkness fell with shards of glass. The large window near us shattered. Everything slowed. Emergency lighting fired up, bathing the immediate vicinity in an eerie orange glow. I turned my head to see someone throw something toward us. Kurt's arm flung over my head and shoved me to the ground. I pushed him off and crawled to my feet, ears ringing.

Chaos enveloped me. I shook the white noise in my head away, it left a shrill ringing that I fought to ignore. Through broken shards of glass, I identified our target. He reached inside a large glass, or perspex box. Viral contamination symbols lit up. I took a breath and held it. My aim steadied at his head. Not on my watch.

"Ng," I said. "STOP!"

The world slowed like a stilted movie. His fingers lifted a flap over a yellow switch.

I squeezed the trigger. A bloody splatter erupted from his head, spraying across the box. Ng turned as he fell. A robotic voice said, "Ten."

Fuck.

Bullets whizzed by, smashing into walls, splintering timber. Someone was still playing to win.

My voice missed a beat as I tried to speak to my teams, "Get out!" Then to Cooper. "Call the strike."

I could see my people moving and sent encouragement, "Move!"

Kurt grabbed my arm as Cooper said, "Danger Close."

We ran. Through the building to the darkness beyond, as the robotic voice counted. "Five ... four ..."

Kurt dragged me behind the perimeter brick fence. Shadows moved fast in our direction. The sky lit with a massive explosion. Everything broke into pieces and rained down upon the area, covering us in glass, broken wood, bits of steel, and assorted pieces of building material.

My ears rang. Below the disruptive noise, I struggled to hear voices.

They were there somewhere.

Concentrate.

I cleared my throat. A dry dustiness in my mouth made swallowing difficult. "All teams this is Echo,

Radio Check, over," I said, hoping our comms still worked.

Sirens sounded in the distance, wailing under the explosions that continued from behind us. We had to move. There was no way we could be found near this mess. Flames leaped skyward from the wreckage of the building. Another explosion rocked the area. Please let that virus be gone forever.

A voice crackled, then made another attempt. "Echo, this is Lima and Delta, Roger out."

Thank fuck for that.

Another voice, Kurt, "Echo this is Kilo, right beside you, Roger out."

Then another, "Echo, this is Juliet, Roger out," said Josef.

The sirens grew in volume.

Cooper spoke, "Echo, this is Charlie and Sierra, Roger out."

Then Rawiri, "Echo, this is Romeo. Foxtrot and Charlie One are injured but mobile, Roger out."

"All Tango. Oscar Mike to Foxtrot Hotel, how copy?" I replied, knowing everyone could still hear me.

"Good, copy," came back from everyone.

"Romeo, this is Echo. You lead, can you get us out of Upper Hutt without coming across those sirens? Out."

"Echo, this is Romeo. Affirmative. Stick close, over."

We ran. Anyone looking, and I bet there were plenty of people looking after that explosion, would've seen sketchy dark shapes race from the fence line, to cars parked a short distance away.

Engines fired. Rawiri and Fran led the way. I looked over my shoulder and watched the burning facility fade into a smokey background. I removed my comms equipment and dropped it into the console between the seats. Kurt had done the same. Silence filled the car and the void in my brain. It wasn't soothing, it was just silent. Did we win? Did the release happen before the explosion? Were we infected?

My phone rang. Sean's ring tone.

"Sit rep from my people," he said. "Drone took out the facility. Two casualties from my force, not serious. No survivors from the lab."

"Thanks Sean."

"That was a good shot back there."

"Head shot or no shot, Sean."

No one wants zombies.

As soon as Sean vanished, another call came through. Josef.

"The mission was success," he said.

"Your men?"

"They did job. Destroyed lab and virus."

"Thank you for your help, Josef."

"It is what friend does."

You can't make old friends, felt like a misnomer now. I had a feeling, I just did. Another incoming call caused a glance in my direction from Kurt.

"Eyes on the road, pal," I mumbled, before answering the phone.

He chuckled. "Gotta be Cooper, we've heard from everyone else ..."

"Haven't heard from Crockett."

But yeah. It was Cooper.

"Cooper, what have you got?"

"No movement amongst the wreckage. The Reaper registered flames hot enough to destroy the virus."

"Let's hope the warhead hit in time."

"I got a good feeling," Cooper said. "You okay?"

"Never better." So, I lied. Sue me.

"Relax Iverson, objective achieved. I'm prepared to call Operation BAR a success."

"BAR?"

"Beyond All Reason."

The call ended.

I let the night close in. Blackness swallowed me, spinning slowly like a pathetic tornado that couldn't make up its mind which direction to go, until it knocked me sideways into a pencil sketch and Chances arms.

His arms wrapped tight around me. "You did it," he whispered.

"I hope so."

"El, big bang, virus burned. You. Did. It."

This time. Maybe.

"There will always be a next time."

"Can we celebrate this success, before you start thinking about the next lunatic, or government sanctioned act of lunacy, that threatens our world?"

"I'm leaving."

"Knee jerk reaction?"

"No. I told Mitch I was ready to retire as an active agent, and live in Marlborough, before we left on this mission."

"Serious?"

I leaned back in his arms to see his eyes. Concern radiated from his core.

"The what-if's are too big now. I owe my husband and our daughters a chance at normal life."

"Now that makes it hard to argue, you know."

"Ever watched *Frozen*?"

Chance shook his head. "Not a lot of movie watching happens in comic books, El."

"The girls love it. Thing is Chance, this is the next right thing. Me, living life, without the FBI, and with my family. It is the next right thing."

"We'll still talk though, right?"

"Of course."

With one last squeeze he let me go. Wind swirled around us and pushed Chance to the edge of the page, where he waved as the book closed.

I opened my eyes. Streetlights flashed past. We were on the motorway. We'd passed Petone and were cruising along the harbor's edge. The water lay dark, flat, and still. A ship near the entrance to the harbor, caught my eye. A white shape that rose out of the dark sea.

The view changed to docks and the stadium as we

neared the city. Then it happened. So close. and yet so far. A car came the wrong way down an off ramp, speeding, being chased. The blue and red lights were just visible from behind the car, as it dodged Rawiri's car. I saw the driver so clearly. Chinese. His contorted expression a mix of rage and disgust as he floored the accelerator.

"Fuck," Kurt said, as he tried to maneuver out of the driver's way. There was nowhere to go. He smashed straight into us.

The world slowed down. Kurt was somewhere under the air bag. I pushed against the white in front of me. Trying to move it aside. Nothing cooperated. Red and blue lights seeped into my eyes.

Someone wrenched my door open and cut the seat belt. I toppled toward the open door without the seat belt to hold me. Hands grabbed me and lifted, pulled, pushed parts of the wreck away, to get me free. Warmth ran over me, out of me, all around me. Someone wiped wet from my eyes and face. I looked into Lee's eyes.

"Kurt." It sounded like my voice, but a long way off.

"Dane and Josef are getting him free. I think he's okay."

Another noise that sounded like a door. Metal scraped on metal. Someone yelled, "Catch."

Lee threw a hand up in the air. He caught whatever it was and lowered it to the ground next to me.

"What?"

"Kurt's backpack," he replied. Zips opened. Then packets ripped.

"Just when I was starting ..." Speech took so much concentration. "To believe, my life ... wouldn't end bloody ..."

"Don't El. It's not. This ..." He pressed harder. "... it's not going to end here."

The world drifted on a red and blue haze, as cold took over. Black lines drawn by an invisible marker outlined my world. The marker shook and the line wobbled.

I let it happen. Lines became furniture and a door. Through the door, stepped Chance. He knelt next to me. "Get up, El," he said, taking hold of my hand, his heat burnt into my rapidly cooling flesh. "Cowboy the fuck up. It's just a flesh wound." Sadness leaked from his fading blue eyes. "Get up."

"You know I can't," I said. "Tell me something."

"Anything," he leaned in, and kissed my forehead. "Anything El."

"Am I alive?"

Chance drifted backwards, a tear slid down his face. I watched him dissolve into a puddle of color and closed my eyes. There was nothing. No pain. No noise. Nothing.

Confusion hit me like a baseball bat, knocking the breath out of me. I fell, tumbling through the nothing, until arms grabbed me and stopped the spin. A voice I knew soothed my soul. "It's okay, Chicky Babe, I got you." Sam wiped dirt off my face with the corner of his shirt. "You gotta go back now. You're not done yet."

"I want to stay. I miss you."

"It's not time. Lee's trying so hard to get you back."

Sam turned my head with his big gentle hands. There was Lee beneath us, working to start my heart. I heard him humming *Another One Bites the Dust* as he did compressions. On the other side of the car, two police officers worked on another bleeding body. Kurt. Mangled in the wreck, was the Chinese male. My memory worked. It was the male from the museum. Fuck him and his bullshit. He's not killing me. He's *not* taking me from my babies.

"El! Come back," Lee said, his words slipped through cracks in the hum that overrode everything. A sudden roar from traffic. Then a bolt of lightning jolted through me. Blinking lights flashed in my eyes. Sam faded into a group of incorporeal beings that emerged from the night and surrounded him. Luminous. Beautiful.

Shrouded in white light. An ethereal pencil gathered momentum on an inky canvas. It drew images of everyone I ever loved, every person I helped, every loss and every triumph. My life sketched out in pastel scenes, and hung together by the slimmest of filaments tethered to a single moment. One decisive instant. Now.

Lee's voice smashed into the drawing. It sent the pencil careening into Sam and off the edge of the canvas. "You need to fight El. We need you here."

No. You don't need me, but two little girls do.

Chapter Thirty-seven
Dance Me to The End of Love

An American Naval helicopter waited for us on the tarmac at Wellington Airport. The rotors turned slowly in the gray drizzle. Droplets of moisture spun into the air.

One last thing, or maybe this was the next right thing. Five days after we dealt with the virus. Five days after the car wreck.

Lee whispered in my ear, "You ready?"

"Yeah."

He made a forward motion with two fingers on his right hand. Dane rolled out first, pushing Kurt in a wheelchair across the damp ground. A light misty rain fell. Marines jumped from the helicopter and stood ready.

We waited until Kurt was helped from the wheelchair, and into the helicopter. Dane returned the wheelchair. Rawiri took possession of it.

They shook hands, Dane ran back to join Kurt. Rawiri moved to stand in front of me, then he dropped to his knee.

"Thank you," he said with a warm smile, that made his brown eyes twinkle.

"And thank you for all your help and support. Maybe I'll see you again one day."

"If you're really keen on staying in Marlborough, the fishing is excellent, and I'm up for a trip down."

"I'd like that. Tell Fran I'll be in touch."

"Will do. Take care, Agent Iverson." He leaned in and kissed my cheek before he jumped to his feet and threw a half-assed salute at me. I laughed.

"Let's go," Lee said, helping me stand. He knew I wasn't going to tolerate being pushed to the helicopter. He handed me elbow crutches. I'd gotten adept at using them over the last twenty-four hours. It was that or stay in hospital. Easy choice.

Two marines waited at parade rest for us to make our way across the tarmac.

"Go easy, El. The drizzle is making it greasy underfoot," Lee said.

"I got this," I replied.

The walk was slow and uneventful, but damp.

"Agent Iverson let's get you on board," said the first marine.

"Thank you."

A voice rang out from the hangar. I turned to see Dave Crocker running toward us, more of a skip and drag involving an elbow crutch, than a real run. He'd copped some chunks of shrapnel in his right leg.

"Got room for me?" he said as he neared.

The marine closest to me turned. "Yes, sir."

The marine helped me onboard, Lee assisted with the harness and passed me the headset from the back of the seat. At least we could talk to each other. Crocker boarded with help from a marine.

Everyone settled. The noise increased as the rotors picked up momentum. The pilot told us they'd land at the biggest of the helipads on Moetapu Road. We would be met by two cars and driven to the house. He expected us to land in twenty-five minutes. As the helicopter lifted off, I looked down. Peter Cooper stood next to Rawiri. They waved.

Twenty-minutes of beautiful deep blue water, green mountains and hills, valleys, islands, and stunning scenery flew by. No one spoke until the pilot told us we were five minutes out, and we'd fly up Mahau sound between the hills, then cross inland to the helipad at the top of the road.

As we neared, I saw the cars driving up. Military transport. Everything we needed to aid our recovery was already in-situ, including a doctor on loan from our navy, and a physiotherapist, also on loan.

The FBI were picking up the tab. Caine signed off on everything.

I thanked our transport, before I disembarked with help.

Don't knock back help. Kurt taught me that. Took him years to get that little nugget through to me.

I watched from the car, as two marines assisted Kurt, and got him in the back of the car with me. His door closed.

"You doing okay, Iverson?" He said, with a small smile.

"Yeah. You?"

"Been better." He leaned his head on the headrest. "Definitely been better."

I smiled. "Yeah, but it could've been so much worse."

"All right, Pollyanna." His smile ringed his words with little rainbows as they hung in the air.

Our driver looked over his shoulder at us. "We'll take it easy Agents."

***

The drive was the slowest five minutes of my life.

"We'll be going all the way down to the bottom entrance, Agents," the driver said, as he turned left into the driveway.

Awesome. The stairs up through the house were a better option than the stairs down from the driveway, and then down into the house again. Maybe.

At the bottom of the driveway, the main entrance door was open. Mitch and Grace, Dad and Isabella, waited. The girls waved and squealed as my door opened.

"Mommy! Mommy!"

I eased myself from the car, took the crutches from the marine who opened the door for me, and nodded at him.

"I'm good, thank you."

He saluted. "It was an honor, Agent Iverson."

I let his words hang in the air for a split second,

before carefully moving through them, and toward my family.

Chapter Thirty-eight
Who Says You Can't Go Home

Three hours after arriving home, Delta A sat around the large table in the dining room, with cameras and screens. The screens and cameras were arranged in a triangle and controlled by my laptop. We could all see each other on the screen, and we could see Caine, and Director Thomas.

Director Thomas bore an unreadable expression. Caine's lip twitched several times, his version of a 'glad you all survived smile'.

"Special Agent in Charge Iverson." I recognized the voice as Director Thomas, but his lips didn't move right away. The internet out in Mahau wasn't the best. Still copper wire and laggy as hell. We were testing it to its limit with this call. "It is good to see you and Delta A."

"Sir," I said. I had nothing else, and his out of sync words and lips were a lot for my brain to cope with.

"We have the report on the Chinese male who crashed into your car."

I waited for his lips to finish moving before I spoke.

"Might be best to email it Sir, the internet is struggling out here."

"Will do, Agent Iverson. This, I'd like to tell you face-to-face."

Screen-to-screen. Whatever. The images coming

from the USA pixelated.

I imagine the reverse happened for them.

"Go ahead, Sir. We can still hear you."

"They hacked into the police vehicle with you and used their GPS coordinates. You didn't have the only drone in the sky in the Wellington Region that night."

"I recall police lights behind the car driven into us?"

"Yes. Police saw him drive onto the off ramp. You were lucky they were there to help save lives."

Yes. We were. I looked at the square on my screen that showed Kurt. He smiled and nodded.

"Sir," Kurt said.

"Yes, Agent Henderson?"

"I'd like to speak to the officers who saved my life."

"Of course. That will be arranged when you are fully recovered." Director Thomas's voice crackled, then returned. "The medical briefing, I was given, said both Henderson and Iverson are healing, but require on-going support for the foreseeable future. The decision from our end is for you all to remain where you are, until such a time as Agent Henderson can travel home."

Did he just issue a sneaky shelter-in-place order? I scanned the faces of my team on the screen.

"Director, is this a quarantine?" Because my kids are here, and I don't want to endanger them, or Mitch, or dad. No one who assisted in our travel wore personal protective equipment. Jeez. He'd better not be talking about quarantine. His image remained pixelated. "Sir?"

"Agents, we do not believe you came in contact with the Qu17p pathogen."

Air rushed over my lips.

"Do not believe, or know for sure?" I asked.

The pixelated image cleared. Director Thomas stared at us. "You have medical staff on hand. I hear that Doctor Whitehorse and Doctor Schneider are in New Zealand. They will be monitoring you, and in constant contact with your medical team."

My kids are here.

MY KIDS ARE HERE.

Caine looked on in horror. Guess Thomas hadn't mentioned anything to him either.

"Sir. That was something we needed to know before potentially putting military, civilians, and children in danger." I wasn't done. "If you have endangered anyone by not sharing this information, I will find you and ... I. Will. Fucking. End. You. Sir."

I slammed the laptop shut.

End call.

"Iverson, take a breath." Kurt struggled to his feet. "We're a team. We will be right beside you."

Dane and Lee's voices united, "All for one."

THE END.

453

"One of the greatest discoveries a man makes, one of his great surprises, is to find he can do what he was afraid he couldn't do." - Henry Ford

Acknowledgments:

I am so grateful to have some amazing friends who keep me sane, point out madness when they see it, answer my questions, challenge me to do better and generally encourage me and cheer me on.

Without a cheering section I wouldn't have been able to type this at the end of the twelfth Byte novel. TWELVE! Holy moly!
You all know who you are, but in case you've forgotten ...

Geoff Inwood, an excellent and much trusted sounding board who puts up with the crazy and loves me anyway.

Pete Turner for cheering loudly, your expertise, and having my back.

Nicky Hurle - a wonderful friend and editor.
The amazing staff at *Upper Hutt Central Library*.

My kids especially *Caoilfhionn* and *Breezy* who have to put up with me while I'm writing for their entire lives, thank you.

Rebekah for reading everything I write, wrangling of weirdos on my FaceBook Page skills, and also for coming with me to speaking engagements and for tequila!

Josephine for her cover design skills and patience. (And for telling me glitter could be a thing!)

Sue Linton, because without Sue none of this would have happened and there certainly wouldn't be any chickens. Sue was the first person to read anything I'd written (as an adult) and when we stopped laughing we looked at each other and realized the potential was there. (Mrs G - thank you for reading my words.)

Mrs H, *Pip*, and *Charlie* - much love.

Special thanks to the amazing readers who took the time to beta read this book and offer insight and clarity. Also, to the people who read and sent me wonderful blurbs!

When I'm writing a book it is a process that requires concentration and uninterrupted time. To everyone who understands I can't just stop and turn my attention to something else, even briefly, thank you. During the initial writing phase, I don't talk much about the story as a whole. I mention things I'm researching and do a lot of listening to people who know shit but I don't talk much. I've been very lucky over the years to have some wonderfully knowledgable and generous friends who are quick to help and make the final product a team effort. Thank you team!

It doesn't feel write closing this out without mentioning Ellie. She walked into my life 15 years ago, sat, down and told me a story. And those stories kept coming, as they did she introduced me to Delta A. Thanks for trusting me to tell your stories. It's been a blast!

Stay Frosty,
Cat xx

About the author:

Cat Connor is a crime thriller author, New Zealander, and instigator of trouble. By day she's a warm body in Writers Plot Bookshop in Upper Hutt, NZ where she spends time answering questions from authors (budding, new, and established) and sharing the joy of kiwi authors with kiwi readers. By night she writes crime novels; wrangles teenagers; enjoys the company of Bucky Barnes & Timmy the guinea pigs and wrestles Patrick the kitten. She flourishes on coffee, tequila, travel, knitting, reading, binge watching Netflix series, and loud music - not necessarily in that order and usually not all at once.

The Byte Series: Follows FBI Special Agent Ellie Conway on her journey as a member of an elite FBI team that functions on dark humor, close relationships, and strong coffee. Each book is a standalone story with the same core characters.

The Byte Series Novels by Cat Connor:
Killerbyte, Terrorbyte, Exacerbyte, Flashbyte, Soundbyte, Snakebyte, Databyte, Eraserbyte, Psychobyte, Metabyte, Qubyte, Cryptobyte and Vaporbyte

You can stay connected with Cat in the following places:

FaceBook: @cat.connor
Twitter: @catconnor
Instagram: @catconnorauthor
Website: www.catconnor.com

We would be ever so grateful if you took five minutes and reviewed this book - preferably via the platform where you purchased the copy!
Thank you, reviews are super important to getting authors work noticed.

Stay tuned for the [Veronica Tracey] Spy/PI Series set right here in Upper Hutt

www.ingramcontent.com/pod-product-compliance
Lightning Source LLC
Chambersburg PA
CBHW022017050726
47499CB00004BA/1028